PRAISE FOR
THE TRUTH ABOUT HORSES

"What an irresistibly readable novel Christy Cashman has written! Her young heroine, Reese, is an astonishing creation, warmly sympathetic, impulsive, unpredictable, brash, loyal and loving, endearing, exasperating, most of all memorable—a triumphant portrait of tumultuous adolescence in our time. *The Truth About Horses* plunges us into a beautifully evoked rural world in which horses are both magnificent beasts requiring human love and devotion and iconic creatures out of mythology."

—JOYCE CAROL OATES, American novelist, short story writer, and essayist

"In her first novel, *The Truth About Horses*, Christy Cashman proves herself to be a worthy successor to Harper Lee. Cashman's protagonist, Reese, instantly captures the reader in the same way that Scout does in *To Kill a Mockingbird*—and takes the reader with her into her world for a magical examination of the human heart."

—ARTHUR T. VANDERBILT II, author of *Fortune's Children: The Fall of the House of Vanderbilt*

"*The Truth About Horses* had me hooked on page one. I set aside everything else and just kept reading, sleep be damned. It is a timeless story about growing up in a world that is less than perfect and trying to figure out who you are through all of those challenges—something each of us faces at some point. Reese's strength, wit, wisdom, and vulnerability offer up a multifaceted character and a person I would like to know. The novel is a tour de force."

—JUDITH LASTER, festival director of The Woods Hole Film Festival

"The truth about *The Truth About Horses* is that it is impossible to put down. With simple ingredients of hay and humor, family and fury, Christy Cashman has spun an unstoppable feast. She shows us how hooves and hearts beat the same truth to light and reminds us that laughter and tears need not be served as separate courses."

—SALLY TAYLOR, singer, songwriter, and founder of Consenses

"Unforgettable and evocative, *The Truth About Horses* is a masterful journey into the heart of a young girl's love for horses, the resilience of family, and the silent language that binds us to the natural world. Christy Cashman has woven a tale of loss, triumph, and redemption that is as captivating as it is poignant. From the pastoral charm of the Big Green Barn to the mystical allure of a ghostly herd, this stirring narrative gallops with unforgettable characters and heart-stopping drama. *The Truth About Horses* is a must-read."

—BEN MEZRICH, *New York Times* best-selling author of *Dumb Money, Bringing Down The House,* and *The Accidental Billionaires*

"Christy Cashman has written a beautiful, thrilling tale about a teenaged girl's journey from fear to courage, from anger to forgiveness, from broken-heartedness to openness. *The Truth About Horses* is so much about the mysterious forces, within us and around us, that are always there to guide us, and the way in which people enter our lives exactly when we need them—if only we'll let them."

—JANE SEYMOUR, actress, author, and cofounder of the Open Hearts Foundation

"There are few people who won't be swept away by this beautiful, gritty, and gripping story about the renewal of life and relationships. Reese takes the reader on a journey of raw emotions, from pain to joy, in this wonder of steadfast perseverance. Being a midwesterner myself, I could almost smell the sacred and magical farmland in her pages. *The Truth About Horses* is a must-read."

—SHANNON PASTUSZAK, media executive, publisher, and founder of The Newbury Cup

"*The Truth About Horses* is a beautifully written and engaging story. Christy Cashman easily sets the tone with her terrific descriptions of the land, the horses, and her teenaged protagonist, Reese. This is a tale of loss, grieving, believing in dreams, and being true to yourself. Reese's voice is spot-on, and you will find yourself alternately worried, frustrated, and awed by her. I quickly became invested in the story and anxious to read on!"

—JUDITH BELUSHI PISANO, producer, uke enthusiast, author of *Samurai Widow*, and coauthor of *Belushi: A Biography*

"Christy Cashman has written a powerful story about loss and grief. Wonderfully evocative and with the author's passion for horses shining through every page, this is a rich and deeply felt novel. Eschewing easy answers, *The Truth About Horses* is strong on how even the small choices we make, sometimes rashly, can so easily hurt those most important to us, and how struggling on through each day can bring enough hope to light the path toward redemption and new beginnings."

—KIERAN CROWLEY, author of *The Misfits* and *Mighty Dynamo*

"This is so much more than a book about horses, and anyone who thinks otherwise is missing out. It is about loss, mental health, families, a love for animals, relationships, finding your place in this world, following your dreams, trials and triumphs, forgiveness . . . and so much more!"
—CHRISTINE WARD, executive director of
Raising A Reader MA

"What a ride! *The Truth About Horses* is the terrific story of a young girl dealing with the trauma of grief while finding herself and a place for her own dreams in the unpredictable world of horses. A really enjoyable roller-coaster journey that never lags—there is always a surprise waiting for Reese and the reader."
—ALAN DEVINE, actor in Netflix's *Valhalla* and
BBC's *The Tudors*

"*The Truth About Horses* is in many ways also the truth about things we hold dear in life. And if that includes captivating writing, Christy Cashman supremely succeeds."
—PATRICK KABANDA, author of
The Creative Wealth of Nations

"Don't waste another moment reading these simple lines of praise. Go straight to the horse's mouth. By the way, it's a winner."
—CARLY SIMON, musician, singer,
songwriter, and author

THE
TRUTH
ABOUT
HORSES

THE
TRUTH
ABOUT
HORSES

a novel

Christy Cashman

SPARKPRESS

Published by SparkPress, a BookSparks imprint,
A division of SparkPoint Studio, LLC
Phoenix, Arizona, USA, 85007
www.gosparkpress.com

Published 2023
Printed in the United States of America
Print ISBN: 978-1-68463-212-1
E-ISBN: 978-1-68463-213-8
Library of Congress Control Number: 2023905250

Interior Design by Tabitha Lahr

"Jesse"
Words and music by Carly Simon and Mike Mainieri. Copyright © 1980 UNIVERSAL MUSIC CORP., QUACKENBUSH MUSIC LTD. and REDEYE MUSIC PUBLISHING CO. All rights for QUACKENBUSH MUSIC LTD. administered by UNIVERSAL MUSIC CORP. All rights for REDEYE MUSIC PUBLISHING CO. administered worldwide by KOBALT SONGS MUSIC PUBLISHING. All rights reserved. Used by permission. Reprinted by permission of Hal Leonard LLC.

For Mom
And for my first horse, Rambler

PROLOGUE

"It'd be a miracle if he raced again," the vet told Mom. Then he added, a little more quietly, "Be kindest to put him down."

For days after the race, Mom walked around the barn like a robot, doing only what had to be done. I knew one day soon she'd wake up and be herself again. I knew it wouldn't be long before she'd stop seeing Treasure's fall every time she closed her eyes. Mom always got back up. Sometimes it just took her longer than other times.

"Come 'ere, boy." I reached my arm over Treasure's stall door. He'd always been the most curious horse in the barn. He'd reach his nose out for a pat or stick his top lip up for attention. He loved to play. When I'd hang his halter and lead shank on the hook outside of his stall, he'd grab them with his teeth and toss them into the aisle just so I'd have to come by to pick them up. I'd always laugh at him, put them back, twist his forelock, and call him a devil. Twenty minutes later, he'd have tossed his stuff back into the aisle again. But after the race, he kept his nose in the corner, even when there was a full rack of freshly cut hay. His halter and lead shank stayed neatly on the hook.

I tried to tempt him with an apple slice.

"Look what I got for you, buddy." I held the apple out as far as I could. He didn't move. He lowered his head even farther, his nose in the shavings. I felt Mom's hand brush through my hair and rest on my shoulder.

"He's on some pretty strong meds for the pain, hon," she said. "He'll be more alert tomorrow."

She opened the stall door and walked over to Treasure, letting her hand drift along his side up to his neck. When she got to his head, she hugged it into her chest and rested her cheek on his forehead.

"You did good, my beautiful boy." She held his head with both hands and kissed him on his faint star. "So good."

My throat tightened and my eyes stung.

"You'll race again," she whispered in his ear. "You'll see."

"Come on, you two," Dad called from outside the barn. He was holding the pickup truck door open for Mom. "Let's leave the barn and its worries behind for a while."

He said it like it was that easy.

Mom slowly slid Treasure's stall door closed, and I followed her out to the truck.

"Mom?" I tugged on her sleeve. She turned to look at me. I couldn't even say it.

"Don't worry, Pun'kin. We're not putting him down."

Dad gave Mom a smooch on the cheek before closing her door. Then he walked over to the driver's side, singing, "Jesse, I'll always cut fresh flowers for you. And, Jesse, I'll always make the wine cold for you. And put on cologne and sit by the phone . . ."

Sometimes we drove so we could "reset" after a horse had a bad race or came up lame or we'd had a pain-in-the-ass client. "It's best to put things behind you and move on,"

Dad would say. He didn't like to dwell on things. Like the race we were all trying to unsee. As if a drive could stop those last few seconds from looping around and around in our brains. As if we could forget how close we'd been to winning the Black Elk—the race that every horse person around here dreams about. How we were all just about to leap a giant chasm together—the one that separates the people who talk about doing things from the people who do things. How around the dinner table, "maybe next season" became "this season." Suddenly we were talking about race day, every conversation filled with words like *the pace* and *the cutaway* and *the going*.

❧

The day of that drive, the air was so clear it almost hurt my eyes. Everything had a sharpness that, most of the time, wasn't there. We pulled out of the driveway in the pickup, them in the front, me in the back. I looked back at the barn and saw things I'd never noticed—chipping paint, the sagging roof, uneven doors, unstained boards patching up holes. For so long, just seeing the barn made me feel like everything would be all right. Now, all I saw was a tired old building that looked like it was trying to lie down and let the grass fold into it. I rolled my tongue around to find the sweet, buttery taste from the caramel apple I'd had the day of the race. But there was no taste. My mouth was dry as a moth's wing.

We never had a plan. We'd just drive. Dad pretended, like he always did, that there was some magical force making his hands turn the steering wheel this way or that. At an intersection, he asked me to guess which way the magic force would take us next.

"Left," I said.

"Let's see if you're right," he said. "I mean left." Then he pretended like he was fighting with the steering wheel to make the magic go my way. But it was too old and stupid a joke to make me laugh.

We headed out of Birdwood and took the road that follows along the Ghost Hawk River, which widens and narrows before it forks. In some places, it gushes with white rapids, but in other places, it creeps so slowly you'd swear it wasn't moving at all. We drove past where the river feeds into the black mirror of Horse Thief Lake. At Ghost Hawk Park, Mom waved goodbye to the river. "There it goes," she said, like it was a person walking out the door. I watched the rolling water rush off into a forest of giant pine and craggy rock.

Dad kept steering the truck farther and farther from the barn, through the grasslands and croplands and toward the Badlands. We passed picnickers and campers. Then he started singing the South Dakota state song. Mom rolled her eyes and shook her head at his awful singing voice. That only made him sing louder. "Come on! Everybody!" he said. "Hail! South Dakota, the state we love the best, land of our fathers, builders of the West, home of the Badlands and Rushmore's ageless shrine . . ."

Dad kept singing on his own while he pulled around big rigs and livestock carriers and bullet-shaped campers. When he finally took a breath, Mom looked at him and said, "Joe, I never knew you couldn't sing." The three of us laughed, mostly because Mom finally made a joke.

We drove through lush, dense forest. When we passed the cliffs that are home to the pronghorn, two of them leaped across the road in front of us. But then the road wound through wide-open plains. I could see Smuggler's Rock in the distance. We kept driving until there was nothing else to see but pink rock and a gray road ahead, straight as a pool stick, the kind of boring scenery that always puts me to sleep.

I woke from my nap to see Dad looking at me in the rearview mirror.

"Did you enjoy your nap as much as I enjoyed mine?" Dad is the king of stupid jokes. I didn't laugh. I looked out the window instead. The same pink hue tinted the air.

"Rose quartz," Mom reminded me.

"But how does the pink in the rock make the air pink?"

"It's all about reflection," she said.

I looked at her reflection. Mom's face was perfectly framed in the side mirror. Her dark brown eyes focused on something we passed, let it go, then followed something else. She kept tucking her hair behind her ears, but the wind lifted strands and pulled one whole twist of it right out the half-opened window. It lay flat against the glass of my window, a giant black wing.

"I think they're close," Mom said. "I can feel it in my bones."

I always sat up when Mom felt something in her bones. It'd always be something I wouldn't want to miss. And when we rounded the bend, there they were. Wild horses. Like Mom's thoughts made them appear.

Dad pulled over to the side of the road. We got out of the truck and walked to the flat plain's edge. I stood between my parents. They were each holding one of my hands like they did when I was little. The horses were about a football field length away. Most of them ignored us. They grazed and ambled from one patch of dusty grass to another. Some raised their heads to look at us, then lowered them to graze again.

Seeing horses in the wild is like glimpsing another world you knew about but forgot existed. Seeing them gallop across thousands of acres of open land is nothing like seeing horses in a fenced-in field, peaceful and content, like decorations in a pasture. Here, the land looked made for them. Like the wind had flattened the plains just for their hooves to gallop along. Like the mountains saw their glistening coats and powerful legs and moved aside to make room enough for all of them to gather.

One black horse, much taller than the rest, threaded his way through the herd. He nipped some of the mares on the haunches, telling them it was time to move on. A dust cloud followed his gallop. His stride was monstrous.

Then he galloped toward us.

"Oh shit!" Dad said. He reached his arm across me and grabbed hold of one of Mom's wrists. "Whoa, buddy. No one wants to hurt you."

But the black horse kept moving closer.

"Don't run," Mom said. "Stay still."

Then he stopped. Right in front of us. He raised his head and looked at me. Straight at me. His eyes were dark pools, and his mane fell like a curtain against his sculpted neck. Then he turned, tossed his head, and charged off with the rest of the herd. Dad's hand shook a little when he let go of Mom's wrist.

"He didn't dare mess with me," Dad joked.

Mom started laughing. Really laughing. "That was crazy!" she said. "Kind of scary and beautiful. Like a dream!" Her eyes sparkled again. Mom was back.

We watched the horses until they were specks on the horizon.

"Well, time to make like a bread truck and haul buns," Dad said, trying to get Mom to laugh again. I climbed into the back seat. The race was still with me, but it was less vivid now. Less in my face. Like all those miles magically gave our minds just enough room to think other thoughts.

"You were right about the drive, Dad."

"Yep," he said. "Nothing like getting scared to death to make you forget your troubles."

But for some reason, the horses hadn't scared me. I could have stood there forever, my hair whipping across my face, my feet feeling the rumble from the herd's hooves, my back feeling the warmth of the sun.

Dad reached over and squeezed Mom's knee. He left his hand there, and Mom put her hand on top of Dad's. Then she turned and smiled at me. I could feel her thoughts. She was getting ready again. Ready again to dream.

Then Dad swerved the truck to the right. Huge chicken crates were falling from the truck in front of us. They crashed open on the road in an explosion of white feathers and sawdust, like some whacked-out piñata. One crate tumbled by my window, breaking open as it landed. Chickens scattered into the road. Another crate fell in front of us, breaking into pieces with every roll. My body leaned as far as the seat belt let it. My shoulder kept slamming against the door. Something hit our windshield, and Dad steered hard to the left, our tires bashing into rocks and banging into holes.

I saw everything inside the car. Mom's hand reaching up and clutching Dad's arm. Dad's arm, straight as a board, trying to hold the steering wheel steady. A spilled coffee cup rolling around on the floorboard. The barn key swinging from the rearview mirror. My parents' heads tilting and nodding like bobblehead dolls. Everything was in slow motion.

But outside, things rushed by so fast I couldn't tell rock from sky.

I knew we were off the road when I saw nothing but pink dust.

I knew we'd been tumbling in circles because I felt like throwing up.

I knew we were upside down because I was hanging from my seat belt.

I knew I was alive when I looked at my dad.

I wanted him to crack a stupid joke.

But I knew, from the look on his face, that Mom was dead.

PART
ONE

CHAPTER ONE

TWO YEARS LATER

You might miss the driveway to the Big Green Barn if you weren't looking for it. Just ahead is the scraggly oak, the landmark I used when I was younger—before I could get here with my eyes closed. Just ahead of the driveway, on the shoulder of the road, a sign sits at a slant. For Sale or Lease. I pick up some speed and run over it.

Most of the run-down farms around here have already sold to developers. The Buttonwillow cattle farm is now a BMX track. The pig farm on Old Pine Road is becoming a brewery. But not this farm. This farm will have horses on it again. Our horses. Dad says developers don't want it because there's too many rocks and most of the front pasture is in the flood plain. And he says Gibson, the owner, doesn't really want to sell it, for sentimental reasons. He already turned down a couple of offers. Dad said we'll be back here someday. But I'm not waiting until someday.

I lean into the turn down the driveway. My bike's tires spit out tiny bits of gravel and dust. I stop and unzip the pocket of my hoodie, pull out my phone, hold it lengthwise, and take a picture. Most people photograph things that are there, but I photograph things that aren't there—the gaps and blank spaces left by the broken rails of the sagging split rail fence, the horses no longer behind it. And things that are there because something else isn't—the field's thick tufts of grass that should be bare patches of dirt, where horses used to stand peacefully, nose to tail, tail to nose.

I bike alongside the battered fences—two giant S's that follow the curves of the driveway for the quarter mile to the barn—the perfect distance to cool a horse down. I stop again to take another picture and zoom in on one corner of the barn—the windy corner, Mom called it. Boards are missing, and the chipped green paint has peeled, leaving giant blotches, gray as dead skin. A red-tailed hawk skims the roof of the barn, circles the open field, then tilts and plunges for a mouse or a rabbit.

It's pathetic, but visiting this abandoned farm is what I do every day after school.

The driveway widens out and makes a circle. I follow it to the back of the barn and lean my bike against the box elder Mom and I planted when I was four. I know the sliding door will be open a crack. We left it not quite closed two years ago, and it stayed that way, rusted on its metal track. I wedge my body through the opening. If I'd finished my school crap-eteria chicken Alfredo, I wouldn't fit.

Daggers of light shine through the barn's gaps and criss-cross down the center aisle. I walk through the cloudy columns of sunlight, passing door after door of open stalls, now empty and cleaned of shavings and hay and smell.

I remember every name of every horse we had here. Rosie, the sweet mare with one eye. Ernie the machine, who did everything from barrel racing to show jumping. Byron, who liked listening to rap at night. Tank, the tiny pony we used as a companion for nervous horses. Oscar, who loved to roll in the river. Mildred, who was so patient she could practically give kids a lesson without an instructor. So many horses in and out of these stalls ever since I can remember. I've missed their soft nickers. Their anxious pawing for attention. Their munching. The busy mornings. The slow, sleepy afternoons.

At the last stall on the left, I stop. It belonged to Trusted Treasure. Outside the stall door, a wood-framed photo of him still hangs at a slant. The nail it hangs from is bent down like it's giving up. In the photo, Trusted Treasure is racing in the Black Elk, jumping over the last fence so high he looks like he's flying. He looks certain to win.

This is where it will happen, I thought.

Just minutes before, I'd dropped my half-eaten caramel apple as Mom and Dad and I ran to the finish line where, any second, the horses would round the bend, charge up the hill, and head toward the last series of fences. The sweet, buttery taste still filled my mouth as Trusted Treasure galloped into view just behind Voodoo. Treasure's jockey was doing exactly what Dad had told him. "Stay in Voodoo's back pocket. He'll lead the whole race. Let him wear himself out, then pass him in the last stretch."

"That's it!" Dad yelled. "Make your move!"

Mom had one hand up like she was hailing a cab and one hand over her mouth like, if she made a noise, she might mess the whole thing up. The horses were galloping up the hill to the last four fences. At the first fence, Voodoo took an extra stride. Trusted Treasure took it long.

"Yes!" Dad yelled. He fist-pumped the air in front of him.

Mom took her hand away from her mouth. "Go, Treasure!"

While the three other horses were in a tight pack just getting to the first fence, Voodoo and Trusted Treasure were duking it out up the hill to the second. The crowd had moved around us with a pulsing, chanting roar. This was a two-horse race. We watched Voodoo sail over the third fence. Treasure was just half a length behind him.

"Push now!" Dad yelled. "Ask him for everything!"

Then as they headed for the last fence, the fence right in front of us, hoofbeats rumbled through the soles of my shoes. Both horses were using every inch of their bodies as they charged toward us. Their hooves ate up the ground in front of them. Their heads moved up and down like levers working their legs. *Push, pull, stretch, push, pull, stretch.* Mom and Dad were almost climbing the fence with me, yelling and pounding the air. Mom had gone wild. Her long black hair was blowing in her face, and she was sweating like she was running the race herself. For a second, the horses were so close to us I could look into Treasure's eyes. "Please" was all I said. I wanted to yell, but it came out as a whisper.

Trusted Treasure's body launched up into the air. He was going to pass Voodoo. Clumps of mud exploded from the horses' hooves. Trusted Treasure's giant body stretched out like he'd sprouted wings. Voodoo's neck was reaching. Both jockeys gave every inch of rein.

But a split second later, there was a muffled clatter of metal and hooves. Voodoo's front legs had hit the fence. He nosedived to the ground right in the path of Trusted Treasure. It felt like forever before Treasure's body stopped rolling and skidding along the muddy track. He groaned, like a train trying to stop, until he landed in a heap.

Then the sound of nothing.

Bzzzzzzzzzzzzz. Bzzzzzzzzzzzzz. My phone buzzes like a bee caught in my back pocket.

Going out with a friend for dinner, Dad texted.

What a surprise. I don't mean it. I'm not surprised at all.

Want me to bring you anything?

He doesn't mean it. He wants me to answer, *No, I'm fine.*

I squeeze back out through the barn door, then I text, *Oh, yes, can I please have a medium rare sirloin and a cheese soufflé with asparagus and hollandaise on the side? Thanks a mill.* Smiley face, smiley face, smiley face, fork.

I watch the dot pulse while Dad thinks. Then it disappears completely.

CHAPTER TWO

My ride home takes seventeen and a half minutes. Nineteen if it's windy or rainy. I pedal into our driveway. No lights on in the house. No Jeep in the driveway. Nothing new. It's odder if Dad's Jeep is here when I get home. He says he's taking up new interests, like he told me to do. But the only interest he's taken up since Mom died is sleeping around. Basically, he's sleeping his way through town.

I don't think he even waited a month. One night, he just came downstairs with his hair combed and his nice shoes on. "I'm meeting a friend," he told me. Then came a whole avalanche of new friends. I couldn't keep up with their names, so I gave them nicknames. There was Big Bird, a tall blonde with a pointy nose; Miss Snail, a manicurist; Airhead, the flight attendant; and a bank teller I called Summer Squash because of her long neck and wide butt. He even slept with my second-grade teacher, Miss Skunk, who has a white streak of hair straight down the middle of her head. And she smells.

I leave my bike on the front lawn—not because I don't care about my bike but because Dad hates it when I do that.

I feel for the front door key in the cowboy boot he doesn't wear anymore, and I let myself in.

Dad's not being here is actually a relief. I prefer to be alone at home. No awkward passing in the hall. No getting pissed off that he's pretending to be interested in how my day went. No pretending like I'm interested in his boring job. Even when he's here, he's not really here. He asks me things just because he thinks he should. He doesn't really listen to the answer.

I don't bother turning on the lights. I go to the kitchen and open the refrigerator door. It's the only light I need. Something feels good about leaving the door open while I dig around in the kitchen and make my dinner. Of course, Dad yells at me for doing it. But the light is cheerful. And I like how, if I forget something, I don't have to open the door again.

Today I have enough energy to make something different. "I'm feeling gourmet," I say to Mom's blue cow butter dish. Instead of the usual Honey Bunches of Oats, I do a blend. A trio mixture. "One for the record books," Dad would say, back when he was funny. Golden Grahams mixed with Honey Bunches of Oats and a sprinkling of Cocoa Crunch with, again, a blend—it's all about the blends—of chocolate milk and regular milk. "And then, the pièce de résistance," I announce like Dad would, pretending to talk to a TV camera. He'd hold the bowl up with his pinky finger sticking out like he was Gordon Ramsay.

I press a minute and thirty seconds on the microwave. "Don't knock it till you try it," Dad said about hot cold cereal. It's something he was actually right about. Cold cold cereal is just inferior. Hot makes it feel like a meal. I slide the bowl out of the microwave. Why a minute and a half, you may ask? Because that extra half minute gives just the right ratio of soggy to crunch. I take a picture of it and head to my room.

I sit on my bed, munching away, eating so fast I let the bowl catch the milk that dribbles down my chin, which no one is around to say anything about. I scroll through some videos, sliding by other lives—a bear is caught on camera eating out of someone's refrigerator, a baby seal lands in a fisherman's boat, a man catches a drunk fan by her underwear before she almost falls over a balcony at a concert, a ninety-five-year-old woman is getting a tattoo on her ass. Then some more cereal recipes. *Low battery* pops up just as a brave dude attempts a six-cereal combo. "And I will go where no man has gone before," the kid says as he pours the cereals into a mixing bowl.

"Genius!" I comment.

One more thing to do before my phone dies. The charger is just across the room, but I don't feel like getting up. All I need is five minutes of search. It's time for my nightly Treasure hunt.

For the first year, I knew exactly where Treasure was. Dad basically gave him away to Delia Boyd, who had a retirement ranch for injured and old racehorses. Delia thought she was some sort of a horse psychic. One time I heard her tell my mom that a young horse she'd just adopted was a plant in a past life and still had memories of being eaten by a wild boar in the wetlands of Pakistan. Aside from her higher-than-average dose of cray cray, she was a nice lady. She knew how sad I was to lose Treasure, so she sent me a video of him in a wide-open field, grazing with a herd that looked like they came from the island of misfit toys—fat ponies, shaggy donkeys, and a couple of overworked mules. Then, ten months later, she got divorced and sold her ranch.

I fluff my pillow to prop up my head and type *Trusted Treasure* into the search bar. The same pages always come up. A wedding dress store, a chocolate cherry company, and a church bulletin that says, "For where your treasure is, there your heart will be also." Nothing about a horse. I already know that. But I can't sleep unless I check. Next, as usual, I type *Trusted Treasure horse* and, as usual, the search engine asks, "Do you mean Trisha's Pleasure?" *What a stupid name for a horse*, I think every time. Nothing has changed on the next page either. He's listed for an auction that happened a year ago in Elkhart, Texas.

Last, I check Horse Tracker, the auction app Dad never unregistered from. I guessed his password on the first try. Mom's name and birthday. Jessietucker1111. Duh. Since then, it's pinged me its tiny neigh just once— *one notification on a horse named Trusted Treasure*—for that auction last year in Elkhorn. The trail ended there. Horse Tracker couldn't even tell me who bought him. I didn't think the app would be this useless.

But I can't give up. Even though his injury means he can never be ridden again. Even though I know what usually happens to retired racehorses with injuries. I don't even like to think about it. I tell myself only the good stories. He's in a big field with shade trees, a gurgling stream, and all the grass he can eat. Or some rich kid is spoiling him rotten at her fancy ranch. I imagine him hanging out with a nice herd of horses, rolling in the dirt, enjoying life.

Wherever he is, something tells me he's not far.

I can feel it in my bones.

I tip the bowl and drink the last of the sweet milk. The spoon clatters when the bowl lands near the rest of the empty bowls on my bedside table. I switch off my lamp. I wait and listen. Then a beam of light sweeps across my horse-patterned wallpaper. I hear the sound of a motor, tires on gravel, muffled Def Leppard.

Shit. Dad's home.

His Jeep door closes. Then there are a few seconds of silence while he feels around for the key in the boot on the porch. Front door opens. Front door closes. Keys thrown on the table. Fridge opens and closes. Footsteps creak the wooden kitchen floor, then get muffled by the living room carpet, then creak the stairs as he climbs to the second floor. My door opens.

He loud whispers, "Reese?"

I pretend to be asleep.

"You OK?"

I still don't answer.

He clears his throat. "Night," he says, then softly closes my door. The stairs creak again. A beer can pops. The TV goes on. He surfs the same channels in a loop. News. Sitcom. Sports. News. Sitcom. Sports. I start counting the loops. News. Sitcom. Sports. One. News. Sitcom. Sports. Two. News. Sitcom. Sports. Three.

Sleep feels so far away. News. Sitcom. Sports. Four.

It becomes a ball I'm chasing. News. Sitcom. Sports. Five.

Each time I get close, it bounces up and away. News. Sitcom. Sports. Six.

I chase the ball, but I can't move fast enough to catch it. News. Sitcom. Sports. Seven.

It becomes a dot on the horizon and then starts rolling back to me again. News. Sitcom. Sports. Eight.

But it's not a ball. News. Sitcom. Sports. Nine. News. Sitcom. Sports. Ten.

It's the herd of horses.

They're back.

They gallop toward me across a wide-open field. A burst of wind brushes across my face as they pass. Bays and grays and paints and chestnuts. Buckskins and piebalds and duns and palominos. Each one is more beautiful than the next. But I'm looking for just one. The black one. The biggest, most powerful. Then I see him, and he sees me. He separates from the herd. He runs close to look at me. This time I want to ask him a question, ask him why he's here again, ask him what he wants. But I can't form the words.

He stares at me like he understands my question anyway. Then I hear his voice. It seems to be coming up from the ground, mixing with the thundering sound of hooves.

"You will see," he says.

Then he turns and gallops off with the others. They disappear into a canyon.

You will see. You will see. You will see.

I open my eyes.

News.

CHAPTER THREE

The more I try to put last night's dream back together, the less I can see it. It's like trying to sew a cloud together or shape something out of ashes. But the parts I do remember make my heart speed up. The horses running toward me. How fast they moved. How the black one stopped right in front of me. Looked right into me.

"Reese!"

The class's chuckling jolts me out of my daydream. Mrs. Roth is staring at me. Her louder-than-usual voice means she's been asking me a question more than once.

"Explain why we should care about dangling participles," she asks me. Before I can answer Mrs. Roth, Lexi Peterson, who sits right behind me and is already easy to hate with her perfect teeth and her big boobs, says, "Her dad sure doesn't care where he dangles his participles."

The kids laugh. I would have laughed, too, if it wasn't about my own dad.

"Shut up, Lexi, or I'll crammar my foot up your ass."

"I beg your pardon, young lady," says Mrs. Roth, who's about a hundred and ten and practically deaf and the only teacher who still uses a chalkboard.

"I was just asking," I say, "if anyone really cares about grammar?"

That sets her off. It's like she turns into turbo granny. She flourishes her piece of chalk and goes on a rant about the importance of punctuation. How a simple comma can change the meaning of a sentence. Chalk chips fly as she writes a huge-lettered sentence on the board.

She turns to stare at me and slowly says each word.

"Let's eat grandpa."

Then she slashes a comma into the sentence, breaking the chalk in half.

"*Let's eat comma grandpa period* is quite a bit different from *Let's eat grandpa period*. Isn't it, Miss I-don't-care-about-the-rules-of-grammar?" Then she says, "Punctuation saves lives!"

"Anyone with a brain would know that you don't eat your grandpa because of one missing comma," I mumble. Then Mrs. Roth slaps me with a detention. Apparently, she's not as deaf as I thought.

Two hours and twenty workbook pages later, I dig my battery-challenged phone out of my backpack. Not only will my dad not spring for a new phone, but ever since I dropped it in the toilet at Tasty Burger, the battery only holds half a charge, even on a good day.

I text Dad the same lie I've been texting him for a week now. "Headed to track meet." I've also used "going to the mall with friends," "staying after for extra help in biology" (what a joke), and "school play rehearsal" (an even bigger joke). Most dads would freak if their daughter texted two hours later than usual. But lately, my dad doesn't pay much attention to details like time.

I walk out of the building as fast as I can, past the gym full of screeching sneakers and yelling coaches, toward the sports field full of kids pathetically chasing after the same ball. I unjam my bike from the crammed bike rack and pedal around the yellow wall of late buses, away from the building that's made of the same boring brick as the state prison. Sometimes I think I'd learn something more useful in prison, like welding or how to operate a forklift. Or at least prison might have nicer people and better food.

As I leave the parking lot, I arc around the puke-green Beulah High School sign. Just one more month at this glorified babysitting trap until summer vacation. I take a few deep breaths to clear my lungs of the stale smell of the halls. I need to unclog my brain of the jumble of Joan of Arc, the value of *x,* and those stupid rules about dangling participles.

I didn't always hate school. It all started when Dad said, "You have to forget about horses for a while, Reese." But the only reason I tried in school was so I could ride. Dad was always like, "Studies come first. Blah, blah, blah." And he'd make me do my homework before I could even sit on a horse.

When he told me to forget about horses, he was looking me square in the eye. It was the day of Mom's funeral. Everyone had finally left our house, and we were cleaning the kitchen. I skipped past pouting and went directly to full-on silent cry. I looked away fast so he wouldn't see my face. "Have to?" I pretended I was looking for the sponge. "What do you mean, have to?"

He tried to change the subject. "Who's gonna eat all this?" He dumped the fourth casserole out of its dish and into the trash. I stood beside him in front of the sink, ready to rinse, but when he handed me the dish, I couldn't take it. I just stood there, crying, staring into the trash at something that looked like broccoli throw-up. I had to gasp for breath. Asking me to forget about horses was like asking me to forget about Mom.

"I'm sorry, Reese. The horse business is . . ." He let his voice trail off, but I wasn't listening anyway. He tossed another casserole into the trash.

"But, Dad, that's all we've ever done."

He poured two half-empty glasses of wine down the drain and clunked the glasses onto the sideboard.

"I'm going to drop the lease on the barn. I decided to take another job," he said, like he was realizing it himself for the first time.

"But . . . we don't know anything else."

"I start Monday down at Keystone selling windows."

"Windows?" I couldn't let him make this mistake. "You're gonna be so shitty at that. You've said like a million times— you'd rather be outside or in a barn than anywhere else. You told me anything else would give you brain rot."

"That was when I thought I had a choice!" He threw away the last casserole, plate and all, and walked out of the room.

Two days later, a convoy of trailers lined up along the driveway like the circus had come to town. I watched as every horse I loved and cared for was taken out of its stall, loaded onto a stranger's trailer, and hauled away. Petunia, one of the mares that Mom had raised on the farm and trailered all over the place, wouldn't load. She kept backing off the ramp and rearing. Something she'd never done before. It was like she knew—this time, she wasn't coming back.

Some buyers were standing outside of their trucks, pacing back and forth like greedy, hungry hyenas. Dad let every horse go for dirt cheap. He didn't negotiate. Didn't haggle. Just took the first offer like he was unloading a heap from his attic.

When Delia headed toward Trusted Treasure's stall with her lead shank, I stepped in front of her.

"Not him. He's staying here."

She leaned down to me like she was talking to a child. "Honey, I know it's hard, but sometimes these things happen."

I went for the lead shank, but she held it away from me.

"He's going to a good place, sweetie."

I ran to Dad.

"Please, Dad. Not Treasure! He can't be ridden! You know what happens to horses that can't be ridden!" Dad didn't look at me. Didn't look at Trusted Treasure. Didn't look at Delia Boyd. Instead, he piled horse blankets and pieces of tack into the aisle, saying to whoever came in, "Take what you want."

When Delia closed the trailer ramp behind Trusted Treasure, I ran up to her one more time.

"Please don't take him. He belongs here with me."

She dusted off her hands and tilted her head to the side. "He'll be OK. You'll see."

I reached between the slats of the trailer window and grazed Treasure's neck with my fingertips. He looked at me like he was asking me why. *Why am I on this stranger's trailer? Why am I being taken away?*

"Don't worry, buddy. I'll get you back. I promise!"

Then Delia climbed into her truck and pulled Mom's Treasure away from me. As her trailer drove away, all I could do was stare at its bumper's red-letter warning. Caution. Horses.

"Mom would never forgive you for this!" I spit the words at Dad.

"Baby, sometimes you can't do what you want. You do what you have to do." He flung a worn-out halter onto the pile. "This place would eat us alive without your mother helping to run it."

I picked up as much as I could from the pile and put things back where they belonged. That's when he said it. "Look, Reese. Maybe we can get the barn back someday. It's just going to take some time."

That was our last day at the Big Green Barn.

I tried doing a lot of other things, like Dad asked. Things that, until we get back to Big Green someday, will help me forget about horses. As if. Hip-hop dance lessons just taught me I have absolutely no rhythm. I gave up on pottery class after the vase I was building splatted off the wheel and onto the studio floor. Lacrosse felt like there was the team, and then there was me.

I did pick up swearing, though. A lot. Which Dad hates, so I do it every chance I get. Because Dad was wrong. Trying new things didn't "help me meet friends" or "make me less lonely." And it didn't help me forget about horses. It just made me realize even more that I'm good at nothing else.

So fuck that shit. Without telling him (he wouldn't notice anyway), I quit it all. Except for the swearing.

Instead, every day now, I get on my bike. I know the way to the barn so well sometimes it feels like I don't even have to steer. Like the barn pulls me. Like a dream.

I turn left down Cekiya Drive. Like most streets in the town of Birdwood, South Dakota, which is smack dab between two reservations, it has a Lakota name. Mom always called it Camel Hump Road. Its two hills rise and fall in front of me like a ride at the park. I pedal fast and then raise my feet. The wind howls past my ears. I lower my body and raise my butt. I'm a jockey on a horse. I'm in the home stretch. I position my feet on the pedals again as I get ready to zoom past the driveway that used to lead to Scott's dairy farm but now leads to a new development. Ten big square houses with ten big square yards. I look for the dogs. The little scruffy one and the big slow one. They always hear me coming before they see me. Sure enough, they charge around the corner. I pedal faster. I've got some downhill speed, but the little dog is gaining on me, yapping and snapping at my back tire. The big dog is loping behind him, cheering him on with his deep, booming bark.

Then I hear something. A drumbeat. I look left and right. What am I looking for? A band? A car with a blaring radio?

Then I hear a breath. A deep, surging sort of breath. It spooks the dogs. They turn on a dime and run home, tails between their legs.

The drumbeat gets louder. The earth shakes under my tires. The sound of breathing gets louder and louder too. I pedal faster and faster. Then I glance back over my shoulder.

There are horses behind me. Like a shitload of them.

I'm losing my grip on the handlebars. My front tire wobbles. If I fall, I'll be trampled. If I slow down, the horses will turn me into mush. I steady my bike and pedal as fast as I can. My heart goes from a fast thumping to a racing in my chest. Right next to the tires of my bike, I see hooves.

A black horse is right beside me. He leads the entire herd. He raises his nose and tosses his head, like this is fun. Like it's some sort of a game. He's so close he could reach out his nose and touch me. He looks at me, stretches his legs even farther, and passes, leading the herd that is now surrounding me. There are so many. Their bodies move like they are connected by an invisible rope. Whipping manes and twisting tails are everywhere.

My feet slip on the pedals. Then a horn blares. A car is coming toward me. I'm in the middle of the road.

"Git the hell out the way! You crazy?" a man yells out of his pickup truck.

I move to the right and slam on my brakes. The horses move to the right too. But they don't stop. They swerve and veer and then gallop off the road, past mailboxes, onto lawns, weaving around houses and swing sets. The air is thick with dust. I stand on the side of the road, gripping my handlebars.

Then the horses are gone.

The back of my spine tingles and my neck feels weak. The dust that had nearly choked me has settled back to earth. *What were they doing here? And where did they go?*

A grasshopper bounces across the scarred black asphalt and disappears into the grass. A plane leaves a white ribbon in its wake. A WE BUY UGLY FARMS poster flaps against a telephone pole.

My eyes follow the line of white paint that edges the road to the top of the hill and then back to where I'm standing. The asphalt is broken. I'm standing where it meets the earth. In front of my foot is a small sinkhole. In its center is a grayish-white stone. I pick it up. I turn it around in my hand. It has some rough, pointed edges. There is a speck of pink at one of the ridges. I try to rub the stone clean with my finger, but it stays the same. It feels pitted and raw. I lay it in my palm to inspect it. Nothing special. But I like the way it feels in my hand.

Another car slowly passes by. The driver is messing with the radio. The girls in the back seat wear earbuds. Their lips are moving to different songs. Everyone's in their separate world. I want to yell, "Hey, did you see . . . ?" I open my mouth, but my voice is gone.

I push my foot down on the pedal and slip the stone into my pocket.

CHAPTER FOUR

When I was eight or nine, I heard Dad's friend Flip Dixon say he saw his dead father one night just standing in the doorway of his double-wide. Dad and Flip were fixing the hitch on the horse trailer. Flip said, "I got up to use the john, and there he was, wearing his boxers and his Sioux Falls Canaries sweatshirt." Dad and Flip kept working while they talked. No different than if they were talking about horses or cars or the weather.

So I figure if Flip can talk to Dad about a ghost, I can talk to him about the wild horses. Besides, who else am I going to tell? It's not like I can talk to all the friends I've met in dance class.

Dad is in the kitchen wearing a new shirt. A friend of his is coming over for dinner. He's got the Bluetooth speaker ready to play their stupid playlists. He's making spaghetti sauce, the kind from a jar, which he just adds shit to and calls homemade.

"So today I was on my bike on Camel Hump Road, and out of nowhere, a herd of wild horses surrounded me." I stop to make sure he's listening. "Dad?"

"Yes, you were on your bike . . ." He tastes the sauce and adds some salt.

"And out of nowhere, there was this herd of horses."

He laughs. "You're so much like your mother. Such a great imagination."

"No, Dad. I'm serious. I was surrounded. There was this big black one, right next to me. And then the entire herd surrounded me."

I want to explain more, but he's shaking his head and stirring the spaghetti sauce.

"Reese, not now. I remember the wild horses too. But, please, just not now."

"But, Dad, I'm not talking about the drive. I'm talking about today."

Dad slams the wooden spoon onto the counter. Red specks go all over his nice shirt.

"Reese. Please." He looks down at his shirt. "Shit."

❧

The next day, it happens again. I'm in the middle of a science project, and though it's not uncommon for me to daydream or even fall asleep and literally dream in science class, this time I'm pouring something into something to see if it will do something, when I hear a rumble. A drumbeat. I figure it must be marching band practice. But when I glance out the window, there they are. The horses. Running across the football field. I drop my vial, spilling copper chloride all over our useless data, and my lab partner calls me a dildo. I know I'm not just seeing things. I have to try again to tell Dad.

When I get home, Dad's drinking a beer in the kitchen. He hands me a root beer float. "Snacks are in here," he says. I follow him to the living room. He plops down on the couch.

I'd forgotten tonight is a game night. Something the three of us used to do together. I never cared about the score, but the snacks could make it worthwhile. Mom made me all the treats she loved as a kid. I take a swig of my float but don't have the heart to tell him it doesn't come close to Mom's. How can you mess up a root beer float?

He's placed a tray of microwaved pigs-in-a-blanket on the coffee table. He pops two into his mouth at once. I push the blob of ice cream down to the bottom of the glass with my spoon and watch it float back to the top. Dad has his I'm-so-excited-it's-finally-baseball-season-again face.

"They look good this year," he says, nodding at the TV. "Thank the Lord they traded that no-good schmuck."

"That's good." He means the pitcher. He always means the pitcher. He yells at the TV for an entire inning, then a commercial comes on about a truck that's so nice and roomy your kids and dogs and grandma and camping gear can all fit inside. Everyone in the truck is happy. Dad looks happy too.

"Hey, I saw the horses again."

He's in the middle of draining his beer. He puts it down and gets up for another.

"Horses?" he says as he heads to the kitchen.

"Yeah, you know, the ones I told you about? The wild ones I see."

"Oh, the imaginary ones." He laughs and rummages through the fridge.

"Well, they don't seem imaginary to me."

He pops the can as he walks back to the couch.

"Hon, Miss Garland told us those vivid dreams are definitely because of the accident. Remember what you're supposed to do? The five-four-three-two-one technique.

Focus on five things you can see, four things you can feel, three things you can hear, two things you can smell, and one thing you can—"

"Taste. I know, Dad. But I see the wild horses. I see them when I ride my bike. I see them out the window at school." I try to sound a little excited.

He looks at me for such a long time that I have to pretend like I want another gulp of my root beer float. I was hoping he'd say, "Who cares about the game? Tell me all about it." Or "Let's go try to find them." But he looks at me, at the TV, back at me, and back at the TV five or six or seven times. I look down at a splotch of root beer foam on my knee.

A couple more commercials yap at us. One is about medicine for enlarged prostates. In the other one, Mr. Gibson, the Birdwood realtor who's also a wannabe TV star, is saying, "Is your farm so ugly it could make a young child cry? Is it so ugly you'd cover it with a paper bag if you could find one big enough? Don't worry, we buy ugly farms. Just call . . ."

Finally, the game comes back on. Dad pretends to watch, but I can see his eyes shifting around. Nine times out of ten, I'd say don't talk to your dad about anything. I should have said ten times out of ten. I was an idiot for thinking Dad would want to know about the horses.

For the rest of the game, things are weird between us. He's acting this different way with me, like we just met or something. In the middle of the night, I go downstairs for a bowl of cereal. I open his laptop. It's still warm. He hasn't closed the screen. I check what he'd been searching. Schizophrenia. Depression. PTSD.

I feel like my insides drop right out of me. He thinks something's wrong with me. Like seriously wrong with me.

Apparently, my dad thinks it's all cool and fun for his friend Flip Dixon's dead dad to show up grinning about a baseball team. But when just *one* herd of actual horses shows up just for me, my freckled butt lands in the counselor's office once a week quicker than you can flick a booger. It pisses me off. Why is it cool when Flip talks about this kind of shit but not when I do?

CHAPTER FIVE

TWO WEEKS LATER

"Have you seen them lately?"

I don't answer. Miss Garland puts a folder in a file drawer and then sits on the other end of the couch. Without the desk between us, she feels too close. She licks her fingers and turns a page in her notebook. I try to glance at the page as she turns it, but I can't make out any of the words. I'm not a great upside-down reader.

"Mrs. Roth told me about the poem."

My face feels hot. She must see my ears turning red. My right knee starts to jiggle. I put my hand on my knee to steady it, but that makes me want to bite my nails. So instead, I bite the inside of my cheek. I want the desk back. I want it there to hide at least a part of me.

"I just misread it."

"Misread it." Miss Garland has a bad habit of repeating my words. Like she wants me to use different words. Thinking about my words makes my knee bounce again.

In English class, we'd been reading poems out loud—one of the most dangerous things you can do as a fourteen-year-old aside from messing around with dangling participles. When it was my turn, I read, "There are beautiful wild horses within us. Let them turn the mills inside and fill sacks that feed even heaven." I thought I did OK. I even remembered to name the author. "By Saint Francis of Assisi."

Then the laughing started. I looked around to see what was so funny, but I should have known they were laughing at me. Mrs. Roth wouldn't have even noticed if Lexi Peterson hadn't yelled out loud enough for even the class across the hall to hear, "She said *horses*!"

My stomach tightened. My throat burned. If I'd tried to talk right then, my voice would have broken. All I do lately is give these assholes ammunition. I looked down at the words again. "Forces, not horses. Wild *forces* within us."

Miss Garland uncrosses and then re-crosses her ankles.

"You know you can come see me even when we don't have an appointment."

"I know. Thank you."

"And your dad? How are things with him?"

"Dad? He's good. You know. He's Dad." I smile at her.

I'm learning that you don't tell the truth to a therapist. Short, fast answers are key. I give the answer she wants to hear. Otherwise, there'll be hours of testing, more therapists, and prescriptions that can make you feel weirder than you do already.

"Your grades seem pretty good."

For me, she means.

"You enjoying track?"

"Yeah, it's good."

"Running can be a great outlet."

"Yeah."

She smiles a little and stares at me without blinking. I tuck my hair behind my ear and look around the room at nothing in particular. She's waiting for me to say something.

"Is there anything you want to talk about today?" she finally asks.

She's still trying to find out if I see them. So she can tell my dad. So he can freak out again. "No, things are, you know, OK."

"OK?"

"Normal."

"Normal?" She sits up straighter. She stares at me. She's supposed to like that word. I bite my cheek harder and clench my toes.

"Well, things are . . ." I need a word that will get her off my back. "Healing."

"Healing." She sits back in her chair. Her shoulders drop. She tilts her head and gives me a sweet smile.

Nailed it!

"Yeah, healing."

"Reese, I am so happy to hear that you feel things are healing."

"Yeah, me too."

Miss Garland takes three deep breaths. She never tells me to, but I know she wants me to breathe with her. When she's done with the breathing thing, she speaks more quietly.

"Sometimes it's easier to process what you feel when your eyes are closed. Why don't you sit back and do that."

I scooch back on the couch and squeeze my eyes shut.

"Last session you told me you didn't cry at your mom's funeral. Why was that?"

I have to think for a minute. I remember my dad in

the truck before the funeral, then sitting next to me in the church's hard pew while the pastor talked about Mom in the past tense, then as her casket lowered into the ground, and then later, cleaning up the house after all the people had gone.

"Because my dad didn't cry."

"You didn't cry because your dad didn't cry."

All this repeating is annoying me.

"Can I open my eyes?"

"Sure," she says.

Silence. She blinks ten times. So I blink twelve.

"Sometimes people try to send a message through their actions, but we misinterpret. I think maybe your dad was trying to be strong for you. I don't think he was trying to tell you not to cry."

"I guess I was waiting," I say.

"Waiting for your dad to cry?"

"No." I look around. "Waiting to feel like she was really gone." I get the jittery feeling of wanting to run. My knee bounces. "I didn't want to blubber at the funeral like an asshole, then turn around and see my mom standing right there behind me."

Miss Garland shifts in her chair and leans on an armrest.

"Why do you think you're beginning to heal?" She frowns a little and presses her lips together. "Did you and your dad do what we talked about? Honor your mom in some special way?"

"Yes." *Not really.*

"That's great. Do you want to tell me about it?"

"I wrote a letter." *No I didn't.*

Miss Garland slowly nods.

"We did a ceremony." *All bullshit.*

Miss Garland nods and smiles.

"We sang songs."

Miss Garland does a soft sigh. *I'm on a roll.*

"We danced the Macarena."

Miss Garland stops nodding. *Too far?* She lowers her chin and jots something in her notepad.

"Tell me more about the letter," she says.

"I just filled her in on what we've been up to. You know, that Dad is a serial dater now who forgot he ever had a wife and wishes he didn't have a daughter. That I started my period during PE and was really stoked that the gym teacher had to tell me how to use a tampon. That was awesome."

Finally, the bell rings. I get up and leave.

"Have a good meet," she calls after me. "Let's talk more about this next time."

❥

On the way home, I decide I've had enough. Talking doesn't help. Her questions just make my head spin. As soon as I get home, I drop my backpack inside the front door.

"Dad?" I call from the kitchen. "Where are you?" I call from the bottom of the stairs.

I find him outside, trying to fix the old push lawn mower Grandpa Tucker gave him. Even though it's broken more than it's not, he won't get a new one. He's got it upside down, and he's turning the blade slowly with his finger and scraping gunk out from under it with a screwdriver. I march right up to him.

"I don't want to go anymore. I don't need counseling. I'm sick of it. Besides, she's like twenty. What can she know?"

He stands up to stretch his back.

"You can talk to her about things that you and I can't talk about, Reese." He leans over again to give the blade one more twirl. "I mean, things you might not feel comfortable talking to me about."

I laugh. "*Me* uncomfortable?" I know he's the one who's not comfortable, so I try to make him even more uncomfortable. "You mean about things like sex and condoms and my period?"

He straightens. "And other stuff."

"So, you think a therapist can just wave her magic wand and all of our problems will go away?"

Dad tosses his screwdriver into the grass.

"That's not what I'm saying. I'm not sure what else you want me to do, Reese."

"I want you to stop wasting my time," I tell him. "Her office smells like farts, and all she does is stare at me."

Dad flips the lawn mower back onto its wheels and reaches for the pull starter.

"Look, just give it a few more weeks. It's not gonna kill you."

He yanks the pull starter, and the lawn mower jumps and shakes as he forces it back to life. Dad moves the lever up fast to keep it from stalling. The mower vibrates and I have to cover my ears. He lowers the blade speed and smiles.

"Anything can be fixed."

He pushes the mower onto our patchy lawn like he just figured out the cure for cancer. I walk back to the house, but right before I open the door, I hear a huge bang and look back at Dad. The mower is possessed, jumping around and making a rattle that sounds like it's trying to throw up a hammer.

"Goddam piece of shit!" Dad turns it off again and goes back to performing surgery on its undercarriage.

"Hey, what's with the naughty words, Mr. Swear-Word Police?"

"I mean gosh darn piece of crap."

All week, Dad's been home when I get home from school, just hanging around, not once going out for dinner with a friend. He keeps doing the humming thing he does when he's nervous about something. When he comes in from the garage, he watches me eat a peanut butter and jelly sandwich, offers to pour me some milk, and then follows me upstairs.

"What are you doing?" I ask him.

"Just, you know, hanging out with you." He's standing in the hall acting like a big, awkward weirdo, and he's looking at me way too much.

"Well, you're kind of freaking me out with all the eye contact."

"Oh, sorry. I thought we should, you know, spend more time together."

"Oh, well, I'm going to my room now. So . . . good talk."

I close the door behind me and lean back on it. *What a total loser.*

A few minutes later, he texts me . . . from downstairs.

I hear walleye are biting over at Crow's Neck. Thought we could pack a lunch on Saturday and see if we have any luck.

Now I know there's something fishy going on. Dad doesn't even like to fish. So when I hear him walk up the stairs and close his bedroom door, I sneak back down to the living room. I open his laptop and scroll through his email. And there it is. Just what I thought. Private and confidential from Francine Garland.

"In my opinion," she wrote, "Reese isn't hallucinating. However, she feels as though she has to say something fascinating and outrageous to get your attention. I find that teenagers who've experienced the loss of a parent often feel emotionally abandoned by the other parent, primarily because each family member deals with a loss so very differently. It is important to validate her feelings and not deny them, as she is still processing the tragic loss of her mother and is seeking your attention. Meanwhile, I'd like to continue seeing Reese every Friday during the last half of sixth period as well as start her on a prescription for an antianxiety medication."

I slam his laptop closed. If that's not the biggest crock of shit, I don't know what is. But it definitely explains Dad's newfound commitment to eye contact.

CHAPTER SIX

It's a half day at school because of some teacher con-
ference. The principal is encouraging kids to stay and
meet in the gym to organize teams for Birdwood Pride,
the Friday-before-Memorial-Day tradition where we play
dumbass sports that the same kids win every year. I feel
"encouraged" to get on my bike and head toward the barn.

I cruise down Camel Hump Road, looking around for
the horses. I pull over, get off my bike, kick a rock off the
road, and watch a couple of cars pass. I listen for a rumble
in the distance. Nothing.

It's cool today. Most of the snow on the Black Hills
falls in March and keeps the whole valley chilled until the
middle of May. I zip up my hoodie and get back on my
bike. My face and hands are cold. Close to my turn, a
small dust devil swirls around the scraggly oak. The flimsy
FOR SALE OR LEASE sign is back in the ground, tilting forward. I mow it down again, then stop. Red block letters
are bannered across the words *Gibson Real Estate*. DEAL
PENDING.

I'm home so fast I don't remember the ride. Dad's Jeep
is in the driveway. I leave my bike on the lawn, on its side,

front tire spinning. I leap up the stairs two at a time and explode through the front door so fast I scare myself a little. Dad almost drops the glass he's holding.

"You said someday!" I stand with my hands on my hips and my feet wide and, for a second, Dad looks scared. Then he sets his glass down and shakes his head.

"Aren't you supposed to be at a track meet today?"

"You said someday!"

"Someday?" He tugs at his earlobe.

"Someday we could go back." I'm trying to keep my chin from wobbling.

Dad's head does mini circles like he's flipping through pages in a book trying to find a place he's lost. Then he finds it. "Oh," he says. "The barn. Yes, *maybe* someday. I did say that."

"It's sold!" My voice gives out like a popped balloon.

"Well, I'm sorry, hon. I can't do anything about that. Mr. Gibson can do whatever he wants. It's his barn. His land."

"But you told me no one would ever buy it. You said the barn was too old and had too many problems. And you said the property was too far away from anything. And the land was in the flood plain and had too many rocks, and that Mr. Gibson . . ."

"That was two years ago, baby. I never guessed anyone would want that run-down old property."

"Why did you even say it then? Why did you say someday?" My stupid, weak chin can't hold it together any longer. It feels like my face might break open. I can already feel the skin on my cheeks tighten. My mouth spreads out and my nose runs. I'm seconds away from blubbering like a two-year-old, so when Dad walks toward me with his arms out, I punch him. But all that does is hurt my wrist.

Dad ignores it. I choke down a sob, and he holds both my arms down in a tight hug. All I can do is stand there and let him hug me.

"I know you want things to be like they were." He pulls my head into his chest and lets me wipe my boogery face all over his flannel shirt. "But we have to move on. We have to—"

When I breathe in, I stop hearing his words. I smell something. A scent. A perfume. It's not a smell I know. It's not the smell I should be smelling. It is *other* and I hate it. Instantly, I have a headache. And then it's like my brain does a replay of the things I saw but didn't pay attention to when I came flying through the door. I push my dad away while he's still talking. He tries to hold on to me.

I look around the room. This time, I notice everything. The wineglass Dad was drinking out of, the empty one on the table, the strange denim jacket draped over the chair, the soft jazzy music. My stomach flips inside out. I can taste the hot dog I didn't want but had at lunch anyway because I was so sick of pizza.

"Reese, there's someone I'd like you to meet."

He's looking over at the hallway. Someone is coming down the staircase.

"This is Sherri."

I know you're supposed to say "nice to meet you" when you're introduced to someone and she's standing there smiling with fresh lipstick and her hand's reaching out for you to shake. But seeing this person in my mom's kitchen—with her high heels and her red shirt and her boobs popping out at the top like a second ass—makes the tiny bit of beginning-to-be-OK-with-things I'd started to build over the past few months shrivel into nothing.

"It's nice to meet you, Reese," Sherri says in a voice that sounds like she has a cold, but she's just one of those forty-year-olds trying to sound like a twenty-year-old. I don't answer. I do the blank stare I've gotten really good at and walk right past her.

"I thought she was at a track meet," Dad says in his loud "quiet" voice.

Words are on the tip of my tongue, but I don't say them. Not out loud anyway. Not until I get to my room.

Short. Blonde. Weird mouth. Ugly hands. Dressed like a slut. Fake boobs.

From my bed, I can hear their voices blend with the lame, smooth jazz. I can't make out what they're saying, but I can get the gist from their conversation's ups and downs. Dad tries to apologize. Up. She says she needs to leave. Down. Dad tries again. Probably with another reason why what she just saw wasn't normal. Up. She still says she needs to leave. Down. Dad doesn't argue anymore. Down. Sound of keys, sound of closing door, sound of car starting, sound of being alone. Down.

Tomorrow, I won't go to the barn. I'll go see Mr. Gibson and get the information straight from the horse's mouth.

CHAPTER SEVEN

When I eat my Cinnamon Toast Crunch the next morning at the kitchen table, a hint of Sherri's stinky perfume is still lingering. I'd rather smell like a goat than wear that shit. Dad is snoring on the couch. The TV is still on. He doesn't wake up even when I let the door bang extra loud behind me.

I peek at him through the kitchen window. He hasn't budged. I ruined his little fling and now he'll be all cranky, nursing a hangover. But I have more important things to worry about. Like my talk with Mr. Gibson.

Gibson owns most of the land that surrounds Bird-wood. He buys it off farmers and sells it to developers for double the price. He's the reason Doe Run Farm is now a condo development. His family has owned the land Big Green is on for generations, but that didn't stop him from putting it on the market.

I pedal to his office, which is on a side street downtown right next to the bus station where I could get a ticket to Texas for $138, which I'll do if I ever get another notification on Treasure being at that Elkhart auction again. I park my bike just beneath the rectangular sign that has Gibson's picture on it, which, if you ask me, it shouldn't. He has one brown tooth, and the rest don't look great either. But that doesn't keep him from smiling like he's a huge movie star or something. He's also one of those people who wears flip-flops ten months out of the year, and if there's anyone who should cover his feet, it's him. His toenails look like curdled cheese. But as bad as his teeth and toenails are, the thing Mom liked least about him was that he mixed his metaphors.

Through the window, I see Mr. Gibson on the phone. The door dings when I open it. He looks up at me but keeps talking.

"Yes, yes, that's right. I can just see a pool there . . . would look great. You bet. I think it's only forty-five minutes from the airport, so that makes it easy, and they don't have to go by the reservation if they take Beaver Glen . . . uh-huh . . . uh-huh . . ."

Finally, he hangs up.

"Miss Tucker, how lovely to see you. What can I do for you today?" He flips through some papers on his desk. His voice sounds like he's smiling, but his face is not.

"Who bought the barn?"

He tries to pretend like he has to think about what I'm talking about.

"The barn . . . the barn . . ."

"Our barn. The one Mom and Dad ran a business out of for twenty years."

"Big Green Barn?"

"Yes, Big Green Barn."

"Oh, a nice young man came in. Didn't really say . . . anything. Just pointed to the property on a map, signed some documents, and wrote a check for the deposit. After someone's check clears, I don't go poking into their bees-wax." Mr. Gibson laughs, but I don't think there's anything funny about it. He sits back in his chair and slowly plays an invisible keyboard on the edge of his desk.

"But I've told you that my dad and I are going to buy it one day."

"With what? Your babysitting money?"

Mr. Gibson doesn't try to be an asshole. He just is. He acts like everything I say is funny. He looks around the empty room like he's laughing with an audience. Then he does that thing where he pretends he's taking me seriously.

"It's been two years, young lady. You never made an offer. Look, if this Indian can't make his payments, we can talk. He's not a developer. And he's only leasing it, just like your dad did before he broke his contract. And he's in the horse business, just like your family was. So you know how that is. Anything can happen. Prince and pauper living."

"Leasing? Horse business? He's in the horse business?" A horn blares outside on the street and it sounds like a celebration. My heart stops. The barn alive again with horses and horse people flashes through my mind like a light blinking on.

"Thanks, Mr. Gibson!" I call over my shoulder as I head toward the door. He's still saying something about how horse people aren't the most reliable, how they're such big dreamers, but I've stopped paying attention.

I pedal away. Out of nowhere, I feel sorry for his wife.

I head straight to the barn.

CHAPTER EIGHT

Something is already different. Someone has stapled a piece of paper to the scraggly oak. *For boarding and training, email Wes at.* The curled-up bottom corner hides the address. *Pretty lame.* I advertise my very average babysitting skills way better than this.

Something's off. I'm getting a definite sketch vibe. Maybe this Wes guy has tons of money, and horses are just a hobby. But if he has money, why would he be interested in this old farm? I bet he doesn't know the first thing about running a horse operation. Maybe the farm is a ploy. Maybe he's hiding something. I bet he's a total lurk.

I coast my bike down the sloping driveway. Bright sections of straight new rails flash by me on either side. Fresh dirt sits in piles near sturdy new posts. *Sketchy Dude has made some improvements, I see.* Horses graze together peacefully. Some stand in the shade under the giant pines.

In the distance, I spot him, and I brake. He's bringing a young horse in from turnout. I must admit, the colt looks well-bred. Nice lines. Good face. When he enters the barn, I let my bike creep forward again, and then I lay it down in the tall grass and duck behind the honey locust. I plan to pay close attention to his every move, anything that seems *sus.*

He walks in and out of the barn, shaking out dusty horse blankets and filling water buckets. When he has a smoke outside, he looks around like he knows someone's watching him. What's he hiding? Where'd *he* get all these nice horses, anyway? Why's he the only one here? Why hasn't he hired anyone? A groom? A stall mucker? Where's his wife? His kids? Maybe he killed them and buried them in a shallow grave in a cornfield in the middle of nowhere.

He takes a long drag of his cigarette, lets the smoke float from his nostrils, tosses the butt into a puddle, and heads back inside. I bet he does more than smoke. Tobacco is a gateway drug—everyone knows that. Just look at Tommy Clemmons from school. He started smoking when he was eight. Now he's addicted to oxys and meth. I bet Sketchy Dude is a drug dealer. I once heard about a drug dealer who stuffed horses' dead bodies with drugs, loaded them in the back of his truck, and crossed the border. *Is that what you're up to, you sicko?*

I sprint to the oak tree and spy from there for a while. Then I watch him from the field at the top of the hill. I lie in the deep grass while he rides one horse after another. I'm pretty sure he spotted me a couple of times—once when I tripped on a rock while running back to the oak tree, and once when I crawled through a patch of pigweed and couldn't hold in a sneeze. But if he did, he pretended he didn't. *Weirdo.*

I get close to the back of the barn so I can get a better look at the horses inside. I figure I'm safe because he's busy with a horse in the ring out front. But then the back door opens, and there he is, leading a bay colt down to the small paddock. The only place I can hide is behind the manure pile. I drop onto my stomach, my face hovering over a fresh pile of shit. Before I can army crawl to the pine tree, I spook the colt. My head is in plain view.

This time he can't pretend I'm not here. If I lower my head any farther, I'll be eating shit. So I wave, like it's natural for me to be sitting here behind a giant mound of horse droppings—me looking at him, him looking at me. He doesn't wave back, just stares at me, the colt dancing around him on one side, then the other.

A pitchfork is stuck in the ground a few feet away. *If he makes one move, he'll be wearing it between the eyes.* My body tenses as I prepare to dive for the weapon. But Sketchy Dude just shakes his head like he feels sorry for me. There's nothing that irritates me more than that. *Bastard.* He fixes a few things around the barn, and then he leaves in his beat-up old truck.

The next day, I get up enough nerve. Even if he chops people up and stores them in his freezer, I need to know his plan for the barn and all these horses. Just in case, I've got the whistle with the pepper spray that Dad gave me on my last birthday. It's pink, it's attached to a key chain, and it's not even the weirdest gift Dad's given me.

I lean my bike against the chokecherry and then poke my head into the barn. Sketchy Dude is untacking a pretty little Appy mare. He seems so comfortable here, which makes me even more uncomfortable. I clutch the pepper spray. He looks at me. I wave. He doesn't wave back. He juts out his chin at me but stays busy, like it's no big deal I'm here. Like he's been expecting me.

"Hi. You must be Wes." I jam both my hands in my pockets and shoulder-point toward the road. "I saw your sign at the end of the driveway."

He ignores me as he heaves the saddle off the mare's sweaty back. She stomps her front foot to shake a stubborn fly off her knee. I take a step into the aisle and wait to see if he tells me to stop. He doesn't. I keep going. Slowly.

I walk down the familiar aisle, breathing in the smells. Those smells. Even empty barns smell great. But nothing is more amazing than the smell of a barn when horses are in it. It's a sweet blend of hay and fresh-cut grass and worn leather and the musky smell that is a horse's alone. I take a deep breath and try to seal it into my lungs. I don't like being a stranger in a place that's put its giant thumbprint on me, but the smell is enough to make me feel like I'm slipping my feet into a pair of comfortable old shoes that still hold the shape of me.

The horses' big, kind eyes track me as I walk down the aisle. A brown muzzle sniffs at me through the bars of a stall. I reach my hand in, and his soft breath curls up my arm. My fingers graze his nose. It all makes me smile. A real smile. If you think about it, most of the time, you smile to be nice or polite or because you should. A real smile is different. Real smiles are very rare. Like pink pigeon rare. And when they happen, they are better than french fries. Better than chocolate.

I turn to look at the man who seems so at home here, scrubbing down the mare, dipping a rag in a bucket of steaming water.

"I'm Reese. You might have seen me around."

He looks at me and smirks. I'm relieved to see a flash of nice white teeth. *Probably not a meth head.*

"I don't live too far away. I used to spend a lot of time here."

He has a young face but old eyes. His hair is almost to his shoulders, but most of it is hidden by his floppy-rimmed cowboy hat. He still doesn't say anything. I walk closer, passing a tall gray horse in a stall across the aisle.

I want to tell this man he's in our space. How dare he settle in and touch all the things that still have Mom's and Dad's and even my own fingerprints all over them. He's been walking around in his scuffed cowboy boots like he's been here all his life—opening stall doors, filling hayracks, cranking the water hose that still moans and shudders when it first comes on. He's been scrubbing the place up like he's washing away our time here. Like it doesn't matter anymore.

He brushes the mare down with one hand and curries sweat spots with the other. I feel better now that I see what a good horse groomer he is. *A murderer wouldn't brush a horse with such meticulous care.* I loosen my grip on the pepper spray. I still want to tell him to stop. But instead, I say, "I'm looking for a job."

He stops brushing and goes into the office. I stand in the barn's main aisle, looking around at what still needs to be done—the wheelbarrow should be emptied, the wash hose isn't hanging properly, and stall guards are missing latches. Then Wes clears his throat. He's standing right under Dad's old sign, which is still tacked above the office door: Let's assume I'm right. It'll save time. He's got a look on his face like he's been waiting. He hands me a yellow piece of paper. He's written a note on it in cursive.

"You have nice handwriting."

He does a short breath out of his nostrils. A nose laugh.

I panic for a second. The swirls and curls that connect the letters always make cursive look like another language. Finally, letters pop from the swirls: *I can't afford help.*

He holds his hand out for me to give the paper back, but I hang on to it and stare at him. When he raises his eyebrows and widens his fingers, I hold the note closer.

"How about I just do a couple of things for free? You can pay me when you get the money."

He gives up on getting his note back and starts brushing the mare again. I crumple the note into a ball.

"My parents used to run this barn. I practically lived here. I can start right away."

I start pushing the wheelbarrow toward the compost pile. He drops the brushes, takes three giant strides toward me, and grabs my arm. His grip isn't tight, but I can feel the strength in his fingers. Like they have more power than my entire arm.

"Hey, use your words!" I say, shaking his hand off my arm. He loosens his hold. I lower the wheelbarrow. His fingers uncurl from my arm.

"I'm not really looking for a job. I just want to be here. I can't take one more hip-hop lesson. I can't even pretend to dance or sing or do any of that shit. I don't get sports, and I think clubs are for assholes." I look down at my orange sneakers. They look so out of place here. *Why didn't I wear boots?*

His lips stay tight, like they're knit together.

"I won't get in your way. Cross my heart a zillion times."

His face softens a little.

I slowly push the wheelbarrow down the aisle. I can feel his eyes on my back. I try my hardest to act like the wheelbarrow isn't heavy, like I'm not about to die of pain from the skin on my hands pinching up against the wooden handles. Wes ignores me while I clean tack and scrub some buckets.

"Don't worry. I won't bug you asking where things go. I already know." I feel for my pepper spray just in case he pulls a nutty. I mean, what's up with the no talking thing anyway?

He just keeps ignoring me. He doesn't seem to care anymore that I'm there. While he tacks up a young horse for a ride, I organize the feed and clean the supply room. I unpack some of the tack and gear from dusty old trunks and boxes. I soak metal bits in warm water and hang tack properly. I fold blankets and make a pile of dirty saddle pads. I even climb a stepladder to get the cobwebs down.

That's when I spot a box on the top shelf of the supply closet. A box of things Dad forgot to give away? One he didn't see? Something of Mom's? I reach for it and pull it down. It's filled with photos of Wes.

I dust them off, but some are stuck together. I plug in the floor heater and blow warm air on them, like Mom used to do, and gently pry them apart. Each photo has the date and the name of a horse and a race or a show written on the back. And in every one, the rider is Wes. Wes in a race in Arizona winning by at least five lengths. Wes in a show in Oklahoma going over an oxer as wide as a car. Wes jumping a huge hurdle in a race in Montana on a horse called Money Maker. He's obviously one of those rare horse people who's good at every discipline. The way Mom was. Every horse person I know would have these pictures framed and hung on a wall, not thrown into a box for who knows how long. I place them all carefully on a shelf.

After I look around, pleased with my good work, I find Wes outside, fixing the hole in the corner of the barn. The windy corner.

He still hasn't said a word.

"You hoarse?" I say. He doesn't seem to get the joke, so I try a couple of others. Dad jokes. "What the hay? Why the long face?"

When he finally looks up, he doesn't even crack a smile. He's got a row of sixteen-penny nails between his lips and a stack of two-by-fours at his feet. He holds a long board in place, plucks a nail from his lips, and keeps pounding. He's good with a hammer. It only takes him three whacks. Sometimes two. And none of the nails bend. They sink right into the splintery plank like they've always been there.

"But, seriously, if you have laryngitis, maybe try gargling with salt water. And you're not supposed to talk at all because you can strain your voice, which will make it worse."

He looks up for a second, takes another nail from his lips, and makes a face like I asked him if he'd like a shit sandwich.

"Sorry." I take a step back. "Just trying to make conversation."

He does a headshake—the universal kind that means he's annoyed—and continues whacking nails.

"I, uh, guess I'll be heading out." I raise my voice to make sure he hears me over all his hammering. "See you tomorrow then." I stare at the top of his hat. "And I cleaned all the tack."

He dusts off another two-by-four.

"See you tomorrow," I say again because I can't think of anything else to say, and it's hard to hold up both ends of a conversation.

There's another bit of silence while he reloads his lips with nails and positions another board. Already, the opening that was there is now just a slice of light.

"Bye, Wes." I turn toward the open door. I wish he'd stand up and look at all the work I've done. I wish he'd do something to make me stay a little longer.

"Oh, by the way, I saw one of the pictures of you in the race. The one in Dad's—I mean, your—supply room. The one where you're jumping a *ridiculous* fence with Money Maker."

His lips are still full of nails. One of them drops out.

"Pretty cool. That really was a ginormous fence." I want him to know I recognize good horsemanship. "Let me know if you need me to exercise any of the horses. I used to ride every day. Jumping is my favorite." I want him to know I can really help him out. But he just picks up the nail and shakes his head again while he places another board into position.

For two years, teachers and therapists and my dad have been trying to get me to *communicate*. I haven't wanted to. Not until now. Being around someone who doesn't talk and doesn't want to listen makes me suddenly have an epic case of diarrhea of the mouth. Words start seeping out of me. I want Wes to know how Treasure almost won the Black Elk. I want him to know about my mom and how she had faith in a horse that no one else believed in.

"We had a horse like Money Maker. His name was Trusted Treasure." I almost choke on his name. I haven't said it in two whole years. "His picture's right over there." I run down the aisle and grab it off the wall. When I try to show Wes the photo, he doesn't look up.

"Mom said he was the best horse we ever had."

I look down at the top of Wes's hat. I want to tell him the whole story, even though my voice is starting to catch again.

"We had to sell him when we left the barn. He's probably sitting in someone's field somewhere getting fat." A quick little laugh tumbles out of me at the same time tears sting my eyes. "The vet said we'd never be able to ride him again."

Wes stops hammering, but he still doesn't look up.

"I know," I say, like I'm responding to something Wes said. "I should probably just forget about him. I don't care about not riding him. I just think my mom would want him back here where he belongs."

Suddenly, I feel stupid talking about old dreams. Babyish. My chest tightens. I'm grateful when the hammering starts up again because I can't hear the sound that the frame and glass make when I throw the photo into the trash.

"See you tomorrow," I say, even though I know he can't hear me.

CHAPTER NINE

The barn is quiet. The photo of Trusted Treasure is back on the wall, hanging from a new nail. The glass protecting the photo is gone. Without it, the picture looks clear and new. For a second, I feel light and bright too. But without the glass, the picture will get dirty and smudged. It will fade faster. *Good. Let it. The sooner the better.*

But something else is new. Something that wasn't there yesterday. Wes has written all of the horses' names on duct tape and stuck them to their stall doors. I feel a warmth in my chest. Like something melted. He must have done that so I'll know their names. *So he does want me to stay.*

A big, beautiful flea-bitten gray leans his head over his stall door and reaches his muzzle toward me, reminding me to introduce myself. The name *Bob* is scrawled on the tape.

"Hello, Bob. That's a plain name for someone so fancy." He nods his head like he agrees.

On a whiteboard outside the office, something is written in Wes's handwriting. *I don't talk. It's a choice.*

"Good to know." I pat Bob and let him smell my cheek.

I move down the aisle to the next stall. Treasure's old stall. I know he won't be there, but I can't help thinking he somehow might be. I peek over the stall door. A tall liver chestnut is standing in the middle of the stall, looking like a gorgeous bronze statue. The tape on his door says *Sir Drake*. He turns toward me and pushes his muzzle into my belly. Treasure did that when he wanted his forelock scratched. Sir Drake stretches his neck out so I can get under his jaw.

"How's that?" I ask him.

He makes me laugh because he's so demanding. Then, when he's had enough, he shakes his head and blows out his nose, leaving black specks of dirt all over my arm.

"Thanks, and you're welcome, Sir." I fill his water bucket and stuff his hayrack with fresh hay. I slide his door closed behind me. "Just call room service if you need anything else."

I move down to the next stall. The tape says *Stinky*.

"What's up, Stink Man?" He looks like the oldest horse here by far. I don't walk into his stall right away. He lifts his head out of the bucket. His nose is covered in brown mash. I'm guessing Stinky doesn't have all of his teeth, so Wes must add water to the grain to make it mushy enough for him to digest. Otherwise, it would come out the other end looking just like it did going in. Stinky puts his ears back at me and dives into his mush again.

"Don't worry, I don't want your bran. I had Honey Nut Cheerios for breakfast, so I'm all set." When he calms down, his ears come forward. I wait at his stall door. "What's up, old man? You lose the bingo tournament last night?"

He looks at me as he munches on his mash, then bobs his head up and down, letting me know it's OK to enter. Mom taught me that before you enter a stall, you should stand for a minute to make sure the horse sees you. Like you're looking at the horse asking, "May I come in?" I mean, you wouldn't barge into someone's house without asking. It's the same thing. I freshen up Stinky's hay and top off his water.

I move down to the next stall and see a note tacked on it. *Olive—vet visit 3:30 pregnancy exam.* I stop breathing. There is absolutely nothing more exciting in the entire world than a newborn foal. I know exactly what needs to be done.

I grab a pitchfork and strip Olive's stall, clearing it of everything, even the cleanish shavings in the corner. When the vet arrives, I want it to be spotless. I empty two clean bags of shavings into the center of the stall and spread them around evenly with my feet. I scrub her feed and water buckets and replace the timothy hay in her hayrack with some deep green alfalfa.

Mom treated our pregnant mares like gold. "They're pregnant for almost a full year," she told me. "And if humans think it's a problem when their babies kick, imagine four tiny hooves kicking around inside you."

I bring Olive into the wash stall, fasten the clips on either side of her halter, and let the water run until it's nice and warm. I start on her legs to get her used to the temperature. Olive lowers her neck as she begins to doze. Her eyes close and her bottom lip hangs loose while I give her a relaxing warm bath.

Her belly is just beginning to swell. The skin pulls around the barrel, and the veins look like the bottom side of a leaf, raised and pushing up on the skin. I scrub softly under her belly, give her a nice warm rinse, and towel her off before draping a mesh sheet over her and leading her back to her clean stall.

The next two stalls say *Jasper* and *Marge*. A note says, *Whatever you do, don't separate these two.* I stand on Jasper's threshold, waiting for permission. He does a little pretending-to-be-tough act and stomps around a little. "Hey, Jas. Someone wake up on the wrong side of the bed this morning?"

Marge, Jasper's neighbor, looks like a big Percheron-cross, and even though she's three times his size, Jasper is acting like he has to protect his woman. They don't really look like they belong together. Marge is a big girl, and Jasper is under fourteen hands—pony size—but, apparently, they don't care. We used to have a couple just like them. Art and Ethel. Art, the pony, was obsessed with Ethel, one of my mom's big jumpers. Mom called them the old married couple even though Art looked like he could have been her baby. When they got separated, all hell broke loose. I introduce myself to Marge and clean both stalls while they finish their breakfast.

I do the same with Elvis, a bay thoroughbred; Bailey, a rose-gray filly; Marty, a seal-brown colt; Leo, a big sable gelding; and Wyatt, a gentle blue dun. There are at least ten more horses turned out in the paddocks and fields. I can't wait to meet them all.

I clean and dress some bridles that Wes left hanging on the hook next to the sink and wash out feed buckets. While I'm replacing the buckets, Wes walks by the feed room. He stops and looks in at me. I can't read his expression. Is he mad? Did I do something to upset him? I stop scrubbing and wait. For a moment, I think he's actually going to start talking and tell me to get the hell out, that he doesn't need me and I'm just in the way. But he raises his eyebrows and nods his head, and his lips slightly creep up in the corners into what barely passes as a smile.

It's a mic-drop moment. I hold out the bucket-scrubbing sponge and let it fall to the ground.

CHAPTER TEN

Wes has let me stay on at the barn for over two weeks now. Mainly because one of my best traits is begging. A close second is making myself useful.

On weekends, I arrive before Wes, but today he's already fed the horses. Some have even been turned out. Dirty tack hangs on the hook over the sink, and the wash stall has a brown puddle near the drain. He doesn't have to say anything. I know I'm supposed to clean things up. For someone who doesn't talk, Wes communicates pretty well. Sometimes he just walks up and hands me the pitchfork—hard to misinterpret that. There's less guesswork than I thought there'd be. His delivery's pretty clear. Clearer than most talkers. But I still wonder why he doesn't talk.

Dad's no help, as usual. I asked him why he thought someone might choose not to talk, and he asked Siri and Siri said, "Someone may not want to talk to you because they are mad at you." Then Dad looked at me and said, "Is that helpful?" And I said, "Not at all."

Anyway, I spend less time thinking about it the more I'm around him. I figure one day he just got sick of it. Just said to himself, why bother? I can see that happening. Like just sort of realizing that talking is a big waste of time. Especially when it's so hard to pick words that match how you feel. There are only so many, after all. Then there's the whole mess of deciphering what people actually mean. Half the time, people don't say what they mean. No. Ninety percent of the time.

In science class last week, Mr. Yutu told us that trees secretly talk to each other using something called the Wood Wide Web, an underground network of organisms that helps them share nutrients and warn each other of threats. No words necessary. I think Wes has already figured out that stringing a bunch of sounds together is way less useful than we think.

Outside, Wes is riding Sir Drake, who's looking like a champion. At least three people are interested in him for the Black Elk. He has the attitude it takes to win. He sizes everything up just so he can jump it.

This time of year, Mom and Dad would dream about finding the perfect Black Elk horse. Every night, their horse talk would float above me, drift down across my shoulders, and seep into my pores. I'd curl up in my chair, listening to story after story about all the horses who'd almost won— the amazing animals who could soar and glide and fly.

Then they'd talk about the horses they were dreaming up. Dad would say, "If I could find a horse that has Mr. Cleveland's legs, Sotheby's body, and Lady Darby's brain . . ."

"That would be some horse," Mom and Dad would say together.

Wes is thinking Sir Drake is some horse. He's big. He's solid. He has strong feet. And he can jump the moon. He's also a nine-year-old, which, as Dad used to say, is the perfect age for this race. Not too young, not too old. Just enough experience and still plenty of stamina. Wes looks amazing on any horse, but on Sir Drake, he looks like he could do anything. If Wes aimed him at his old truck and asked him to jump it, he would. He'll definitely be able to sell him for the kind of money that lets you buy four or five more horses at auction.

I go down the aisle, shoveling, spreading fresh shavings, and filling water buckets stall to stall. Now that I've gotten to know everyone inside, I spend time just talking to them, making them comfortable. I'm asking Elvis how his life is going when the stall door rumbles behind me. Wes is standing at the door, shaking his head. I know he thinks I blab too much when I work. Then he hands me an envelope. I can tell by the feel of it there's a nice wad of cash inside. On it he's written, *It's a good thing I don't talk. You talk enough for the both of us.*

My first payday. Everything changes in an instant. Wes sees this isn't just a hobby for me. He thinks my work is worth something. I'm not just a kid who loves horses and gets underfoot. I have to stop myself from throwing down the pitchfork, slinging my arms around Wes's neck, and squeezing him as tight as I can.

"Thank you, Wes." I pat Elvis's neck. "I've noticed you're really busy with Drake. Just let me know if you need me to exercise any of the others."

Wes nods.

"I'll try to talk less if it bothers you."

Wes shrugs a little, like it's not a big deal.

"I don't know why I do it."

But the truth is, I know why I talk so much when I'm here. Useless as words might be, they fill the space between then and now and muffle the question that seems to yell at me whenever I see Treasure's old stall: *Where is he?* And words dull the sharp pain I feel in my chest whenever I turn a corner, expecting to see Mom.

With this barn so full, why does it still feel so empty?

CHAPTER ELEVEN

I must have zoned and not noticed Dad's Jeep parked outside the house. My mind was too busy racing with ideas
for helping Wes's business. Now that I'm on payroll, with
a fat wad of cash in my back pocket, I feel like I matter.
Like I can make a difference.

"How'd it go today?"

Dad is sitting in the living room in his chair, staring at
me, eyebrows up, wearing a goofy grin. I can't remember
what the hell I told him I was doing today. Keeping track
of lies is a lot of work. He's waiting for an answer. Where
did I say I'd be? Dance class? Some after-school thing? The
mall? A friend's house? *Shit.*

"Those don't look like track-meet clothes," he says.

The meet! Oh yeah!

"Yeah, I . . . had a . . . sprained ankle so I couldn't
compete. But I went with the team. It was mandatory. You
know, team stuff. There's no *I* in team," I say, imitating the
coach. "So I just watched, you know, to be supportive."
I'm talking too much. Explaining too much. Which isn't
natural for me. I should shut up.

"That's good. I'm glad. I got a lot out of being on the baseball team when I was your age."

I sense one of his stories coming on, the kind that makes me feel like my toenails are being peeled off, slowly, one by one. He started talking at me this way after Mom died. His voice goes all TV dad from a show called *How to Talk to Your Teenage Daughter*. He sounds more like he's reading than talking. I want to run, but I make myself stay put. I do a big yawn.

"I should probably put my ankle up."

"Right. Good idea. Yeah, rest it. Rest is important. And maybe some ice."

He gets up to go to the freezer. I walk past him as quickly as I can. I remember to do a slight limp.

"You hungry?"

"No. Just ate."

I head toward the stairs.

"Hang on a sec. Take this." He hands me a bag of frozen blueberries.

"Thanks."

"Ten minutes on, ten minutes off," he says, using his fingers in case I don't know what ten is.

"K. Night." I try to make my voice sound like there's nothing to look at here. *I'm still your bratty daughter, and I'm not hiding anything.*

"Oh, Reese?"

Shit. I close my eyes tight. I hover one foot over the first step and wait for him to call me out on my fake limp.

"I, uh, I've been wanting to mention. There's someone I'd like you to meet."

"Sherri? I met her. Remember?"

He swipes at the air like a fly's buzzing around him.

"No. Someone else."

"Another friend with benefits?" I wink and elbow-jab the air.

"Uh, no, we . . ."

"A phoner and boner?"

"Reese, stop it. I'm being serious."

"Me too."

"Knock it off, Reese. This is different. I'm seeing her kind of seriously. Her name is LeeAnne. I want to have her over for dinner some night when you don't have play rehearsal or a track meet or choir practice. I mean, I can't keep up with all of your after-school activities."

He really doesn't have a clue. Part of me wants to shake him and tell him how clueless he is, and another part of me—the part that wants to stay alive—is relieved he's so busy with his own shitty life he doesn't pay attention to mine.

"OK. I'll try to make it."

He smiles another goofball-looking smile. "Great. I really think you'll like her."

Before I climb the stairs, I look over at him. He's gone back to looking at his phone and drinking his beer. Then he puts his headphones on, the ones he uses when his tinnitus gets bad.

About a month after the accident, he started having a constant roaring in his ears. Sometimes it's low, sometimes it's so loud it makes him crazy, and only he can hear it. Dad says maybe it's a delayed reaction from going to all those Def Leppard concerts and standing too close to the speakers. The doctors say there's no cure, but he's always trying to find something that will help. Once, he put an oil that smelled like rotten eggs right into his ear. It didn't help, but it stunk up the place for days. Sometimes tinnitus gets better on its own. Sometimes it gets worse. And God help us if it gets worse, because you'd already think the doctor told him he had cancer of the ball sack.

"Night, Dad," I say, but he can't hear me. I want to tell him about my first payday. I want to sit him down at the kitchen table and make it rain fives and tens and show him how hard I've been working. But the one thing I want to brag about is the one thing that he'd totally lose his shit over.

He tugs on his earlobe and then sticks his finger in his ear and opens his mouth like he just went swimming and he's trying to get the stuck water out. Then he walks toward the kitchen for another beer but stops to look at himself in the hall mirror. He smooths his beard with his hand and turns his head this way and that until he sees my reflection. He takes off his headphones.

"Oh, night," he says, not really looking at me, still checking himself out.

He stopped really looking at me about a year ago. Even worse, he stopped giving me *the look*. The one that meant, *You OK?* We could have been out at the grocery store or going to a movie or just hanging by ourselves at home. It was just a glance. And it was just enough. But *the look* stopped. He started looking past me or just to the side of me or over the top of me.

He also became a weirdo with a beardo. His beard went from a dirt-on-his-face stage to a patchy-Amish-guy stage to a lumberjack stage and lots of stages in between. The worst part is, he doesn't look like Dad anymore. It's like he thinks he looks hot or something. What man in his forties thinks he's hot? It's just wrong. It's legit gross.

I fake limp all the way up the stairs.

In my room, I take the cash from my back pocket. I

stand on my bed and take down the terrible paint-by-numbers of Man o' War that's been hanging over my headboard since I was eight. Last year, I made a hole in the wall behind the painting so I'd have a place to hide my stuff. It started pretty small, but it's now the size of a dinner plate. I filled the inside of the wall between the studs with old towels to keep things from falling to the baseboard.

I reach into the safe for one of Mom's hummingbird stationery envelopes and place the cash inside. On the front of it, I write *barn* and add it to the stash of envelopes I've labeled *babysitting*, *dog walking*, *birthday*, and *Christmas*. Before I put Man o' War back on the wall, I reach in for Mom's old barn notebook, then plop down on my bed.

The only reason I have this notebook is because I found it in the trash when Dad was cleaning everything out of the barn. Seeing that Dad had tossed the notebook Mom always had tucked under her arm or stashed on the truck's dashboard or opened on the kitchen table was even worse than finding out he'd given all her clothes away to Goodwill while I was at school one day. He'd asked me the night before if there was anything from her closet I wanted to keep, but the question made my insides feel like they were all squished together. I should never have to answer that question. So I didn't.

But the notebook was different. I hid it under my shirt in case he tried to talk me out of keeping it. In case he said it was full of a bunch of useless stuff like the rest of the boxes he was filling.

I sit up in bed and, for the first time ever, read every word. I flip through pages full of Mom's handwriting. She made lists of clients and sales and training logs and pretty much anything else that went into running the barn.

Every inch of the page is full of information. Sick horses' symptoms and treatments and dates. Every auction where a horse had been bought or sold. Feeding instructions for picky eaters. Training notes for anxious horses. The ranches and farms that bought horses from her for years.

The last two pages are laid out like a spreadsheet. She has columns for revenue and expenses. The prize money and purse money from shows and races were barely enough to carry the place for a month. The sales, boarding, and lessons were their income. That's how they survived. That's what kept their dreams alive.

I close the notebook and slide it under my pillow. I can't believe my dead mom is more help to me than my living dad.

CHAPTER TWELVE

On my way downstairs to breakfast, I almost forget to limp.

Dad has two bowls of cereal ready on the kitchen table. Every morning, before we head out the door in different directions, Dad and I have our cereal together. But when I say *together*, I mean we're eating at the same time while we both look at our phones. Today, there's Fruity Pebbles for me and some nasty-looking high-fiber thing for him that I wouldn't even feed to the horses because it would probably give them the runs for a week. It's usually cold cold cereal in the morning. Hot cold cereal is more of a dinnertime thing.

"Wanna watch the game tonight?" he asks. Then he gets up, puts his bowl in the sink, and grabs his jacket from the back of the chair. He's trying to act normal, like he's not all I've-got-a-girlfriend goofy.

"No thanks."

"OK. I'll be right here tonight if you change your mind." His mouth is full of cereal and whiskers. "Don't forget to lock the door on your way out."

He's pretending like he didn't ask me, just last night, to meet someone he's "seeing kind of seriously."

"OK. Bye, Grizzly Fatums." I've come up with a slew of nicknames for Dad and his latest beard. He looks down and pulls his belly in. Grizzly Fatums is the name that pisses him off the most because he's become sensitive about his weight gain. If he misses a run or two, he gets a muffin top fast.

He grabs his keys off the sideboard and is just about to close the door behind him when I say, "Hey, Mutt Face. You've got a dinglebeardie." He swipes at his beard where half a flake of his gross cereal is dangling from where his chin should be.

"Thanks," he says.

He's so used to the name-calling that he doesn't tell me to stop it anymore unless it's one of the really bad ones, like Pube Face. I know his tactic. He thinks if he acts like the name-calling doesn't bother him, I'll just stop. But he doesn't realize my tactic is to not stop until he finally shaves and looks normal again. Old Dad was fun and funny and gave a lot of hugs and didn't try to act cool. He just *was* cool. I miss old Dad.

"Is it play rehearsal today?" he says, like he's proud of himself for remembering.

"No, choir practice."

He nods like he remembers. He believes my most absurd lies. Choir practice. I don't even sing in the shower. But he falls for them all because he doesn't really care anymore.

From the window, I watch him get into his Jeep and pull onto the main road. As soon as he makes the turn, I dump the rest of my cereal. I make sure I've got Mom's notebook and run to my bike. I pedal as fast as I can to the barn.

Horse owners start to get nervous about three months before the race. That's when the real nervous nellies start looking for a replacement horse. They start overthinking. They worry that the horse they were planning to run doesn't really have what it takes to win the Black Elk. Dad said he could pretty much mark on his calendar the date they'd start to call. "Another fussbudget," he'd say when his phone rang. Sometimes a horse really had developed an injury or some sign of weakness, but usually it was just an owner who started to doubt. This time of year, the doubters come out in droves.

Worrywarts, skulkers, fainthearted whiners, cow-babies, and pansy-asses are just a few of the words my dad used to describe these owners. Owners like Ty Sedgwick, who wants to meet with Wes at the Twin River Ranch today. Ty is from Big Horn, Wyoming. Wes is showing him Sir Drake. I'm tagging along because I begged Wes until he let me.

Twin River is the only property in the area that has jumps anywhere close to Black Elk jumps. Here, Wes can prove that Drake has the goods. I'm guessing selling a horse like Drake would be ten times the profit of the average sale. It's like hitting a gold mine.

Wes was hoping for a 6:00 a.m. slot, but all he could get was noon. Which means I'm playing hooky. Which means if I get caught, I get a detention. Worth it. But practicing as late as noon kind of sucks for Wes. By that time of day, rails will be knocked or broken, the footing will be cut up, and too many other trainers will be in the field.

I have plenty of time to do a few barn chores and help Wes get the trailer ready. I hide Mom's notebook in a safe place until there's a good time to show Wes. Timing is everything. I don't want him to feel like I think I know more than he does or something. You have to move around horse people the same way you have to move around young horses. "Slowly and deliberately," Mom used to say.

I remember Twin River Ranch being nice. I was here a few times when Dad schooled here. But I swear it seems swankier every time I see it. It's owned by Sid Barker, the wealthiest rancher in the area. He's a breeder and an owner. He also has cattle. "Just for fun," Dad says.

Wes is checking the place out from the road. I can see him scanning the expensive fencing and the manicured grounds. He looks over at me, raises an eyebrow, sticks out his bottom lip, and nods. *Not too shabby.*

"Nice crib," I say. Wes laughs.

Wes pulls up to the driveway entrance and stops in front of the giant wrought iron gates. They're monogrammed. We stare at the *T* and the *R*.

"You have to press the buzzer. Then just look at the camera. They're expecting you."

Wes gives me a *no-shit* look, then reaches out and presses the button. He tips his hat to the camera, and someone buzzes us in. The gates slowly open, and we continue down the driveway, which runs alongside the schooling field.

I expect we might run into a few people who knew me when I was younger, the kind of people who are nice to your face and then turn around and say, "That horse hasn't got a shot." I'd hear crap like that all the time. They'd say it right in front of me after my parents went out to the field, like I was invisible or deaf or something. I hold in a laugh when I think of how they'll all shit themselves when they see Wes on Sir Drake. They'll all have to run home and change their Depends.

Today, Patrick Miller, one of the best jockeys around, is in the field. He's originally from Australia, where riders are known to ride "hurt." Broken bones and injuries just make them want to win more. He's the jockey who was on Storm Dog, the winning horse the year Trusted Treasure almost won Black Elk.

Sid Barker is paying Patrick to ride in this year's race. He'll be on a big gray, Sunday Secret, who's known to fly over fences and leave six inches to spare. Patrick just so happens to be out on that gray today. He gallops up alongside our old truck as we putter along. Instead of saying hello, he taps his whip to the brim of his helmet.

"Schooling field closes in an hour. May want to come back tomorrow." He inspects the truck while the big gray yanks on the bit.

Wes nods. He isn't going to waste his time with so much as looking at this guy. Patrick's already playing some power game. Wes acts like he doesn't even notice.

"That's all we'll need," I say, trying to play it cool like Wes.

"Park in the back of the barn. Got a trailer coming in," he says.

Wes nods again. Patrick gallops off behind us, and I crane my neck to watch. The gray flies toward a jump and careens over it like he has an extra gear. I try to keep my jaw from hitting the floorboard—the animal Patrick's riding is amazing. For the first time, I wonder if Sir Drake is good enough.

We pull around to the back of the new barn, which has padded stalls and air-conditioning. I've heard it has a therapy pool for injured horses. Even the light fixtures look expensive. It doesn't really look like a barn at all.

The truck hiccups and sputters, like if we turn it off, it might not start again. Wes shakes his head and pats the dashboard as if the old truck could love him back. We both climb out to unload Drake. I hold him while Wes grabs the tack out of the bed of the truck.

"I bet these horses speak French and shit roses," says a tall man walking toward us from a shiny white dually pickup. He takes off his baseball cap and holds his hand out to Wes. "How you holdin' up, Wes?"

Wes shakes his hand and does his tight-lipped smile-nod.

"I'm Reese," I say, holding my hand out too.

"Nice to meet you, Reese. Sedgwick. Ty Sedgwick." He squeezes my hand so hard I make a face. He looks back at Wes.

"That little mare you sold me last year won Prairie Meadows. Thinkin' of breedin' her next year." Then he turns his attention to Drake.

"Looks nice. Let's see what's under the hood."

Wes and I tack up Sir Drake next to the trailer. I tighten the girth and hold the reins under the horse's chin tight while Wes does a one-bounce from the ground and swings his leg over Sir Drake. Ty and I watch as Wes has Drake jog a few figure eights. He canters a circle in one direction, then the other.

I lean on the board fence rail, then stand on the bottom rung to get a better view. My skin itches from the rail's whisker-like splinters. I would be lying if I said there wasn't a tiny tinge of jealousy creeping up my spine. I hate sitting on the sidelines.

Out on the schooling field, Sir Drake's coat shines like

copper. The sun highlights every muscle in his chest and haunches. He prances sideways. A horse can sense when something big is about to happen. Drake knows he's going to run. Wes stays solid and still over Drake's withers and pats his neck to calm him.

Drake cruises over the easier jumps, and Wes lets him size up the more challenging ones. The jump at the top of the incline is the most treacherous of all. Just like in the Black Elk, it's the last jump in a series of four. How you meet the first sets you up for the last. Drake will have to jump a good foot higher than the height of the jump, and if he's too tired to leave the ground early, he won't have the rhythm he needs to clear it.

"Leave something in the tank" is what Dad always said. Treasure wasn't the first horse to make it through almost the entire race, have a shot at winning, and then crash at the last fence. And he won't be the last. Drake needs to get it right the first time. After he gets a few good looks at that jump series, Wes will approach the incline with him like they've done it forever.

As I watch the magic that's happening between Wes and Drake, my tinge of jealousy fades away, replaced by the feeling that happens when you let yourself think, *What if?* I imagine race day. The parking lot full of cars. Bands playing. Sparkling horses painted on kids' faces.

Then a voice booms in my ear, and my daydream is over.

"May as well forget about any horse this year except the gray Patrick's on."

I hadn't noticed anyone standing next to me, let alone Bill Gander. I recognize him by the mole that sticks out of his neck.

"Makes that chestnut the deaf guy's on look like a plow horse."

Dad called him Bill Goiter. He trains for Sid, and every year tries to buy him a horse to race in the Black Elk. But it just never works out for Bill, and he doesn't like it when it works out for anyone else. Two years ago, he tried to buy Trusted Treasure from Mom and Dad two days before the race. He knew they were having money problems, but they still wouldn't sell. After Treasure's fall, when we were all still in shock, Bill went right up to Dad. "Thanks for not selling," he said, then walked away laughing.

I can tell he doesn't recognize me. He's the type of person who looks past anyone he thinks is "unimportant." I almost tell him that Wes isn't deaf, he just chooses not to talk, and maybe he should consider doing the same, but I bite my tongue.

"Put him dead center," Goiter yells. "Jayzus, Patrick, keep ridin' like a split-tail and I'll get you a sidesaddle."

Patrick's got his horse moving like the race is next week. He's pushing him into all the high panels in a row of four hurdles and driving him on with his whip. Wes is out in the far end of the schooling course, and Patrick has just charged past him, making Drake shy to the side. Wes acts like nothing's happened. He lets Sir Drake pick up a nice canter, and they do some big circles before heading for another jump. But Patrick gallops up behind Wes even harder than before. He passes too close, then takes the jump first. Again, Wes acts like nothing happened.

Wes moves to another area of the enormous field, but Patrick follows. The gray yanks and pulls on the bit. He's already lathered. His bit is cranked up with more attachments than I've ever seen. It's clearly irritating him, making him stick out his tongue and bob his head. I'm sure the gray's nerves are getting to Sir Drake.

Wes doesn't show any reaction.

Patrick takes out his whip, thwacks the gray's rump hard, and gallops uphill at top speed. Wes holds Drake back for a moment, but when he loosens his hold, Sir Drake goes from a walk to a dead gallop in a split second. I run along the fence line with Ty and Goiter and watch Wes aim Drake up the hill and almost catch up to the gray.

They're both heading directly for the incline jump.

"Holy shit," I say too loud. I feel like a fish is flipping around my insides.

"That's what I'm talkin' about," says Ty.

"Drive on!" yells Goiter. The sun is hitting his mole just so, and it looks even bigger with his chin raised up while he's yelling.

The horses stretch out at racing speed. The gray is only four strides out from the jump. Drake is two strides behind him. The gray takes off an extra stride before the jump, but Drake passes him in the air. The gray hits his knees hard at the top of the jump, catapulting Patrick over his head. The gray's horseshoes flash in the air as he nosedives to the ground. But Sir Drake clears the jump like he wasn't even trying. Wes pulls him up after a few strides.

I run through the field. Someone from the barn is driving toward the accident in a pickup. I get there first and grab the big gray by the reins. Wes, still holding onto Drake, goes to help, but Patrick waves him off. One of his shoulders sits lower than the other.

"Same damn collarbone," he spits out with a laugh, then pulls a bottle of pills from his pocket. "It's broke more than it's not these days." Patrick doesn't ask about his horse. He just calls him a daft mule, empties the pills into his mouth, and crunches them in his teeth.

"Poor baby," I whisper into the gray's muzzle. Patrick will blame the fall on him. But I know it was Patrick's fault. He pushed the horse to do too much too soon.

As we lead Drake back to the trailer, we pass Goiter sucking on a cigar. He's already on the phone about another horse.

"Have him here by Sunday and I'll pay cash," he says.

"He sure has a lot of fun throwing Sid's money around," says Ty. "He'd do better using it to wipe his ass."

Wes laughs.

"I'll be by your place tomorrow to vet him," Ty says as he climbs into his pickup.

"You rode great today," I tell Wes. "If I was riding that gray, I would have asked for another stride. He took it way too long if you ask me." I'm hoping if Wes hears how much I know, he'll let me ride soon. I'm trying to be patient. But when there's an opportunity to drop a hint, I try not to miss it.

On the ride back to our barn, I feel a flutter in my chest. Selling Sir Drake will suck. But knowing how much we need the sale makes it OK. And just thinking about him running in the Black Elk is enough to make me feel like my feet won't quite touch the ground when I walk around telling everyone, "I know that horse."

CHAPTER THIRTEEN

When I arrive at the barn the next day, I'm still trying not to think about what happened at Twin River. My mind replays the gray's body hitting the ground the way Trusted Treasure's did. How everything happened so fast. How he was so perfect and full of energy one second and crippled the next. How he struggled to stand after he fell and hung his head. Worn out. Finished.

Unlike my mind, the barn is quiet. The only sound is the rumble of construction equipment more than half a mile away where they're leveling the pig barn and the old farmhouse that stood next to it. Then they'll rake and groom the land that's been raising pigs for a hundred years. When the wind blows in this direction, a plume of brown dust drifts across our pasture, then spreads out and disappears.

Drake is the only one inside, and he's pacing back and forth in his stall.

"No turnout for you, handsome? Don't worry. Soon you'll be heading to a nice big ranch where they'll treat you like a king."

Then I notice that Wes left a note on the stall door. *Cool down 20 mins. Hose down.* Wes trusts me with Sir Drake, the most important horse here. It's a major step up from stall cleaner and water bucket filler. He's asked me to cool down some of the other horses before, but never Sir Drake.

Dad would call this a marigold-orange-1955-Ford-Thunderbird-with-a-removable-hardtop-carrier moment. When he was just fourteen, his grandpa handed him the keys to the car he called his baby. "All I did was park it," Dad said, "but it changed my life forever. Made me feel like an adult." It's one of those stories he tells so often I can mouth the words.

"Hey, gorgeous." I slip Drake's halter over his big, beautiful head. "You and I are gonna take a walk." I clip on the lead and walk him out of the barn. He's tired but still raises his head to look around. He's probably wondering about the change in the routine, just like I am.

"It's OK, buddy." I pat his neck and shorten up on the lead. "We can have some nice private time." Mom always liked to take a horse for a walk before it went to a new owner. She never said so, but I know it was how she said goodbye. The horses in the field run to the fence line to say hello as we pass. Sir Drake doesn't really care. He knows he's part horse, part god. I think he's mostly god.

"Too important to mingle with the commoners?" I ask when he ignores the other horses, who are craning their necks over the fence rails, wanting his attention.

When his breathing slows, I slide my hand under his cooling sheet to feel for heat. His nostrils flare for a bit longer than I expected, but a longer cooldown is fine by me. A warbler with a patch of yellow feathers—a butter butt, my dad would call it—perches on the top rail and then hops along, catching insects. A puddle duck flies to its nest. "Something about being alone with a horse makes you notice more," my mom used to say.

By the time we're halfway back, Sir Drake's head has lowered, and his breathing is normal. There's a white crust of dried sweat on his neck and behind his ears. I bring him into the wash stall and let his legs feel the cool water from the hose. Not as good as bringing him into the river, but I don't want to do anything Wes didn't ask me to do. The water warms, and I curry the sweat marks away and sponge off his face. Then I squeegee the water out of his coat and towel off his face and legs. He does a contented blow out his nostrils as I lead him to his stall, which I've prepared with deep, clean shavings, fresh hay, and water.

"Should you require turndown service this evening, please call the front desk," I say in a terrible British accent. I pat his neck and slide the door closed behind him. I make a note for Wes about the longer cooldown and head for the wheelbarrow.

Twelve stalls. That's how many I have to clean. It's not easy. After the eighth stall, I lean the pitchfork in the corner and take a break. My fingers are curled into my palms like they're still gripping the handle. I push them against the tops of my thighs to straighten them. I walk to the open window and lean my elbows on the sill to take a breath. Outside, the light is bright and the air is cool.

Wes is in the training ring riding Percy, one of his young fillies. Only a week ago, she was trying her hardest to buck him off. She's still green, but Wes is already making her look like she's "one of those," as Mom would say. One with the X factor. Her every turn seems effortless, her every stride a part of a beautiful dance. I know Wes must be giving body commands, but I can't see them. His hands hold the reins slack. His legs are still but not stiff. His shoulders are square over his hips as Percy stretches her neck forward and back. I feel hypnotized.

When they approach a jump, Percy doesn't even hesitate. Each obstacle just seems part of the terrain to her, even the oxers. She takes them on simply—no fuss, no funny business, just boom, boom, boom. Canter, jump, canter, jump, canter, jump. Wes looks calm enough to be eating his lunch or reading a book while he rides. Percy has nothing but trust for Wes. I've never seen anyone train a horse so fast. One thing is for sure. Wes is the real deal. He's got the natural talent and the eye for a good horse.

I shake my head out of my trance. *Four more stalls to go.* The next couple aren't so bad, but I'm definitely slowing down. I step outside to get some water. I run the hose to flush out the rubbery taste before I let the water splash my face as I slurp from its fountain. The back of my hand is the only semi-clean part of me, so I brush it across my mouth. I crank the hose off, and just as I'm about to head to stall number eleven, I catch sight of Wes leading Percy into the barn.

I run to grab her from him. I put her on the cross ties to untack her and throw a mesh sheet on her for a cooldown. When Wes sees my note, he walks into Sir Drake's stall. He leans down and places his hand on Drake's abdomen and holds it there while he stares at the ground. Slowly, he stands up straight, frowns, and pats Drake on the neck. He takes out his phone to text someone, and I lead Percy out for a walk up the driveway.

On my way back to the barn with Percy, Sedgwick's white pickup and Dr. Pane's gray van pass by. I put Percy in her stall and join Wes and Sedgwick while Dr. Pane listens to Drake's heart, lungs, and gut. He slides the stethoscope behind Drake's left elbow, lowers his head to listen, looks at his watch a couple of times, and then places the stethoscope back on Drake's throat. He listens again, adjusts his earpiece. After listening a few more times to the airways, Dr. Pane shakes his head.

"Take him out for a little jog," he says slowly, then picks something out of his ear like he's bored and Drake is the hundredth horse he's seen today. "I'll be able to hear more with his breathing accelerated."

He's not the vet my mom and dad would've used. Dad said the way Dr. Pane moves in slow motion reminds him of a drunken sloth. That if Pane got paid by the hour, he'd earn a hundred bucks just walking to his truck. But he's the closest vet to Birdwood.

Wes leads Sir Drake out to the ring and lunges him at a trot a few times in each direction before bringing him back to the barn. Dr. Pane bends down and slides his stethoscope around Drake's abdomen and listens again. The quiet hurts my ears. Wes is waiting with his chin tucked in and his arms crossed.

Drake's nostrils are wider than they should be, and his sides are moving too much, like he's trying to force air out.

Dr. Pane stands up straight.

"Heaves," he says and then walks back to his truck and fills a syringe with the medication that Sir Drake will probably need to take for the rest of his life. "This is pretty severe. He needs antibiotics and something that will relax his throat muscles."

He says it the same way he might say, "I'll have fries with that," or "Isn't it a rainy spring?" But I hear the sound of screeching tires and breaking bottles and exploding things. Wes pats Drake's shoulder and then hugs his big head and scratches his forehead. It's like he's telling Sir Drake it's OK. Like it's just another day. Another day at the barn.

"Well, damn," says Ty, holding his hat and scratching the top of his head with his thumb. "I was already countin' my win money." He spits into the shavings. "'Show me a dreamer and I'll show you an idiot' is what my Gran used to say. Maybe next time, Wes."

CHAPTER FOURTEEN

My dad knew the answer to almost any barn problem, and I could really use his advice. He used to give a lot of it—mostly when I didn't ask. When he and Mom had a horse business situation, they always came up with a solution while they were cooking dinner or cleaning the dishes, and then things would run smoothly again for a time.

Now that I'm stepping up at the barn, I need to pick his brain about lessons and board and who to do business with because, with Wes, I have to act like I know what I'm doing.

But talking to Dad depends on whether he's had a good tinnitus night, which means he noticed the noise in his ears but still got a decent night's sleep, or a bad tinnitus night, which means the slightest thing is too much for him to think about, and the morning after isn't the time to ask him about anything, not even if we're out of toilet paper or if my jeans are in the dryer.

"Hey-oh," he says when we meet halfway up the steps.

"Hey-oh." I imitate his fake excitement to see me.

"There's a new box of cereal in the kitchen," he says, like he baked a three-course meal.

"Dee-licious." I say it like I'm impressed. I stop midway up the stairs, and he keeps walking down. I get a whiff of soap and a cologne that makes me think of an ad with a howling wolf or fighting lions. But he doesn't have the two-line groove he gets between his eyes when he's had a bad tinnitus night. His face has the softer look of a good tinnitus night.

"Hey, Dad. You have a minute?"

He doesn't answer right away. He stands taller and widens his eyes like he's trying to listen with them.

"What?"

I've been wanting him gone more than wanting him around lately, and he doesn't know what to do with the sudden change. It does feel weird.

"Can you talk?" I can tell he thinks I'm going to say I've seen the horses again. "It's a business question."

He nods fast, like he's relieved.

"Oh, yes, of course . . . um, here? Or . . ."

"Let's go to the kitchen." I point like he doesn't know the way and follow him back downstairs.

We sit at the table. I pull out Mom's notebook from my pocket and take the pen out of the spiral binder. I need as much advice as I can get without letting him know I'm actually already at the barn. It's going to be tricky.

I start with his favorite word. "Someday . . . when we get the barn back, I just want to be prepared. You know, hit the ground running. And I have a few questions about stuff like what to charge for board, what to pay for hay first cut, second cut, how to cut down on vet bills, and since—" I stop. Dad's looking at the notebook, staring at it like it put a spell on him. Mom's handwriting covers the entire page. For a minute, I'm not sure he's breathing.

"Dad?"

He blinks and looks at me, but his eyes are empty.

"No."

"What? What do you mean? I just have a few questions. Please, Dad."

"Reese, I said no." He stands up. "I told you to try other things."

"I am. I have. I just want to be prepared for someday, like you said."

"It hasn't been long enough." He walks toward the door. "Lock up after me."

I imagine tiny spears flying out and hitting him in the back. He opens the door to leave. My stomach feels the way it always does just before I say something I know I'll regret, but I let the word spears fly anyway.

"Who is it tonight? Airhead? Big Bird? Summer Squash?"

He turns around to look at me.

"You need to stop giving my friends nicknames, Reese. It's not right."

"What's it matter? They aren't around long enough for me to bother learning their real names. It couldn't possibly still be Miss Serious."

He shakes his head.

Here it comes. His tinnitus always starts with the head-shake. It's the reason he can't sit for too long or have things too quiet or too loud or eat spicy food or drink too much coffee or talk about things from the past or think about the future. I know exactly what he's going to say. After the headshake, it's always, *I'm sorry, Reese. I had a bad tinnitus night, and I just can't deal with a lot when—*

"I'm sorry Reese . . ." Here we go. He's nothing if not the most predictable man on the planet. I start saying it with him . . . *I had a bad—*

But he doesn't say what I predicted.

"LeeAnne and her boys, Cody and Kyle, are coming for dinner Friday night."

I close Mom's notebook.

He says, "I've been trying to tell you."

It's amazing how just a few simple words can change your world. Dad looks up at the door like he's measuring it with his eyes. He doesn't look at me. But those words keep coming at me like meteors tumbling through space. *LeeAnne and her boys.* He's had a lot of *friends.* He's had a lot of friends over for dinner. Bringing kids into it is a whole other thing. *LeeAnne.* I hate her name. Way too pretty. Pretty names always make me suspicious. What is she hiding? And Cody and Kyle? What is she? A freak for alliteration and cheesy '90s TV shows?

"Reese, I promise it won't be terrible . . . and you might even like them. Look out for that! That could be dangerous. Don't like them whatever you do . . ." Dad does a nervous laugh. "So, what do you think?"

"She has boys?"

"Yes, Cody and Kyle. They're good . . . good boys."

"They're coming here?"

"We really want you guys to meet."

"Gee, that sounds like so much fun, but I have to stick toothpicks in my eyes that night."

"Well, I'll text you a reminder." His voice catches in his throat when he says, "And please, no more nicknames."

He shuts the door so quietly I don't even hear it click.

I close my eyes and repeat Dad's words. *We really want you guys to meet.*

Wow. They're a *we.* So the noise in his head is so bad he can't take me out to eat anymore because the "din" in a restaurant makes it even worse? And it's a noise no one but him can hear? A noise that makes him act like he's on his period half the time? But he can go out with this *LeeAnne* he's seeing kind of seriously?

I call bullshit.

CHAPTER FIFTEEN

Since Wes can't sell Sir Drake, he'll have to sell at least four others to make up for it. He'll get a good chunk of cash for Olive's foal, but she's not due for at least six weeks. Of the horses that are close to being ready for sale, Cleo will go the fastest. She's basically bombproof. When Wes rode her the other day, a bulldozer on the main road made so much noise it sounded like a war broke out, but she barely looked up. Most horses would have lost their shit and bolted, especially around here, where you hardly ever see equipment heavier than a hay baler.

Most of the other horses are still too green or have an issue Wes needs to work them through. But they'd better sell fast if we're gonna pay the bills here. Dad used to say that if you're not selling, you're spending. "It's a thousand bucks a day just to turn the lights on."

Wes left me in charge of the barn for the day. He was off showing a horse to a rancher in Pierre, but he should've been back a long time ago. The horses are pacing back and forth in front of the paddock gates. Even they know Wes is late. By now, I should be home eating cereal and scrolling through videos and posting my horse pics of the day.

I check my phone. The low-battery window pops up. It's seven o'clock. The sun will be setting soon. Normally, Wes would have brought everyone in for dinner by now. I sweep the aisle for the fourth time. At every sound, I poke my head out to see if Wes's truck is finally turning down the driveway.

Since I've been waiting, the clouds have turned from light pink and orange to deep red and purple. I take another look toward the road. No Wes.

I'm worried for the horses, but I'm also worried that my dad will be wondering where I am. Assuming he's thinking about me at all. It's the first time I'm grateful he's dating LeeAnne. He's always so busy now getting ready for their next date that he still hasn't figured out that I stopped going to track a long time ago. I should call to tell him I was at a meet out of town and the bus broke down or something. But just when I try to call him, my phone goes dead. Of course my charger is at home. I run back to the barn to use the landline in the office, but of course Wes hasn't hooked it up yet.

Now the whole sky is just-before-dark lavender. There's nothing left to do except bring the horses in for their supper, something I've never done for Wes before. It's a lot more complicated than breakfast, when horses are already in their stalls. It's especially tough to do alone. No matter how well-fed a horse is, dinnertime is serious. They can be in a field full of grass, but if there's a bucket of grain anywhere in the vicinity, they'll act like they've been starving on a desert island, and that can get scary.

I search around the office to see if Wes left me any special dinner instructions, but I can't find a thing. I figure if I can get all the horses in and have a handful of grain waiting in their buckets, they'll at least have a safe snack before Wes can give them their normal dinner. I start pouring out small amounts of feed, but when the horses hear the sound of it hitting the buckets, they get even more riled up. They start whinnying and kicking out at each other. A couple of them look like they might jump the fence and charge toward the barn. I try not to let on that I'm terrified.

"Hang on, guys!"

I dribble the pellets into the bins as slowly and quietly as possible. I'm half hating Wes for not showing up and saving me from this chore. I check the office clock. It's now three hours later than the normal evening feed time. I've waited as long as I can. Wes would want them all fed and put in for the night.

I grab the pile of lead shanks and halters and walk toward the anxious horses. I try to disguise my racing heart by talking low and drawn-out like Mom did when the horses were about to get out of control. "Eeeeeeasy, eeeeeeasy." But I don't sound calm. My voice is too loud and sharp. "Just take it easy, guys. You're all going to eat. No one's going to starve."

The nine that are in the big pasture move toward me, stirring up a big cloud of dust. The horses that are already near me are acting like they're playing King of the Gate. Penelope nips Buster, leaving a wet smear on his haunches. Juno pins her ears back and swings her head from side to side, pushing through to the front. Boris hangs his head over the gate until he's pushed out of the way by Slim and Bailey.

I need to separate the horses, two at a time. Penelope and Buster are doing most of the kicking and biting, so I go for them first. Once they're safely out of the pasture, the others will be easier to control.

I slip Penelope's and Buster's lead shanks around their necks and get their halters around their noses and over their ears. The other horses are crowding around me, pushing against the gate. I try to shoo them away so I can slide the gate's metal pin latch out and up. If I can shorten up Buster's line, I can hold his lead close to his head. Then I'll lengthen Penelope's lead by letting it slide through my fingers to give her space enough to come out on Buster's heels.

Just as I'm about to get them through the gate, I hear hoofbeats charging. Jasper is torpedoing toward me. The other horses part to make room. His ears are back and his mouth is open, baring his teeth. He's warning everyone, including me, to steer clear. Right on his heels is his big girlfriend, Marge. I need to latch the gate, but I'd have to let go of the leads of the two horses who are already halfway through to the other side.

I hear Mom's voice. "Never let go of your horse." Then I hear Dad's voice. "When a horse charges, you have two choices. You stand your ground, or you stand your ground. They'll turn at the very last second."

I plant my feet. I clench the lead shanks in my fists. I spread my feet wider. *Don't move, don't move, don't move.* When Jasper sees the sliver of space between me and the gate, he aims at it like he's an axe and I'm on the chopping block. Marge flashes her big yellow teeth.

I have no choice. I step to the side. Jasper and Marge bust open the gate I'd been so close to latching. Two more horses gallop out. Elvis sideswipes me, and I land on the ground. The lead shanks slide from my fists. I may as well have been trying to hold tight to shards of glass.

The rest of the herd is now bucking and kicking up the hill to the barn, sparks lighting the dusk as their shoes strike the gravel. Every single one of them is hell-bent on getting to the barn first.

"Shit!"

I run behind them, knowing how fast things can get dangerous when horses run loose in a barn. If two or three horses crowd into a stall after the same bowl of food, you can bet there's going to be a fight.

Then I hear the rattling engine I've been waiting for. Wes's truck. He drives up close enough to see me but doesn't stop for me. Doesn't even look at me. He pulls right up to the barn and practically drives through the open doors.

By the time I get there, he's already got a couple of the horses in their stalls. Most of them are still all wound up, trying to find their homes. They zigzag back and forth down the aisle. Wes almost gets kicked in the chest when he passes between two of them. I know I should help, but I stand there, frozen.

The barn is a wreck. They've strewn bales of hay down the aisle from one end to the other. A door is broken, a bucket of feed has been stomped into the ground, and specks of blood cover one of the boards. Cleo has been injured.

"I'm so sorry."

Wes only looks at Cleo. She has a horseshoe-shaped cut just above her knee. She'll need stitches. Wes will need to sterilize the wound and cover it until morning. The horses' munching fills my ears.

"I'm so sorry, Wes."

Crying about a stupid thing you've done is something horse people should do on their own time. And anything else I could say would sound stupid and empty. I stare for a long time at the top of Wes's hat. He stands up and walks by me like I'm not even there. Then he picks up the feed bucket and the blood-specked board and shakes the dirt from some halters. I grab the rake from the feed room and start to pull the hay into piles, but Wes grabs it from my hand.

"Please, Wes. I didn't mean to."

He doesn't budge.

"I want to help."

He is stone-faced. He grips the rake in one hand while his other hand points toward the door.

CHAPTER SIXTEEN

My bike is where I left it that morning, leaning against the barn. I sit for a minute before I press my foot onto the pedal. When I'm about halfway up the driveway, a pair of high beams rolls toward me. I feel like I'm falling into a canyon with no sides to grasp on to, no ledge to stop me, nothing to break my fall. Dad stops the Jeep and then reaches over to open the passenger door.

"Get in."

He gets out, puts my bike in the back, then climbs back in and jerks the gearshift into first. He's gripping the steering wheel like he's trying to strangle it, and he's breathing like he just got back from one of his sprints. I'm afraid to look at him, but when I do, he's doing the underbite thing he only does when he's really mad. I jump when he yells, "You didn't think to call?"

"My phone died." I keep staring ahead.

"Your ph . . . That's all you have to say? Your phone died?"

The barn lights are still glowing, getting smaller and smaller in the distance.

"Do you know that I came this close to calling the police? Do you know how long I've been looking for you? I called the school. I felt like a complete idiot after I asked about your track meet. They said you stopped going to track meets months ago! You're not on that team, not on any team!" Dad keeps looking back and forth from me to the road.

"I thought you'd be out, anyway." My throat feels like sandpaper.

"You thought nothing." A wave of light passes over us from a car's beams. "I suppose this means you haven't been going to the mall with friends either? And you didn't really join the glee club?"

I actually have to laugh. Dad knows I'm the least likely person to ever join a glee club. I mean, even the word *glee* gives me the creeps.

"What part of this do you find funny?" he says in a spray of spit.

"Nothing. Nothing is funny."

"And the rehearsal you said you had for the school play?"

I stare down at my hands in my lap.

"Jeezus, Reese. When have you told the truth? Why did you lie?"

I want to say that telling him the truth wouldn't even have been an option. He hasn't wanted to so much as look at a horse since Mom died. And I knew he didn't want me to either.

I shrug. "I didn't think you'd notice."

"Really? So did you ever do any after-school thing?"

I stare straight ahead. I'm too tired to lie.

"I mean, what kind of parent will people think I am if you're off doing whatever you want? Huh? Reese? What kind?"

A sourness rises from my stomach. Words start spilling out of my mouth.

"I guess the kind that's busy fucking anything that fucking walks after Mom fucking died and you don't fucking care about anything important anymore." I know how much he hates that word, and I just want to keep on saying it.

Suddenly, the back of my head hits the headrest. There's a white spot in my vision. I'm still not sure if he really hit me. He's never done anything like that before. Not even once. But I don't see anything else in the car that could have popped me in the lip.

"Reese, I'm sorry." He's staring at his hand the way a newborn baby does, like it's not part of his body. He reaches out to check my face, but I back away from his hand and keep my face turned away from him. I swallow the lump that's growing in my throat.

"I'm fine." I stare at my reflection in the glass. A glistening red ball the size of a pea slides down my chin and lands on my arm. I touch my puffy lip. My tooth razors against it.

"We should put something on that. I'm sorry, Reese. I don't know why I did that." His voice is shaking. There's total silence for the rest of the drive. I stare at his reflection as he takes his hand off the steering wheel again and again, looking at his palm and stretching out his fingers.

He parks the Jeep in front of the house, and I go straight to my room and sit on the edge of my bed. I hear him running water in the bathroom, getting things out of the medicine cabinet, talking to himself.

He knocks and I don't say come in. He cracks the door. "Reese?"

I'm still sitting on the edge of my bed.

"Baby, I'm so sorry. That was so wrong of me. We should put some of this on it." He has a bottle of hydrogen peroxide and a tube of some ointment and a bag of ice.

"You can leave it there. I know what to do."

He stops and looks around for a place to put them down. "I, uh, I want to . . ."

"It's just superficial."

"Superficial," Dad says. That's a word horse people use a lot when a horse isn't hurt badly enough for them to call the vet. Dad used to say it a lot. "Good. I'll put these here. And I'm sorry." To make room on my cluttered bedside table, he pushes aside my stack of bowls and spoons. My pill bottle rolls off the bureau and falls to the floor. He picks it up and shakes it. He opens his mouth to say something, but instead, he holds the bottle out in front of him. It's like I can hear him sifting through his thoughts.

"I stopped taking them," I say before he can ask. "They made me feel funny."

Dad breathes hard out of his mouth. "I don't think it's something you should mess around with, Reese. I mean, you should have told me . . . or Miss Garland . . . before you just stopped."

He puts the bottle down. "Reese, you know I love you, right?" He has that look that feels like it burrows into a weak spot. It cracks me open. I nod.

"I mean, you don't have to make things up to get my attention. About seeing the wild horses. I know I've been distracted and . . . you know, kind of trying to figure things out. But you know that I love you."

I nod again.

"So, can we agree that from here on out, you tell me the truth?" He pulls on his earlobe. "Even if it's painful?"

I nod.

"When you first told me about the horses, I didn't know what to think. I thought something might be really wrong. But then it all made sense. You were trying to get my attention. I get that. And then I started thinking, you're right. I haven't been paying attention. I shouldn't be dating so much. I should settle down. You know, with someone. So we can start over again . . . as a family."

He looks at me like I should like what he said as much as he does.

"I don't see them anymore."

He breathes in and looks up at the ceiling. He breathes out and looks down at me.

"Not since I've been going to the barn."

He steps toward me with his arms wide. He wants to hug me. I sit there like a rock but I let him. He sits on the bed next to me and pulls me into his chest. He's doing gulping breaths, like he might cry, and he doesn't let me go. I'm kind of embarrassed for him. Finally, he lets out a big sigh.

"So, it's OK if I go to the barn?"

Dad does a lip-flutter laugh.

"I don't think it's a good idea, Reese. You hanging out there all day with a very odd guy. He doesn't talk. I mean, that's weird."

"He's not weird. He just doesn't talk."

"When I saw Mr. Gibson at the hardware store last week, he said the guy was very strange. That he doesn't seem to have any family . . ."

"Mr. Gibson doesn't even know him. You always said Mr. Gibson was weird and you wouldn't trust him as far as you could spit."

Dad shakes his head. "Better ice that."

I put the pack up to my lip. I'm not sure why I feel so protective of Wes already, but I do. Wanting to protect him is all of a sudden making me feel like I could cry. I'm thankful the ice pack is hiding my trembling chin.

"I'll call you from the barn. Every hour. And I'll share my location. We can even do the face thing if you want." He knows how much I hate to do the face thing with him. He can't remember that he doesn't need to put the phone to his ear. "Please, Dad. Please."

He looks around my room and then glances down at his hand.

"Reese, hon, you don't understand. I know what the horse world is like. It's a hard life. We weren't living in the real world, your mom and I. We were living in some crazy dreamworld where all you do is think about *someday* and *what if* and *if only*. For what? Why would I want that for you? You'll never make it in that world. Almost no one does."

"You don't know that."

"But I do. It takes too much. It's a constant struggle."

"What else am I gonna do?"

He stares up at the ceiling.

"Please, Dad. I just want to be there."

He looks around my room at all my horse things, and his face softens.

"Fine," he says. "Every hour."

"Every hour."

He closes the door, then opens it again. "And you have to tell the truth."

"Fine."

But I was lying. I still see the horses.

I unplug my phone from the charger. Along with the twenty-seven missed calls from Dad are three texts from

Wes. All during the time that I was wondering what to do with the horses.

7:01 p.m. *Had an emergency.*

7:27 p.m. *Just throw the horses some hay. Make sure to spread it out so they don't fight.*

8:17 p.m. *On my way.*

CHAPTER SEVENTEEN

I sleep like a baby. Literally. I'm awake every couple of hours and I'm restless and I want to cry. I realize that making an effort to go to sleep is making sleeping even more difficult. So I try not to think about sleeping, and then all I can think about is not sleeping. I say a quick prayer that Wes is getting a good night's sleep and that he'll be well rested and more understanding tomorrow.

When I get to the barn, there's a note tacked on the door.

DO NOT ENTER. ESPECIALLY YOU!
(YOU KNOW WHO YOU ARE!)

He's placed it exactly at my eye level, which somehow makes his point even stronger. The door feels heavier than usual as it scrapes and stutters on its metal track. I slide it open just wide enough to get my body in sideways and put one foot in.

"Wes?"

I hear only horse sounds—munching, a few nickers, muffled hooves in deep shavings. I can't see Wes, but I can feel that he's here. Then I hear the sound of shoveling and manure landing in the wheelbarrow. *Scrape, phoop, scrape, phoop, scrape, phoop.*

"Wes?" I call out again into the dark aisle and take a couple of steps forward. "I'm really sorry about the mess with the horses. My phone died and I didn't see your texts until I got home. I thought I could handle it myself and I wanted to impress you . . . and be useful. And I thought maybe you just took off . . . like for good."

The shoveling noise stops.

"I have an idea. One that I think will make up for the . . . kerfuffle the other day." He probably won't like that word, but it sounds so much better than *disaster.*

Wes darts out of Bob's stall. He stops right in front of me and jabs his finger in the air, pointing toward the door.

"Yeah, I saw your note."

He's blocking me from walking into the barn any farther, his arms spread wide. Then he steps back like I have some disease and he's afraid he and all the horses will catch it.

"By the way, that note's not the least bit inviting. I doubt you'll get many boarders if you keep it there."

He tilts his head to the side and looks at me, his lips pursed, his eyes narrowed.

"You mean it. I know."

He nods quickly.

"Just give me a minute, Wes. You won't regret it. I promise. I'd like to propose something I think could work for both of us."

He shakes his head and looks up at the ceiling.

"No, I know. I get it. You want me to leave." His stone-faced expression doesn't change. "Like right now. But if I can just—"

Wes points to the door and steps toward me like he's going to push me out. I back up. He doesn't touch me. But he doesn't need to. He's hunched forward, hovering over me. I slowly back out of the barn through the opening I made less than ten minutes ago. He slides the door shut so hard that chips of paint fall at my feet.

"I'm pretty sure that means stay out," I say out loud. My nose is barely an inch from the closed door. I stand there staring at the grain and grooves in the wood. Above me, swallows weave in and out of their hiding spots in the eaves. There's nothing else to do now but turn around and go home.

A gentle wind moves toward me across the field, making the weeping willow shudder. Then it rolls up the hill, rustles some leaves, and stirs up some dirt. There's stillness for a second, then it washes over my face. *You can't see the wind, but you can see what it does*, Mom used to say. I close my eyes and breathe in all the smells it brings with it—of the river I played in while Mom gave riding lessons, of the sweetgrass I sat in while Dad trained a young horse.

This place. I'm not ready to leave it.

I stand as tall as I can, take a deep breath, and brace myself for what I'm about to do next. I have to go back in.

I use all my strength to slide the door back open. I start talking even before I spot Wes fixing a stall door midway down the aisle.

"I hate to tell you this, Wes, but you pretty much need me." I take one more step closer to him. "I saw the pathetic sign you stapled to the scraggly oak. Really, Wes? You're amazing at a lot of stuff, but advertising is not your forte." I keep talking, each word making me feel a little braver.

"Ever since I've been here, not one person has driven up to ask about training or even how much it would cost to board. You're in the middle of nowhere in the back of beyond, and you think that sign on the tree with your email written so small no one can see it will bring in business?"

Wes is replacing a pin latch on a stall door. He's screwing it into place like I haven't even come back in.

"I've looked you up online. There are some great articles and some awesome photographs of you as a trainer, but you don't have a website. You've invested in some really nice horses. I can see that." I point to the stalls like I'm a flight attendant showing the exit signs. "But you have a hefty payment hanging over your head for leasing this place every month, not to mention the bills for the vet and the farrier and the hay and the grain."

Wes slides the door open and shut to check its alignment.

"I'm not sure what your plan is, since you couldn't sell Sir Drake, but one thing I know for sure is that if you don't get this operation up and running, every day you'll be digging out from the day before. You need a database, Wes. You've got to get yourself out there. And in between the big sales, you need to board. Boarders are going to be your bread and butter while you train horses to sell." I stomp my foot to accentuate the urgency.

Wes drops the pin latch into place and turns to look at me.

I pull out my mom's notebook from under my jacket and flip through the pages. "I have this. Each page is crammed full of numbers and email addresses and every name of every person who ever boarded or trained when my parents ran the barn. My mom was old school that way. She kept it on the computer, too, but after a few crashes where she lost everything—and I mean *everything*—she just wrote it all down."

I point to a few highlighted names. "This guy sells good hay, and it's cheaper than the place you buy from now. That guy's a real douche. I can't tell you how many times he delivered moldy hay before my mom switched. Sadly, Big Larry, their farrier, died, but Little Larry took over the business. Little Larry is actually bigger than Big Larry, but everyone still calls him Little Larry. Anyway, I hear he's even better than his old man, God rest his soul."

I point to heaven and pause to remember Big Larry—and to buy myself some time. Wes takes a step toward me, looking like he's going to kick me out again, so I start talking even faster than before.

"The vet you're using is decent but not always available, and besides, Dad said never trust a vet with a weak chin. I'd recommend Sue Landry. She can bring a horse back from the dead. And she'll show up at three in the morning if you need her." I pull out my phone. "I have also followed every single horse site that exists since I was eight years old."

Wes's eyes start to wander like he's looking at all of the problems I've caused him. I can't stop talking. He takes the pitchfork and starts walking toward me.

"Don't say no, Wes. You need me. I'm your golden ticket. Your secret weapon. Your—" He's getting closer. I won't let him make me leave again. I try to think of something else to say. Anything. "I'm that little thing you didn't know you had on your Swiss Army knife. I'm that special sauce that you use on . . . everything. Even a peanut butter sandwich. I'm the super, duper, triple layer . . ."

Wes reaches his hand out toward me, which I'm hoping means we have a handshake deal. But when I reach out mine, he doesn't take it. Instead, he stops in front of me and, once again, points his finger at the door.

CHAPTER EIGHTEEN

I let a whole day go by without going to the barn. Then another. I want to go back, but I don't have a plan. Four whole days drag by like four whole years. I don't even bike past it. Every morning I think, *Maybe this will be the day he'll realize how much he misses having me around.* I check my phone every ten minutes. Nothing.

So every day I just bike around until dark and then eat cold cold cereal in the empty house. On day four, I bike toward something reddish brown that's lying in the ditch by the road in front of one of the new developments. Is it a blanket? A scarf? A small dog? A large cat? I stop my bike and stare down at it. A fox. A vixen. She looks like she's squinting. Her mouth is open, showing the sharp, pointy triangles of her teeth. The breeze parts her thick coat in sections, showing the soft white fur that lies beneath the shiny auburn layer and two lumpy rows of swollen teats.

She was probably headed for the hill. But where are her cubs? How long has she been dead? When did she last feed her babies? Their little faces are probably still covered in a gauzy fluff, big eyes blinking open in their den, empty stomachs that should be full of milk.

Stupid trucks. Stupid cars. Stupid everything.

On the way home, my phone buzzes. Wes! I skid my bike to a stop and look at the cracked, chipped screen.

One missed call. One voice mail. Dad. I sink back onto my seat and press PLAY.

"Hey, Reese. Just reminding you about dinner. Lee-Anne and her boys are here. They're really looking forward to meeting you."

It's 6:05. I told him I'd be home at five.

I ride the brake downhill trying to think of reasons why I can't show up. I'm on my period. I was hit by a car. I was abducted by aliens. Maybe all three.

When I finally get home, I drag myself up the porch steps. I can see them through the kitchen window. Dad and Lee-Anne are making a salad. The two boys are teenaged. One has brown hair that falls in his face. The other has a blond mohawk. They're sitting at the table, looking at their phones. Dad leans against the counter while LeeAnne slices tomatoes.

LeeAnne. She matches her name. She probably does a lot of yoga. She has a slightly messy reverse bob that says, *I just went to a salon but I don't want it to look like it.* Nauseating.

Dad playfully nudges LeeAnne out of the way so that he can finish the slicing. She puts up a fuss and tries to stay put. Dad pours her some wine. She smiles at him, takes the glass, and lets him slice. Dad carves into a roast chicken. LeeAnne fills a bowl with mashed potatoes. Then she and my dad join the boys at the table.

I'm watching them through the glass like I'm watching TV with the volume down. They look like they aren't missing anything or anyone. Like they're complete. The brown-haired boy says something. Dad scruffs his hair.

The boy and LeeAnne laugh. When the blond-haired boy spoons some peas onto his plate, one pea falls off the spoon and rolls toward Dad. He pops it into his mouth, and they all laugh. I begin imagining ads for their new sitcom. *Ditch the Daughter.* Or *Everyone Forgets Reese.* Or even better, *Mom's Dead so Let's Just Get a New Family.*

When I walk through the door, everyone gets quiet.

"How was your day?" Dad uses his put-on excited voice. As if he'd actually listen. Lately, it's like someone's hijacked his brain. Who does he think he's fooling, helping in the kitchen and wearing those stupid loafers and growing that beard? I want to start a fight. Miss Garland says *hurt people hurt people.* One of her many annoying little phrases.

I walk around the table, and the moment I sit in my chair, I wish I hadn't. I should have gone right to my room. They're still all quiet, like I interrupted their fun. Then Dad clears his throat.

"This is LeeAnne. And these are her two boys, Kyle and Cody."

He spoons mashed potatoes onto my plate. When he shakes off the gloppy, lumpy slop from the spoon, the burrito I had for lunch starts making a second appearance. The two boys grunt something at me. I look past them. I couldn't care less. Then LeeAnne holds out the salad bowl with her manicured hands. Mom never had a manicure. Not even when she was a bridesmaid in her cousin's wedding. LeeAnne tries to act like she doesn't notice the rim of black dirt that lines each of my nails, the scratches and calluses on every one of my fingers.

"I'm not hungry." My voice comes out in a whisper. I slide out of the hard, cold chair and don't bother pushing it in. Before I turn for the stairs, LeeAnne starts up.

"I've found that if I've had a really long day, I don't think I'm hungry until I start eating, and then I realize how hungry I am."

"Yes. Great point, LeeAnne. Why don't you just have a couple of bites, Reese?" Dad nods like LeeAnne just said something truly amazing.

"Your dad tells us that you spend a lot of time at a barn. That's so cool. Right, Cody and Kyle?" Her smile is too big when she looks at her boys.

"Yeah, super cool," says Cody.

"Rad," says Kyle.

LeeAnne is still smiling. She hangs one elbow over the back of her chair and swings her top crossed leg back and forth too fast.

"He also says you're absolutely horse crazy. I mean, what teenage girl isn't? Right? They're so beautiful."

"Please stop talking." It just comes out. Everyone at the table looks at each other as if someone shit their pants.

"What?" says Dad.

"Oh," says LeeAnne.

"Ouch!" says Cody.

"Burn!" says Kyle. "Mom just got dunked on."

"I'm sorry. I'm just really tired and I had a late lunch and I just want to go to my room." I walk up the stairs, leaving them all to their chicken and their gloppy potatoes and their dumb expressions. My bedroom door barely closes behind me when I hear them start up again. Their laughter. Their comments. Their chatter.

"Can I have more chicken?"

"Who's watching the game tonight?"

"Teenage girls. What can you do?"

I want to block their sounds, their smells, their stupid happy bullshit out of my life. I close my eyes. Then someone knocks quietly on my door.

"Reese?" My name always sounds softer when Dad says it with his wine voice.

"What?" I yell. He and his timing are really pissing me off.

"Can I come in?"

"No."

"Can I just—"

"I'm sleeping."

"You don't sound like you're sleeping."

"Ughghghgh," I grunt as I get up and stomp over to open the door. Dad has one arm reaching up on the doorjamb.

"Yes?"

"You're not coming down?"

"And join in the insta-family party? No thanks."

"It's not an insta-family, whatever you mean by that." Dad takes a couple of steps into my room. I act like I'm busy looking for something.

"I told you about LeeAnne. Several times. I told you that I'm serious about her. That I wanted you to meet her. That she happens to have two nice boys, and I have . . . you."

I know Dad doesn't mean that to sound so insulting, but I'm not about to let it slip.

"Right, you have me, the crazy daughter who doesn't have friends and works all day at a barn and smells like shit." I wait for him to get mad and say I'm putting words in his mouth.

"Reese," he says, then his cheeks puff out as he tries to hold in a snicker.

I'm not prepared for this reaction.

"What are you laughing at?" I stand there looking at him. I'm holding a shoehorn, pretending I found the thing I was pretending to look for.

"Nothing. It was just the way you said it, and I've . . . I've had a few drinks, you know, probably because I was nervous about introducing you all and . . ."

I don't know what to say. I was used to our old script. The one where he says something, then I get mad and give a snarky response, and then he gets mad and says I'm in trouble. No snarky response is coming to mind for this giggly, not-mad Dad.

"I dunno, Reese." Dad slurs a little. "I mean, first you didn't like that I was dating . . . a number of different women."

"A number? Like seventy-eight? Ninety-two?" I say it loud enough for everyone in the house to hear.

Dad puts his finger to his lips, glances behind him, and pulls the door closed.

"Shshshshsh. Now I have LeeAnne. One person I really, really like. I mean, I think we could all get along great . . . you know . . . like do some fun travel and cramping tips and—"

"Cramping tips?"

"Come on, Reese. Will you please come back down? Maybe join in a game or two?" Now Dad is slurring a lot. He's having a hard time focusing his eyes, which is actually a welcome relief from the intense stares that make me feel like every inch of me is potentially in trouble for something.

"Fine."

"Great." He claps his hands together, and I follow him to the living room, where they're playing—of all the stupid games—charades. LeeAnne is sitting on the couch.

"Reese, so glad you're going to play. I can't get this one. Do you know what Cody is doing? The category is movies."

Cody is obviously a jockey on a horse, and the movie is obviously either *Seabiscuit* or *Secretariat*, and they're obviously doing this for my benefit. I cringe everywhere. It's annoying enough that they're using this particular method to try to welcome me—in my own house!—and that it's what you might do for a ten-year-old. But there's something else.

Sure, the boys are playing the game, and their mother is all smiles. But are they making fun of me? Cody and Kyle catch each other's eyes. Cody raises his eyebrows. Kyle smirks. LeeAnne doesn't catch any of it. She's just so excited to have everyone playing this fun little game. So I give in and plop down on the chair. While Cody beats away on his imaginary horse with his imaginary whip looking like he's humping an imaginary thing, I make some guesses.

"Oh, is it *Beauty and the Beast*?"

"No."

Cody shakes his head, and his hair somehow lands right where it was, in his eyes again.

"*Superman*?"

"No."

"*Marley and Me*?"

"No."

"Geez. I'm stumped." They look at each other like maybe they should have picked an easier one.

"*Crouching Tiger, Hidden Dragon*?"

"No!" they all practically yell at me.

Finally, Cody can't stand it any longer. "It's *Secretariat*!"

I act like I'm a big old dummy. "Oh, yes, of course it was. Duh."

Dad looks at me with his wine-buzz-is-wearing-off face.

We play a few more rounds. They don't choose any more movies that are even remotely about horses. I'm grateful. It finally ends. LeeAnne has to get the boys home to do whatever they do.

I go back up to my room. But it feels like I'm leaving the scene where a crime of epic proportions has just taken place. Because while we played charades, Dad sat on the couch next to LeeAnne, right where Mom used to sit. And his arm was around her. And her hand was on his knee. And she draped one of Mom's throws over her shoulders.

And I was part of it.

CHAPTER NINETEEN

In English class, we're taking turns reading aloud a story about Joan of Arc. But I've tucked something else to read inside the textbook's pages. Mom's notebook. The one I thought held all the answers to my new life at the barn. But I realize now it's just a lot of scribbled information I'll never be able to figure out. Pieces to someone else's puzzle. I crumple the first page in my fist. When Mrs. Roth calls on me to read the next section aloud, it takes me a few seconds to find my place.

"Every man gives his life for what he believes. Every woman gives her life for what she believes . . ."

Then, in the middle of reading, I hear it. *The tiny neigh.* The sound I've been waiting months to hear. Under my desk, my phone is lighting up the inside of my backpack. The neigh is muffled and soft. Sweet and gentle. Like a whisper. But it gives my heart a jolt. I rush through the rest of the reading.

"One life is all we have, and we live it as we believe in living it . . . and then it's gone. But to surrender who you are and to live without belief is more terrible than dying—even more terrible than dying young . . ."

When I'm done reading, I look at my phone. *To be auctioned in Casper, Wyoming, Saturday, May 27. Trusted Treasure.*

My scalp tingles. I smooth the crumpled notebook page and hug it to my chest. I forward the link to Wes and text, *He's coming back.* And then I add Mom's line. *I can feel it in my bones.* Even though Wes thought he was kicking me out for good, I know that the moment he meets Trusted Treasure, he'll change his mind. Treasure is a special horse, and a good horse person can tell a special horse just by looking at it.

Every hour I check for a text from Wes. No response. I text him again. *See you there.* There's no way Wes won't see how obvious it is that Trusted Treasure needs to come back to Big Green Barn. Horse people are practical people. We're also not idiots. We know that when fate is practically hitting us upside the head with a two-by-four, we better pay attention. This is definitely meant to be. And when something is meant to be, it works out.

Like how it just so happens that this weekend, Dad is taking LeeAnne and the crapheads on a camping trip—or cramping tip—which I now won't ever let him live down. He invited me, but did he seriously think I would go? And it also just so happens that there's a bus that can get me to Casper. And it just so happens that I've got more money stashed away than I've ever had in my life. Which means I'll go with or without Wes. If I ignore all these arrows pointing me to Trusted Treasure, then what business do I have being a real horse person? Real horse people know when something is meant to be. We feel it in our bones.

I've taken the bus on my own once before to visit my aunt Jerri in Plainsville. I was ten. The station still smells like someone peed in an armpit. And the guy handing me my $128 ticket looks like he might be the latest culprit.

I board the bus and choose a window seat. Before I put my backpack under the seat in front of me, I unzip the side pocket to make sure my money is still there. A wad of cash makes me feel large and in charge. I've got a whole $500 to bid on Treasure.

The bus merges onto the highway. The engine hums. I feel for the stone in my pocket and take it out. I don't know why I like this stone, but for some reason, I always want to have it on me. If I don't feel it in my pocket, it makes me anxious. I hold it up next to the window. In this light—in that one spot where the stone is most translucent—I see flashes of rainbows.

Mom loved rainbows. She'd scream and practically scare me to death if we were driving and one of them arced overhead. She'd crane her neck up to see where the rainbow stopped and started, and I'd grip the door handle thinking she might drive right off the road.

One time we saw the whole entire rainbow.

"Look! It starts there," she screeched, "and there's the end over there!" She always ended with "A miracle, just a miracle."

It's not that I didn't think rainbows were beautiful and amazing, but that was back when I was a good student and paid attention in science class. I'd just learned that rainbows happen because light bends. It's speeding along, and an obstacle gets in its way, and the result is this incredible thing. But it's not a miracle.

I told Mom as much one day. "It's just physics." I was

cranky and looking at an oncoming pickup while she was looking at the rainbow and not the road. "Light bends. That's what makes a rainbow."

She laughed and said, "Well, that doesn't make it any less of a miracle to me."

I slide the stone back into my pocket.

Lazy cattle speckle the fields. Barbed wire fencing runs beside us like it's trying to keep up. Mom and Dad and I took so many trips down this road, but there's only one day I remember. Like it's the only day that matters. But I don't remember it in order. I remember the chicken crates crashing on the road. Mom saying, "I think they're close. I can feel it in my bones." The coffee cup rolling around on the floorboard. Dad putting his hand up when the black horse got close. His hand on Mom's wrist. My hair whipping in my face. The rumble of the horses' hoofbeats.

The sound of snoring brings me back to the bus. The woman across the aisle has her head back and her mouth open.

I force myself to think of another day. The day we got Trusted Treasure. Mom bought me a cinnamon churro, and I almost ate the whole thing before we even sat down. We had a good view of the ring. Dad raised his paddle for a couple of nice fillies but got outbid every time.

Most of the colts were snatched up pretty fast. But one colt wouldn't even come into the ring. He was bony and gangly. He kept his head up in the air. His eyes were bugging. When his handler swatted him hard across the rump with a whip, he just dug his hooves in even more. As if he was saying, *Hit me as hard as you want. If you think I'm going in there, you're crazy.* Then he sniffed the dirt before he stepped backward and pointed his nose in the air again, acting like he was being asked to walk into a snake pit.

"Stubborn little shit," Dad said.

It took two men looping their ropes around his rump to get him into the ring.

"Soon as he gets his feet to work, we can sell this colt," said the auctioneer.

Everyone in the stadium laughed.

"This is Trusted Treasure and that name fits him about as well as my size 36 Wranglers fit me. Badum tish." The auctioneer thought he was a stand-up comedian or something.

"Poor baby," Mom said. "He's just afraid."

"Just afraid?" Dad said with a big laugh. "I know you like a challenge, Jessie, but this one is . . ." Dad didn't finish his sentence. He just shook his head.

Mom always said horses had to learn to trust. Dad always said they had to earn it. Mom's theory was, the more afraid they are at first, the better they turned out later. She said if you could get them to trust just a little, you couldn't hold them back if you tried.

"Trusted Treasure," Dad snarled. "He'll never trust anyone."

"Looks like he has some growing to do," said the auctioneer. "A bucket of oats could do him some good."

Treasure fought every step of the way. A cowboy rode into the ring on his Appaloosa and tried to calm him down, but that just made him more anxious. He reared up, pulling the lead out of his handler's grip, and started bucking and galloping around the ring. People started yelling and clapping like he was part of a show.

"Can I get five hundred?" the auctioneer tried. But people were having too much fun watching the young horse fly around the ring to pay attention. "Five hundred? Anyone for five hundred?"

That's when Mom held up her paddle.

"Sold!"

When we pulled out of the auction house parking lot with Trusted Treasure in the trailer, it was already dark. It had taken four hours to load him. No one was talking. Dad kept angry-tapping the steering wheel with his thumb.

"What got into you, Jessie? We can barely feed the horses we have. You know how long it'll take to sell him. Years!" Then his hand came down hard on the steering wheel.

Mom stayed quiet. I wasn't sure if she already regretted buying Treasure. Did she really see something in him?

"Give him a little time, Joe."

"No, you give him time, Jessie. I'm not touching that animal. If he kills you, don't tell me I didn't warn you!"

Out the bus window, the brown, flat plain meets the pale blue of the sky. I take a deep breath of the hot chocolate and coffee in the air. I feel cramped and too hot. I just want to get where we're going. For a second, I'm nauseous. I keep my eyes on the horizon, knowing that, pretty soon, the bus will be part of a long line of trucks and trailers. On a good day, this auction can draw people from as far away as Texas.

Finally, we pull into the auction lot. Parking attendants point with their orange wands. As soon as the bus doors open, I jump and run the quarter mile to the entrance. Music booms from inside the stadium. I slow from a run to a walk and join a fancy-boot-big-hat group funneling into the arena. I'm hit by the smell of new leather and aftershave and manure that always hits me when I'm about ten feet from the entrance. Men laugh and holler back and forth and slap each other on the shoulder. "Country Girl" blares from the speakers, and the bass drowns out the sound of my heartbeat. For a while, I'm happy again. I'm just part of the crowd.

I stand on my tiptoes and try to spot Wes. His floppy hat will definitely stand out. I crane my neck, but I can't see through all the hats and flannel shirts ahead of me. I walk through the gigantic entrance doors. There's a line for Registered, another for Unregistered. I stand in Registered. When I get to the front, a frizzy-headed lady in a pink cowboy shirt looks at me, and I just stare at her. I hadn't thought this far ahead.

"I'm picking up my paddle for my dad. Tucker. Joe Tucker."

"I'm sorry, sweetie. We'll have to wait for him. We need an ID."

I start sweating nervous sweat on top of the sweat from running.

"He's in the bathroom," I blurt out. Then I lean closer. "He has"—I remember a commercial that always plays during the game—"an enlarged prostate." She does a yikes-but-I'm-sorry look, then waves up the next person in line.

"Joe Tucker?" says a tall man with bowed legs. "You're Joe and Jessie's kid?"

"Yeah."

"Flip," he says. "Flip Dixon." Even though he has a farm just down the road, I haven't seen Flip since he and Dad were fixing the trailer hitch. And I'm pretty sure Dad slept with Carla, the owner of the Bread Pit, who Flip was kind of dating.

"I know your dad. Sorry about your mom. I haven't talked to him since. He here?"

I point to the bathroom.

"Aw, dang. Well, I'm runnin' out to Telusca for the afternoon auction. What's it you're lookin' for?"

"Uh, our paddle. It's under his name." He files through

the box with the registrations. "Tell him I said hi. Glad to hear he's gettin' back in the business. Be good to catch up." He hands me the paddle, and the lady doesn't even notice. She's too busy helping someone else.

"Thanks, Flip!" But he's already out the door.

⌄

The only seats left are in the back rows. I step through a narrow aisle and around a lot of legs and boots and beer cans. My foot squashes down on a pouch of Beech-Nut chewing tobacco that's next to a clear plastic cup filled to the brim with brownish spit. I stand in front of my chair and scan the arena row by row looking for Wes.

It's still early, so the crowd hasn't gotten too crazy yet. Mom and Dad and I always left when it seemed like just breathing the air could make you drunk. The auction pamphlet says that Trusted Treasure's lot will be up toward the end of the second section. I put the pamphlet under my leg and sit back to watch. Then the auctioneer's voice booms from the speakers like God.

"Ladies and gents, we have an amazing selection of bloodlines here today. And one of the largest representations of thoroughbred and quarter horse stock in the country. So get your checkbooks ready and let's get started!"

A beautiful, sleek black horse is led out and goes for big money. A gorgeous brown-and-white paint sells for $50,000, a number I can't even understand. I know it's a thousand fifties or fifty thousands. It definitely wouldn't fit in my Man o' War hiding spot.

Most of the horses at the auction are fancy, well-bred horses that I know Mom and Dad wouldn't have dreamed of bidding on. They were always looking for the diamond in the rough, or like Mom called it, the unlicked cub. The next is a gorgeous gray mare and her baby, who follows her around the ring like there's an invisible rope between them. His tiny head bobs up and down, and he makes people laugh when he does a little buck to show off. The bidding frenzy ends at $35,000.

After all the fancy horses are auctioned off, the ones with a "dicey past" are brought out. Some of them look like they've never seen a barn. The yearlings—with their baby coats gnarled in burrs and thistle—were probably just rounded up off a ranch, loaded onto a cattle truck, and shipped here without ever having been handled. But bidding for them is strong. Even the horses that look a little lame or old get bought for way more money than usual. It's like the bidding has become more about the ranchers showing off to each other than it is about the horses. The paddles pop up and down all day long like gopher heads.

While the auctioneer rattles off more names and numbers, I sit up on the edge of my seat and search the crowd again for Wes. I keep checking the entryway, but there's no sign of him. The man to my right elbows me. "They're scraping the bottom of the barrel now, I'll tell ya. Love to hear how the auctioneer talks up this one." He puts his hands to his mouth like they're a megaphone. "Here we have a big-eared, ewe-necked, rib-protruding, shaggy-haired, good-for-nothing excuse for a horse."

"Ladies and gents," says the auctioneer, "this guy is just looking for a good home. Who will start the bid at four fifty?"

People laugh and shift in their seats.

"Four hundred?"

The usual yelling and chatter quiets. A tall man with not much hair on his head and a face that looks like he ate a fart leads the frail-looking, sunken-eyed, dull-haired chestnut around the ring.

"You digging horses out of graves now, Ethan?" a man yells. Everyone laughs. A woman shakes her head.

"Put him out of his misery," another man yells from across the ring.

"What are you wasting our time for?"

"Dog food!"

Now the stands are full of people laughing and shaking their heads. The meat factory man grips his paddle. I'd rather not watch what happens to this sad-looking horse. I figure it's a good time for me to stretch my legs and grab a quick snack before Treasure comes up for bid, so I get up to leave my seat, thinking about caramel apples and cinnamon churros. Then, suddenly, everything goes as quiet as if someone's clamped his hands over my ears. I don't hear anything around me—not the horse who's kicking up dirt in the ring, not the man next to me who opens his mouth wide to laugh.

But then I hear *them*. The crashing waves of their breath, the drumbeat pounding of their hooves. Even through the blur of their kicked-up dust, I see their colors—chestnuts and grays and paints. The herd circles the ring and then gallops back out through the stadium doors.

All except one. The black horse.

No one else seems to notice him. I track him as he moves behind the seats on the other side of the stadium. I lose him. Find him again. My view of him is broken up by the metal bars and rails, like he's pieces of a puzzle. I see glimmers of his eyes, flashes of his rippling mane and tail. He passes some bidders close enough for them to feel his breath, then he charges toward a man in his path. The man looks like he's been hit by a sudden gust of wind, as if the horse galloped right through him. His huge Stetson blows off, but he just picks it up and continues walking as if nothing weird just happened.

When the black horse comes into full view, I freeze. He looks straight at me, rears, and paws the air. His tail pours onto the ground. When he stands on his hind feet, he reaches halfway to the ceiling. He tosses his head, stomps the ground hard, then stands in the center of the ring, right beside the sad, frail horse I didn't want to watch get auctioned off for meat. The black horse stays right there, even when the silence ends, even when sound matches up with motion again, even when I return to the world around me and I hear the sad horse whinny.

The auctioneer clears his throat. "Now, this horse has definitely seen better days. Not a bad bloodline though. He's out of Daring Greatly . . ."

Daring Greatly, I think. *What a coincidence. Same as Treasure.*

"Move this along, for Chrissake!" someone from across the stadium hollers. "Ain't got all day!"

The crowd is losing interest. Some leaf through their pamphlets. Some stand to stretch or leave to get drinks. The black horse keeps looking right at me.

"He won at Lone Star and Fair Hill as a six-year-old," the auctioneer continues. "And went on to run in the Black Elk."

Holy holy shit.

The audience laughs, like they think it's a joke, but I feel like I just snapped out of a dream. The black horse rears up again. But just before he bolts back out through the doors and gallops toward the herd in the distance, he stops and looks at me. I nod to him. I want to thank him. Without his help, I'd have been off eating a cinnamon churro and would never have realized. That sad horse, that frail horse, that sunken-eyed, dull-haired, about-to-be-auctioned-for-dogmeat horse . . . is Treasure.

"Here! Over here!" I jump up, waving my paddle as high as I can, but a fat-ass Wrangler lady stands up and stretches, blocking the auctioneer's view of me. He thinks he's got no bids, so he just talks louder, trying to get the energy in the stadium back.

"Whatdya think, folks? He could make a nice trail horse. A companion horse. Three fifty? Can I get three fifty?"

I wave my paddle, but he still doesn't notice me. Then one of the meat men raises his paddle.

"I've three fifty here. Can I get four hundred?" Another man raises his paddle for four.

"Can I get four fifty?"

I step over legs and cans and spit cups to get to the aisle and hold my paddle high in the air. He finally sees me.

"Four fifty. Can I get five?"

I'm starting to get scared. The most I can bid is five.

"I got four fifty. I need five."

I raise my paddle again.

"Five!" the auctioneer looks at me and yells into the mic. "Five fifty, folks. Any new bidders at five fifty?"

No one else raises their paddle. It's really happening. I'm going to buy Treasure for five. Then the auctioneer looks high up into the back rows. A short, stumpy man with a huge cowboy hat raises his paddle.

"Shit," I say out loud.

I lower my paddle. It's over. *I'm out of money.* Six hundred. A paddle goes up. Six fifty. Another paddle. Seven hundred. My chest tightens.

"Seven fifty. Can I get seven fifty?" Again, the skinny meat man holds his paddle high.

I can't watch. I throw my paddle to the ground.

"I got seven fifty. Can I get eight?"

Then a hand reaches for my paddle. I look up.

Wes.

He's smiling his biggest smile—the one that covers his whole face. And he's holding my paddle high.

"Eight hundred dollars. I got eight hundred. Can I get eight fifty? Eight fifty?"

The auctioneer looks around the stadium. The skinny meat man tosses his paddle to the ground.

"Going, going, gone for eight hundred to the man in the floppy hat."

I don't walk toward Trusted Treasure. I run.

Just before I reach him, I stop. It's true. He doesn't look like himself at all. But the moment my eyes meet his, I know. It's him. "Treasure." I speak as softly as I can. He raises his head, pricks his ears toward my voice, then reaches his nose to my cheek. I wrap my arms around his big, bony head. His coat is dull, and his neck is so thin it looks like it shouldn't be able to hold up his head. Bite scars and kick marks cover his whole body.

"Poor baby." I kiss his nose. "You've been cramped up with monsters."

"Hey, kid." Ethan, the wrangler, stands beside me with his hand out. "You gonna pay for this horse or just make out with him?"

I reach into my backpack and pull out a large cash-filled plastic baggie. "I only have small bills." I count out in tens and fives.

Ethan looks at the loose, wrinkled bills and counts

them again himself. His face screws up like he ate another fart. "That's only five hundred."

I wave to Wes as he weaves his way toward me through the crowd. He tilts his head and approaches Treasure slowly, then slides his hand down Treasure's neck and looks into his big eyes. He moves his hand over Treasure's withers and down his bony spine. He runs his hand down each leg, presses softly, shoulder to knee, then wraps his fingers around the thin cannon bone.

When Wes is finished, he stands, nods his head, and slowly reaches into the back pocket of his jeans. He pulls out his money clip, peels off three hundred-dollar bills, and hands them to me.

"Thank you, Wes. Thank you, thank you, thank you, thank you. I will work my butt off at the barn." I give Ethan the rest of the money.

"Congratulations," he says without smiling. He hands me Treasure's dirty, frayed lead. I don't ever want to let it go.

"Hello again, Treasure." He nudges my hand. His nose feels like velvet.

❧

On the way home, we drive into a burst of blood-orange sky. Wes shifts gears and looks in the rearview mirror.

"Just wait until he's fattened up. Wait until you see him then."

The orange fades and a lavender color appears and then disappears into the night. Wes's face seems softer, less strained than before. Like he might open his mouth any second now and speak. My mind is humming with something else I want to tell him.

"Wes, have you ever seen something that you can't explain? Something that you know is there, but it's not real for anyone but you, and you feel like it's trying to tell you something really, really important, but you don't understand it because it's from another, you know . . ."

Wes looks at me out of the corner of his eye and circles his finger around his ear, making the cuckoo sign.

"Yeah. Me neither."

Wes shakes his head and changes lanes. When his truck finally jostles down Big Green's bumpy driveway, the glow from the barn light dances. Wes parks the truck and goes around back to open the ramp. Treasure steps from the trailer and stumbles a little.

"Good boy, Treasure. Welcome home." I lead him into the warm barn. Whoever said you can't buy happiness had it dead wrong.

CHAPTER TWENTY

My mind is a tangle of thoughts. One swaps for another before I can finish the first. All I can think about is Treasure. How did he feel about his first night back in the barn? Did the other horses accept him? How did he sleep? How much does he remember his life here? How much has his injury healed? Is he really the special horse I thought he was? Did I make a huge mistake?

When I enter the barn, I feel a whole kaleidoscope of butterflies in my stomach. The first thing I see is Trusted Treasure. He's looking out of the stall door like he's been waiting for me. I run to him. He looks alert. His eyes are brighter. His halter is lying in the center of the aisle.

"Back to your old ways, you big stinker?" I scratch his forehead and pat his big cheek. He nods his head up and down like he always did. Like he never left. I peek into his stall. "Looks like you had a good night and a good roll." He lets me pick some flecks of shavings out of his mane. I pat his neck.

"And one nice, big poop. Not a nervous poop either, huh? Nervous poops are a big, runny mess!" I'm talking with my teeth clenched, which I only do with him. Then someone taps me on the shoulder, and I jump. I hadn't heard Wes walk up behind me.

"Oh, hey, Wes."

He shakes his head a little.

"Treasure is acting like he never left. And he already looks better than he did at the auction."

Wes pokes his head over the stall door, nods, and scratches Treasure behind the ear. Then he heads out to the tractor, and I begin my morning routine. When I finish the feeding, I decide to take Treasure out to the big field.

Whenever we brought home a horse that looked like it had hit a rough patch in life, Mom used to say, "Turn him out." We had our fair share of those horses—skinny things that looked like they'd never seen a field or a currycomb. She said the best thing for a horse like that was the nothing schedule. "Don't mess with him. Don't even put a halter on him. Let him go in a big field with lots of grass and fresh water. Let him remember who he is." It sounded silly to me then. But now I wish I'd asked her. How do you forget who you are? How do you remember?

I pick up the halter that Treasure's now thrown on the ground four times and grab his lead shank from the hook. I open his stall door slowly. He blows through his nostrils, his signal that it's all right for me to come in.

"Hey, bud. How 'bout a little walk?" He lets me attach the lead shank, then follows me out. I'm actually leading my own horse through the barn. It doesn't feel real. But each time I look back to prove I'm not dreaming him up, he's there, clomping along behind me.

"This is Trusted Treasure, everybody." The horses all crane their necks out of their stalls to get a good look at him.

His hooves make the hollow *clop-clop* that is probably my favorite sound in the world. His ears move forward and back as he listens to the other horses, who are stomping around in their stalls, wondering where we're going. I lead him out of the barn, through the grange area, and past the old silage bunker. He stops and looks up the hill, taking in his surroundings. I give the lead a gentle pull to bring his head back down, and we continue on toward the field.

It's a beautiful morning. The mist is stitched to the fields below in wispy threads. The pine trees look soft from a distance, like tepees of green wool. The brown, rusted gate opens to the biggest field we have, at least fifty acres that roll down to the Ghost Hawk, where deer drink at dusk and dawn. When we walk through the gate, Treasure raises his head high and looks around like he's crossed some threshold into a strange new world.

"You know this place, Treasure. This is where you belong."

My arm barely reaches his halter. I crawl my fingers up the lead shank to the latch. I don't have to wait any longer to let Treasure loose in the field he spent most of his life in. I click open the halter's metal fastener. I drop the rope to my side. I set him free.

He shakes his head, almost looking like a happy, normal horse, and then heads down to the river. He skims his muzzle over the top of the water and takes a long gulp, raises his head to look around, then takes another.

"Good boy, Treasure!" I tell him, even though he's probably too far away now to hear me.

While Treasure is getting reacquainted with the far meadow, I notice movement near me up on the hill. A reddish-brown animal is pouncing on something. When I move closer, I see not one but two skinny fox kits scrounging around for grubs. They look weak and frail. The breeze almost knocks one over. When they see me, they dive into their den. The carcass of another smaller kit is only a few feet away, covered in flies. I find a flat piece of bark, scoop up what's left of it, and throw it into the woods.

These babies are too young to be without a mother close by. Then I remember the dead vixen I saw in the ditch. I kneel down and take my half-eaten granola bar out of my pocket and toss it near the den. A moment later, a tiny twitching black nose pokes out. The baby stares at me for a few seconds, leaps for the granola bar, then dashes back inside. I hear muffled baby growls, and then it's quiet. I imagine them feasting away. Probably the most they've eaten since their mom was killed.

"I'll be back with more tomorrow, guys!"

I head to the far meadow, where Treasure is already making the most of his new old home, chomping away on the sweet grass by the river like nobody's business.

"Looks like you're making up for lost time," I tell him when I'm just close enough for him to hear. He turns toward my voice and trots up the bank toward me, lifting his feet high and tossing his head. He looks around again and then heads to a mound of dirt. I know just what he's going to do. He circles the mound, sniffs around, bends his knees, lets his body down with a groan, and lies down on the cool dirt. Then he waves his hooves in the air, rolling back and forth like a big dog having the time of his life. He's just a big goofball. I have to laugh. Even my skin feels happy.

Wes's truck turns down the driveway. He putters up, gets out, and stands next to me. Trusted Treasure jumps up from his roll and shakes his whole body.

"Wes, he loves it! Look at him! He's so happy to be back."

Treasure shakes his head and blows dust out from his nostrils. Then he paws the ground for another roll. Wes and I look at each other and laugh.

Wes smiles and walks over to Treasure, who touches Wes's cheek with his muzzle. Wes puts his hand on Treasure's forehead, right over his faint star. It's like Trusted Treasure is saying, "Thank you, Wes," and Wes is telling Treasure, "I'm glad we finally met." Wes knows a good horse when he sees one. Sometimes he knows right away and sometimes it takes a moment. This is that moment.

Then Treasure looks at me. Leaving him on his own for a whole month—the best thing in the world for his healing—is going to kind of break my heart. "Go! Go stand in the river, eat some more, and lie in the sun. Be a horse!" It's like he knew exactly what I was saying. Because that's exactly what he did.

***

When I get home, Dad's Jeep is in the driveway. I leave my bike in the yard and walk up the front steps until I hear a scraping sound around the corner of the house.

"Dad?"

He's on a ladder, wearing his headphones, tossing wet leaves and gunk from the gutter that hangs over my room.

"Dad!"

He pulls one side of the headphones away from his ear. "Hand me that hammer, will you?" His tar-covered fingers wiggle toward a toolbox on the ground. I climb the first three rungs and hand it up to him. But when we're both holding on to it, I don't let go.

"Dad. I got Treasure back."

Silence. An acorn rolls off the roof and pings the aluminum ladder before it hits the ground. I let go of the hammer, and Dad's hand disappears.

"He's still special, Dad. He's skinny as a rail. He doesn't look like the same horse. But I'm doing what Mom always said. Let him remember who he is. Just let him be. I know he's going to be great again. I can just tell. Will you come and see him? I don't think it would be breaking Mom's let-him-be rule if we just watch him from a distance."

I know what he's going to say before the words even come out of his mouth.

"This is my only day off, Reese, and there's so much to be fixed around the house." He claps the headphone back on his ear. The hammer starts sliding off the roof, but he catches it. "Maybe in a coupla days."

But I know what "maybe in a coupla days" means. Dad has so many ways of saying no. I love Treasure more and hate Dad more, all at once. I won't ask him again. Not until I get Treasure back into shape. Then Dad will wish he'd been part of it. Then he'll shake his head and say, "Why didn't I listen to you, Reese?"

I know he thinks I'm still standing there. He asks me for the flathead screwdriver, but I pretend I don't hear him and walk into the house.

PART
TWO

CHAPTER TWENTY-ONE

I'd like to spend all day staring at Trusted Treasure enjoying himself out in the field, but we have horses to sell. When I get back to the barn, Wes is already out in the ring. Hank Derkin is on today's calendar. He's a rancher who bought a horse or two from Mom and Dad every year. Wes has ten good sales horses to show him.

We've also got some auctions coming up in Wyoming and Nevada at the end of the summer. Once Wes sells a few horses, we can buy more, train them, and keep selling. Then we can pay the bills that aren't exactly disappearing off the desk, and Wes can get back to normal. I take a deep breath. A tightness in my shoulders melts away. Wes has such a good eye, and he's done such an amazing job training, I have a feeling these horses are as good as sold.

A fancy Cadillac SUV pulls in. The doors open and close and three men stand next to it, looking around. Hank always brings along his ranch stockman and his jigger boss. The stockman stretches and yawns. I walk out to greet them. "We're looking for Wes," says the jigger boss. I lead them to the ring. Hank doesn't recognize me, even though, just a few years ago, his daughter and I built a fort in the hayloft.

Wes is trotting a little bay mare around the ring. The men watch her calm working jog. Wes waves. He wants to show them Shorty first, so I go check that he's already groomed and tacked. Wes did a lot of work this morning while I was out with Treasure. He's fed the horses, given them fresh hay and water, and swept the aisle. Jasper, Marge, and the older horses are already turned out in the paddock.

Wes rides one horse after another into the ring to show how it moves, how it can turn on a dime, back up, and start a gallop from a standstill. The men are admiring the Appaloosa that Wes is showing now. He has her canter on the proper lead and do a figure eight. Then he has her stop and back up and canter off the halt. We named her Spot, which is about as original as naming a chestnut Red or a black horse Midnight. The men comment on Spot's lines and muscle, her bones and soft mouth. I think they're going to buy her right out from under him.

Wes looks up at me and holds up four fingers. That means Trudy. I nod and walk down the aisle. She's also fully tacked. Her usual halter is over her bridle and tied to the metal bar, but her saddle is English. That's different. We've never shown horses in English tack. I lead Trudy out to the ring. Hank and his crew don't notice me. They're in a tight circle talking horses and cattle and weather.

"Why that daughter of mine wants to ride in one of those silly little saddles, I'll never know," Hank says.

"It's just a phase," says the stockman. "She'll come to her senses and ride the right way again in no time."

Wes motions for me to get on Trudy.

"Me?"

He nods.

OMG. This is big. He not only wants me to show a horse to clients, something you only have your best riders do, but wants me to ride in the ring *with* him. Yeah, I might be his only rider, but that doesn't stop me from feeling like I'm chosen to do a very important job.

"Let me get my helmet, Wes." I jog back up to the barn like if I don't hurry, I'll mess this opportunity up. I grab it from the hook and run back to the ring still fastening my chinstrap. Wes is changing Spot's saddle from Western to English in the middle of the ring. She stands patiently while Wes tightens the girth and adjusts the stirrups.

I bring Trudy to the mounting block and put my leg over her. Wes motions for me to walk her one way and then the other. I try to show off my perfect form, imagining a straight line from the back of my head to my seat to my heels. I wait for Wes's signal and then ask Trudy to trot, which she does perfectly in each direction. The ranch guys are paying more attention to each other than to anything going on in the ring. They're still talking about the Appy. The stockman says he likes her low head carriage and that she might be just right for Hank's daughter, but nothing yet about Trudy.

Wes waves his hand for me to fall in a few strides behind him. I urge Trudy on with a little pressure from my outside leg, and she canters smoothly. I feel my nerves fall away with every stride. Wes and I take another turn around the ring in each direction, doing figure eights and lead changes. That gets the men's attention. They start pointing and I can tell they like both horses. They nod, like they're giving each other some serious we-should-make-an-offer glances.

Wes guides Spot into the combination jump along the far side of the ring. He wants me to do the same with Trudy. I'm finally getting to do the thing I love to do most on a horse. It's like I can already feel myself over the jump. I do a half circle and keep my eye on the obstacle. Trudy has a nice, soft stride that's sure to get the right distance to the jump. But when I square up to the first jump in the line, my shoulders seize up. My legs go weak. My focus blurs. I steer Trudy to the outside of the jumps. Wes canters a smooth half circle ahead of us.

"Don't the other horse jump?" Hank calls out. Wes nods to him and then rides up to me so we can trade horses and he can take Trudy over the jumps, but Hank stops us.

"I know Mr. Horse Whisperer guy can jump her, but what about the girl? What's your name, hon? You're about my daughter's size."

"Reese." My voice sounds far away, even to me.

"Why don't you jump her for me, Reese?"

Wes looks over his shoulder at me. He gives me a look, a one-sided smile with a quick nod. *This is your chance. Show me.*

I give Wes a slight nod back. He motions for me to fall in behind him. We take another lap around the ring. Once again, I'm fine at the canter. Wes guides Spot into the uncomplicated combination along the rail. I follow about six strides behind.

Trudy gets strong right before the jump. I should sit back and make her slow, but I lean forward, my leg telling her to go faster. When she pulls me into the jump, I may as well be a sack of feed on her back. My body does the opposite of what it's supposed to do. Trudy goes over the jump, but I land right at the base of it. She's galloping off to the far side of the ring, her leg caught in the hanging reins. She bucks and wheels and breaks the bridle. Then she leaps out of the ring, one leg still tangled in the reins, and breaks the top rail.

Now Spot is acting up, rearing and whirling as Trudy charges around outside the ring, shaking her head and whinnying like she's pissed off. When she runs off to join the other horses in the lower field, I start to chase after her. But Wes gives me an I'll-handle-this look, so I just open the gate for him as he kicks Spot into a dead gallop. The men start mumbling.

"Clive is gettin' up there. He'd never be able to stay on her."

"She's night-mare-ish, I'd say."

"She's too green for Emily, and I'm not interested in the App."

In a few minutes, Wes returns, ponying Trudy. I open the gate to let him through. He seems determined not to miss a beat. He goes straight to the barn to pick another mount to show Hank, but the mood in the air has changed. The stockman checks his watch; the jigger boss digs the toe of his boot into the dirt, and Hank is talking on his phone.

I blew it. It's as clear to me as when the sun goes behind a cloud, but Wes hasn't realized it yet. He comes back into the ring on one of the newer horses, a young palomino, and I finish tacking a nice little roan gelding. But when the gelding and I pass Hank on the way back into the ring, he looks right at me.

"Unnecessary," he says.

I know exactly what he means—that he's already seen every horse he wants to see. But it feels like he was only talking about me.

Unnecessary.

I put my hand up to cover the lump that's growing in my throat because it feels like something they can see. I try not to blink. One blink will turn me into the crying little girl I am trying so hard not to be.

"Thanks all the same, Wes," says Hank, "but we'd better get going. Keep me posted about anything interesting."

The men walk past me to their air-conditioned SUV.

"Let's stop at that ribs joint."

"Maybe ask the girl from the auction in Aberdeen, the one with the beautiful chest—I mean chestnut—to join us."

I can still hear them laughing through their closed doors as they drive off.

Unnecessary. The word settles in my brain like a puddle of mud. I don't know what happened to me. I don't know why I suddenly froze doing something I used to do all the time. Something I felt born to do. Whatever it was, it came out of nowhere. And I will never let that happen again.

It's always hard to apologize. When you're embarrassed, it's even harder. When you feel embarrassed and unnecessary, it's pretty much impossible. I want to tell Wes a million reasons why it wasn't my fault. I find him in Trudy's stall, wrapping up one of her banged-up legs.

"I think maybe Trudy was in heat, Wes. I think she—"

Wes stops what he's doing but doesn't look at me. He just holds the wrap of cotton bandage in place at Trudy's cannon bone.

"It could have been the wind. You know, the wind has been carrying all kinds of dirt and dust from . . . or something could have spooked her."

Wes doesn't move. It's like someone pressed his pause button. His stillness makes me feel trapped.

I keep spitting reasons, rapid-fire, hoping one of them sticks. Maybe Trudy sensed a storm front moving in. Or she heard the sound of a bulldozer not too far off. I don't want Wes to focus on what happened with me and the jump. I want him to think of anything but that. I want him to think of all of the other reasons it's possible the sale didn't happen.

"It's not my fault the bottom fell out of the horse market."

Wes stays still. Still as a statue. He's waiting for something. And I know what it is. He does this when he wants me to listen to myself. He just waits. He won't move until he hears what he knows I should say. His stillness is worse than getting yelled at.

"It was my fault. I'm sorry, Wes."

His fingers continue to slowly wind the wrap around Trudy's leg.

"I should have been able to help you make that sale."

He finishes the neat wrap and stretches the Velcro strap out and around, then moves to the other leg.

"I should have—"

Wes's hand goes up, stopping me. *Enough.*

"I—"

He raises his hand slightly higher and keeps it in the air. *No more excuses.*

CHAPTER TWENTY-TWO

"Nobody's buying horses these days. At least not for what you're asking."

I see the text just before Wes picks up his phone and deletes it. Then he grabs the list of ranchers I'd written for him and draws a line through the last name left. Hank Derkin. Wes drops into his office chair and traces that line over and over and over. He doesn't look up. He just keeps going back and forth with his pen, creating a groove so deep the paper tears.

I walk down the aisle of the barn. I'm not supposed to be even a little bit happy that sales are down, but I am. Most of my favorites are still here. Only Bailey's and Elvis's stalls are empty. Wes sold them for almost no profit at all. Since land is worth more cut up into lots for developments, even wealthy ranchers are bailing, which means you can get your hands on a well-bred horse for next to nothing now. No matter how good his horse is, Wes can't make a profit.

When I stop at Olive's stall, she pricks her ears toward me and reaches her nose out for a pat. According to her file, Olive is fifteen. Her real name is Olivia's Illusion. She won at Prairie Meadows as a two-year-old, set a new track record at Elko County, and narrowly lost at White Pines to a horse that went on to win the Manor Downs. She's had two foals—Whispered Illusion, a filly too young to have a record, and Holiday Illusion, who won the Black Elk three years ago. With Olive's breeding, her foal will sell for silly money—even in tough times. Wes already has a buyer who also wants to contract Wes to train the foal. Then the money problems will go away. But Olive still has at least a month to go. The question is, what do we do between now and then?

"Some things you can't rush," I tell Olive while I scratch her forehead and give her another flake of hay.

Doing my best to steer clear of Wes, I continue with chores—hay first, then grain, then scrubbing and refilling water buckets. I'm hoping the work will help me forget how our troubles are partly my fault. How I blew the deal. How I froze before a two-foot jump. How I was afraid of something I used to do all the time. How things would be different if I hadn't told Wes over and over what a good rider and jumper I am, even though I hadn't jumped once since the crash. *It won't happen again. That was just a silly moment of nerves*, I tell myself.

I'm praying for something to change our luck. Maybe a billionaire rancher who has seen the good horses Wes turns out, or a loaded heiress with an empty barn to fill. I'm scrubbing a bucket with a handful of straw when a brown minivan jostles down the driveway and parks in front of the barn. Just someone coming to get paid, I bet. A woman with long black hair gets out. Definitely not an heiress. I leave the bucket and wipe my hands on my jeans.

"Can I help you?"

She holds out her hand. "I'm Ellen." Her eyes are dark and deep-set.

"Reese. You lost?"

She laughs. "Well, maybe a little."

Then the minivan door slides open.

"Can I ride a horse here?" a girl shouts from her seat. She looks like she's around nine. She stares up toward the sky, her milky eyes unable to focus. Ellen helps her out of the minivan and leads her over to meet me.

"Zadie, hon, this is Reese."

"Nice to meet you, Zadie."

"So, what's the deal? Can I ride here?"

"Zadie took lessons at Whispering Oaks," says Ellen, "but they closed last month. It was the only place that taught kids with . . . this ability." She glances down and runs her hand through Zadie's hair.

"Mom really means disability. She thinks it makes me feel better to call my blindness an ability. I think it's stupid."

"Do you do lessons here?" Ellen asks. She looks tired. Like she already knows the answer that's about to come out of my mouth. The same one she's been hearing from everyone else. "We'll sign a release, of course."

"I'm not a beginner," Zadie says. "I can even tack the horse if you leave the saddle over the stall door." Then she leans in like she's telling me a secret. "What I really want to learn is how to jump."

Ellen looks at me and shakes her head.

"Zadie, we mostly train horses at this barn," I explain. "You know, to sell. Wes, the owner, goes to auctions to—"

"Can I meet Wes? I bet he'll say I can have a lesson."

"Well, Wes isn't in a great mood right now. He might have to trailer all the way to the auction in Oklahoma tomorrow."

"Are you just making stuff up like the guy at Fox Meadow did? He said he couldn't do lessons because his back was out, but Mom thought he looked fine."

"I was getting a little tired of all of the excuses people had," Ellen says. "They're all so afraid to let her ride. But really, she rides better than most kids."

"Better?" Zadie laughs. "I can ride circles around them."

"She doesn't need to be in a special program. I mean, once she's on the horse . . ."

"The horse has eyes!" Zadie says.

"Ellen, the problem is, we're not that kind of barn. And Wes . . . doesn't talk."

"He can't talk?"

"No, he . . . just doesn't talk. It's a choice." I sound frustrated when I say *choice*.

Ellen looks at me like she's sure I'm just making shit up. "Come on, Zadie. I guess a man who chooses not to talk can't give you a lesson."

"Maybe Stony Brook will do it. If you want to wait a minute, I'll call over there."

"We already stopped there. They said they don't have an *appropriate* horse."

"I'm sorry, Ellen. I hope you find a place. I really do."

Zadie holds her middle finger up behind her back as they walk away.

I'm making my way back to the bucket I was scrubbing when Wes jogs out of the barn. He shoots me his irritated look and heads over to Zadie and Ellen. I had no idea he was listening. Great. I've probably blown it again. Like, as far as Wes is concerned, I can't do anything right.

Wes reaches them just as Zadie is buckling her seat belt and Ellen is about to slide the minivan's door shut. I make my way back over.

"Ellen, Zadie, this is Wes."

"We'll be out of your way in just a minute," Ellen says, glancing at Wes. But Zadie slides her door back open.

"Wes? Are you gonna let me ride?"

"Zadie, don't worry, we'll try another farm," Ellen says, trying to slide the door shut again. But the door won't budge. Wes is holding it open.

"Wes, am I riding or what?"

Ellen looks at Wes. Wes nods.

"Is it happening?" Zadie asks.

"It's happening," says Ellen.

Zadie leaps from the minivan and practically drags her mother behind her.

"Whoa, whoa, whoa! Slow down! You don't even know where you're going." Ellen pulls Zadie to a stop.

"I'm going with Wes."

"Well, in that case, you better wait for him. You ran right past him."

When Wes catches up, Ellen guides Zadie's hand from hers to his.

"Are you really gonna let me ride, Wes?" asks Zadie.

Wes places Zadie's hand on his chin and nods. Then they go right up to Marge's stall. Wes guides Zadie's hand from Marge's diamond-shaped forehead to her velvety muzzle.

"That's Marge." I take a few steps toward them.

Wes slides the bridle over Marge's ears and then puts the reins in Zadie's hands. She leans her head toward the clip-clop of Marge's big hooves. Together, they lead Marge into the ring.

Wes stops in the middle of the ring and guides Zadie to Marge's side. He places her hand on Marge's huge shoulder, and she traces Marge's body from neck to tail, down one side and then up the other. Zadie looks focused, like she's listening to Wes. Then he puts both of her hands on Marge's withers and places her foot on his knee. Zadie understands. She steps up and slides her small leg across Marge's back. A smile stretches across her face, then she leans forward and hugs Marge's neck.

"Marge is solid," I tell Ellen. "Very calm and sweet."

Ellen presses her palms together just beneath her chin, like she's praying.

"No one has ever let her sit bareback."

Wes positions Zadie's fingers around the reins, leads her halfway around the ring, and then lets the reins go. Zadie is on her own now.

"Should she be doing that?" Ellen takes a step toward the ring. "They always held the lead at Whispering Oaks."

"Marge will take care of her. Don't worry."

Zadie's smile has grown even bigger, which didn't seem possible. Wes signals for Marge to pick up a slow walk. Zadie's body relaxes and moves with Marge's—way better than most beginners I've seen.

The phone in the office rings, but I ignore it. Instead, I watch Ellen watch her daughter. Ellen's fearful, but she's holding herself back from charging into the ring. She can't take her eyes off Wes and Zadie. Wes looks at Ellen and gives a slow nod. *Don't worry. She's OK.*

I feel a plan coming out of nowhere. Like Dad used to always come up with, all of a sudden, when we were driving along or watching TV. It always seemed so random, like something just plopped into his brain out of nowhere. Like when he spent hours twisting and turning a Rubik's Cube. He'd put it down for days, then one night, after a long day at the barn, he burst through the door shouting, "Here's what we need to do!" That scared me so bad I spilled my Cocoa Corn Puffs down the front of my shirt. Then he picked up the Rubik's Cube and in four swift moves, he solved it.

I'm having a Rubik's Cube moment. I know what we need to do. But knowing is one thing. Convincing Wes will be another. I take out my phone, hold it steady, then press SLOW MOTION, RECORD.

CHAPTER TWENTY-THREE

A couple days later, Wes and I are on the tractor, heading out to the back pasture to clear a fallen tree. I'm sitting on the wheel well, gripping the back of the seat, while Wes drives. The motor's trembling and shaking is making my fingers go numb. Wes stops, jumps down, and attaches a chain to the back to pull the tree's giant stump out of the ground. While the tractor's wheels churn the deep, dark mud, and the bark crumbles from the pull of the chain, I start clearing away the brush.

I trip on a knot of a root that's poking up from the chopped, churned earth. I pull on it, but it doesn't give. I twist it one way and then the other, but it feels like a rubbery, wiry rope. I yank on it some more and then try stomping on it with the edge of my heel.

My face feels hot. It's like things just got real with this root. The more I pull on it, the more I lose my grip. I try digging around the root to get a better hold, but my hands slip and I get cut. This root is not about to come up. Like it's challenging me, making fun of me.

"Ahhhh!" I get on my hands and knees and punch the root. "Damn it, damn it, damn it, damn it!" Then I start

yelling all these thoughts I didn't even know I was thinking. "Unnecessary! I'll tell you what's unnecessary! You are
now, you stupid root! And so were my cousin's tonsils and
my uncle's appendix and my old cat's extra toe. Why were
they even there if they weren't necessary? What the fuck!"

I am a muddy, sweaty mess. But I don't care. I pick up
a rock and throw it as far as I can, but it hits the trunk of
a nearby tree. It ricochets and almost hits me in the head.

"Fuck Hank fuckin' Derkin. Unnecessary! I know he
was talking about me. He can just go and fuck himself."

I start pulling on the root again. Then I just sit down
beside it. "Ugh. The thing is, I know I'm actually *not* necessary. I mean, I could bite the big one right now and the
world would keep on turning. Just like it did when Mom
died. And Wes will do just fine at the barn without me.
Probably be better off."

Behind me, the tractor goes quiet. Without the engine's
rumble, the chirps of the birds are back. My ears are ringing from all my yelling. Then Wes's hand is on my shoulder.
I want to stand or turn or run, but I can't. My body ignores
me. Wes lifts me up by the armpits. The last time someone
lifted me like that, Dad was helping me up off the hot
pavement after I fell off my bike. I hate myself for feeling
like a kid again. Helpless.

Before I know it, Wes's big arms are wrapped around
me, and he's patting my head with hands that smell of
diesel and mud and horses. The tightness in my throat
begins to loosen. My fists begin to unclench. Then we hear
the honk of a horn. A black Tahoe is making its way down
the driveway, trying to steer around the muddy ruts.

"Gibson." I wipe my nose with the back of my hand.
Wes nods. We leave the tractor where it is and walk through

the field to the barn. We climb over the fence just as Gibson is pulling up to the entrance. The driver side of the Tahoe is newly emblazoned with his big, rotten-toothed-smile photo and, in huge letters, WE BUY UGLY FARMS.

"That's a good way to ruin a nice-looking ride."

But I can't make Wes smile. He waits for Gibson to open his door and get out. First thing we see is his flip-flopped foot, which he hesitates to put down in the muddy driveway. He looks around, grimaces, and then crinkles his nose as he walks toward us.

"Wes, I think you know why I'm here."

Wes doesn't nod or look down or do anything. I can't tell if he's looking at Mr. Gibson or looking past him.

"I know the predicament you're in. Horse sales are down. That's a real fact. And that's just not ideal for a horse operation. Look, I'm not gonna mince-coat anything here. It's just a matter of time. You and I both know that. All you have to do is look around." Gibson hunches his shoulders and spreads his arms out like he's not sure what he's displaying. "Unless you're gonna pull a rabbit out of your cowboy boot here or some such thing, this place is—"

Wes holds up his hand to stop Gibson from talking.

"Look, I know it's hard to admit when you've made a poor choice. But I think it's time to cut your losses. You know, chalk it up to bad timing. No one knew that land would be developed way out here, that the bottom would fall out of the horse market. But what's bad news for you is great news for me. Doesn't make sense for me to lease land to someone who can't make the payments when I could sell this dump for a small fortune. To a spa developer! These assholes think there's something special about the quartz deposits around here. Some kind of magic mojo. Can you believe that shit?"

Wes's jaw muscle pops in and out. I follow him into the barn. Gibson follows us both. Wes stretches his neck from side to side as he paces in his office. Gibson doesn't give up. He stands in the doorway and keeps on talking.

"Pivot, Wes. That's the new word. Most people have to at some time. It's the kinder, gentler way of saying you failed. I don't know. Raise alpacas. I hear people are raising them in Lewiston now—land is cheap there. Sell the wool for blankets and stuff. Or spin it and weave it yourself. Make your own blankets. Try something new. But then again, don't your people already know a lot about selling blankets? Could be big. You know, that thing about closing windows and opening doors?"

Wes walks over and slams the door in Gibson's face. His voice is only slightly muffled through the closed door. "OK then. Last time I cast my pearls among sewer rats!"

Wes picks up the stapler from the desk and throws it at the door.

"Jeez, simmer down in there, Tonto. Things don't have to get ugly." Gibson nervous-laugh-mumbles to himself before he yells, "Actually, they already are! It'll sure be tough for you to come back from being two months behind on your payments, Wes. Soon you'll be three. Three's pretty much impossible. Unless you think you can win the Black Elk." We can hear him laughing all the way back to his Tahoe.

Wes shakes his head and sits down at his dusty desk. I turn a bucket upside down and sit on it. I can hear the new-Dad voice like it's right here in the room. *Reese, I told you so.* Blah, blah, blah. *The horse business is full of one heartbreak after another.* But like old Dad, the one who believed solutions can pop into your brain out of nowhere, I have an idea. And it's a great one. But I have no idea how to tell Wes. He's a horse person. And horse people are the proudest, most stubborn-ass people you'll ever meet. I'll lead up to my big idea slowly, starting with an idea I know he's already thought of.

"What if we went to Texas? The big auction in Amarillo? They must still be getting good prices there."

Wes just stares down. I know the answer. It's too competitive there. Almost impossible to make your horses stand out. It wouldn't be cheap getting there either. Wes starts tapping at the calculator, adding up money he doesn't have.

On the shelves and walls, Wes's pictures are now mixed with some of our old ones. There's Treasure when we brought him home from the auction. What a skinny, awkward, stubborn thing he was. What did Mom see? How did she know he was special? That she could break him of his stubbornness and get him to trust her?

I think about how Mom went over and over the same lessons with him when he was a young colt. Like the puddle lesson. "This puddle's not gonna kill ya, see?" she said. Then she walked into it herself and stomped around. She did it as many times as it took, and it felt like forever. But three weeks later, he actually followed her into a tiny little puddle. Back then, I still couldn't imagine him ever being bold enough to face the obstacles of the Black Elk. "It's not that I don't think it'll happen, Jessie," Dad told Mom when Treasure started to show some promise, "but what are we gonna do to make money if you're spending all your time training that colt? We've got a barn full of horses I can't sell, and they're just sitting here getting old." But Mom didn't give up, and things worked out.

I pull my phone out of my pocket and find the video of Wes teaching Zadie. Somehow, the moment, the light,

and the slow motion makes everything look shimmery and
beautiful. It might be the most professional-looking video
I've ever shot. I go to his desk and hold the phone out so
he can see the screen.

"Wes, look here. When sales were down, Mom gave
lessons."

Wes grunts and does one of his lip-flutter laughs.

"Seriously. It's what they lived on until they could sell
horses. That was their bread and butter. I remember Mom
standing in the center of the ring, kids riding in a circle around
her while she instructed. I didn't think it was an option here
because I thought you needed words to be a teacher. But I
was wrong. Somehow, you can do it without them."

Wes looks at me like I'm crazy.

"It's something, Wes. It's something we can do."

Wes pushes my hand away and stands up.

A drop of sweat slides down my back. "I will hunker
down in the office and call every number in Mom's notebook and get as many people as I can to come here for
lessons and boarding. It's lessons and boarding that we
have to push until the time is right for selling again. I'll
answer all the calls and emails. I'll keep up with the grooming and tack cleaning and mucking out stalls."

He shakes his head and kicks an open drawer closed.
I follow him into the aisle.

"I know you're thinking how horse people talk about
other horse people. That if you have to resort to giving
lessons, you're not a serious horse trainer. That you're not
a trainer worth his salt. But we don't have any options
right now." I run ahead of him so I can look him in the eye.
"You've done an amazing job training these horses. You
could put any rider on any of them." He keeps walking

forward, so I walk backward and keep talking. "I know what else you're thinking. What parent's going to sign their kid up for lessons with some dude who doesn't talk?"

Wes pulls his chaps down from a hook and heads back to the office. I stay in front of him.

"I watched you with Zadie. I don't know how you did it. But you did. And you did it even better than someone who talks." My right leg catches on the handle of the full wheelbarrow, almost tipping it. I catch it just in time. "I'll post about you and say how you train and teach, you know, in this new, cool way . . . without . . . talking." Wes passes me. I run past him again and keep talking. "And I'll push it out there like it's this new, super-successful way of doing things. Because riding is a feeling and it can't be explained anyway. And I'll say how horses like it and kids pay attention because it's not like someone's yelling at them all the time."

I keep going because Wes is in his chair again, looking at his pile of bills and tapping his thumb fast on the desk. He looks around the office. His thumb slows to a heartbeat rhythm, and then he does one final loud tap and stands.

"We have to open for lessons, Wes. Please. We don't have time to do anything else."

A horse whinnies in the paddock. Jasper bangs on his stall door. Olive nickers. Wes walks past me again. His shoulder brushes my shoulder. I don't follow him this time. I don't have anything else to say. No more ideas. I step back and drop down onto my bucket seat. I can already picture a wrecking ball blasting through the barn wall. My throat feels like a vine is growing around it. I blink fast to keep my tears back, then I get up and walk slowly out to Wes.

He's in Stinky's stall, brushing him. Dust swirls through shards of light as Wes flicks the bristles with every stroke.

"What now, Wes? You just gonna let some buyer turn this place into a spa where fancy-ass city people come to find their center and get their toenails polished?"

Wes keeps brushing.

"I don't have any more ideas. Other than, maybe, join the circus? Train the horses to do backflips? Teach them to skydive?"

Wes takes a saddle off the stall door and looks at me. He tilts his head toward the board across the aisle. He's written something. *It's not me I'm worried about.*

"What? What else? You're all that matters. People will be curious. Like I was. They won't believe it at first, but then . . ."

He opens Stinky's stall door, walks past me to the board, and writes something else. *You're not much of a people person.* He puts the marker down and smirks a little as he walks back to Stinky's stall.

"Me?" I step backward like I've been shoved.

"Seriously, Wes? You're worried about me?"

He looks around. *Do you see anyone else here?*

"OK, look. I may come across a little, you know, over-enthusiastic at times. And I don't have many friends."

Wes furrows his brow and looks at me sideways.

"Any friends. But I can make friends if I have to. I can be the nicest kid anyone has ever met if it means keeping this place going. I know I have a tendency to swear a little. But that's just us, you know, horse person to horse person."

Wes attaches the girth on one side and moves to the other.

"OK. Maybe you're right. I know I have to work on that. And I will. If I have to. I'll be a people person better than any person has ever been a people person with people before."

He reaches under Stinky's chest for the girth. He pulls up on the billet strap to tighten it and lets the stirrup leather fall back down.

"I'll be patient and kind and sweet if it kills me. Wes, please. If that's what you're worried about, I promise I'll be so nice you won't be able to stand it."

Wes stops a minute and rests his hands on either side of the saddle.

"I know lessons weren't ever in your plan. You're better than that. I know. Your horses are too. But can we just give it a try?"

I stare at Wes. He stares at the ground. Finally, he looks up at me.

"Can we?"

Dust motes swirl in the air between us. Even the horses are waiting.

Then Wes nods.

CHAPTER TWENTY-FOUR

I used to know nothing. I used to be an empty-headed dope like my dad is now. But ever since Wes gave me the good-to-go five days ago, I've noticed that I actually know stuff. I wouldn't say I know *everything*, but I know a lot more than Dad does. For instance, I know that one picture can be liked and shared and reposted. Which mine are. And the right picture with the right message can reach hundreds—if not thousands—of horse people. Which mine do.

It hasn't hurt my marketing plan that, for an older dude, Wes is kind of hot. He could be thirty-five, or he could be twenty-five. Probably, like most horse people, he's never heard of toner or moisturizer. People who work outside every day get a little older a lot faster. He's most likely way younger than he looks.

I've been posting a new pic of him every day. #horse whisperer #teachwithouttalking. And under the pic of Wes jumping the huge stone wall, #wheretheresawalltheresaway. I include the video of him teaching Zadie. After only half an hour, we've got followers. It's only a matter of time before the phone rings and it's a customer, not a bill collector.

I hold my phone out the barn window and video Wes in the training ring, riding on a young quarter horse named Chester. The horse seems like a handful. He has a bit of a crazy eye, but Wes looks like he's relaxing in a lawn chair. He holds the reins long and loose. You can tell the horse is paying attention to him. I post another pic of Wes shoeing Jasper. I thought the sweat on Wes's biceps and his old, worn-out chaps could sell some lessons. I want to portray him as a sort of approachable horse genius.

At magic hour, when the sun is low and the colors are warm, Wes is lunging Harper in the ring. I sneak closer, crouching down to include the big sky behind them. It's totally cowboy-and-his-horse. Wes slowly turns his body. Around him canters Harper—neck arched, chin tucked, hind-end engaged. When I'm just about to get the perfect angle, Wes sees me. But instead of getting mad and shooing me away, he tilts his head just so and flexes a bicep. Not the shot I was hoping for, but usable.

"It's better if you don't pose!"

He nods and relaxes. I grab a few more shots before the sun goes down. Back in the office, I scroll through them and show Wes my faves while he scribbles out some checks for the few bills he can pay.

"Pretty good, right?"

He sticks out his bottom lip and nods.

"If I can get that new lens attachment . . ."

And then it happens. The phone rings. Not Wes's phone. The office phone. The one on the desk with the cord and the actual buttons. I'd forgotten how it sounded. The ring's vibration disturbs layers of dust. It keeps ringing. Wes looks at me, then back at the phone. I pick up, but I have no idea what to call the barn now.

"Thanks for calling Willow Creek Farm."

Wes glances at me. I shrug and cover the receiver. "We need to come up with a name." I've been doing all of the promotion using Wes's name, but a real operation has to have a farm name.

"Why, yes, we most certainly do give lessons here. How old is your little one? Oh, for you? Is Wes single?"

Wes looks at me sideways and shrugs.

"Yes, he's single." I cover the receiver again and whisper, "Better for business if you're not attached. Anyway, I got this. No, he just rides horses . . . Yes, he rides with chaps . . . No, he's not on Tinder . . . Hey, what are you? Some kind of a weirdo freakin' asshole?"

I slam the phone down. "Don't worry, we're going to get some riffraff. It's all part of the—" Then I see how Wes is looking at me.

Shit. I'm supposed to be a people person.

Almost immediately, the phone rings again. I grab it fast and answer in the sweetest voice I've ever used. It doesn't even sound like me.

"Crooked Oak Farm."

Wes doesn't like that one either. He gives me two thumbs down.

"Sure, we could do a birthday party."

Wes shakes his head no.

"I mean, it would have to include riding lessons, of course."

It doesn't take long for legit customers to start calling. One wants a lesson for her eight-year-old son, another for his twelve-year-old daughter. By the end of the day, I have Wes set up to teach a group lesson for eleven kids on Saturday morning at ten.

My plan has worked. I feel like my feet might come off

the ground. All those posts I blasted out into the cyber abyss have paid off. In my notebook, I list every caller's full name, number, email address, and riding ability. Wes leaves, but I stay and work. I have two days to get everything ready for the people who'll be showing up on Saturday. I need to print out release forms, start a file for every client, and update posts.

I look around at the barn—full of horses and tack and feed and hay. I breathe in the smell. The smell that's back again. The smell of a barn full of life. And soon, people will be back. Just like before. People I found without an ounce of help from Dad. People who will see that this place is finally back in action.

❧

I can't sleep. I'm staring up at the ceiling, feeling like I just drank eight cups of coffee. I could get up and pace, but my legs are too tired. I think about scrolling through videos on my phone, but why would I need videos when a movie keeps playing in my head? People are filling the barn. Adorable kids are falling in love with the horses. Parents are signing them up for lessons. Rich show people want Wes to train their horses. We are making so much money, we paint the barn, get new doors, and build a better ring. Wes even gets a new truck. And Wes starts to talk. He tells me it's all because of me. He makes me stand on a bale of hay while he talks to a big crowd. "She's the one who noticed my eye for amazing horses. She's the one who saw my talent for teaching. She's the one who knew this place could thrive. We couldn't have done it if she wasn't so nice."

Then I remember that horse people are always suckers for the latest and greatest thing. My posts have intrigued them, which is good. But what if they think the place is too run-down and doesn't have nice enough wash stalls or any heated therapy pools? That could be bad. My eyes are getting heavy.

Or maybe, just maybe, I've made something awesome happen. I think of how the day will go tomorrow. How I'll feed and tack the horses Wes wants to use. How I'll wait for the cars to start pulling down the driveway. How nice I'll be—how nice everything will be—when I greet all the new students arriving at the barn.

CHAPTER TWENTY-FIVE

Complete chaos. Monstrous shitstorm. That's what it feels like at the barn. I even showed up early to get everything organized and ready for the day, my most important day here so far. But last night, there was a torrential downpour, and the stupid roof gave out directly over the tack room. All of the saddles and saddle pads and bridles are soaked. There's an inch of water on the floor. Every piece of tack we have is completely drenched.

I can't put soaked saddle pads on horses, so I'm making trips back and forth between the tack room and the fence, hanging dripping saddle pads on the fence line outside. But I know it won't even begin to help. When leather gets this wet, it takes forever to dry. Then it needs to be conditioned and treated. But I don't know what else to do. And people are already showing up.

I'd planned to be out there, welcoming everyone and directing parking. But with water everywhere, my big plan for Wes and me and the barn has been shot down before it could even get started. Parents are parking in the wrong places, blocking the entrance and getting stuck in the mud.

Kids are yelling, running around, and getting the horses all worked up. I have to act nice, like everything is under control, even though I'd like to yell at these brats and tell them they're not going to so much as touch a horse if they don't calm their shit down. But I can't lose any customers. So I fake smile and say crap like, "Wow, aren't you a crazy little cowboy," and "Look at you, all fired up for your lesson."

My phone vibrates in my back pocket. I know who it is even before I look. I press ACCEPT, and there's that giant, useless ear again taking up the entire screen.

"Dad, I can't talk right now."

"I tried calling you three times."

"Sorry, there's a leak here and . . . please, Dad. It's just not a good time."

"Reese, we made a deal that you'd call every hour."

"Dad, take the phone away from your ear for a sec and look. This is what I'm dealing with." I turn the phone around to show him the hole in the roof and all the damage.

"Oh, wow. That's bad."

"Yes. And I have people showing up for lessons. I really need to go."

"Just real quick . . ."

I consider throwing my phone. "What?"

The kid commotion amps up. I run to the aisle to make sure they aren't messing with the horses. One of the boys is throwing horse turds at a girl. She's screaming and hiding behind some hay bales. Five or six kids are laughing hysterically.

"Hey, guys, can you please stop? I have . . . Dad, I gotta go."

"Wait a sec, Reese. Remember when I mentioned I wanted you to start having family nights with LeeAnne and her boys?"

"Yes, I remember." I wonder if he can hear my eyes roll.

"I was wondering if next Tuesday would work. Lee-Anne mentioned she'd like to come over again and cook us dinner, and I thought—"

"Next Tuesday?"

"Yeah, I think it would be great for us all to spend more time together. You know, just casual and fun."

Dad is yakking away like he's all of a sudden got all the time in the world for me.

"Dad, I don't know."

Kids are screaming from somewhere in the loft. It sounds like their stomping feet might come through the boards at any second.

"OK, fine, Dad. Whatever."

"Call me when you're—"

I throw my phone on the desk and run back to the tack room.

I look up at the rafters and see even more sky than before. *Fuck, fuck, fuckity, fuck, fuck, fuck.* I grab a pile of pads and head outside.

Wes is on the roof, peeling back the shingles and pulling off the rotten wood. I can tell by his face that he's adding up the cost of a new roof. I just hope he stays up there until I get things in order down here on the ground.

Back inside, one of the moms is standing in the doorway of the tack room. Her sweats are bedazzled with the words *Hot Mama Jama*. She doesn't seem fazed by the water on the floor or, for that matter, the gaping hole in the roof. "Tristen needs new paddock boots. Any recommendations?" she asks.

"Hi, Mrs. . . ."

"Oliphant. You can just call me Cookie."

"Yes . . . sure, Cookie. I prefer the lace-ups. Mud and sweat can make zippers pretty useless."

"That's what I thought." Cookie seems very pleased with herself.

I lead her out to the ring so I can clean up the mess without any more interruptions. I don't have one horse tacked, and the lesson is supposed to start in ten minutes. But first, I grab the release forms and the information sheets off Wes's desk. I pass them out to the parents, who are standing around with their coffee cups, talking to each other like this is some kind of a party.

"If you could please just fill these out and sign, your kids will be up on their horses in the lower ring in about ten minutes." I know it will be half an hour at best. I still don't know what to do about the kids who are climbing into the loft. Their stomping is making streams of dirt and dust fall from between the planks onto the parents and the horses below.

Shit, shit, shit.

I go back into the tack room to wipe off the saddles. When I discover that every single towel is already wet, I take off my sweater and use it to rub the seats dry. I go from one saddle to the next until I have to hang my sweater up to dry too. Everything hangs limp. Most of the pads are still dripping wet.

Back inside, a strange kind of quiet hangs over the barn. I don't hear the parents chatting and bragging. The kids aren't stomping their feet in the loft. Wes is in the ring, and the kids are lined up behind him. No horses. Just Wes and the kids. He breaks into the kind of trot that I used to do when I was little, pretending to be a horse. The kids all follow him. He circles to the left and slaps his left leg.

He circles to the right and slaps his right leg. *He's showing them leads.* Some of the kids laugh and slap their bums instead, like it's too silly for them. But most of them are having fun.

I run to the fence rails and start pulling down some of the saddle pads. They could use an hour in a dryer, but I don't have an hour or a dryer. I also don't have a choice. I have to use these pads, wet or not. Jasper shudders when I place his pad on his back.

"It's OK, buddy. Just a little cool."

I quickly add his saddle before he makes too much of a fuss. One down. Then I race back to the tack room and saddle up three more unhappy horses. I give them all extra hay so they won't take their unhappiness out on any of the kids.

Out in the ring, things are still quiet. Around the perimeter, some of the parents are talking quietly. Outside, a few are wandering around in the driveway, talking on their cell phones. Others are leaning against the rails, chatting. When Wes sets up some cavalettis and small jumps, the parents stop talking and pay close attention again. But there's still no horse. Wes makes the kids take little steps and big steps, then nice, even, comfortable steps to get them into the rhythm they'll use before a jump. He doesn't make them count, like most trainers would. Wes is showing them that you can feel when you need to release for a jump, just like you can feel when you need to step over a branch on the ground or step up onto a stair. He trots like a horse toward a jump. Then he goes over it without breaking his stride. The kids follow. Wes catches my eye and holds up seven fingers.

"You want Bob?" I yell.

He nods.

"Tacked?"

He shakes his head no.

I slip Bob's halter over his big ears, do a once-over with a brush. "Come on, bud. It's showtime." I lead him down to the ring. All the kids act like he's the first horse they've ever seen.

"What's his name?"

"How old is he?"

"How tall is he?"

Before I can answer their questions, Wes takes him from me and leads him to the center of the ring. The kids form a circle around Bob. When Wes drops his lead and takes off the halter, Bob moves away, but when Wes holds up his hand, he stops. Then Wes walks to Bob's side and pushes his palm out. Bob follows him as if he's still wearing his halter and lead. They walk around the ring, side by side. The kids ooh and aah like they're at the circus. When Wes rolls his hands, one around the other, Bob walks in a circle around him. When he rolls his hands faster, Bob picks up a trot, circling wider and wider, then breaks into a smooth canter. When Wes makes a circle with his finger, Bob turns and does the same thing in the other direction. Then Wes's hand movements become smaller and smaller until it looks like he's controlling Bob with just his thoughts.

The kids don't say a word. They watch Wes like he's a magician. The smallest girl, Naomi, has been watching his every move, eyes wide. He taps her once on the shoulder. She looks around, stretches herself as tall as she can, and walks toward the center of the ring, stepping right into the footprints Wes has left in the dirt. Bob is waiting for them patiently.

Wes takes Naomi's hand and holds it up in the air. She keeps it raised, and Wes moves away from her and toward the rail. Bob starts to follow him, but he gestures for Naomi to stay put and hold her hand higher. She does, and Bob stops. Soon, Naomi is directing Bob to walk around her in a circle. When she rolls her hands like Wes did, Bob trots. Little Naomi can't be more than fifty pounds soaking wet, and here she is, controlling eighteen-hundred-pound Bob without a lead, without words. Just signals.

Next, Wes shows the kids that standing tall makes a horse pay closer attention. When he closes his body by hunching his shoulders and looking down, Bob puts his nose to the dirt, blows out air, then starts to wander. But when Wes straightens up and raises his hand, Bob pays attention again. Wes is showing the kids that a tall stance and a raised hand means *Look at me. I'm the boss.* Then he shows them that moving both hands together like you're tossing the contents of a bowl means *trot on*. Wes is like a conductor of an orchestra. I'd like to stay and watch the rest of the lesson, but my thoughts go back to the dripping, drenched tack. I hustle back into the barn.

"He's amazing," a mom tells another mom.

"To think they had such a fantastic lesson and didn't even sit on a horse," a dad in a sweater vest says to a mom in yoga gear.

"I've never seen Tommy pay such close attention," says another mom.

"Somehow, he makes words seem useless."

"I didn't even know you could teach a horse without voice commands."

"I wonder if he'll come to my house and train the kids."

The conversations get louder as the parents walk in a

small, compact herd up to the barn. They are ripping off checks and digging into their bags for cash.

The barn is quiet again. Wes is back on the roof. The saddle pads are finally dry. I've conditioned the last saddle with leather milk and have the bridles hanging in a cool, airy spot. Bob is happily munching sweet-smelling hay with all the other horses.

My phone vibrates in my pocket. I accept the call and see Dad's ear.

"I'm done, Dad. I'm on my way home."

I pedal out of the muddy driveway. Its deep ruts are all that's left to show for the first day's awesome chaos. That and the fat envelope of checks and cash I handed to Wes. It's almost dark. I wave goodbye to him, but he doesn't see me. He's too busy pulling another tarp over the gaping hole in the sagging roof of the Big Green Barn.

CHAPTER TWENTY-SIX

ONE MONTH LATER

I should be thrilled with how things are going at the barn. We have lessons booked straight through summer break. We've started leasing some of the seasoned horses. Wes has new horses to train for clients from as far away as Utah. One of the horses is a contender for the Black Elk. And the local channel sent their crew out to film Wes giving a lesson. Apparently, Hot Mama Jama works at Channel 7 as a part-time reporter. She thought Wes was a perfect local story for Birdwood. So did everyone else. "Local trainer teaches without words."

I'd be lying if I said Mama Jama's little PR piece, which is now linked on our website, didn't help business. We've even had to turn some business away. Wes gets stopped at the gas station and the feed store by people who recognize him. They take selfies with him, post them, share them, and then I can't keep up with the calls. The "weirdo loner guy who doesn't talk" is now the "genius horse trainer," and everyone acts like they know him. Some reviews even mentioned how nice I was. I really was excited when kids started showing up at the barn. But now, it just feels like they're a bunch of barn rats I want to keep out.

The good news is, we now have a lot of boarders. The bad news is, we now have a lot of boarders. And the worst intruder of all is our newest boarder, Lexi Peterson, the same loudmouthed chick from English class. Lexi enters the barn like she is the reason it exists. She walks around like the world should wait on her. And at Big Green, that world would be me. As if I don't have a million other way more important things to do. Like rehab my horse.

Lexi has a lesson with Wes this morning. I plan to get my barn chores done early so I can be gone when she gets here. I'd rather have my front teeth drilled than hear her voice. And I don't want her to ruin today. Today is the day I can finally bring Treasure in from the field. It's been four and a half weeks since I first turned Treasure out. I did exactly what my mom used to do. I didn't bother him. I didn't make an excuse to walk out to see him. I simply let him be. Just the medicine a horse needs after a rough spell. I can't wait to see him, but I'm a little nervous because I don't know what I'll see.

When I get to the gate, I lean on the top rail. I scan the field, but I don't see Treasure anywhere. He must be by the river. I whistle. Nothing. The birds quiet for a few seconds, then start up again.

"Treasure! Come on, boy!" There's still no sign of him. I climb through the rails of the fence and trudge through the deep grass. "Buddy!" I make a megaphone with my hands. "Where are you hiding?"

Then I hear hoofbeats. I look toward the woods, the open field, the river. Finally, over the top of the hill, I see him coming toward me in a balls-to-the-wall gallop. He is flying. In just a few seconds, he's right in front of me. He's tossing his head, trotting around in the tall grass, raising his legs high. His body has filled out. His neck has thickened up. His ribs are only slightly visible. Even the hollow spot above his eye has filled in. His mane and tail have grown long, and patches of his coat gleam in the sunlight. He raises his head in the air and does a big snort.

"Whoa, boy. Whoa." I reach my hand out to touch him. "Look at you! Look who's back!" I pat his neck. He prances a little from side to side. He knows I'm paying him compliments.

"This month did you some good, huh, boy?" I attach his lead shank. I can't wait to show him off to Wes. As I lead him through the gate, the early morning heat is already making the air feel thick.

We head toward the hill. It's a good size—steeper than it looks. While Treasure grazes, I find the entrance to the den and pull out of my pocket one of the napkins full of leftovers I brought from home. I toss pieces of bacon and some pizza crusts onto the mound at the opening. Then I wait. Pretty soon, two sets of fuzzy ears poke out.

The babies have been getting fatter since I've been feeding them. It was nice having them to care for during the month I was letting Treasure care for himself. Every time I visit, no matter what time of day, they're already there waiting for me, their tiny heads popped out of the den's entrances like they knew I was coming long before they could possibly have heard me. Do they feel the vibration of my footsteps? Do they sense me? How do they know?

I unwrap the other napkin. "Hope you're in the mood for some dry meatloaf. Dad says it's delicious, but he'll eat anything." I throw them a few chunks. Both kits crawl out, eyes wide, noses sniffing the air. They snatch up the pieces and dive back into their den. Treasure pays no attention to them. He just keeps on munching grass, lazily swatting flies with his tail. Pretty soon, the kits pop their heads out again, looking for more. I throw the rest of it into the grass. They dive for it like it's going to run away.

"Sorry, guys. That's all I got."

I pull the currycomb out of my back pocket and start brushing Treasure in big circular motions. His dull, dry coat starts coming off in clumps. I pull his matted fur out of the bristles and toss it into the grass. Birds fight over it for their nests. One of the kits darts to a clump, probably thinking it's food. He sniffs it, then lets it blow away.

I want to sit and admire the scene for a while, but the only place I could possibly do that, other than the ground itself, is on the rock at the edge of the pasture. But I won't, not even for a minute, because of something else I've seen sitting on that rock. Snakeskins. Lots of them. Thinner than paper. More like ghosts than flesh. They are wispy and dry but somehow hold the snake's shape for days before they blow away. I take a deep breath and wipe my hands on my jeans. I get back to brushing Treasure. With each swipe of the brush, a glossier, softer layer of his coat shines through.

"You're shedding your skin, too, boy." He raises his head out of the deep clover, then rubs his nose and mouth on my sleeve, leaving behind a long smear of green horse saliva. "And, obviously, snot. Thanks a ton, Treasure."

Then he stands statue-still and pricks forward his ears. He's spotted the kits. He stares for a long time at all their hopping and rolling around. They come a little closer.

"Guys, this is Treasure. Treasure, this is . . . I'm not sure."

When I told Sue Landry, our new vet, about the kits, she said, first of all, don't feed them. Second of all, don't name them. And third of all, if you feed them and name them, at least make sure you keep them afraid of you. Well, I've already fed them, so I might as well name them. Something Mom would appreciate. She loved classic country music. Johnny Cash. Hank Williams. Waylon Jennings. Dolly Parton. Merle Haggard. But her favorites were Conway Twitty and Loretta Lynn.

"Conway and Loretta," I tell Treasure. "That's what we'll name them." Then I stomp my feet, clap my hands, and growl, scaring them back into their den. "It's for your own good!" I call to them.

I wish I could make Kyle and Cody fear me that easily. I want them out of my hair. But I don't frighten them in the least. They already walk around my house like they own it. They leave their shit around. They grab whatever they want out of the fridge.

"I'd rather have Dad go back to dating three girlfriends a week than have to put up with those assholes," I tell Treasure. He nods his head. Either he agrees with me or he's trying to avoid the sneaky sweat bee that keeps buzzing around him. I shoo it away from him and attach his lead shank.

"Time to get back to the barn." I give his line a tug, and he raises his head and follows me down the hill. When we're almost back to the barn, I hear an engine roaring behind me. Blaring from the radio is Trace Adkins's "Honky Tonk Badonkadonk," pretty much exactly the kind of song that gives country music a bad name. Damn. Just my luck. They're early. Lexi and her lame-ass boyfriend, Blake. They don't care that Wes hates it when people drive too fast near the barn. Blake's black monster pickup blazes up the driveway anyway, chrome bumper gleaming in the sun, super-sized tires rotating to the thumping bass.

When they get near Treasure and me, they slow down. Blake's hunting dog leaps at us, smacking the closed back window. His teeth flash and gnash. His slobber smears the glass. He snarls. His enormous front paws seem like they could come plunging through the glass at any moment. Treasure spooks. Blake jerks the dog down by the collar.

"Down, Rattler! You listen!"

Lexi rolls down her window. "Who's that poor thing?" she says and laughs.

"My horse. Trusted Treasure." The exhaust pipe breathes like a rabid dog next to my leg. I try to walk a little faster.

"Awwww. Trusted Treasure. That's so cute." Lexi is using her baby-talk voice, which makes my teeth hurt. I have to say something. Something that lets her know that Treasure was a serious racehorse. He isn't just a silly hobby horse like hers.

"He raced in the Black Elk." I quickly regret telling them.

"They let you enter mules now?" Blake asks.

Lexi laughs again. That voice. If I close my eyes, she could be Alvin the chipmunk.

"Don't be mean, Blake," she says. "He's probably just super old. Is *Trusted Treasure* . . . really old?" She giggles, saying his name as weirdly as she can, like it has air quotes around it or something.

Blake shoots his arm across Lexi to push her back so he can get a good look at Treasure. "Hey, isn't that the horse that fell?"

If I could sic Blake's own hunting dog on him, I would.

"He only fell because the horse in front of him fell," I tell him, somehow without adding "ya douche."

"Holy shit. I thought he was dead!"

"Well, he might be," Lexi mutters. "Have you checked his pulse?"

Blake's arm presses hard across Lexi's chest, squashing her big boobs while he examines Treasure. "I mean seriously dead a long time ago."

"Hon, I can't breathe." Lexi pushes Blake's arm off her chest. "And I want to get to my lesson."

They drive on past us to the barn, and I can breathe again. I'm not sure how they can suck up all the available air, even when we're outside, but somehow they do. It's like their evil superpower. They breathe it in until everyone around them feels like crumpling up and keeling over.

Yup. The couple from hell. Blake and Lexi.

Blake's the type of guy who's handsome from far, but far from handsome. He looks good in silhouette. He's tall. His jeans fit right, if not a smidge too tight. And he wears nice cowboy boots. He goes to the gym—like a lot—but I doubt he's ever lifted a bale of hay or gripped a pitchfork in his life. He always has duck blood on his Sunday clothes. I swear he tries to live his life to the lyrics of a country song.

And Lexi. She thinks a hundred different things at once and says them just as fast as she thinks them. Since I'm a person who might think forty things and say just one, I have trouble keeping up. Sometimes I think I must be stupid because, instead of hearing her words, I just get caught up in the sound of what she's saying, in the up-and-down of her voice. If she's mad, you know it. If someone upsets her, that person is a vicious sociopath who's liable to chop you up into bits. Anyone who wrongs her is "psycho" or "mental" or "deranged." And by "wronged," she means someone didn't compliment her on her new sweater, or asked her to babysit for an amount "ridiculously lower" than Lexi thinks she's worth.

"Hey, Lexi, I hope you grow a third nipple! On your back! And Blake! I hope you grow a donkey dick out of your forehead!" I know they can't hear me above the music, the engine, and the dumb dog. But it still makes me feel better to say it. And to not have to be so fucking nice all the time.

CHAPTER TWENTY-SEVEN

I dread going to the barn knowing Blake and Lexi are already in there. But it looks like Sue Landry, the new vet, is here too. And I really like Sue.

There's already lots of activity when Treasure and I walk in. I can hear music and voices and the moving around of horses. It's always exciting when Sue and her girlfriend, Carol, show up. Sometimes, if Carol doesn't have to be at her health food store, she comes to assist. Especially when it's not an emergency, just routine stuff. And today is routine stuff. Sue's here to vaccinate all the horses and check on Olive.

"We're fragile creatures, aren't we?" Sue says as she pats Olive's big jaw. Sue is a tiny thing, not much taller than I am. Her bright green eyes stand out against her brown skin. She's from Louisiana and moved out West to go to vet school and never went back.

"Why's it taking so long?" I ask her.

"Just lazy," Sue says as she holds her stethoscope way underneath Olive's belly. "Babies can be lazy about moving on. They act like, 'I've got everything I need right here, so why should I leave?'"

I give Olive a fresh bucket of water and scratch her forehead. "Don't worry, girl. Soon." She blows out a long sigh, and I think about how many times this week I've told her the same thing. Then I follow Sue to her next patient—Blake's horse, Gator. Carol carries Sue's tackle box of supplies and sets it down in front of Gator's stall.

Carol and Sue are a great team, which is funny because they're total opposites. Carol has short red hair, always has a mega cup of iced coffee, even in winter, and wears high-top sneakers with shorts cut just above the knee, again, even in winter. Sue is kind of quiet, especially when she's thinking about what's making a horse sick or behave differently, but Carol is a talker. Sue is serious, but Carol is fun. She brings an easy mood to the barn and plays happy music.

And today, like always, she brought a box of donuts. She opens the box and holds it out toward me like it's full of expensive jewelry. Half of the dozen is rainbow sprinkled, the kind she knows I like. I pick a middle one—they stay softer than the ones on the sides. When I take a big bite, I can feel the sprinkles sticking to my lips and dribbling onto the front of my shirt.

"I like your thing," Carol says, one cheek full of donut. She's looking at the stone I'm twirling in my free hand. Sometimes I forget I'm holding it.

"Just a stone I found on the road."

"Cool. Can I see?"

I hold out the stone. It's looking smoother, like it's gotten polished from being in my pocket. The gray is almost gone, and pink is peeking through in lots more places. The center is glassy and catches the light, like a little rainbow is trapped inside.

"It didn't look like that when I found it."

"Nice," she says. She holds it up to the light and turns it around to see all of it. "This isn't just a stone," she says. "It's got some old concrete and asphalt stuck to it, but this is a piece of rose quartz."

Rose quartz. I remember Mom saying those words on the drive. I remember how the air across the plain seemed pink. But I'd never seen rose quartz. I'd only heard her talk about it.

"It's really translucent, so I'm guessing it's gemmy rose quartz. Has some kind of crazy good energy," she says, rubbing one side of it with her thumb.

"What if you don't believe in that stuff?"

"Probably wouldn't matter what you believe. The energy doesn't go away just because you don't believe in it." Carol hands the stone back to me. "Anyway, it's pretty. Should make a necklace out of it." The light bounces off it even more than I'd noticed before.

"Yeah." I roll it around in my hand and then slide it back into my pocket. I don't know if it's warm from my body or if it has a heat all its own.

Blake walks toward us, and I cringe. He's wearing an outfit that looks like he just stepped out of a country music video. I can't remember the name of the musician he's trying to look like, but it's the one who wears his bootleg-cut Wranglers just a little too tight and a little too long. Blake looks at Carol's box of donuts. He plucks one from the edge and snickers before taking a bite.

"Hey, Carol," he says. "How nice. You sell these at your health food store?"

Blake likes to tease Carol. He acts like he's being playful, but he's always got some kind of a hidden zinger. I can tell by Carol's face that she's not in the mood for him.

"Ah, Blake. You know what bores me? Predictability. For instance, you with those muscles and tight jeans and the big zilch going on upstairs. Most interesting people are a walking contradiction. Should try it out sometime. You get me?"

"What the . . . ?" Blake laughs, but it's just because he doesn't know what else to say.

Sue presses her stethoscope into Gator's girth area right behind his left elbow to listen to his heart rate. She adjusts her earpiece and slides the stethoscope to the triangle area between his shoulder and his rib cage and listens to his respiratory sounds. Then she moves her stethoscope under his barrel to listen to his gut sounds. Finally, she lifts his tail, inserts a thermometer, and leaves it for a few seconds.

Gator is a good patient. He barely flinches. He's an eight-year-old, big-boned chestnut. A thoroughbred cross. A true sport horse. He's got a slightly Roman nose and a shortish neck for his body. He's not as stunning to look at as Sir Drake was, but he's smart and bold and fast. Blake came across him by chance at an auction in Utah, bought him, and hauled him back. Now Gator is Blake's contender for the Black Elk, and he wants Wes to train him. He didn't even ask Wes what he thought. He just unloaded him, handed the lead shank to Wes, and said, "This horse could win the fuckin' race with his eyes closed."

Wes handed the lead back to Blake and shook his head. He'd rather hang from his armpit hairs or eat cat shit for breakfast than train a horse for Blake. But Blake keeps bugging him, shoving money into his face. He says Gator is Wes's only shot, that Wes has got a stable full of cart horses that ain't gonna do jack. The truth is, with any other trainer, Gator would be lost. With Wes, he'd actually have a chance.

All the while Sue is examining Gator, Carol is yakking away. She barely takes a breath, going from one story to the next. Sue calls her the Queen of Non Sequiturs. While Sue runs her hand down Gator's back leg, Carol is blabbing about the amazing and fascinating African dung beetle. No one is really paying attention to her, but she doesn't seem to mind.

"Those little bastards are something else. They live in Africa. I'd like to go sometime. Probably never will. But if I did, I'd make a beeline for that dung beetle. I'd skip the zebras and the lions and the rhinos and head straight for that crazy little bug." She rattles the ice in her cup and waits for me to ask why.

"Why is that, Carol?"

"I'll tell you why." She hustles to the center of the aisle and acts like she's holding something tiny in her hand.

"Because this little beetle spends its life rolling a perfectly round piece of poop across the hottest scorching sand—get this—with its back legs." Carol acts out like she's pushing a poo ball by balancing on her hands and putting her feet on a bale of hay. "That's right. They've got their face down in the dirt the whole time, and they push the poo ball with their back legs, day in and day out."

I'm not sure I'm appreciating the African dung beetle in quite the way Carol wants me to, but I'm definitely entertained by her storytelling techniques. Sometimes she adds sound effects. Sometimes she puts on a different voice to become a character.

When Carol stops talking for a minute about the African dung beetle, Sue says, "Carol, that has absolutely nothing to do with absolutely nothing."

"I'm glad you learned something."

"How about puttin' a sock in it, Carol."

"Well, aren't you a crankasaurus?"

When Sue sticks her fingers in Gator's mouth to look at his teeth, he puts his upper lip up and turns his head in a half circle. He looks like he's smiling at us. We all laugh, and Sue and Carol forget to argue. When Gator gives Sue a little love nip, she swats his muzzle and tells him no. Carol does a low voice and pretends to speak for Gator.

"Well, if you didn't smell so delicious, I wouldn't bite you."

Sue talks back in her normal voice. "One of these days, you're gonna bite the wrong person."

And Carol-as-Gator says back, "Do wrong people taste as good as you do?" Carol uses a low voice that makes her sound more like a dumb, old hound dog. They both laugh, and I laugh too.

"Ladies, I hate to interrupt comedy hour, but how does my horse look?" Blake still has a green sprinkle on his lip. Sue and Carol notice it too. We all give each other a look that means, *Don't tell him*.

"He looks good, Blake," says Sue. "No glaring issues."

Lexi walks up to Blake, wraps her arms around his waist, leans in, and just as she's about to kiss him, stops.

"Babe, did you actually eat a donut?"

Blake looks at her like she just accused him of reading a book.

"Me? Of course not," he snarls.

"Then what's this?" Lexi picks the sprinkle from his lip and shows it to him. "You know it's just like eating plastic."

"Matches his personality," Carol says. Then she gulps her coffee and follows Sue to the next stall. While Sue works, Carol tells another funny story. She coaxes a beautiful smile out of Sue with another one of her imitations.

I realize I don't feel pulled to a place in the past so much anymore. Now, it's hard for me to imagine the barn without Sue and Carol. Without Wes. I want to stay right here, joking and laughing on this beautiful warm Sunday. It's a day that feels right. Even knowing that Dad is out with LeeAnne and her boys isn't spoiling the day for me. Blake and Lexi over in the distance fussing with some new contraption of a bridle doesn't even bug me. They are part of this new world, too, even with their shiny boots and their perfect hair.

Sometimes I still feel guilty when I'm laughing and having a good time. Like I forgot about Mom or something. It makes me feel bad. The same way I felt when I played charades with the insta-family. But knowing that Trusted Treasure is back in his old stall is enough to take my mind off just about anything. Having a barn full of horses makes me feel like the world makes sense again. There is an order to things. If a stall needs to be cleaned, I clean it. If a horse needs to be groomed, I groom it. If a horse needs to be fed, I feed it. I know what chores need to be done, and the next day they're all there to do over again.

I tune in to Carol talking about wampum.

"I mean, what's the difference really? They traded with beads made from shells. We trade with paper or"—Carol looks over at Blake, who's flexing a muscle he'll never use—"plastic."

The three of us burst out laughing, but Carol laughs the hardest. She snorts at the end, which is what she always does when she laughs hard.

"So, Reese," Carol says, "you seem to do a lot around here. Do you have an official title?" She's being playful, but I can also tell she's truly interested.

"Nothing official. But it's not like you could fit everything I do onto a business card. I'm part barn manager, part groom, part PR advertising guru, part exercise rider, part grand poo-bah poo picker upper."

Wes walks into the barn. He's leading Darcy, one of the newer gray mares, in from the ring.

"The only thing I won't do is windows." I say it loud enough for Wes to hear. He throws us a smile and uses one hand to make a yapping mouth.

"But my biggest job," I say, leaning in closer to Carol, "is Wes translator. I can read his face pretty fast. And his body language. Everything means something. See how he takes that saddle off? He lifted it. He didn't slide it. That means it was a good ride. See how he scuffs the ground with the tip of his boot with every step? Not a lot. Just enough to notice. That means he's behind. He's still got four horses to ride and not enough daylight."

"Very interesting deduction." Carol nods.

"He's also happy because he sold a couple of horses this week."

"Really?" Carol says, studying Wes's face. "And how can you tell that?"

"Cuz I saw it happen." I laugh.

Carol laughs harder. "I was beginning to think you had a real gift."

Wes stops brushing. He looks up over the back of his horse and shakes his head, like he can't believe we could possibly have anything more to talk about. When Carol opens her mouth like she's about to start another story, Sue gives her a look that says, *Please shut up for the fourteenth time*, but throws her hands up instead. She knows it's no use. And it's OK. It's all OK. Right now, I'd like to freeze this feeling. I know that things aren't perfect. Things are different at the barn. And that's OK.

After I help Sue pack up her things, she and Carol head to their truck. Wes hands Sue a check on her way out. I finish the last of the chores for the day. Blake tries again to convince Wes to train Gator. But Wes just shakes his head and pushes away the wad of cash that Blake keeps shoving into his chest.

"I'm giving you the chance of a lifetime, Wes. My horse would make you famous." Blake walks backward out the barn doors. He spits into the shavings and tucks his cash into his back pocket. Then he turns and trips over his pant leg.

"Goddam fuckin' . . ."

I want to tell Blake it's not about the horse. It's about his owner. After Blake leaves, Wes rolls his eyes, points his finger at his head, and pretends to pull a trigger. We both laugh.

When the water hose hangs in neat loops on its hook and the aisle is swept of hay and manure, I stop to say goodnight to Treasure. He sticks his nose out of his stall. I reach for his forelock and let my hand slide down his face. All day, he acted like he was used to all the fun and commotion. His lower lip hangs loose, and I wobble his chin up and down.

Wes passes us on his way home for the night. He hands me three envelopes to pop into the mailbox and one check with my name on it. He does his goodnight wave, and a few seconds later I hear his old truck argue with him about whether to start up again. Then the sound of its motor slowly slips away, and only barn noises are left, faint and low. The quiet is like a soft cushion for me to land on at the end of a day. Treasure lowers his head and sniffs my pocket.

"Whatcha lookin' for, bud? It's just my stone in there." I reach into my pocket to show him. The stone is warm. When I place it in my palm, I look for that tiny rainbow prism of light. I let the stone rock back and forth in my hand. I hold it right up to my eye and see a maze of white flecks. Slashes of smoky chambers. A galaxy of milky bubbles. And something else. Deep inside. Something moves. Shadows pass in and out of gauzy caverns. I feel a rumble. Then suddenly, Treasure's big lip covers the stone, and it disappears from my hand.

"Hey!" I startle him and he drops it from his mouth. "It's not a treat, you silly boy."

I pick it up and wipe it off on my jeans. Treasure lowers his head and blows his nose on my arm.

"It's not your fault," I laugh.

The thought of the stone being lost scared me. Like I'd be lost without it. If he'd swallowed the stone, I'd have done just what Mom did once when a pony ate her wedding ring—frantically dig through horse poop to find it. And with my luck, right in the middle of doing just that, Lexi would surely show up.

CHAPTER TWENTY-EIGHT

Lexi Peterson isn't a Big Green Barn type of person. She actually wears makeup to the barn. Her boots are more expensive than a year's worth of board. She has big boobs and a boyfriend who's a senior. This is a dangerous combination, even from my perspective. I don't care about the big boobs part. They actually look uncomfortable when she rides. But those boobs definitely get a lot of attention when she starts trotting around with them jostling like they want to escape the tight shirt they're strapped into. She tries to act like she doesn't notice everyone staring.

When Blake isn't around, Lexi poses for Wes. She'll lift up her shirt a little to show her tanned waist, right when Wes is passing. One time she asked me if her new riding britches, which looked like they were doing their best to contain a bowling ball, were too baggy. "They look OK," I said. Then she watched Wes pass like she didn't even hear me.

The worst thing about Lexi is, she always shows up when I'm doing about twelve different things at once. Like right now. I have tack to clean and stalls to muck, and I'm keeping a close eye on Olive. Since she's in foal, I'm in her stall, giving her extra-nutritious alfalfa.

As usual, Lexi is jabbering on to someone about something. And, as usual, I'm tuning her out. Then I realize she's talking to me. Or at me. I missed her first few sentences, so I'm already lost. Then she stops talking and looks at me sideways. She must have asked me something. I feel like I'm coming out of a trance. I rewind her voice in my head until I get to the last thing she said.

"Your new halter is in your trunk," I tell her. "I wasn't sure if you wanted to use it right away."

She cocks her head to the side like she's talking to a child.

"That makes sense. Putting a brand-new halter in the trunk. I mean, why put it on my horse, right? That's a silly idea."

She turns on her heel, then walks away, shaking her head like she's shaking off flies. Even if Lexi spent twice the time working on her personality as she spends putting on her makeup, she'd barely make it to tolerable.

If it were up to me, I'd screen everyone who comes to the Big Green Barn. I'd turn people away at the slightest hint they'd be more trouble than they're worth. But, like Dad always said, it's all about providing a service. And when you provide a service, you have to smile and nod and always remember that's what you're getting paid for.

So today and every day, when the barn opens its doors wide, I welcome Lexi and Blake and all their chattering and clattering. But I keep wishing Lexi would step on a pitchfork or get trapped under a bale of hay. But if that ever happened, she'd probably get CNN to cover it. And then I'd end up getting blamed for leaving the pitchfork out or letting the hay bale land on top of her.

I have way more important things to think about than Lexi's little ass-aches. I finish making Olive's stall soft and cushy with extra shavings. Her legs look thin under her big, round belly, like they shouldn't be able to bear the weight, and her skin looks stretched as far as it will go. She holds her tail out at an angle like she's ready for something to come flying out of her at any second. "Come on outta there," I say to her baby. "Come out and play with me." But the baby's being stubborn. Olive's belly is taut as a trampoline.

"Reese, for like the tenth time, I have a lesson with Wes in fifteen minutes."

"Oh, sorry. I wasn't listening." I remind myself over and over that Lexi's not worth the time I spend thinking about her. The best way to handle Lexi is to keep my head down and just keep working. But for some reason, she grates on my every last nerve. And at the end of a long day, I have zero patience for her. It's not just that she's as annoying as a spoon caught in the garbage disposal. She's just so "there," so in my face. Like literally.

"Whoa, what is that on the side of your nose?" She has an expression on her face like she's watching a decapitation. "That is one whopper zit you got there. You gonna raise it and pay for its college education?"

"Ha ha. Very funny, Lexi."

"Actually, I'm serious. That thing is a mirror splatterer if I ever saw one."

"Thanks for your professional advice."

"No charge. Just trying to help."

⌣

The mirror in the barn bathroom is pretty gross. I use the towel to wipe away some of the dust and grime, and there it is. This sucker could be Queen of Zitdom. *Shit.* Was it there last night? Another thing Dad would never notice. It feels like something's burning under the skin of my left nostril. I put a finger on either side of the bump and press. White pus explodes onto the mirror. I examine the little hole that keeps filling with blood, then I press it with a tissue to stop the bleeding. Now, my entire nose is red and my eyes are watering. I splash some water all over my face, but the hole keeps filling with blood. *Stupid fucking zit.* I press a tissue down on the zit hole as hard as I can, but as soon as I take it off, blood fills the hole. I stuff some tissues in my pocket and get back out to work. While I'm picking out stalls, I dab my nose every so often with the red-speckled tissue. The bleeding finally stops.

Lexi. I bet it's her fault the zit is there in the first place. Like she literally got under my skin. I wish she'd never come here in the first place. Her voice fills the barn from the time she arrives until the time she and Blake drive off into the sunset. I swear there's an echo of her voice in the barn even after she's gone. I also swear my tongue has bite marks on it from all the times I stopped myself from telling her what I really think about her and her fancy clothes and her expensive shit and her doting, dumb-as-a-stump boyfriend.

I know we're running a business. I know I'm supposed to be nice to her. But I can't take it anymore. Wes doesn't see how awful she and Blake are. He just tunes them out. I'm the one left dealing with all their stupid shit. It's time. He needs to know. I stab the pitchfork into the shavings and unbend my cramping fingers. Then I march out to the ring where Wes is setting up a course.

"Wes, I, uh . . ."

He studies my face. When he notices the crater in my nose, he does a *yikes* look.

"I, uh, scratched myself by accident."

Wes nods, pretending he's going along with my lie.

"OK, yes. I had a pimple."

He uses both hands to pretend-pop something and then puts his hand to his nose like he's in agony. Then he acts out a volcano eruption by shaping a mountain with his arms and then letting his hands fly up in a blast. He points at the sky and then ducks his head like he's going to be covered with lava pus. I'm trying my best not to laugh, but when Wes falls to the ground like he's being drowned in the pus, I can't help it. He squirms around on the ground, clutching his throat. Then he lets his tongue hang out like he's dead.

"OK. Now that you've had your fun, can I tell you something?"

Wes stands up and brushes himself off, laughing at his little performance. He bows and pretends to introduce me, like I'm next onstage.

"Wes, I'm serious! Stop messing around."

He nods, waiting for me to spit it out.

"There's something I've been wanting to talk to you about."

Wes gestures—*Get on with it.*

After he was being all playful, I'm going to sound like a whiny twerp. But I don't care.

"It's Lexi. I . . . there's just something . . . I don't trust about her."

Wes looks at me with a closed-lip smile and raised eyebrows.

"Wait. Wes, seriously . . . What? . . . You think . . . You think I'm . . . *jealous* of her?" My neck is getting hot.

He shrugs and then tilts his head. *Maybe just a little? I can see why. I know how girls are.*

"Well, I'm not! I'm definitely not jealous of *her*."

He nods, but it's a nod that means he doesn't believe me. "Wes, she doesn't—"

He rubs his fingers and thumb together.

"Right. She's loaded. But I'm not sure how much we should continue—"

He pats my shoulder as if to say he's done with the conversation. Or maybe he's trying to comfort me just a little. Then he waves his hands out around him. *Look what we have. Look at the big picture. Don't think so small.*

"Maybe you're right. I guess I should put up with her as long as she's paying her bills. But the moment that payment is late . . . like by two seconds, she's outta here."

Wes does a little laugh.

Ppppppfffff. Jealous of Lexi Peterson. As *if*. She may be rich and pretty and own all those cool things and know what to wear and have all kinds of fun with her big boobs, but I have Trusted Treasure. She'll never have a horse like him. Injury or no injury.

Wes looks up at the mountains behind us. Just above them, a thick gray cloud smudges the blue of the sky. A storm. This time of year, a cloud like that could mean hail the size of golf balls. Wind and lightning could hit us in less than an hour. I see Wes's thoughts bump into each other. *We have to clean the trailer, we have to get the horses in, we have to load the hay . . .* He heads for the barn, but before I follow him, I look for Treasure. Horses know when there's a storm coming. They find a spot in the field and point their butts into the wind. Treasure is down in the corner, tucked in behind the hill, ass in the wind. I catch up with Wes and take an armful of halters and lead shanks. He's fast-walking back into the field. I pick up a jog.

"Dad used to say that it's the damndest thing how

they'd rather stay out in a storm than come in." The wind starts whipping around us. "Dad said that, ten years ago, he didn't worry about storms so much. He says storms have gotten worse. He says you can ask any rancher. We never used to get these supercell storms. We just had storms. Storms that livestock could handle. Now we get storms on steroids. Now a hailstorm with high winds can wipe out an entire herd. He says you gotta bring all the horses in, even when they don't want to, unless you want your horses looking like Swiss cheese."

Wes gives me a look, the kind that means I'm talking too much.

"Sorry. Probably just nerves."

He does a circle with his finger, telling me to turn around, and turns off a fake switch at the back of my head. I act like it worked.

The hail peppers the ground around us. We climb over the gate and start catching horses and leading them back, four at a time. Rice-sized hail stings my hands and face. Lexi and Blake pass us on their way out of the barn, but they don't bother asking if we need any help.

We get all the horses in right before the hail grows to pea size. It bounces off the ground and ricochets off the side of the barn. Wes puts my bike in the back of his truck. On the drive to my house, I tell Wes how we lost one of our best mares and her five-month-old filly three or four years ago when a storm came out of nowhere and the mare wouldn't come in. How the hail got as big as grapefruits that day. How, during the storm, the mare and the filly were nowhere to be found. How, after the storm, Dad discovered that the coyotes found them first. How there wasn't much left to bury.

By the time we get to my driveway, the hail sounds like it's having a BB gun war.

"I think I was talking too much again."

Wes crosses his eyes and rubs his head like it hurts.

"I know. Sorry." But he doesn't really look annoyed. He pats me on the back and hands me an auction magazine so I can protect my head from the pellets that are shooting down and covering the front yard.

"Thanks, Wes!" I yell and make a dash for it.

CHAPTER TWENTY-NINE

Marble-sized hail isn't that big for around here, but when it hits my bedroom window, it still sounds like it could break the glass. I figure I might as well straighten up the mess in my room. It would be nice to see my floor again. Besides, wandering around the house could lead to bumping into Dad, which is about as fun as getting your period twice in one month.

Under some clothes that have fallen between my bed and the wall is a white plastic bag. Tucked inside are a ball of lime-green yarn, a pair of knitting needles, and a set of instructions. They explain casting on, the knit stitch, and the purl stitch. Someone has scribbled in the margins. *Keep your hold loose.*

Mom.

I used to get angry if Mom gave me anything that wasn't a horse thing—horse book, horse shirt, horse blanket. One birthday, she gave me a lamp with a ceramic horse-head base. But a few years before she died, she gave me a knitting set for Christmas. I couldn't understand why she was giving me crazy-old-lady gear. *I'm a serious horse person, not a hobby person*, I wanted to tell her. I felt hurt, like she must not really know me at all. I threw those big pearly gray needles and that lime-green yarn clear across the room. "This is a stupid gift," I said.

She didn't get mad or anything. Just continued glazing the ham. "Well, put it away until it's not stupid anymore. Life's not always about horses, Reese."

Why did I have to say the gift was stupid? Why didn't I just put it away and say nothing? Why did I say so many mean things? A pang is in my chest, like someone is poking at it from the inside.

Outside, the hail is now mixed with rain. It's coming down in buckets. A branch scratches the outside of my window. I hear the high-pitched squeal of Dad's bathroom faucet. I close my door, sit down on the edge of my bed, and open the bag. I pull the skein out by its floppy end, loops falling this way and that. I lay out the instructions on the floor. *STEP 1. Casting on.* The drawing of the hands-that-belong-to-no-one shows how to loop the yarn around the needle.

I turn on the horse-head lamp to get a better look. I position my hands just like the ones in the drawing. But the loop I'm supposed to make is so small that my clumsy fingers feel like five big toes. I must be gripping the needles too tight. It's weird that a tight grip forms loose stitches. My first three stitches, which I worked so hard to loop, unwind.

"Crap."

I throw the yarn and the needles across the room, just like before. They fall into a nasty little heap that tries to look all innocent. I want to grind them into the floor. But almost right away, I feel ashamed. Why do I get so angry? Why can't I be more like Mom? I think about her glazing the ham. Not even getting mad at my snotty comments.

So I pick the yarn and needles up again. I find the tied loop that took me a good fifteen minutes to make. Then I figure out how to keep it on my needle without it twisting and unraveling every time I try to create a stitch. Who does this lame-ass hobby anyway? And why? But now, I'm determined. Like if I can do this, it's as good as telling Mom I'm sorry.

Keep your hold loose.

I pinch the needles together with one hand and wrap the yarn around with my other. "There. Casting on. Done." Then I slowly inch the top needle out of the X position and simultaneously loop the next piece of yarn. While I'm finishing one stitch, I'm beginning the next one. Ha. I'm starting to get it. But my fingers are used to doing big things like gripping the lead shank of a thousand-pound animal or lifting its leg to scrape out a hoof. Holding this yarn and these needles feels like I'm trying to make something out of air or breath or clouds. I finally have three stitches again, but am I at the beginning of a new stitch or at the end of the last one? *Shit.* Mom would know what to do.

Keep your hold loose.

She said that when I rode too. It worked every time. When I loosened my hold, the horse stopped pulling. *Jeez, Mom. How many other things did you tell me that I might have missed completely? What else will I never know because I wasn't listening to you? And what about all the things you never had the chance to say to me?*

I put the knitting down and look through the photos of her that I keep in the chipped Seabiscuit soap dish on my bedside table. When I find the one I'm looking for, I try to wipe it clean by rubbing it on my jeans. This one is especially smudged because I've thrown it into my wastebasket and dug it back out at least three or four times. I love it of her, but I hate it of me.

Dad took this picture of the two of us on the day she gave me the knitting set. We're standing in front of the Christmas tree. I was nine years old. I look like a spoiled little brat, but Mom's got a big smile. She's wearing the pink toolbelt Dad bought for her that year. She could fix anything.

Since she died, the place has been falling apart. Like the leak in the roof. Like how the dark stain on the ceiling in my room gets bigger after every rain. Like it is right now. Like what started out looking like a caterpillar is now looking like a giraffe. Dad knows there's some perfect roof-fixing tool in Mom's toolbox, but if he opens it, all he'll see is Mom. And then he'll have to explain to himself why he's going out with someone who will never be Mom. So instead, he grows his beard thicker and wears clothes that don't look like they belong to him. Like the only way he can find someone else is by becoming someone else.

"What'cha lookin' at?"

I hadn't heard him open the door. Weird how your hearing turns off when you're thinking about another place and time. I show him the picture.

"She was laughing at you in that picture. You were so mad. Remember what you said?"

I pretend not to know. Dad puts his beer can on the dresser and chuckles. It feels strange for him to be here.

"You said, 'Thanks for the knitting stuff. I'm sure I'll enjoy it in the nursing home.'" The beer can crinkles as he takes a sip. "She told you that knitting was good for thinking. You just didn't get it. You had a one-track mind. If it wasn't about horses, it wasn't worth your time."

I can't help smiling. I want to be tough and not show

him anything I'm thinking or feeling. But with him talking the way he used to talk, it's just impossible.

"You were so upset you told us you were going to bed early and maybe next Christmas would be better."

It feels good to know that maybe she thought my mad face was just funny, not bratty and mean. A short laugh bubbles up and then turns into more of a sob. I put the picture down.

"It's OK, Reese." Dad sits next to me on the bed. His weight on the mattress makes me lean into him. "I know, I know. But you have to understand that things will never be the same. And we're all doing the best we can."

The annoyed feeling I expect to have from hearing Dad's canned crap isn't what I feel at all, even though he sounds like he's in one of those cheesy teen movies where you're supposed to think the characters are learning a valuable lesson. He's not even doing a good job with his lines, but I realize something I never realized before. Because, while he's looking at me, really looking at me, I want to tell him I've missed him. Not just Mom. I've missed him. So much. It's him I've been wanting to talk to. Not a therapist.

Then he clears his throat and tugs at his ear. "Damn tinnitus," he says as he wiggles his jaw back and forth. "I wanted to tell you, Reese. LeeAnne and I are thinking about . . . what it would be like if we . . ."

I feel like I've swallowed a rock. I'm so glad I shoved down all that sentimental bullshit that was ready to spill out of me. I know what he's going to say.

". . . tried living together."

"Seriously?" I can hardly talk.

"I mean, I didn't think this would go over well with you now, but once you get to know LeeAnne better, I know you'll like her. I just wanted you to know that it's the direction the relationship is going in and . . . and I'm not talking about right away. I mean eventually, like in the next . . . few weeks."

What an ass I would have looked like if I'd shared my feelings.

"Her kids too?"

"Well, they are her kids. What's she gonna do? Have them go live with their father?"

"Can I go live with their father?"

I stand up and walk to the window. Rain pelts against it. Drops from the ceiling gather and drip onto the floor. Dad uses his foot to slide my wastebasket under the leak.

"It'll all be OK, Reese. I promise. I'll find another therapist for you to talk to about our new . . . home life."

He tries to catch my eye, but if I look at him, he could hypnotize me into agreeing with him about thinking this is a good idea.

"We have to move on. I know your mom would want that. For you."

My room starts to feel smaller. He feels like an invader. My head aches from avoiding his stare. I look at everything but him. The branch that's knocking on the windowpane. The dirty pile of clothes. The photo. Then I pick up the yarn and throw it at him.

"Get out!" I yell. "Get out of my room!"

I can feel him want to yell back at me, but he doesn't. I'm sure Miss Garland must have told him not to. He comes over and puts his hands on my shoulders. I just keep looking away, hoping he'll leave me alone.

"It'll be OK," he says again.

"OK? What does that even mean? There's not one single part of this that feels OK."

After he leaves, I keep watching the beads of rain swell and fall and swell and fall. The *click, click* of the drops hitting the wastebasket fills the room. *Click, click, click-click-click-click.* The stain on my ceiling seems to grow before my eyes. I realize I'm shaking. I pick up the photo again and fall onto my bed. I'm holding the photo so tight I've made a tear into Mom's smiling face. *Shit. Shit. Shit.* I tape up the rip and place the picture back in the dish. I look up at the leaking ceiling.

Keep your hold loose.

I can see now that it's not a giraffe. It's a horse. It's Treasure. Then it's the black horse. Then it's Treasure again. I close my eyes. He's in the race. He's charging up the hill. He's approaching the last fence. He takes off.

CHAPTER THIRTY

"I don't feel any signs of an old injury." Sue slides her hand down the front of Treasure's injured hind leg. Then she glides her hand down the back of his hock and pinches his cannon bone between her fingers and thumb. She feels his good hind leg and then returns to the injured one.

"Do you have records from back then, Reese?"

I hand her Treasure's file, one of the few things I was able to save from Dad's purge of the old days.

"Who was the vet?"

"Dr. Higgs. He's dead."

Sue leafs through the file.

"Higgs was old school," she says, looking at the image. "Yeah. I see it. There's the suspensory. Definitely not pretty." She scrunches up her face while she runs her finger along the white X-ray line of Treasure's tendon and bone. "I didn't feel it at all, but injuries like this don't usually miraculously disappear."

"You mean it could have? It could have miraculously disappeared?"

"I'll know more with an ultrasound. But either way, a beanpole like you isn't gonna hurt him by riding him."

"Riding him! Really, Sue? Are you sure?" This already feels like a miracle.

"I'm sure. No reason not to. He should be getting some exercise anyway."

She's saying it all casual, like, "Yeah, go ahead and wear that hat." But for me, it's like a parade should march through the barn and a man playing the fiddle should jump down from the hayloft and everyone should start line dancing. I grab hold of Treasure's neck and hug it to my chest. Then I do-si-do around him, bow, and start up again. Treasure blows out his nose and shakes his head. Sue laughs.

"He's saying, 'Chill out, kid. You're wrecking my vacation.'"

"There's a saddle at the feed store. I've walked by it a hundred times. I always thought it would be perfect for him, but I never thought he'd be able to actually use it."

"Well, I think he deserves his own saddle. He is famous, after all."

Wes walks in, probably annoyed by all the happy noise we're making. His jaw is set just slightly to the side, meaning he's got something on his mind. The air in the barn immediately changes.

"Fly in the spiderweb," Sue says, giving me the side-eye. She once said that a young horse's brain is like a spider's web. It's all perfect and intricately designed. Until something bad happens. Then it's like a fly gets trapped inside that beautiful web of a brain forever. Lately, we've both noticed Wes's brain is all wrapped up around something. Now it's kind of an inside joke between me and Sue.

"Yeah, I can't look at Wes lately without thinking of that spider's web."

"The fly is most likely money."

Sue's right. That's probably all it is. The lessons aren't enough to make up for our horses not selling. And horse farmers, unlike ranchers and dairy and pig farmers, don't get government subsidies when sales are down. You'll either get through the rough patch or you won't. Lately, it seems like we won't.

Sue brushes her hands off on her already dirty pants and then adds up the day's charges. "Wish me luck," she says as she heads toward Wes.

"OK," she tells him. "We're all set."

He motions for her to follow him to his office. I can hear Sue talking.

"That's cool, Wes." Her voice is high and singsongy, like she's discussing a meal she had or a band she likes. Anything but money. "You can pay the rest next week."

When Sue comes out of the office, she tosses the hoof tester into her tote and packs up the rest of her supplies. Then she points toward an open window. I don't see anything until I walk closer. Thin strands of a spider's web are suspended between the window's top corners. And there's a big hole in the middle, like a tear in a screen. A spider is working away to repair it.

Sue clears her throat. "I'll be back next week to check on Olive. Or sooner, if she drops her foal. Might need to hold off on everything else for a bit. Unless it's an emergency."

"OK, right. But what do you mean, everything else?"

"You, Reese, are totally capable of doing the routine stuff." Sue pulls her stethoscope from her neck and puts it around mine. She opens Bundy's stall door and stands next to him. "If you're worried about a horse, you can start by listening."

"Listen for what?"

"Come here. First you need to know how a healthy heart should sound. Like if it goes *lubbadubdub* instead of *lub dub, lub dub*."

I stand on Bundy's left side. Sue places the stethoscope behind his elbow.

"What do you hear?" Sue asks.

I hear a sound like a shower running and a rhythmic thumping. "*Lub dub, lub dub*."

"Good. If it sounds different from that, call me. There's no reason you can't check for dehydration too. It's just a simple skin pull test." Sue pinches Bundy's skin at his shoulder and lets go. "If it doesn't pop back into place right away, he's dehydrated."

I watch Bundy's skin go back to normal like it was never pinched.

"Not dehydrated."

"Correct. Here's another test." She lifts Bundy's upper lip to expose his pale pink gums and then presses her thumbs down on them just above his front teeth. "When I take my thumbs away, the gum will be blanched white. If it goes back to pink after a couple of seconds, his circulation is normal. If it stays white, he's got poor blood flow." When Sue takes her thumbs away, the white fills in with pink almost instantly.

"Turns pink really fast."

"Keen observation. Now, there are a few more things you can do, like listen to their airflow and gut sounds. And you can do sheath cleanings on the geldings. Do you have a rectal thermometer?"

"Ugh. Yes." I hate the thought of Sue not being here as much. "You'll be back to your regular visits in a few weeks, right?"

"Reese," she says. Then she looks down and shakes her head slightly. "He crossed me off his schedule for the next three months."

"Three months?"

"Yeah. But I won't be far away. Mares at Twin River are dropping foals like hot potatoes."

I feel a pain in my stomach.

"So, why can't you come anyway? Don't you care about the horses?"

"Well, I'd love to," she says, "but I do need to get paid."

Money. It's always about money.

"As it is, I'll be paying off my student loan until I'm"— Sue looks up at the beams and closes her eyes like she's calculating in her head—"a hundred and three. Carol will only be a spry ninety-eight. After that, I'll be able to do whatever I want. And watch out. I might really cut loose and party," she says with a big laugh.

"Why is this so funny to you?" I slam a stall door closed.

"Hey, Reese, you need to chill. It's not funny. I'm just trying to be realistic. Look, if anyone's gonna pull through a rough patch, it's Wes. He's the most talented trainer I've ever seen. And stubborn." She ducks her head and tries to make me look at her. "Did I mention stubborn?"

Sue points past me toward the ring. Wes is riding a rank filly who's bucking and whirling, but he sits on her peacefully, like he's on a pleasure horse. The filly finally gives in, stops in the middle of the ring, and looks around calmly. As if she wasn't just a second ago flying around like someone set her on fire. Wes pats her neck.

"The pat means they have a deal," I tell Sue. "Wes is telling her she passed the test."

The filly shakes her head and blows out dust.

"And she's telling him he passed the test. That's why Wes is Wes," she says. "He lets the horse think it's her idea." Then Sue continues her tutorial, teaching me how to notice anything alarming or abnormal.

"Now, have you ever done a sheath cleaning?"

"Gross! No! You'll never catch me touching a horse's wiener."

Sue laughs. "Well, I'm sure cleaning a horse's wiener isn't high up on your list of fun activities, but you really should learn." She picks up the bucket, but when she sees my face, she puts it down. "OK. You win. We've probably covered enough for today. You can still call me if you need me. If you think a horse is colicky or if Olive looks like she's stressed out, I'll be right over."

She pats my shoulder and tells me to keep her stethoscope. "You've got this, Reese. Just text when you're ready for another lesson." Then she hugs me goodbye.

Sue's truck kicks up a cloud of dust as she backs it up and then moves it forward. When she sees me standing there in the big open doorway, she stops and lowers her window. "I'll come back soon with my new ultrasound machine to get a better look at Treasure. If you can think of anyone else who might need it, I always do guinea pigs for free." She smiles and drives away. I can hear her coughing as her tires kick up even more dust in through the truck's windows.

For the rest of the day, I practice Sue's lessons. Checking for abnormal isn't that easy when you're not sure what normal is. Like everything else around here. But when I listen to Treasure's heartbeat, I hear *lub dub, lub dub, lub dub*. Normal. I press the stethoscope harder, and it feels like his heart is in my hand.

On my way to the field at the end of the day, I see Wes's phone lying in the dirt. He must have dropped it when he was getting bucked around the ring on the filly. The screen is frozen on an old picture of him as a kid. It looks like there are two of him. But the other kid in the picture has a birthmark the size of a dime on his cheek. Except for the birthmark, they're identical.

Wes has a brother. Wes has a twin.

I swipe left. There are more pictures. The two boys in a tree fort. A birthday party where each boy has his own cake. The boys in midair, jumping from a rope swing into a lake. Then the last picture. Wes looks a little older than I am. Another birthday party. Just one boy. Just one cake.

CHAPTER THIRTY-ONE

I put Wes's phone on the office desk and get on my bike to head home. I think of how Wes moves so silently in and out of the barn, sometimes making me jump. He's there, and then he's not. Or he's nowhere to be found, but when I turn around, he's standing there, busy with something, like he was there all along.

As good as I am at knowing what's going on in Wes's brain, knowing a little more would be nice. I've always had questions for him. When things are OK, getting answers from someone who won't talk doesn't feel that important. But now that things aren't OK, I need to know. What has him all so distant and sad and mad? What's different?

And why does he hold everything in? Is there *anyone* he talks to? What happened to his brother? Why has he chosen silence? I imagine myself saying, *Wes, if only you had someone to talk to. Like, really talk to.* And I realize I sound just like my dad.

The picture of Wes alone in front of his birthday cake is stuck in my mind. Daisy-patterned tablecloth. Small bookcase in the corner. Porcelain duck on the shelf. Green-and-blue plaid curtains. And in the window, a reflection of a woman—his mother?—taking the photograph. The cake was square, like it was baked in a brownie pan. White frosting. Less going on than most birthday cakes. And the candles, setting off a fuzzy glow that . . . Candles! Cake! Dad!

I slam on my brakes.

Shit! It's his birthday!

He never makes a big deal about it unless I forget. If I show up empty-handed, he'll know I did. He'll tease me about it for a year. He'll put on his Eeyore voice and say, "Oh, your poor old dad. He's OK. Don't worry about him. He doesn't need to be celebrated on his birthday. Birthdays are for kids. Let me just bust my ass at work, and maybe you'll remember next year. It's just another 365 days." I can't stand his Eeyore voice. I turn around and head into Birdwood.

I pedal quickly past Trudy's Hair Salon & Fine Art, which is where LeeAnne works. I don't see her at her usual station next to the window. When I get to the feed store, I slow down. The saddle is still in the window. There's a line slashed through the original price of $1,200, and the new price of $800 is written in red. A woman is looking at it, lifting the flap to check the billets, running her hand along the cantle and the panel. I watch her through the window until her kid starts screaming. She picks him up and walks away.

I put my hand on the glass. I imagine myself placing the saddle on Treasure's back. But then I see the race. Treasure crashing to the ground. Then how he stood in his stall, his nose low in the shavings. And Dr. Higgs's words. *Be kindest to put him down.* I leave a curved fingerprint smudge on the glass and pedal on toward Phil's Pharmacy. I lean my bike against a parking meter.

Phil's is one-stop shopping for me. It sells pretty much everything. Mom and Dad used to bring me here some Saturdays for a treat because Phil's has an ice cream counter. Brilliant marketing, if you ask me. Mental note. Talk to Wes about having an ice cream truck at the barn in the summer. I decide to get a scoop while I peruse, so I walk up to the case and look through the glass. I usually choose ice cream by color.

"What'll it be?" Phil asks. His mustache is grayer than I remember.

"I'll have the mint chip elk droppings, please."

"Good choice. One of my personal favorites."

Phil doesn't have to ask cup or cone. He leans over the counter to hand me my waffle cone, and I walk down the greeting card aisle. There's a whole row for father's birthdays. I avoid the ones that have fancy lettering and fishing boats. And the ones that say things like "You are my best friend" or "Best Dad Ever" or "Superdad." And the funny ones aren't that funny. I find one on the bottom row that just says "Hi, Dad. I got you a card." Then I grab a bag of licorice and a bottle of barbecue sauce and head to the counter. Phil meets me there.

"Dad's birthday again already? Seems like you were just in here for that." Phil shakes his head. "Time's a funny thing." Which is exactly what he said last year.

"Thanks, Phil!" I head out the door, my bag tucked under my arm.

"See you next year," Phil says and waves. "Oh, and congratulations, Reese. I heard the big news from my neighbor." He points his elbow in the direction of Trudy's

Hair Salon & Fine Art. I stop, my hand on the doorknob. I can tell by Phil's face he can tell I haven't heard yet.

"Oh, just the moving-in news. Your dad and LeeAnne. She says everyone's excited."

I throw my half-eaten ice cream cone into the trash barrel outside and grab my bike. I pedal so fast I can't feel my feet. When I pull into the driveway, LeeAnne's minivan is there. Dad is carrying one of her chairs up the steps to the house.

"Please tell me this isn't happening."

Shitty boy-looking stuff sits in piles on the porch. Skateboards, sweatpants and T-shirts, a gaming system, jumbles of cords, and mini-mountains of controllers.

"How long have you actually known her, Dad? Aren't there laws about not letting people move in together so fast?"

He tries to shush me by talking even lower and quieter than I just did. "LeeAnne and I have known each other long enough. We talked about this, Reese, remember?" Dad has a dumb look on his face, like when he was scared to get on the Tower of Terror at the fun park but got on anyway.

"Beavis and Butthead are actually going to live here? Like in my house?" I look around at all their stuff, which seems to belong to another world where everything's the color of crap. "I hope you're building another bathroom. There's no way I'm sharing mine."

"Don't be ridiculous. Boys don't spend a lot of time in bathrooms anyway."

"They will be shitting in yours then. Not mine. No way I'm putting my bare ass on the same seat they do."

"Reese, you're being incredibly selfish. They're nice boys. We're all going to get along just great."

"How do you figure that?"

"I knew it the night we were all playing charades."

"I was faking. I was doing you a favor. I hated it."

I follow him into the house. The moment I walk in, everything seems different.

"What's that smell?"

LeeAnne walks into the kitchen from the living room. "Hi, Reese. Oh, that's probably apple kiwi." She holds up a bottle of room spray.

"It's disgusting. It's already giving me a headache."

She's replaced the kitchen table. She's stacked matching plates and glasses on the counter. She's hung up a plaque that says LIVE, LAUGH, LOVE. How fucking idiotic is that?

"Please don't hang that in my house," I hiss and head to my room. I pass fartface and shitdoink sprawled out on my couch.

"Hey, sis," Cody says, then laughs.

"*Su casa, mi casa*, get it?" Kyle says, then falls all over himself laughing.

"Oh, Reese. I washed some of your things this morning. This must have been in your pocket. It fell out in the dryer." LeeAnne holds up my stone.

Heat is rising from my chest to my face. I go to take the stone from her, but Kyle snatches it from her hand.

"What is it?" he asks, swiping his hair out of his eyes.

"Give it!" I stand there in front of him with my hand out.

He ignores me, tossing it from one hand to the other. Cody reaches around Kyle and nabs the stone out of the air, mid-toss.

"The eighties called," says Cody. "They want their pet rock back." Both boys think that's the funniest thing they've ever heard, and even LeeAnne chuckles. My head feels like it might explode.

"Boys, don't tease. Give her the rock."

Dad walks in, and when Kyle looks over at him, I lunge forward and grab my stone from his hand.

"Don't ever touch my things again!" I hope my eyes are burning holes into their dumb faces. "I'm going back to the barn. I can't handle another minute of this fucked-up shit." I slam the front door shut, rattling the stupid new welcome sign that's shaped like the sun.

Dad opens the door and steps out onto the porch.

"Reese! Don't be like that."

"Don't be like what?!"

"LeeAnne was just trying to help. And . . . it's my birthday."

"Oh yeah. Happy birthday." I throw him the Phil's Pharmacy bag. When he catches it, the bottom of the bag tears open, and the bottle shatters on the porch step. Dad just stares at the thick puddle of barbecue sauce, brown as swamp water. It creeps toward the second step, then drips over it. I can't think of anything to say. It feels like I'm trying to swallow a small fire. I get on my bike. I can't pedal fast enough out of the driveway.

CHAPTER THIRTY-TWO

When I get to the barn, Wes is giving Zadie a lesson. I slide Treasure's halter over his ears and lead him out of his stall. We walk up the hill in the back pasture. I can finally breathe out all of the apple-kiwi-scented air from my lungs.

"What do you call home when home doesn't feel like home anymore?" I ask Treasure. "The truth is, home hasn't felt like home in a long time."

When Treasure and I get to the top of the hill where the field meets the woods, the foxes are boinging around outside their den. They remind me of popcorn popping. Conway springs up high into the air and turns completely around, landing on some unsuspecting cricket or grasshopper. After he lands, Loretta pops into the air and does her own little acrobatic move. With their tongues hanging out of their mouths and their lips drawn up, they look like they're smiling huge smiles.

"Good morning, little kits!" They trot toward me, wagging their whole bodies. I know I should keep them afraid of me, but they're just too darn cute. Treasure lowers his head toward them and flares his nostrils. Loretta, the smaller, braver one, reaches her tiny snout up to Treasure's, and they touch noses in the softest, gentlest way. Then Treasure snorts, scaring Loretta. She dives back into her den so fast that she scares *him*! Then Treasure raises his head and nods: *I like this game.* Loretta pokes her head out from her den again slowly—ears first, then eyes, then her little black nose.

I reach into my pocket for the bag of dinner scraps I grabbed from the office fridge. I toss over a piece of a hamburger and a few Oreo cookies. Loretta creeps all the way out, her head low to the ground. She grabs a piece of cookie, a piece of meat, and another piece of cookie. Then she disappears again into her den. *These babies aren't gonna starve on my watch.* They make me laugh. And I swear, with the way Treasure shakes his head and blows out his nose, he's laughing too.

I scatter the rest of the food, say goodbye to the silly babies, and lead Treasure back to the barn. Wes is in the ring with Zadie. From a distance, it looks like they're doing a performance. Zadie is sitting on Marge like she's ridden her all her life. When Wes unclips the lead shank, Zadie urges Marge to trot in circles around Wes. Then Wes gives Marge the slightest of hand signals, and off they go, doing figure eights and flawlessly transitioning to a canter. Wes watches them move around him slowly. He clocks them from the center of the ring.

When I get closer, I can't believe what I see. Wes has set up a jump. It's just a pole between two standards, about eighteen inches off the ground, but I've been left behind over smaller. Wes is standing to the side, one arm propped on the top of the standard. Why is Wes doing this? It's like he's setting her up for failure. What if she falls? What if she gets hurt? Is this some twisted kind of joke? Letting a blind girl jump? Is he crazy?

Somehow, Zadie aims Marge directly at the jump. She does a half circle at the end of the ring and then goes over the jump from the other direction. How does she know where the jump is? How does she know when it's coming? How does she know where to turn? Why does she ride better than I do? Wes is watching her, looking like he's not even impressed. Zadie slows Marge to a walk and then pats her neck.

"Wait until my mom's not looking," she says. "Then make it higher, Wes. Marge can practically step over that. Please set it higher. I'm sick of these pansy-ass poles on the ground."

Wes raises the jump another three inches. Zadie and Marge go from a walk to a beautiful collected canter, circle the ring once, and then pop over the jump. Wes smiles. After Zadie jumps it a few more times in both directions, Wes raises the height of the pole again. I try to imagine being on a horse, darkness all around me, feeling the jump. I try to imagine jumping something I can't even see.

On my way back to Treasure's stall, I see Ellen standing in the shade under the oak tree. She waves me over.

"Reese, I just want to say thank you. You know, I've tried to pay Wes for the lessons, but he refuses to take the money. Do you think you can get him to take this?"

"I'll try, but he can be pretty stubborn." I try not to sound pissed. Here we are, struggling every day, and he won't take money for a lesson.

"Well, you have no idea. The most I was hoping for was a trail ride. And now to see her on a horse, controlling it, cantering and jumping, doing all these things, I just . . ." Ellen talks fast, like she's flustered, but I can tell she's trying to find words for a feeling that doesn't seem possible to explain. "The other day, I took a call for fifteen minutes, and when I came back, he already had her going over the jump. If I'd seen Wes put up the jump, I would have insisted he take it down. I would have told him there's no way Zadie can jump an obstacle she can't see."

"I don't know how she does it. I've never seen anything like it. I can't even jump something I *can* see," I tell her. Ellen laughs like I'm just joking.

"When she was born, I remember one of the doctors took me aside. He told me that seeing is only one of our senses. He said that we have many more than five. I thought he was a total wacko. I was like, sure. I didn't want to hear him." She swats a fly away before she continues. "He said she would develop senses of her own and that she'll trust those senses more than a seeing person trusts their sight. He said most people use their vision to strengthen their fear, not to overcome it. And when your sight is taken away, you have to rely on something else. I was totally offended that he was so optimistic and cheerful telling me this. I didn't realize until later that he was blind too."

In the ring, Zadie is laughing at something. Wes has a big smile on his face. He's nodding his head like he just told her a funny joke.

"Since she was born, every day of my life has been about not letting her blindness stand in the way of her curiosity. I've wanted her to feel as free as she can possibly feel. But right now it's scaring the shit out of me."

We both watch Zadie. She almost falls but catches herself and bursts out laughing.

"Make it higher! Make it higher, Wes!"

"I wonder if I was doing the right thing. I wonder if she'd be better off being afraid."

Wes raises the pole a couple more inches.

"Wes!" Ellen marches down to the ring. "That's high enough!"

"Awwww, Mom, please just leave us alone. Wes and I are fine." Then she starts reading her mom the riot act for interfering.

Bzzzzzzzzzzzzz. Bzzzzzzzzzzzzz.

I pull my phone out of my pocket and read Dad's text.

I've scheduled an emergency appointment for you. Dr. Monroe. 6 pm tomorrow. List to follow.

CHAPTER THIRTY-THREE

Dr. Monroe's office is one town over in the Three Moons strip mall, tucked between Doggie Style and Lord of the Wings. Still within biking distance. In the waiting area, I look at the list Dad texted me. Things I'm supposed to talk about.

1. Blended family
2. Sudden outbursts and swearing
3. Hormones and boys
4. Imaginary horses

One of those brain-teaser puzzles, the kind with two rings and a rope, sits on the coffee table. I don't even bother. Happy teenagers smile at me from the covers of magazines. Dr. Monroe opens her door. A boy walks out of her office. He looks like a tool. I almost leave.

"Reese?"

She waves me in, but first, I delete Dad's list.

"Good to see you," she says, like she actually means it.

"You too." I actually kind of mean it too. There's something I like about her right away. Maybe it's her purple hair and purple cowboy boots. Maybe it's the small, cheery room, or her shell collection, or her corny-captioned cat posters.

"Have a seat. Get comfy. Make yourself at home." She looks at her watch. "For an hour." Then she laughs and slaps her knee. "So, Reese, how *are* you today?"

"Lookin' good, feline better. But I might have a cattitude problem."

Dr. Monroe laughs and glances at her posters.

"OK, yes. I love cats. You'll never guess what Stuart and Pearl did this week."

She shows me some pictures. Stuart is playing in a pile of toilet paper, and Pearl is sleeping in a tiny box. I laugh. Which catches me by surprise. *When was the last time I actually laughed?*

"Is there anything specific you'd like to talk about, Reese? Your dad mentioned that your home life has changed a little."

"A little?"

"A lot," she says, agreeing with me. She nods her head and breathes out a long sigh. "I'm sorry, Reese. It must really suck."

"Yeah. It does."

"I'm sure that having strange new people in your home feels like an invasion. Do you want to tell me about it?"

"Not really."

"No?"

"Can we talk about something else?"

"It's your hour," she says, throwing her hands up. "Talk away."

"Well, I want to know why I'm afraid of something. Something I used to do all the time without even thinking about it."

"What's that?" She leans forward a bit.

"Jumping. I don't know why I can't do it anymore. I jumped horses almost since I could sit on them, and now I—"

A spot on the top of my leg suddenly feels hot, like I just spilled a spoonful of soup on it. Weird. I try to ignore it.

"What happens when you try to jump?"

The heat is coming from my stone. I take it out of my pocket and hold it tight in my fist. Dr. Monroe waits so patiently for my answer she looks like she's frozen.

"I don't know. I just panic. The smallest jump now seems like some huge wall that's impossible to get over."

"You panic? Like, your heart speeds up? You break out in a sweat?"

"Exactly!" Wow, not bad. This one might actually be worth the money.

"Anything else?"

"I can't get my body to do what I tell it to."

"Yes, OK. So fear really grabs hold of you."

"Yeah. But I don't have a reason. I mean, I shouldn't be afraid of something I've never been afraid of before. It's not like it's a new thing."

"Have you ever heard the expression 'There's nothing to fear but fear itself'?" She tucks a purple strand of hair behind her ear.

"No."

"Good. It's hogwash. I mean, don't get me wrong. I think we *can* be afraid of fear. But usually the thing we fear most is pain."

I shake my head. "I'm pretty sure that's not me."

"I know it sounds weird, but it's actually way more common than you might think. The hard part to understand is, when is it really about fear and when is it really about pain?"

This psychobabble is getting on my nerves fast.

"Jumping isn't painful for me."

Dr. Monroe looks up at the ceiling and squints her eyes.

"Pain is inside of us all the time. It's sort of just the state of being human. Since humans aren't great at dealing with pain, fear takes over. And we want to, you know, give a face to that fear."

Then I feel a rumble, like a big truck is passing outside.

"Give a face to fear?"

"Maybe for you, fear has attached itself to jumping?"

"I don't know . . ."

Outside the window, a woman clutches her fluffy dog as she walks through the parking lot. The dog is barking its head off.

"Underneath fear can be pain. And the brain knows that pain is . . . painful. So, whenever it can, your brain will divert you from feeling pain. It would much rather feel fear than pain. So, in your case, it's steering you away from the jump. But that also prevents you from healing whatever that pain is—from getting over it. And jumping is literally *getting over something*."

Then the rumbling gets louder. I just know it. The horses are here. I look out the window and there they are, galloping straight through the middle of the Piggle Wiggle parking lot, weaving around parked cars and some people pushing shopping carts.

"Personally, every night I ask myself, what did fear attach itself to today? And as soon as I can identify a fear, I dig a little deeper, and I find pain." She stares at me. "Is there something that might be so painful for you that you'd rather feel fear?"

My eyes stay glued to the window. Some of the horses come close, passing just outside the office. I shrug. Dr. Monroe stares at me, blinks twice, and does a slight nod. The black horse stops right outside her office window. He looks at me through the glass. Then he rears in the air.

"Reese? Are you OK? Would you like some water?"

"I'm fine." I try not to look out the window.

"I'm gonna go out on a limb and say that, when you lost your mom, you also lost your—"

Dr. Monroe's lips are moving, but I don't hear her words. Outside, the black horse breaks into a gallop and charges out of the parking lot. The herd follows. They're gone. I can finally exhale. My heart beats normally again. I look back at Dr. Monroe. She's staring at me.

"Your dad told me about the horses. Have you seen them lately?"

"No."

"No? Nothing?"

"Nope."

Dr. Monroe sits back. She takes a sip of water.

"And how does that make you feel?"

"Good."

"Good?"

"Relieved."

"Because . . . ?"

"Because it's not normal to, you know . . . see things that aren't really there?" I didn't mean to end it in a question. It just came out that way.

"Is that what you think?"

"Yes."

"Creating a herd of wild horses could have been a way to distract yourself from feeling your pain around what happened."

By "what happened," she means Mom hanging from her seat belt. Me and Dad standing at the edge of the road, broken crates scattered everywhere, chickens flapping around while the EMTs cut her seat belt to get her out.

Dr. Monroe is wrong. I feel it like it was yesterday.

CHAPTER THIRTY-FOUR

When I get home from the therapist's, the invaders are crowding the kitchen. Dad looks up from making himself a ham sandwich. I walk past them all without saying a word and go right to my room. Talking is exhausting. I have a pounding headache from thinking about what Dr. Monroe said. Maybe jumping isn't what I'm really afraid of? My brain is trying to not feel pain? *What does that even mean?* I'm beginning to think I was right in the first place. Therapy is a stupid waste of time.

I hear a knock on my door.

"Reese? Can I come in? How was the new therapist?"

"Stupid."

"Oh boy." He does a big sigh like it's soooo hard for him. "Strange . . . her reviews were great. Kids love her. Supposedly they open up more quickly because she has a cool hairstyle and—"

"I hate her!"

"But I've prepaid for your next two sessions. What do you expect me to do about that?"

I can tell he's holding back because he doesn't want LeeAnne to hear us arguing, so I yell as loud as I can.

"Nothing!"

"She has you in her schedule," he says, like his jaw's all clenched.

"Then you go see her."

"For f . . . frank's sake, Reese, why do you have to make everything so franking difficult?" Then he smacks the door. "I'll do another web search tonight," he mumbles as he walks away.

I open my door and yell down the hall. "Don't bother! I am so done with talking! Maybe I should be like Wes and just stop!"

The next morning, I try to imagine what it would be like to be Wes. To never say another word to anyone. It's time for that experiment. I mean, why not find out? I write a few words on a napkin and walk downstairs to the kitchen. LeeAnne is busy killing a small swarm of fruit flies that are hovering over her organic grapes. I hand her my note. She reads it, nods, and for some reason, thinks she has to whisper.

"Laryngitis? Did you gargle?"

I nod.

She opens a cabinet that used to store random mugs and plates but now has rows of oils and vitamins. "I have a tea tree and geranium oil blend. Put a few drops in some warm water and—"

I wave my hand out in front of her.

"No? But it really works. Better than salt water."

I shake my head and open the pantry door. There are boxes and bags and cans of things I don't recognize.

"It's arranged alphabetically. Except for your cereals. They're on the bottom shelf."

My boxes of Cinnamon Toast Crunch, Cocoa Crisp, and Sugar Snaps are lined up on the floor next to the trash can. LeeAnne reaches around me and grabs a box from the top shelf.

"I got you these," she says, "if you want to try them. Flax Flakes. They're so good you'd never know they were healthy."

I shake my head and pick up my unopened box of Cinnamon Toast Crunch.

"Don't open the new box of cereal until the old one is gone," she whispers, trying to take the box from my hand.

I snatch the box away from her and get my bowl from the cupboard. She's so annoying and weird, and I wish she'd mind her own business.

Dad comes downstairs wearing a stupid sweater and loafers. LeeAnne whispers, "Reese has laryngitis." Dad whispers back, "Oh, how did she get that? Couldn't possibly be all that yelling she did last night." The two of them continue their whispered conversation for about fifteen minutes. Then the two clodhoppers come downstairs, their hair sticking up everywhere.

"Why's everyone whispering?" Cody asks, scratching his balls in front of the open refrigerator door. Then he reaches for my leftover pizza and starts shoveling it into his mouth.

"That's my lunch, you asshole!" I blurt out.

So my experiment lasted approximately seventeen and a half minutes. I don't even bother explaining anything. I just say, "I guess I'm better," and leave for the barn.

I make the turn at the scraggly oak and coast down the driveway. I let my bike almost come to a standstill before I start pedaling the rest of the way to the barn. It's the kind of day I just want to be alone with my horse.

I put Treasure's halter over his head and lead him out of the barn and up to the back pasture. We walk through the field and down to the willow tree, its branches draped all over in bright green buds, in spite of the drought. We needed the recent rains, but they weren't enough. The grass in the field is still a brownish yellow. The river makes just a gurgling sound, not the rushing sound you'd normally hear after a good rain.

Treasure likes to graze at the bank, where the grass is lusher and sweeter. He plunges his nose into some clover while I pick a daisy and pluck its petals one by one until all that's left is a bald center on a limp stem. I take a good look at Treasure. A nice layer of fat is now covering his rib cage. His coat is so shiny he almost looks wet. It can't hurt to just sit on him. Sue said as much.

One time, when everyone still thought young Treasure was impossible to ride, Mom just walked into the field and hopped right on him, totally surprising me and Dad. That afternoon was hot, hot, and we'd just come back from trying to cool off in the river. We were in the truck, sitting on wet towels, smelling like river water, driving back to the barn to wrap things up for the day. Mom pointed at Treasure in the field and asked Dad to stop. She got out, climbed the fence, wearing her cutoffs and tank top, and walked barefoot through the grass. Before we knew it, she was on his back, wearing that huge smile of hers. Treasure acted like this happened all the time. He just kept on grazing away like a backyard pony.

"Look, Joe," she said. "Look at the crazy horse you said I'd never be able to train."

Dad was leaning on a fence post, chewing the sweet end of a blade of grass. He shook his head with a worried smile. He parted his lips, ready to tell her to get off before Treasure bolted or bucked. But he stayed silent. Stunned, probably, that Treasure had come so far. Then Mom grabbed Treasure's mane. When she clucked to him, he lifted his head and walked toward us.

"OK, Jessie. You proved your point," Dad said. "You can get off now."

But Mom didn't. She let me pet Treasure's nose. Then she squeezed her leg and said, "C'mon, boy." Treasure took off at a gallop, stirring up the other horses, who followed him and Mom across the field so fast that, in an instant, they were all down the hill and out of sight.

"Shit," Dad said as he threw down his chewed stalk and climbed over the fence.

That's when I grabbed my camera out of the truck. I was just about to climb through the fence and catch up with Dad, who was angry-walking into the field in his wet trunks and bare feet, when Mom and Treasure crested the hill and galloped back to us with all of the other horses in tow.

"Whoa," she said. "Whoa, boy!" Then she pulled back on his mane like she was holding onto reins. She was laughing so hard she was crying.

"Oh my God, Joe. He's even faster than I thought!"

"And you're crazier than I thought," Dad said.

Mom stopped Treasure exactly where their ride began. She leaned back, rested her hand on his back, and let him graze. The rest of the herd settled down and grazed too. She tilted her head back and closed her eyes, feeling the sun on her face. Her bare feet dangled above the earth. A sudden breeze caught her hair and Treasure's tail at the same time. That's when I snapped the picture.

Of all the photos I keep in my Seabiscuit soap dish, I love that one the most. There's a glare from the sun that cuts through the image from the top left corner to the bottom right. It blurs the edges of things and adds a white light that isn't in my memory. In the middle of all that light is Mom. Like the picture was trying to tell me something. I took it only thirty days before the race.

I lead Treasure over to a fallen tree and maneuver his body parallel to it. Then I slowly step onto the trunk, leaning my chest across Treasure's back and gradually resting all of my weight on him. He doesn't do much, other than turn to look at me. With my heart pounding in my ear, I slowly ease one leg over him and sit. I'm on my horse. The world is making sense again.

I've only ever been on Treasure once before. I was nine. Mom lifted me up on him when she was cooling him down. We did the driveway walk, Treasure following Mom like a big dog. I can almost feel Mom here, holding the lead while Treasure grazes. The three of us. Like it used to be.

Treasure's back is warm from the sun. I can smell the wet grass and the riverbank's mud. He keeps munching. I look down at the earth, so far below, and at my dangling feet above it. I'm careful that my calves don't put too much pressure on Treasure's belly. I want him to keep on grazing. Keep him relaxed. Which might not be easy, considering it's been more than two years since anyone's sat on him.

But he's acting like we've done this many times before. I take a hank of mane in one hand and hold the lead rope in the other. His tail swishes from one side to the other. His ears twitch lazily forward and back, forward and back. His hooves rise and fall slowly in the tall grass as he eases forward. He's grazing like I'm not even here.

What if I do what Mom did that time? I could squeeze my leg just a tiny bit and we'd be thundering across the field. But when Mom did it, Treasure was strong and healthy. He won't ever be able to run like that again. Not with someone on his back. I let his mane slide through my fingers.

He keeps grazing peacefully by the river, and then he takes a long drink. A great blue heron suddenly spreads his giant wings and lifts off from its rocky perch, but Treasure doesn't startle. After I'm sure he's had plenty of grass and water, I lean forward and hug his neck. Then I swing my leg around and let my feet slowly touch the ground.

We head down the long, hot driveway. I feel in my pocket for my stone. Before we enter the barn, I hold the stone up to the sunlight. New windows of pink are peeking through the dull gray parts. How can a stone keep changing? I'm wondering this and looking at the stone instead of where I'm going when I almost smack into a lady who must have walked in through the back.

"If you're looking for your kid, Wes is doing the lesson in the ring." I hold out my hand to her. "I'm Reese."

She gives me one of those prissy fingertip handshakes. She's not in barn clothes. She's wearing a fitted navy blue suit jacket with a matching skirt. Her flawless auburn ponytail is so tight it must be hurting her face. And she's walking on tiptoes so she won't ruin her pink suede heels. She is definitely not a horse person. Probably not even the parent of a horse person. Might not even know the difference between a horse and a cow.

"Nope. No kid," she says. Her red lipstick looks very . . . red. "Just wondering if I might talk to the owner."

"That would be Wes, and he's in the ring." I spare her the details about Wes just leasing, not owning, the place. "He won't be done for a while. And he's got a ton of stuff to do. Part of the roof gave out over the tack room and—"

"This place is old, huh?" She looks up at the beams. I follow where she's looking. We seem to have accumulated more cobwebs overnight.

"Yeah, I mean, it's old but it still—"

"My name is Cassandra. Cassandra Murphy. Are you his daught—"

"I'm his partner. Business partner."

"That's . . . very . . . sweet," she says. Not the reaction I was expecting. I don't get what's sweet about an honest answer.

The minute she starts dodging piles of manure, waving away flies, and talking some more about how old this place is, I'm sure Wes won't want to waste his time on this Cassandra Murphy. Like any good horse person, I can sniff out a phony in about the time it takes to add one and one.

On her tiptoey way out, she hands me a pamphlet.

"I wonder if you could give him this. And maybe ask him to email me."

On the pamphlet's cover, little bungalows are superimposed all over the Big Green Barn property. And the title is stupid. "Relax from Ahhh to Zen at Reflections Spa and Wellness Center." Inside, glossy photos show couples in their white robes sitting on their little decks. They're drinking cucumber water, getting massaged, hiking on trails, sitting in a hot tub, and eating greens (also in their robes). The main spa—some awful new building that's trying to look old—looks like it's exactly where the barn is now. If I read one more word like *submerge* or *emerge* or *bliss* or *harmony* or *rejuvenate* or *exhale* or *escape*, I think I might throw up.

I wave goodbye as Cassandra climbs into her red Range Rover. "Pleasure meeting you! I'll have Wes email you ASAP!" Then I rip up the pamphlet into teeny-tiny pieces and let them scatter in the breeze. I guess Gibson wasn't just flapping his gums about having a buyer. This little visit must be a cover for her just poking around the place. People like Cassandra with perfect clothes and flawless ponytails and smooth talk and fancy pamphlets have a way of acting like they're doing a thing when they're really doing another, then making you do things you don't think you're doing.

Like those fancy-pantsers who pulled one over on Cyrus Tibbs down on Camel Hump Road. He thought a nice man in a sharp suit was going to give him money for his dairy farm while he was still running it. He couldn't believe how lucky he was. He thought the guy offered him a deal where he would get paid in advance for his property and then, since none of his kids wanted to take over the farm, suit man would pay it off to his family after he died. He signed on the dotted line. Next thing Mr. Tibbs knew, he was ordered to leave the property because he was in breach of contract for buying more cattle. Now he lives in a tiny apartment in Rapid City. And he's still not dead.

I consider this visit as fate doing us a favor. Now I know that developers really are taking a serious look at this property. Just a matter of time before Gibson starts looking for any excuse to push Wes off this land. Excuses we're already giving him. The only real protection Wes has is getting caught up on the lease payments.

Now I don't have a choice. I have to step it up. Do things I really don't want to do. I text Sue.

I'm ready for the next lesson.

CHAPTER THIRTY-FIVE

"You don't have to be a vet to clean a sheath," says Sue. She's here to make good on both of her promises—to test out her new ultrasound machine, yay, and to give me the dreaded wiener-cleaner lesson, boo. She lugs her tackle box from her truck to the barn.

"Sheath cleaning is pretty basic stuff. No big deal, really."

"That's what she said," Carol says out of the corner of her mouth.

"Carol, why don't you go listen to the Indigo Girls or . . . get another iced coffee." Sue waves Carol off with her gloved hand.

I still can't believe Sue is doing what she's doing with a straight face, like she's combing his mane or cleaning his hoof. It looks like she's jerking Bubba off. In fact, she is jerking him off.

"To do it properly, the horse has to be extended, not soft. You can't clean a soft penis thoroughly," she says into Bubba's flank.

"Is there any way of doing it without having to touch it?"

"Don't worry, Reese," Sue says when she sees my face. "It will feel routine after you've done three or four."

"Routine is taking a temperature or giving a vaccine. I can't imagine that cleaning a sheath will ever feel routine."

"You don't need to put on music and light candles and open a bottle of wine or anything." She does a little snort laugh. "Just enough groping so the penis drops down enough to scoop out the smegma." She holds up her fingers to show me the pasty white goo before she flicks it into the bucket.

"Ewwww. It looks like toothpaste."

"Yeah, I wouldn't try brushing with it," says Carol.

"I mean, how important is it, really? How often do they need it done?"

"Once, maybe twice a year. Depends on the buildup. Come on, Reese. Stinky will be a piece of cake."

Sue closes Bubba's door and heads over to where I'm waiting beside Stinky. She's ready to coach me through it. I slowly reach under Stinky's belly. My first thought is, I'm touching a horse's wiener before I've touched a boy's wiener. I mean, Sue talks like it's just another body part, like a hoof or an ear. But I bet there's not one person who agrees with her, including me. First, I just let the back of my hand hit up against it. Then I rest my hand there. But just before I actually try to grip it the way Sue showed me, I pull my hand away. I just can't do it.

"Why do horses have to have wieners? Wieners are just gross!"

Sue and Carol laugh at me.

"Reese, you can do this. Think about it this way. If a horse's sheath isn't cleaned, he can get an infection or cancer or all kinds of awful things."

I wouldn't want any of that to happen to Stinky, so I try again. This time I just go for it. I grab it and hold it. Stinky swipes at me with his hind foot.

"Shit!" I stand up.

"OK, he doesn't understand that humans have messed-up ideas about certain body parts, so he's not going to react well to your squeamishness."

"OK. Good boy, Stinky. I'm sorry. It's not your fault you have a wiener."

Sue and Carol snicker again. Now I feel bad. My being completely grossed out has made Stinky afraid. I reach back under him and slowly feel for his sheath. This time, I can actually stand holding on to it. I find the ridge and scoop out the gunk.

"Well done," Sue says. "Jasper will be a walk in the park."

I clean four more geldings, and believe it or not, it really does get easier. On a little break between wieners, I pick up the halter and lead shank that Treasure has tossed into the aisle. Then I give him some fresh hay.

"Treasure hasn't taken a lame step since he's been back," I tell Sue.

"Yeah, let's have a look at that old injury." Sue walks toward me, peeling off her rubber gloves. "I'll grab the ultrasound machine from the truck."

A minute later, Sue opens her laptop and plugs in the cord that's attached to the probe. I already have Treasure on the cross ties. He stands there patiently. Sue sits in her collapsible chair, shears the area of his hind leg that she's going to scan, and applies a gel. She smears the probe with some more gel and places it over the suspensory ligament between the hock and the ankle. I place one hand on

Treasure's neck in case he needs calming and lean forward to see what Sue is looking at on her screen.

"I can't stand the suspensory suspense," I tell Sue. "It looks like the Milky Way on a really clear night."

"That's good," Sue says quietly. "The whiter, the better."

She moves the probe around while she looks at the image on her laptop. Then she removes the probe, adds more gel, and places it back on Treasure's leg again. She moves it in tiny circles, one way and then the other. She rotates the image on her laptop.

"I'm looking to see if the fibers connect both vertically and horizontally," she says.

"And?" I ask. I don't understand what she's looking for, and I don't have the patience to learn anything new right now.

"Yeah, just what I thought."

"What, Sue? What did you think?"

"With a front suspensory, you have a chance. But a hind suspensory . . ."

My body goes limp. Why did I even hope? I let my arm drop from Treasure's neck. Sue shrugs as she looks at her screen and wiggles the probe around some more.

"I've looked from every angle," she says, "but I don't see any sign of an old injury."

"What?"

"There's really nothing wrong with him."

"Wait, Sue. What do you mean?"

"I mean, some suspensory injuries can heal. It's possible. But acute hind limb proximal suspensory desmitis? That's usually a hopeless prognosis. Sometimes there's just no explaining things." She winds the cord back around the probe and places it in her tackle box.

"So, he's OK?"

"I mean, to be sure, we could do an MRI. But I wouldn't spend the money. Especially since he hasn't taken a lame step and I don't feel any heat in that spot."

"He's ready for a saddle?"

She pats Treasure's forehead and smiles. "He's ready for anything."

CHAPTER THIRTY-SIX

I'm grooming Treasure in his stall, admiring his shiny coat and healthy layer of fat. If he's ready for anything, then what do I do first? Where, exactly, do I start?

Wes and his young horse Lance leave the ring and walk up to the barn. Wes dismounts, but he doesn't untack. Instead, he ties Lance to the hitching post and walks past me to the tack room. *Must have forgotten something.*

I'm watching the currycomb slip through Treasure's copper mane when Wes comes over and stands just outside Treasure's stall door, waiting for me to open it. He's holding a saddle, which he lifts and slowly lowers onto Treasure's back, and a bridle, which he hands to me. Then he walks back out to Lance.

Wait. Is Wes inviting me and Treasure to go out on the trail with him? Could this really be happening?

I finish tacking Treasure. It doesn't seem possible that I'm pulling a bridle over his ears. That I'll be leading him to the mounting block, swinging my leg over him, and actually riding him. Back when I was still searching for him, I never thought anyone could ever ride him again. I thought I was bringing him back here to retire. To live out his best life in the place Mom brought him so many years ago, when he was so young and afraid and so slow to trust. But Treasure acts like he's always known better.

He stands there patiently. Like he's ready. Like he's been waiting for this day all along. I step into the stirrup and slowly swing my leg over Treasure's back. He turns his ears toward me as I lower myself into the saddle. Being on him feels as natural as walking out the front door.

I sit up and pat his neck, and just like that, we're following Wes and Lance through the open gate at the bottom of the field and heading to my favorite trail. It has a little bit of everything. A nice grade to help a horse get off its front end, several clearings for cantering, and a few obstacles to jump. I've missed it. It's even prettier than I remember. When we climb a little higher up, we look down at the roof of the barn. The river below looks like a black-tarred road winding through the property.

Wes doesn't seem to mind that he's on a horse who's afraid of his own skin. Lance is on the bit, grinding his teeth, already working up a lather, even though we're barely a mile into our ride. But Treasure is a good influence. His cool head and calm disposition remind a young nutjob horse like Lance that he doesn't need to worry about every little thing. Treasure's older and wiser, and if some critter suddenly appeared in front of him, he'd probably keep on going like it wasn't even there. He's seen a lot, so not much can surprise him.

The path keeps to the edge of the woods. In the coolness of the shadows, Treasure takes a nice deep breath. "That's it," I tell him and reach down to pat his neck. In my mind, he's being a teacher. He's showing Lance how to breathe. The farther we go down the path, the more

Lance relaxes, finally letting his neck get long. Instead of his nervous jog, he stretches into a nice walk. Wes pats Lance and lets the reins hang loose, rewarding him for relaxing.

Treasure takes it all in. When a horse knows his job, it's the best. And Treasure doesn't just know his job. He seems to love it—being out front leading, showing the young horse the ropes. It's like he's just out for a stroll, moving in and out of the patches of sunlight, enjoying the foliage and the deep musky smells of the forest.

Then, out of nowhere, a mule deer crashes through some low branches and zigzags around some trees. Even I jump. I pull up on the reins, purely out of instinct. But I didn't need to. Treasure stays calm. Not Lance, though. He wheels around and bunches up like he's about to rear. Wes sits still. He's patient and firm with Lance. He doesn't get mad at him for spooking. Instead, he turns Lance in the direction of the deer and doesn't let him look away. *Stare at it all you want.* After Wes settles Lance down, he pats his shoulder. But where there's one deer, there's more. Sure enough, an even bigger deer careens after the first, its antlers spread out like a candelabra. This time, Lance stands and watches. Just like Treasure. When the deer are out of sight, Wes nods for me to keep going.

When we reach a nice grassy clearing, Wes motions for me to trot. He rides beside me and lets Lance break into a canter. Treasure's canter is like butter. Wes smiles. He takes the lead, and we do a couple of laps around the clearing. On Treasure, it feels more like he's skating than running.

Wes steers Lance along the edge of the woods and motions for me to follow. He's heading toward a log jump, and Lance's eyes are probably bugging out of his head, thinking the jump might reach up and bite him. But Wes's strong leg and generous bend at the elbow give the horse confidence. Lance clears it, no problem.

The moment you think about doing a jump, a good horse will know it. And Treasure is a good horse. I don't even have to ask him. He's already aiming for the log, cantering through the field with the jump in sight, almost pulling me into it. I feel his muscles collect. He knows exactly where to shorten or lengthen his stride so that, when he's at the base of the jump, he'll be in perfect position to leave the ground. I can picture myself going over it. This time, riding Treasure, I know I'll be able to do it.

As we approach, our pace and momentum are perfect. I feel the rhythm. I want Wes to look back and see how unafraid I am on Treasure. But when Wes turns, I tense. Treasure and I are five strides out, and my loose hold on the reins turns to a white-knuckled grip. My shoulders squeeze toward my ears. Sweat trickles under my shirt. *I'm a natural. I was made to jump.*

I lock my eyes on the log. My heart pounds in my ears. My breaths get shorter and shorter. The log jump now looks enormous, but I'm determined to will myself over it. Then a crate breaks open on the road. The barn key swings from the rearview mirror. I'm in the back seat of the truck. Mom's hand reaches for Dad's arm.

The ground blurs by beneath me.

One stride out, I pull Treasure to the right.

Wes looks back, shrugs his shoulders, and shakes his head. The log is a nothing jump. A couple of feet high. He rides Lance past me back to the trail. He gives me an *it's OK* look. But it's not OK. I can see he's disappointed. I'm sure he doesn't understand what just happened.

Neither do I.

CHAPTER THIRTY-SEVEN

It's first thing in the morning, and I'm in my room, standing on my bed. I remove the Man o' War paint-by-numbers, reach into the hidey-hole, and grab the envelope of cash. The price of the saddle I've had my eye on at the feed store just got slashed again. I start counting. I've got $650. Just enough. I'm unsticking a taped-up twenty from a five when I hear Dad yelling his head off downstairs.

"Reese! How many times have I told you not to leave your bike lying around?"

He's still yelling when I run into the kitchen.

"Now you have to help me get it out from under the Jeep!"

The kitchen door bangs shut behind him.

"What are you talking about? I always—"

Dad is on his hands and knees. I kneel down beside him.

"It's caught on the exhaust." He's blowing out his words like dirt's in his mouth. "I guess this is what you get for not putting your bike away." He stands up and brushes off his hands. "You know as well as I do how many times I've told you not to leave it lying around."

"But the bike was on the lawn."

"It wasn't on the lawn, Reese. You left it in the driveway."

"No I didn't."

"What's going on?" LeeAnne opens the front door and stands there like she actually might intervene.

"Stay out of it," I yell.

"Stop being a snotty-nosed little brat," he says. "You did this to yourself, and now I'm going to be late for work and you're out of a bike and you'd better pray it didn't puncture the exhaust system."

"But, Dad, I never leave it in the driveway. I always leave it on the lawn. You know that!"

"Reese, when are you going to actually take responsibility? Huh? When? That's what I'd like to know. Because I'm sick and tired of you always playing the blame game."

"But I'm not! I know where I left it!"

"Right. You left it. You didn't put it away. Like I've told you to do so many times I got sick of saying it."

Dad angry-crawls under the Jeep and tries to untangle my bike. He grunts and swears and finally drags my bike out. The frame is bent back like a taco shell, and the handlebar is backward. The chain hangs off like a cheap necklace.

"Well, there's no repairing that," Dad says. "I guess you'll be walking to the barn from now on."

"But you said anything can be fixed."

He acts like he doesn't even hear me. He gets in his Jeep and guns it. His back tires leave a pair of deep ruts in the driveway's gravel.

I look at the spot in the yard where I normally leave my bike and the spot where Dad backed over it. I know I didn't leave it there. I storm into the house. LeeAnne is in the kitchen cooking some gross-smelling thing.

"They used my bike!"

She ladles some sort of broth into her smoothie and presses BLEND. I press STOP.

"I know they used my bike. I never leave it in the drive-way. I always leave it on the lawn. They owe me a bike."

"Reese, the boys won't even ride bikes. They think any-thing without a motor is a girlie thing. Do you want me to drive you to the barn? It's on my way to work."

"I know they moved it." I wish my glare could make her skin slowly peel off.

"Well, I know they didn't, Reese. I think you owe me an apology."

"Don't hold your breath."

"Exactly, Reese. You shouldn't hold your breath so much. How about we do some nice cleansing breaths together? You're always walking around here all tensed up. That can really get your chakras all out of whack. I think your third chakra especially. I have an inkling it's blocked."

I stare at her.

"Did you seriously just spew that shit at me?"

She laughs like we're having a moment together.

"I know it sounds odd. But breathing is so helpful for clearing blockages. Helps us let go of things."

"Let go of things?"

"Look, I think you and I could really get along. You just need to breathe a little, you know. Get your energy flowing freely." She's using a rubber spatula to push a pile of shitty ingredients into her smoothie. "And it could really help you deal with losing your mom."

"Don't ever talk about my mom."

I stomp out of the kitchen and head up to my room.

"Ya know, I wouldn't mind a little more respect around here!" she calls after me.

"Talk to your chakras about it!" I yell down the stairs. "And I wouldn't get into your eucalyptus stink-bomb minivan if someone paid me a trillion dollars!"

I stuff my cash back into the envelope, toss it into the hole, and rehang the Man o' War paint-by-numbers. Spending all of my money on a new-used bike instead of the new-used saddle is totally gonna suck. I'll have to run the entire way to the barn. I know I'll be at least an hour late.

CHAPTER THIRTY-EIGHT

When I finally get to the barn, Sue is in Olive's stall. That can only mean one thing. The baby is here. My heart leaps. It's like the dark cloud that followed me here has disappeared. Carol is watching from the aisle, hands in her pockets. When she hears me coming, she looks over her shoulder.

"She have it? Is it a filly?" No one answers me. No one is talking.

I just want to get close to Olive's baby. But something, everything, stops me. The way Carol is pressing her lips together, unsmiling. Sue's bloody T-shirt. Her red-streaked gloves, already off. She's kneeling in the deep straw beside Olive.

Olive's sides are heaving in and out. Her nostrils are flared. Her tail is arced up, and just underneath it, wet as a seal, is the lumpy, bumpy shape of a foal. Its tiny rib cage doesn't rise or fall. Mucus and blood cover its eyes and mouth. It looks like it stopped right in the middle of a gallop that was so fast its ears are still pinned back. Then the afterbirth slithers out, and all I can think of are the jellyfish I saw on a field trip to the aquarium.

I kneel beside Sue. I touch a tiny hoof. It reminds me of the smooth black stones at the bottom of the creek. I want to ask what happened, but I can't say the words. It's like I've walked into a scene that's already been fast-forwarded, and I can't catch up. *But why? What happened? Someone, tell me what happened.* I still can't say the words. But when I look at Sue, I know she heard my thoughts.

"Stuck for too long. It was a big boy, and Olive could have used some help."

I stare at Sue. She looks at Olive.

"We have to get her up," says Sue, stepping around the foal. She puts her hand on Olive's neck and starts pushing. Olive's head lolls and dips, like it's too heavy for her body. Then she grunts and tries to lie out flat again. "No, no, girl. Not now." Sue tries again to push Olive upright.

Wes comes in. His boots are covered in mud. He lifts the foal up in his arms.

"Don't take him, Wes," Sue tells him. "Not yet. Let her say goodbye. Let her see him."

Wes lowers the baby back into the straw, and then he helps Sue push on Olive. They rock her back and forth and back and forth. I find a place at her haunches and push on her too. My head starts throbbing.

"Get up," I say, softly at first. But the more I push, the louder I get, until I sound angry. "Olive! Get up!" Her front legs reach out, and then she groans and finally pulls herself up, legs wide, like a baby deer.

"He's beautiful, Olive," says Sue. "He's got your lovely forehead."

I want to punch Sue. I don't want to hear how beautiful the baby is.

Sue pats Olive's shoulder. "It's OK, girl." Then Olive

lowers her head to the baby and breathes in his scent, her soft muzzle traveling down the length of his body.

"That's it," Sue says. "That's it."

Watching Sue force Olive to meet her dead baby makes my throbbing head explode.

"Stop it, Sue! Why are you making her do this? Hasn't she been through enough?"

Sue keeps patting Olive. "If she were in the wild," she says, using the same soft voice with me that she's been using with Olive, "she'd have time with him. No one would take him away. Seeing him will help her process his death. Right, girl?"

Olive looks like she could fall over dead, right on top of her baby.

"How long?" My words hardly make a sound.

No one says anything. Sue just keeps talking to Olive.

"How long was the baby stuck?" My voice is louder this time.

Sue finally looks from Olive to me. "Hard to tell."

I can't watch this any longer. I need air. I walk to the entrance of the barn. My tears feel trapped behind my eyes. I'm too angry to even cry. At the edge of the woods, Wes is using the backhoe to dig a hole. He moves the bucket in and out of the small pit, then tips the dark earth onto a mound.

Carol stands beside me. She's watching Wes too. He moves the backhoe to the side but doesn't turn the engine off. Instead, he swings the arm to another spot.

"What's he doing?" I ask Carol. "Why is he digging another hole?" Before she says anything, I already know the answer. Olive is barely able to hold herself up.

"Just in case," Carol says. "She bled a whole lot."

"But that's . . ." The words feel stuck in my chest.

Carol puts her arm around me and pats my shoulder.

"My granny was a pig farmer."

Shit. I really don't want a Carol story right now.

"One year, she let me raise a little piglet who couldn't get to its mama's milk because it wasn't as strong as the others. Floyd was a runt and just a tiny little thing. So I bottle-fed him. I loved that pig."

Is Carol really telling me about her pet pig right now?

"I carried Floyd around in my backpack until he got too big. Then he started following me around like a Labrador. One day, I got home from school and Granny told me Floyd had been run over by the tractor. A freakin' tractor. I was so mad I yelled at my granny for letting it happen. She said, 'Honey, where there's livestock, there's deadstock.'"

You are not helping, Carol. You're making it so fucking worse.

"I thought that was a terrible thing to say to a kid who'd just lost her pet pig. So I ran away. For two and a half hours."

Please stop.

Carol lifts the lid of her iced coffee and lets an ice cube slide into her mouth. She crunches it, snaps the lid back on, and finishes chomping her ice. She's done with her story.

Thank God.

"Anyway . . ."

Shoot me now.

"When I got back, I'd calmed down a bit. I was up in my room, still missing my pig, when Granny came in. She said, 'When you have a farm, you choose to surround yourself with all kinds of things you fall in love with. The dogs, the barn cats, the pets you didn't even know you wanted. Farm life is about feeling. And there are lots of opportunities to feel. Don't let an opportunity to feel something go by without letting it have its time.'"

Are you done? Please be done. Oh, please.

"I'm not gonna say it's OK."

UGH!

"Nothing that makes you sad is OK. Like Granny said, 'You're never going to like it. But you do have to accept it.' She was a pretty smart pig farmer."

Don't go on. I don't want to hear about pigs or your granny or anything else right now.

"Reese, I know you said you never cried at your mom's funeral. Well, maybe this baby is giving you that opportunity . . ."

I can't take it any longer.

"Carol, shut your fucking mouth! OK? Just shut up! You don't know when to just shut the fuck up! I can't stand your stories anymore. I don't care about your fucking pig or your granny or the lessons you learned. OK? They're stupid to me. Don't you get it? They're stupid fucking stories!"

Carol stands there in her flannel shirt, which she probably has fourteen of, her mouth hanging open like she was just getting ready to start another story. I pick up her iced coffee and throw it against the wall. My chin trembles. Carol's mouth shuts. She looks down in the aisle at her dirt-covered ice and cracked cup. Hurt. I run out of the barn and up the trail into the woods.

I don't go back to the barn until Carol and Sue are gone. Wes is still driving the backhoe at the edge of the woods, operating the bucket in and out of the second pit, making another mound of cool, damp earth. I try to feed some sweet grain to Olive by hand, but she won't even smell it. She curls her nostrils and looks away, so I toss it back into the bucket. I dip my hand into some water and try to force a few drops between her lips. She lets her lips hang loose and looks away. I leave the barn and trudge up the hill to Wes.

He's sitting at the edge of the hole with the baby in his arms. Its long legs are like stalks with big, knobby bumps. They dangle from his arms. Wes slides the small body into the hole and lays him down.

I back away as Wes climbs out and picks up his shovel. I don't want to watch the clumps of earth landing on the foal. Covering its eyes, its nose. Making it disappear completely. Like it was never here. Like all those months of Olive's pregnancy meant nothing. Nothing to show for her tired muscles and stretched belly.

I stay back until Wes has completely filled in the grave. He pats the earth down with the back side of his shovel, making a flat brown square in the grass. Then he disappears into the second hole. I hear his shovel scraping rocks, its blade chopping a root. While Wes keeps working, making cuts and grooves into the clay, I stand at the edge of the pit. He won't give me a look. He doesn't write a note or point at anything. But I know what he's thinking. To him, she's already gone. I know she's too weak to even keep her ears up. But my chest tightens when I think about this grave waiting for Olive while she's still breathing air.

"She's not dead yet." My voice sounds dry. I bite off bits of skin from my chapped lips. I taste the saltiness of dried blood. A coolness is rising from the crumbling dirt. Wes keeps digging.

"Wes. She's still here. Please don't act like she's already gone."

His silence makes me feel like my head could erupt. He swings his shovel two more times. Then he stops. He tosses the shovel up onto the grass and climbs out of the grave.

He gives me a look that says, OK. *You win. For now.*

As I follow Wes back to the barn, I feel a sharp pain, like someone's poking a hot needle into my heart. My legs almost give out. I think about the day. About how things could have gone differently. If only I hadn't been late. If only I'd left an hour earlier. If only I hadn't spent all that time counting my money and fighting with LeeAnne. If only I'd taken her up on her offer to drive me. Then I might have been here on time. Then I might have seen Olive struggling. Then I might have had just enough time to call Sue. Then I might have . . .

I can never be late again.

CHAPTER THIRTY-NINE

I wake up thinking of the foal lying in the wet straw, his legs stretched out like he was in a full gallop. Eyes closed. Blood in the crease of his mouth. The house is quiet. My feet are still hanging off the edge of the bed like I haven't moved since I laid down. In the dim morning light, I can see that the watermark on the ceiling has grown a mane and a tail. It must have rained overnight. Cold. Wet. Like the foal. Today definitely doesn't feel like a holiday.

The first thing I need to do is buy the bike I saw for sale at the hardware store. It's open until noon. It seems like everyone needs to make an emergency run to the hardware store on a holiday. And my bike situation is definitely an emergency.

The tag on the bike said it's slightly used, but from the look of it, I think they might be slightly fibbing. I don't care either way. I need whatever they're selling right now.

I stand on my bed, take down Man o' War, and grab the envelope. I pull on my boots, fly down the stairs, and sprint through the front yard past Dad. He's set up the smoker grill, which looks like a tiny train engine puffing smoke and going nowhere.

"Where's the fire?" Dad calls after me. But I'm too focused to answer. "And a happy Fourth of July to you too," he calls out after me.

I run past Cody and Kyle in their camouflage gear. A pile of dead squirrels lies at the edge of the yard, and their guns lean against a tree. They're both looking up at the sky, heads in sync, following some remote-control thing.

But wait. The envelope in my hand doesn't feel right. It's too light. I open it and see a few fives and tens, but most of it's gone. Must have fallen out when I grabbed it in such a hurry. I run back to the house. The front door bangs behind me.

"Hey, Reese, want a cupcake? Just getting started on the frosting," says LeeAnne as I dash through the kitchen.

I look around my bedroom floor. I toss dirty clothes out of the way. I pull the blanket off my bed, then the pillows, then the sheets. I check the space between the bed and the wall. Nothing. I don't bother kicking off my dirty boots before I stand on the bed and lift the Man o' War painting off the nail. I reach into the hole. Just crumbs of plaster. Did cash get stuck to the back of the painting? Did I hide it someplace else? It must be something simple like that. Something I'm forgetting. It will come to me. I sit on the bed and try to remember.

Then I hear a whirring sound outside. The boys' mini-spaceship thing is hovering just inches from my window. I walk over to get a closer look, and whatever-it-is looks at me with one eye. It tilts and buzzes and circles above the yard, where Kyle and Cody are looking up at me, laughing. That's when I know.

I can taste the hate. It's both sour and bitter, like acid. It dries my mouth and swells my tongue. Not only are they in my home, sleeping in what used to be Mom's sewing room, eating at my table, spreading out on my couch, watching my TV, they're in the fucking air, looking through my window. They're claiming space I didn't even know it was possible to claim.

I leave my room in what doesn't even feel like my own body. Instead of turning left and going downstairs, I turn right and stop at their bedroom door, which is already slightly open. I push it all the way. Their normal pigsty has a new layer of debris—a freshly opened cardboard box, large chunks of Styrofoam, at least four sheets of bubble wrap, a plastic bag the size of a small parachute, and an instruction manual. I step into the room, pick up the bag, and pull out a receipt.

Gatorade $3.50
2 Snickers bars $4.75
DJI Phantom drone $699.00

My legs give out beneath me and I fall to the floor. The drone is still buzzing and dipping and darting. I get up and look out of their window. Cody is stepping around the squirrel kills, controller in hand, while Kyle watches. Dad, clueless, is slathering the brisket with juice. I stomp downstairs and out to the porch.

"Give. Me. My. Money. Back."

"We didn't take it," Cody says.

"I know you did, you little bastards."

"What? Are you calling us liars?" Kyle shoves his phone in my face to show me a picture the drone took of me when it was hovering outside my bedroom window. I'm making an expression I don't ever want to remember, but Kyle has it on his phone forever. "Look who's a big crybaby," he says.

Cody laughs. "Look who's a crazy girl!"

"They stole my money!" I yell at Dad, who's finally paying attention. "I had six hundred and fifty dollars. They must have seen me put it in my spot yesterday."

"What spot? You have a spot?" Then he says, "That's a lot of money, babe," like I'm eight and I'm showing him coins from my piggy bank. He pats my shoulder and even tries to hug me. "But I'm sure they didn't take it."

I want to scream, but if I do, they'll all nod to each other and raise their eyebrows like I'm not even here. *Yup. We knew it. She's crazy.*

"Well, where did they get the money for the drone, then?"

"Their father gave it to them for their birthdays."

"And you actually believe their shit? You actually believe them instead of me?"

Then I do scream. It just vomits out of me. I never should have told Dad about the money. I never should have told him about seeing the wild horses. I never should have told him anything. Why even bother if he never believes me?

Dad orders me to my room to calm down and "get a hold of myself." Even facedown on my bed with my pillow covering my head, even over my sobs, I can hear them. Everyone is having such a fucking lovely conversation. Talking over each other. Joking. Laughing. Like the theft never happened. Like the boys didn't just completely ruin my life. Time to interrupt this brunch. Time to demand some justice. Time to get my money back. I march downstairs. I am ready for this fight with Cody and Kyle and

LeeAnne. But when I open my mouth, it's Dad I tell off. Out of me come words that have been so trapped beneath so many layers for so many months, they seem musty.

"Why didn't you cry at Mom's funeral?"

Everyone stops. Kyle and Cody look at each other. Lee-Anne pushes food around on her plate. Dad stops drinking his beer, mid-sip. He lowers the bottle. I've cornered him.

"It's complicated, Reese."

"Try me."

He looks at me funny because that's something Mom always used to say.

"This is a conversation we should have another time," he says, just like he's reading the words from a book. When he stands to get something out of the pantry, I can't take another second of it. I follow right behind him.

"I hate you!"

I'm not sure what I say next. But I'm sure that my arms are waving in the air. I'm sure that I'm beating on his chest with my fists. I'm sure that I'm screaming. I'm sure that he's just standing there.

"Why?" I yell. "Why are you letting me hit you?"

LeeAnne and the boys are standing, watching.

"Stop this, Reese!" LeeAnne yells. "Joe, do something!"

But he doesn't do anything. The most he does is lift his chin high enough so that my wild hands won't hit him in the face. Then, out of an exhaustion I've never known, I stop. My hands fall to my sides. I can't look at him. I stumble back out of the kitchen and collapse on the living room floor.

"Shit, man. I told you she was crazy," says Cody.

"Dude, she went apeshit," adds Kyle.

"Joe, please, this just isn't right," says LeeAnne.

I get up and run out into the yard.

"Eat shit and die!" I yell as loud as I can. But eating shit isn't anywhere near disgusting enough to make up for what they've done.

CHAPTER FORTY

I take the path through the woods to the barn. My feet know exactly where to go. I avoid the roots, the rocky edges. I know which tree trunks are best to hold on to when I step across the creek. Like I can step into footprints I've already made. Footprints from two years ago.

Thick branches overhead block the sunlight. After I cross the creek, I stop. "Where are you?" I yell. Dad said I'd conjured them up. Well, right now I'm trying to. I listen for the drumbeat, wait for the breathing, but the only pounding is my heart, the only breath my own. Then I hear a noise off the trail. I pull branches back and look beyond the undergrowth and brambles. Nothing.

I run the rest of the way to the barn and head straight to Olive. She's standing in her stall. Ghostlike. Still. Not a twitch of an ear. Not even a swish of her tail to swat away the flies that are swarming and buzzing around her belly. I open the door and approach her.

"What's going on here, girl?" I wave my hand to shoo the most stubborn flies away. One of her teats is swollen. I can feel the heat coming off it. "Oh, poor baby," I whisper. Mom would have made a hot compress for an infection like this. I fill a bucket with hot water and grab some clean hand towels from the tack room.

I dip a towel into the hot water, wring out the excess into the shavings, and place it on the shiny red tissue. Then I dial Sue's number. *Please don't let Carol answer. Please don't let Carol answer.* The wall near the barn door still has a dark stain where Carol's iced coffee landed. I put the phone on speaker and toss it into the shavings at my feet. When Sue answers the phone after eleven rings, she has a raspy morning voice. I tell her about Olive.

"It feels like I'm pressing on a rock."

"Yeah, she was engorged," says Sue. "She might kick because it's so painful."

"I'm so sorry, girl," I say, knowing that what I'm doing must hurt like hell. But she just lays her ears back and lets me press down. It's like she's left her body. Finally, the hot compress softens the blockage in the infected teat, and four straight streams of liquid flow out of her nipple.

"This doesn't look like milk. This stuff is thickish and yellowish."

"Some of that is the infection," says Sue. "But most of it is colostrum. That's what the baby would drink before the milk comes in. It boosts the immune system."

The shavings soak up Olive's precious colostrum. How sad it is that it's become unnecessary.

"She seems so weak."

Olive's belly is still stretched from the pregnancy, but under the stretched skin, she's gaunt.

"Has she eaten today?" Sue asks.

"No. Her bowl is still full from yesterday."

"Some mares have a really tough time after a stillborn.

They don't really get over it. They lose the will to live. She might be punishing herself."

"Punishing herself? Why would Olive ever punish herself for something she can't help?" I run my hand over Olive's bony shoulder. It seems so crazy to me. But Olive did go off her food right after she gave birth. And now she looks like she just wants to let the wind blow her away. "Don't punish yourself, girl. It's not your fault."

"Place the stethoscope over Olive's heart. You're listening to see if her heartbeat is weak or strong."

I listen to the *lub dub, lub dub.*

"It sounds faint. Like it's far away. But it's steady, at least."

"Would be good if you could get her to drink. If I have to, I can give her some IV fluids. But if she's not going to eat and drink on her own, the IV might just be postponing the inevitable."

"The inevitable? Don't say that, Sue. I'm not giving up on Olive. Fuck the inevitable."

"You're doing everything you can for now, Reese. Call me if she gets worse."

I want to tell Sue I'll call her when Olive gets *better.* But I can hear it in her voice. She thinks I should be praying for a miracle.

A couple of hours later, Wes pulls up with a big load of hay. He parks his truck under the loft window near the automated hoist. Sometimes it works and sometimes it doesn't. Today it doesn't. For the hoist to work right, the winch and pully need to slide smoothly on a wooden track. But the nails that hold the track down pop out of the rotten wood on a regular basis. Wes needs to replace a few nails each time he uses it. He'll need the drill and the 5/16 drill bit, so I head out to the supply room, leaving Olive to get some needed rest.

The supply room is like an odds-and-ends closet, the place where everything random ends up. Broken tack. Torn blankets. Rakes with missing prongs. I get to the drill without a problem, but I have to clear a path to get to the bits. When I lean down to move a broken rake, I get a whiff of something foul. It's sort of dead rat with a hint of puke. Then I spot the source. A bucket I'd set in the corner so no one would trip over it while I watched Sue check on Treasure's old suspensory. Yup. That bucket is full of smegma.

Gross.

I hold the bucket as far away from my body as possible and go outside to empty it. Most of the white paste creeps out onto the dried leaves and needles, but the slimiest and thickest stuff sticks to the bottom. I pick up a stick and scrape the gloppy goo until it begins to travel down the bucket's sides. It's completely gross. It's thick as cream cheese frosting.

Then I stop.

I let it slowly ooze back down into the bucket.

Maybe it's just the kind of gross I need to make me happy.

My phone buzzes in my pocket. *It's the Fourth of July! I've been smoking a brisket since 4 am. LeeAnne has been baking all day. Get back to the house to celebrate and act grateful for once.*

Overall, his text is weirdly cheerful and forgiving. As if all I did today was forget to say please and thank you. Do they have some new parental strategy? Did someone actually give them some good advice? Maybe they gave Dr. Monroe an emergency call.

I quickly text back. *Really sorry I lost it today Dad. Just having a shitty day but I shouldn't have taken it out on you. I'll be home soon. Please tell LeeAnne that I breathed into my third chakra and feel much better now. And tell her that cupcakes are my favorite.* Emoji cupcake, cupcake, cupcake, fork, American flag, fireworks, smiley face. And just for me, I add a rocket that looks a lot like a wiener.

I find a Chock full o' Nuts coffee can in the garbage, pour in some smegma, put the lid on, and carry it home.

CHAPTER FORTY-ONE

When I walk into the house, it smells like butter and cream and vanilla. Freshly whipped frosting is sitting in a bowl under the mixer. The beaters are covered in tiny, perfect cones. Blue and red sprinkles for dipping sit next to the plate of golden cupcakes. How fucking festive. I take the lid off the coffee can, but when I hear someone coming, I snap it back on again and stash the can in the dish towel drawer.

Dad and LeeAnne walk in. They're holding hands, which makes me want to puke in their faces. But I smile.

"Happy Fourth," says LeeAnne.

"Same."

"Something smells kind of funky," Dad says, sniffing the air.

"You always say that when I use all organic ingredients," says LeeAnne.

"I can't wait to taste these cupcakes. Can I help you decorate?"

Dad and LeeAnne give each other a quick smile. Dad's dopey smile is all I-knew-she'd-come-around. And LeeAnne's is all see-I-told-you-all-she-had-to-do-was-learn-to-breathe.

LeeAnne lets go of Dad's hand, and she joins me at the counter.

"Of course you can help. What a nice change that will be. The boys just want to eat them. I've been slapping their grubby hands off them all day."

"Well, the cupcakes look so delicious, I don't blame them."

"Joe, why don't you go and get the boys to help with the brisket? Let Reese and me have some girl time."

Dad backs up to go out the door, looking like he can't believe his eyes. He glances at me. It's just a glance. But he catches my eye and raises one eyebrow and gives me a look. I stand there smiling at him, but there's a spot in my throat I can't swallow past. Because he's giving me *the* look. The look I haven't seen in a really, really long time. The look that means, *You OK?*

And I nod.

"Be right back," LeeAnne says. "Just have to grab a few things out of the minivan."

"Take your time," I tell her.

I watch her through the kitchen window. She disappears off the back porch. I look back and forth between the bowl of frosting and the coffee can of smegma. Thirty seconds ago, it was going to make me happy. Why did Dad have to give me the look now? I was so ready to silently cheer as I watched these assholes eat the grossest thing imaginable. And now, when I'm so close to knowing how good it will make me feel, I can't stop thinking of Dad's look.

LeeAnne is saying something to Dad about how good the brisket smells. I peel the lid off the coffee can and stare at the sticky white blob inside. I don't have much time. Dad calls to LeeAnne to taste something. I look through the window. He and LeeAnne and the boys are smiling at each other, looking so happy. LeeAnne kisses him and heads back to her minivan. *Fuck the look.*

I use a spatula to scrape the smegma into the frosting bowl and turn the beaters on. I add extra vanilla to cover the foul smell and then spray the room full of LeeAnne's apple-kiwi room freshener. I use a butter knife to spread each cupcake's top with a thick layer of the goopy white frosting mixture. I dip one of the frosted cupcakes into the bowl of red sprinkles, and another into the bowl of blue sprinkles. Then I dip one into both red and blue.

"I'm back!" LeeAnne says, bursting through the door. "Sorry! I forgot!"

I run past LeeAnne, who's standing there holding a shopping bag and half a dozen party hats. They have shiny silver stars all around, and red and white streamers spew from the tops.

"Gotta go!"

———◆———

When you suspect you've just turned your life to total shit, maybe there's no better place to go than a shit pile. And the barn has one that's practically a mountain. It's in extreme need of shoveling, and I've been shoveling for over an hour. My hands are blistered, but if I grip the handle of the pitchfork tight, they sting a little less, and I can keep going. A blister tears open, and I stop to inspect the red, shiny skin underneath the white flap. Then I hear the sound I've been expecting since I got here. A minivan is flying down the driveway toward the barn, surrounded by a cloud of dust. The muffler scrapes on the ruts from going so fast. Ever since I texted Kyle and Cody the recipe for the frosting, ever since

I sent them a video called "How to Clean a Sheath," I knew it was just a matter of time before LeeAnne came for me.

She's not slowing down.

I don't know whether to keep shoveling or run. So I stand there, frozen on top of this gargantuan mountain of shit. LeeAnne pulls right up to the barn, even though Wes doesn't let any vehicle but his go past the front paddock. She opens her door before she fully stops the car. Then she's out of it and charging toward me. She stops and glares, her eyes narrowed into slits, her lips and jaw so tight they might break. Before she speaks, she takes in where I'm standing, her eyes crisscrossing back and forth around the mound of rotting dung.

"You are a disgusting little brat." Her hands are shaking at her sides. She wants to come after me, but her nose wrinkles, and I can tell the smell stings her eyes. Flies swarm her feet. She takes a step back.

Now Dad's Jeep comes bouncing down the ruts, gathering its own dust cloud. It skids to a stop, and he explodes out of the door.

"LeeAnne!" He runs toward her, loafers slipping around in the mud. "LeeAnne! Listen. I'm sure it's not as bad as you think."

"Oh, really? Really, Joe? Feeding my boys horse semen isn't as bad as I think? She needs help, Joe. I've told you that. Serious help."

Dad looks at me. His eyes are pleading.

"Reese?"

I look back and forth between my dad and LeeAnne. For a second, I want things to go back to the way they were. Back to when Dad wasn't paying me any attention and LeeAnne was just his annoying girlfriend.

"I didn't."

Dad breathes out, letting his shoulders drop. He even smiles. "See, hon. I knew she'd never do such a thing."

"It was smegma." At least I wasn't lying.

LeeAnne bends over and heaves right into my horseshit fortress. Then she reaches into her pocketbook and pulls out a small brown paper bag. She throws it at me, as high as she can, up into the air. Cash floats out of it and lands on the manure pile all around me. The sun hits one of the bills just right. There's no denying it. My taped-up twenty.

"The boys never took your damn money, Reese. Nobody did. After you accused my boys, I went looking for the money myself. I found your *spot*. Your little hole-in-the-wall savings bank. The money was sitting right there on top of the twenty towels you had stuffed down there."

Then Dad gives me a look. Not *the* look, but a look that says he doesn't know me. A look that says he doesn't care if he ever sees my face again.

Fine. Maybe you won't have to. Maybe I'll never go home again.

CHAPTER FORTY-TWO

That night, I gather up some saddle blankets and make myself a bed right next to Olive. For the next few nights, I let my body curl into her big, bony back. During the days, I hardly leave her side. But Olive doesn't get better. She gets worse. She won't eat. She won't drink. She lies down in the shavings, and I can't get her up. There are no more instructions from Sue, from anyone. So I just sit with Olive. I hum to her. I let my cheek press against her cheek. I blow softly into her barely fluttering nostrils. I pray this will give her some strength. I pray that she will fight. I pray that Sue and Wes are wrong. I wrap my arm around her. And I fall asleep swearing that if she goes, I'm going with her.

There's a moment that happens when you ride. First, the horse is in control, then you are in control, then the horse, then the two feelings melt into each other—*that* moment. It's the same with thoughts and dreams. There's that moment when you don't know if your thoughts are melting into your dreams or if your dreams are blending into your thoughts. It happens right when you give up a little control. When you start to let go a little. When you *loosen your hold.*

So I don't know exactly when I go from knowing I'm curled up on the barn floor next to Olive to dreaming I'm a baby in my mother's arms. We're in a field, and she's tossing me up into the air. I go up and down and into her arms over and over. She's smiling. The space between us scares me, but when her arms reach toward me, I smile too. Then I laugh that baby laugh from my belly. I'm having so much fun.

Mom's black hair winds around her like a long, flowing dress. She's telling me something, but I'm in the air above her. Her voice sounds like she's at the end of a long tunnel. Each time I come down into her waiting arms, I try to hear what she's saying. Over and over, her lips form the same words, but I don't hear any sound. Then, just before the last time she catches me, I hear her voice. I make out her words.

You will see.

Then I land on the back of the black horse. He gallops at a speed that blurs the world around me. I am in a tangle of mane. His breath is all I hear. I'm too afraid to cry. He stops in front of my house. Dad is on the porch. Right where I left him. After my rage. He is alone. I reach for him, but he can't see me. The horse's giant mane hides me like a veil. His black coat blends into the night. But I am so close to Dad. If he would just reach out, I could tell him I'm sorry. I could tell him how much I miss him. But he turns and walks inside the house.

Then there's nothing but the black horse and me. Only swirls of color all around us until we stop, and then we are in a sea of wild horses. They make way for the majestic animal that towers over them all, creating a path that leads us to the barn. On either side, horses welcome us. When we enter the barn, the black horse's head almost touches the beams above.

Olive is lying in her stall. The black horse calls to her, but she's too weak to respond. He arches his neck over her door and reaches his big head down to her nose. Her nostrils quiver. Then she is still again.

I scream. I'm beating on the black horse's back with all my might. *Is he taking Olive's last breath?* But I have no power. I want to turn and find my dad, but I'm being pulled upward. I'm warm and light. I hear a whisper. *You will see.* Then a soft tingling runs up and down my spine, and I'm awake. I'm not sure where I am until I see the blades of sunshine that slice between the slats in the stall. Dust particles float and spin in the light. I hear munching and stirring in the hay. I sit up.

"Olive?"

She's up. She's standing. She's eating hay.

"Olive!"

I reach out and touch her. She pushes me with her nose, like she's being playful. I lean into her shoulder. She munches away like nothing ever happened. She's breathing normally. She shakes her head and blows dust out of her nose. She shifts her feet. She looks at me with her clear, sweet eyes that say, *What were you ever so worried about?* If happiness is something you can see, it's the gentle nose of a big dumb horse who has no idea how much you love her.

I hear the rattle of Wes's truck and the slam of the door.

"Wes!"

I don't want to take my eyes off Olive. I'm afraid this is some kind of a trick and if I blink, she'll be replaced by the sick, dying Olive.

"Wes!"

Wes comes running over, looking like something's scared him half to death. The way I yelled must have made him think something awful happened. He looks around the stall like he's trying to find the sick Olive. But as soon as he sees her standing there, his face softens. I laugh.

"She's OK, Wes!"

He stands there, frozen for a minute. He still looks confused. Then he crawls under the stall guard and stands in the deep shavings with Olive and me. He reaches out and touches her, just like I did. Like he wants to make sure she's real. Olive's ears move forward and back, listening to the morning noises. She's alert and content. And the way she buries her nose into the hay makes me so happy I can't help but hug Wes with all my might. It feels like I'm hugging a tree, but I don't let go. Finally, he hugs me back.

"She's OK." I put both my hands on his arms and look him square in the eye. "It was the horses, Wes. The same horses I've been wanting so much to tell you about ever since they showed up at the auction and made sure I saw Treasure. But I was afraid you'd think I was crazy. Well, they were here. In the middle of the night. The big one, the leader, he breathed into her and made her better. Look, Wes. He healed her. She looks like she was never even sick."

I let go of his arms, then I fly around the barn, looking for evidence to prove to him that the black horse really was here. "Tracks . . . there must be . . . there and then here . . . and he was . . ."

Wes is just staring at me. I need to make him understand exactly what happened. "The herd came right up to the barn. They waited for him outside. There might have been a hundred of them. Maybe more. All gorgeous. But the big one. He's the one that walked into the barn and went right up to Olive . . ."

But he stops me. He waits until I calm my hands, which were flapping around like a trapped bird's wings, and leads me to the whiteboard. He picks up the red marker. Underneath *Marge and Jasper turn out 2 pm–6 pm,* he slowly and carefully writes.

She got better because
you believed she would.

Wes caps the marker and pats me on the head. I open my eyes as wide as I can so he can see they're brimming not just with tears but with truth.

"But I didn't believe, Wes. What happened with that black horse and Olive was a miracle. Some things are real even if you don't believe."

The next day, Olive's folder is out on Wes's desk with a note attached. *FOR REESE.* Inside are Olive's papers. Beside the word *owner,* Wes has crossed out his name. In its place, he's written *Reese Marie Tucker.* Sale price, one dollar. I slip three quarters, two dimes, and a nickel into his desk drawer. Then I dance all the way back to Olive's stall.

CHAPTER FORTY-THREE

The only downside to a miracle is that it makes you feel even worse about the crappy things you've done. It sort of forces you to go over in your mind how maybe you could have done things differently. Especially when you feel like you didn't do anything to deserve the miracle at all.

I mean, knowing that Kyle and Cody crammed their mouths full of smegma cupcakes did make me happy for a nanosecond, but it didn't give me the lasting effect I was looking for. I couldn't stop thinking about Dad and the look that day. The one I saw all the time when it was still just Dad and me. When it seemed like we were both on the same track. When we'd end up in the kitchen around the same time in the middle of the night because we both had trouble sleeping. Or when we saw something that reminded us both of Mom. We wouldn't have to say anything. We'd just give each other the look. That's all we needed to do.

Then he started going out. A lot. And the look stopped.

Now I'll never see the look again. Not after what I did on the Fourth.

Worth it?

This is how the shit went down after LeeAnne drove away from the manure pile and Dad forced me to have a "conversation" about what happened. He said no daughter of his would ever do such a horrific thing and I said well I guess that means I'm not your daughter. He said I better straighten up and get my act together and I said thanks for being such a great role model. He said I love you Reese and I don't know why you won't let anyone help you. I said I hate you and I don't need any help. And then I moved into the barn.

Then, a few days after the "smegma thing," I got a frantic call from Dad. He said I had to go home immediately and apologize to LeeAnne because she doesn't know what I might be capable of next. He said she already sent the boys to live with their father, and she's packing to leave. I said in that case I was glad I fed them the smegma cupcakes. He said, that's it! I'm going to pick you up now to take you home to apologize, and then you need to see a therapist every day for a solid week. I said good, they've been so much help so far. He said, do you know what your mother would think? I said I don't care, she's dead.

It's not like I don't know you could take my speech right out of any handbook called *How to Act Like a Teenager*, but believe me, if my body or brain would have let me say anything different, I would have. But trying to save Dad and me would be a lot harder than just letting go with both hands—just letting it be over. Done. I know he doesn't love me. He doesn't give two shits. Why try to save something that feels like it's been torn to shreds? Something that can't be saved? Dad's right. I don't care about anything but myself. And LeeAnne's right. I'm a disaster. And Kyle and Cody are right. I'm crazy. And Lexi is right. I might be pretty if I had a different face.

But still, Dad insisted I apologize to LeeAnne. And in the end, I didn't say no.

❧

Dad's Jeep makes the turn off the main road and pulls down the driveway to the barn. I get in without saying a word. He turns the Jeep around and we head toward the house. He pulls up to a stop sign on Camel Hump Road.

"If only you didn't lie all the time," he says, looking left and right and left again.

"I'm not the only one doing the lying," I whisper, staring out my window.

"What exactly does that mean?"

"You're the one who started with the lies."

"When did I lie to you?" he asks, like he really doesn't know.

"For one, you said we'd get the barn back. But you knew you never planned to."

"I tried to tell you. You wouldn't hear it."

"You lied by having all of those girlfriends."

"OK. It wasn't right, but how was it lying?"

"It's the exact same thing as lying. You lied by walking around with your beard and ignoring me. You never *really* wanted to spend time with me. You only started spending time with me when the therapist told you that you *should*. Not because you wanted to. So don't lie to me. You don't really care. Don't you think that being with someone who's only spending time with you because they think they should is even worse than being alone?"

Dad does a big sigh. He doesn't even want to answer the question. Instead, he answers my question with a question.

"Where do we go from here, Reese?"

"Go fuck yourself."

"Nice."

"Well, what do you want me to say?"

He clears his throat.

"As soon as I find you a new therapist, you need to talk about why you did the smegma thing. Why you thought that was OK." He pulls into the driveway and skids to a stop. "Now get in there and apologize to LeeAnne!"

When I walk through the front door, LeeAnne is surprised to see me. She's sitting at the kitchen table, smoking. I never knew she smoked. She takes the cigarette out of her mouth. Her hand reaches for a glass on the table. She takes a sip. She's still in her nightgown. It has penguins on it. They're playing with a beach ball. Her reverse bob is flat, and the white of her scalp is showing.

"Dad told me you were leaving."

I close the door behind me, but I don't let go of the knob. I pretend like I don't see her cigarette and her drink, like I don't notice she's still in her nightie at noon.

"I just wanted to say sorry. Sorry for the smegma thing."

LeeAnne swirls the liquid in her glass, clinking some ice.

"It's a little late for that, don'tcha think?"

I don't answer.

"Ya know, young lady . . ." She chews the ice in her whiskey or whatever it is. "You haven't cornered the market on pain."

Her eyes are red and puffy. Her voice is raspy. There's a stillness in the kitchen that feels unnatural. No hum of the refrigerator or whoosh of a fan or tick of a clock to take away the heaviness of the silence. It's the first time I really wish I hadn't done the smegma thing. I don't know what to say. So I say, "OK."

"Just know that I never took your father from you. You can push someone away just as easily as you can pull them to you."

"OK," I manage to say again, barely.

"And no one replaces anyone in this life. You just wanted to blame me because it was easier for you to do that than to admit your dad could love someone else. Because you think his doing that would just erase your mother a little bit more."

She takes another drink. This time she gulps it. Then she sets the glass down and pushes her chair back. She slowly stands. Like it hurts her to straighten. She doesn't look at me. Just leaves the kitchen and walks up the stairs. She doesn't bother turning around when she says a few more words, which don't fully hit me until I'm back out on the porch.

"Try to be a little kinder to the next one. We're all dealing with our own shit."

PART THREE

CHAPTER FORTY-FOUR

As it turns out, you can't feed people smegma cupcakes and get away scot-free. Whether you feel bad about it or not, you can't put the toothpaste back in the tube. And you can't put the smegma back either. Horse people spread that kind of news like a bad rash. And it sounds worse every time it gets retold. No matter how much of a pain in the ass the smegma eaters may have been, the general public just doesn't like the idea of someone being fed smegma. It's really frowned upon. The same social media that saved the barn is now my worst enemy. "Reese's revenge cupcakes recipe" sort of went viral. And any way you slice it, that ain't good for business.

When Sue heard about it, she stopped by the barn, hoping it was just a rumor.

"You actually put it in the frosting?"

I nodded.

She looked away with a grimace, then looked back at me. "Seriously?"

I nodded again.

"It's creative," she said, shaking her head. "I'll give you that. But remind me to never eat anything you've baked."

I could tell she was disappointed in me, even though she tried to joke about it. She walked to her truck, still shaking her head, and got on the phone, I'm pretty sure to Carol, who I still owe an apology. The last words I heard Sue say before she closed her truck's door were *smegma cupcakes*.

Smegma cupcakes. Yup. The reason lessons are canceling left and right.

Now the only income we have is from Blake. As dismal as it sounds, he's the reason we can still turn on the lights. Wes riding Gator in the Black Elk is our last hope for keeping the barn going. And Blake knows it. He and Lexi walk around the place giving orders to Wes and me like they own the Big Green Barn. Thank God the race is only a month away. Wes will win the race—everyone knows that—and we'll finally get things back on track.

It's the kind of day that's so beautiful you want to drink in the air. The kind of day that makes you believe anything is possible. If I weren't so preoccupied with thinking about the race, I'd be soaking in the warmth of the sun instead of pushing a wheelbarrow full of horseshit. But all I can think about is Wes collecting his money and us starting fresh.

In Wes's office, Blake has been busy drawing something on the whiteboard. He's standing in front of it, pointing at it with the blade of his pocketknife. I set down the wheelbarrow and walk closer. He's drawn a track that winds and loops around and takes up the entire board. It's the Black Elk course. It looks like a five-year-old drew it. At the top of the board is an outline of the jagged foothills. A squiggly line that I know is the Ghost Hawk River snakes from one end of the board to the other. He's drawn smiley faces where the spectators stand. He's sketched in some obstacles. He's got the fences at the beginning of the track before it winds up into the Black Hills. He's got the canyons. He's got the ravines.

"Then, when you come up in here," he's telling Wes, "give him a breather. Let him catch his breath while the others wear themselves out." He's taking bite-slurps of his apple and storing bits of it in his cheek.

The hair on the back of my neck stands up. Blake talking like he knows more than Wes. As if he has a clue. Steam must be pouring out of Wes's ears. But that's what happens when you take people's money. You have to listen to them.

Blake points the tip of his blade at the head of a stick-figure rider whose stick-figure horse is falling into the Ghost Hawk. "This shit-for-brains took the turn too close to the edge of the bank. Right into the deepest rapids. Better not be you, Wes. And whatever you do, don't let Patrick's horse pass you here. Don't miss an opportunity to check Patrick when you're up in the woods. Slam him into a tree if you have to."

Wes has had enough. He stomps out of the office, but Blake follows him through the barn. He watches as Wes puts Gator on the cross ties and tacks him up for a session.

"Here's the thing, Wes." Blake puts his hands on his hips and jiggles his jaw. "You gotta ask everything of this horse. He can do it. I saw it the moment I laid eyes on him."

Wes doesn't nod. He just leads Gator past Blake and out to the ring.

After a few minutes of warm-up, Wes guides Gator into a combination that ends in a four-foot straight bar with no ground rail. There's lots of air between the bar and the ground. Some of the best horses have trouble knowing when to take off, but Gator makes easy work of it. He flies over everything Wes aims him at. After the last jump, Gator tosses his head and flicks his tail like he might buck, but Wes sits tight, lets him slow to a trot, and then pats him on the neck.

After Wes cools Gator down, he leads him into the barn. He attaches the cross ties, and I slip off the sweaty bridle and fill a bucket with hot water. I sponge Gator off and put a clean mesh sheet on him to wick away the dampness.

Blake is leaning against his truck, watching Wes like he owns him.

"Kick his ass if he acts up."

After I finish the outside chores for the day and dump the last wheelbarrow of manure, I head back inside to say good-bye to Wes. But first I'll have to walk by Blake. My skin crawls just thinking of going anywhere near him, but there's no avoiding it. He's talking on his cell phone and checking out his reflection on the side of his shiny new truck. Kenny Chesney's "She Thinks My Tractor's Sexy" blares from the speakers. Rattler's drooling, panting head bobs out through the open rear window. When I walk by, he's laughing into his phone. Then he leans forward, tilts his head to the side, and blows out a snot rocket. "Tracked that buck for five miles," he brags. "He left a trail of blood you could've seen from a plane . . ." I fantasize about filling his exhaust pipe with manure and watching his truck blow to smithereens.

In the office, Wes is staring at the whiteboard, shaking his head. I stand beside him, but he doesn't seem to notice.

He's too busy looking at Blake's winding map and arrows and circles. His eyes cross and recross the map. Blake walks in and mouth-breathes over his shoulder. Wes grabs a rag, wipes the whiteboard clean, and picks up a marker.

He can jump anything, he writes.

Blake stomps his foot and slaps Wes on the back. "Ha! You got that right."

Wes keeps writing. *But he's not fast enough.*

Blake's face falls. He pushes his chest out, steps toward Wes.

"What the fuck are you talkin' about, bro? Not fast enough?"

Wes holds up a hand and continues writing. *It will depend on the footing, which horses scratch, how hot it is.*

Blake's eyes dart from Wes to me to the board. He looks like a kid who just found out that Santa isn't real.

"Well, there must be something we can do about that," says Blake, like Wes could mix a magic potion to make Gator go faster.

Wes shakes his head no.

And just like that, our only plan goes up in smoke. I feel like a complete idiot. How could I have forgotten all of the warnings Mom and Dad heard when we entered Treasure? Don't put all your eggs in one basket. You're more likely to win the lottery. You're more likely to get struck by lightning. You're more likely to have a two-headed dog. I think about saying something. But I don't. Gator winning was the only thing that could have saved the barn.

"Reese, where's my new soap?" Lexi shouts from the aisle. Her voice sounds like a knife scratching Styrofoam. Just as

I'm about to open her trunk, I hear an awful sound—part growl, part howl. I run outside. Blake is on the ground, his truck door is open, the back seat is empty, and Rattler has escaped to the field.

"The foxes!" I yell to Wes. I can't breathe. I know what that dog has spotted, but still, I pray I'm not right. I'm chanting, "Let it be a rabbit, let it be a rabbit, let it be a rabbit," until the words are not just in my head. I'm yelling them out loud.

Blake slips and slides in his fancy boots before he gains enough traction to chase after Rattler. But with all that speed and force, Rattler must already be halfway through the field. I run as far as the fence line, then just stand there, paralyzed, watching the whirlwind of twisting and snapping, leaping and dragging, listening to the vicious growls and tiny yelps. Then Blake's fierce shout makes the hound look up. "Rattler! Git back here!"

Just beyond Rattler, Conway and Loretta are limping back into their den. The tip of Conway's tail is lying in the dirt. Rattler's big face peers at Blake over the swaying grass, his chest puffed, his tail high. His big, swollen tongue hangs out of his mouth, bouncing with every pant. He wants to be praised. *Look what I did! I'm doing my job! Come and pet me!* He looks proud.

Then I hear a crack. A pink spray bursts like a tiny firework from Rattler's ear. He drops down like the earth beneath his feet gave way, that proud look frozen on his face. Blake lowers his gun and walks toward his dog.

"Ain't no use, won't listen," he says as his boots crunch the grass.

What a liar this bright and sunny day turned out to be.

CHAPTER FORTY-FIVE

The next morning, I scan the field for any movement. I walk to the den, but the kits don't pop their heads out when they hear me coming. No pointed ears listening for my footsteps, no big eyes peering back at me. I reach into my pocket for the pizza crusts I brought.

"Come on, guys. You must be hungry. It's OK to come out now."

But there's no movement. No scurrying out to fight over a crust. Just silence. So I wait. I'd ask Sue for help, but she'd just scold me for not listening to her about leaving wildlife alone. "Don't interfere with nature," she'd said. "It never ends well." And she was right. All that time I thought I was helping them, I was hurting them. I shoo away some birds from the pizza crust and place it as deep inside the den as I can. "You don't have to come out. Just stay in there and eat," I tell them. Then I head back to the barn.

Today, I'm in charge. Wes left early for Yankton, hauling two horses he'll have to sell for next to nothing. I push a wheelbarrow full of hay down the aisle, putting a flake or two into each of the stalls' hayracks. The horses nicker and nod their heads at me when they see me coming. When I get to Gator, he's not pawing or sticking his head over the stall door like usual. He's lying down, and he's not the lying-down type. I open the door and stand close to him. He doesn't get up when he sees me—or his hay. That sets off an alarm.

"Hey, bud. You not feeling so hot?"

I crouch down beside him. His entire body is covered with a rash. Just under his coat, his skin is bubbled up just like plastic does before it melts.

"Ooh, poor guy. This does not look good."

I hold his head. His lids are heavy and his eyes look puffy and dry. I lift up his lip and press my thumb into his pale gums. When I take my thumb away, the thumbprint doesn't fill in with pink. His nostrils are flared and fluttering. When I put my ear next to his nostrils, I hear a rumbling.

"Dehydration, labored breathing, a rash from head to tail, and he's lethargic," I tell Sue on the phone.

"Try to get him up. I'll be right over. I'm just over at Twin River."

I push on Gator and rock him back and forth. He stretches out one front leg, then the other, and pulls himself up to standing. But he's not steady.

"Easy, buddy. Easy. Sue's on her way."

When I see Sue's truck speeding down the driveway, I breathe a sigh of relief. She rushes into the barn and goes straight to Gator's stall. I text Wes. *Gator is really sick. Sue's here.*

Sue already has her stethoscope around her neck, listening to Gator's heart.

"Oh, yeah," she says. "He's got something weird going on."

She places the stethoscope on his side and listens.

"Did he get into any food he's not supposed to?"

"No. I was the last one here last night, and I've been feeding him the same thing every day since he got here."

Sue shakes her head and places the stethoscope on his throat.

"No new supplements or drugs or anything?"

"No."

"Well, this is a pretty classic anaphylactoid reaction. Not sure to what. But you're telling me that his routine hasn't changed?"

"Not at all."

"He's not due for vaccines until . . . ?"

"Next spring."

"OK. I'm gonna draw some blood and give him epinephrine, glucocorticoids, and some oxygen."

Sue goes to work poking needles into vials. She pinches the skin on his neck and inserts a needle that's attached to a syringe. I watch as a plastic vial fills with Gator's purplish blood. She pulls out the syringe, caps off the vial, and places a label on it. Then she puts a portable nebulizer on his muzzle and secures it over his ears.

"Tell Wes I'll put a rush on the bloodwork. Hopefully, we'll hear back by tomorrow. Meanwhile, keep an eye on him. Keep the nebulizer on for at least two hours."

"Thanks, Sue."

I follow her out to her truck. Before she drives off, she leans her head out of her window. "And whatever you do, don't feed him any of your cupcakes."

CHAPTER FORTY-SIX

"What's going on, Wes?"

He's piling horse blankets and saddle pads and tack into the center aisle. I follow him in and out of the tack room. He doesn't even look at me.

"What are you doing? Are you going somewhere?"

I go to Gator's stall. Blake is there, watching Sue finish her exam. She pats Gator on the neck, winds the stethoscope cord, and places it into her tackle box.

"He's stable now, but that was a close one. It's a good thing Reese was here yesterday and noticed something was wrong. He would've been dead in another hour."

"What was it?" I ask.

"Gator's bloodwork showed large doses of a performance drug called dermorphin. It's made from the secretions of poisonous frogs. I don't even know where anyone would find it around here." Sue looks at me, her eyes full of tears. She looks away fast and quickly wipes her face on her shirtsleeve.

"I know how much Wes needed to win this race," Blake says, "but drugging my horse?" He gives Gator a pat, something I've never seen him do before.

"What?" I look at Sue. "You think Wes did this?"

"I found the empty dermorphin box on Wes's desk. I don't want to get the police involved. I really don't. It could mean jail time, and right now it's Blake's word against Wes's, uh, silence."

"Yeah, he didn't even really defend himself," says Blake. "He just shook his head. I mean, how would anyone even know where to find this shit?"

I walk into the tack room, where Wes is scribbling prices on round stickers before putting them on saddles and bridles.

"Maybe it's time to say something. Please, Wes."

He stops what he's doing and stares at me for a long time—long enough for me to notice that his eyes aren't brown. They're amber with tiny flecks of green and black and copper all around. And they're full of a sadness I've never seen in them before.

I wait for him to say something. Anything. But he doesn't.

"Wes, I know Blake is a liar. You're the best person I know."

But I can tell that no matter what I say, it won't make a difference. He just keeps separating girths, breastplates, martingales, nosebands, and bits. My words won't matter. They won't make him stay. Then I think of the thing I should have said a long time ago.

"I'm sorry, Wes. It's all my fault. It's my fault the lessons canceled. It's my fault you have to work for Blake. Please give me a chance to fix things. We'll prove Blake drugged Gator. Please, Wes. Don't give up. Let me try to get the lessons back at least."

I follow him while he empties the tack room and cleans the trailer.

"Wes, please say something."

But he says nothing.

———— ✦ ————

He says nothing when a convoy of trailers shows up. He says nothing while strangers lead his horses to waiting trailers. He says nothing as, one after another, they're driven away to different parts of the country forever. Now, there's only one horse left for sale.

"What about Stinky?" I ask him.

"I'll be taking the money for him," says Gibson, who seems to come out of nowhere. He has a real gift for sneaking up on a person at the worst possible moment.

Wes hands Gibson what little money he's already made.

"This'll make up for one month's rent . . . barely."

"But Stinky? Wes, nobody's going to buy him. Unless they're from a—"

"Don't worry. I have a buyer," Gibson butts in.

"Wes? Wes!"

I run after him as he gets into his truck and closes the door. I press my hand against his window, but he won't turn to look at me. Just starts up his truck. The engine clunks and sputters and the whole truck shakes. My hand vibrates on the glass. I pound on the window, but Wes still won't look my way. Then, just like that, he drives away. I stand there watching until his truck disappears completely.

———— ✦ ————

Back in the barn, a skinny, scruffy man who looks like a rat terrier walks up to Stinky's stall.

"This the one?" he asks Gibson.

"That's him."

Rat Terrier digs into his pocket for a roll of cash that's held together with a rubber band. He unwinds the roll and counts out four hundreds.

"Wait!" I run up to Mr. Gibson. "You can't sell Stinky."

Rat Terrier looks down at me like I'm an annoying fly buzzing around him.

"You making a better offer, Miss . . . ?"

I don't answer him. I swallow a lump in my throat.

"Hey." Gibson shrugs. "I'm just here to pick up the scraps when the dreams come crashing down. No crime in that."

Gibson and Rat Terrier laugh. I try to figure out how much cash I have stashed in my room and who can loan me the rest.

"Mr. Gibson, I'll match his price. I don't have the money yet, but I can figure something out. Please don't sell him. He's—"

"Look. If I can get four hundred here and now for this horse, why shouldn't I?" Gibson reaches for Rat Terrier's cash.

"Because I can give you five."

The men turn around to see who could possibly have shown up to start a bidding war on Stinky, of all horses. But I recognized that voice right away. I've never been so happy to hear it. Carol marches right up and stands between the two men.

Rat Terrier looks at Gibson. "He's old as dirt, but I'll give you six." He peels off two more hundreds.

Carol doesn't take her eyes off Rat Terrier. Rat Terrier stares at Gibson.

"Seven," says Carol.

Gibson looks at Rat Terrier and raises an eyebrow. Rat Terrier peels off another hundred.

"I've got a story about an old horse that I could tell you," Carol says.

Gibson holds up his hands and backs away. "Oh God, Carol, not one of your stories. I've got to get home before my grandkids have grandkids."

Rat Terrier puts his money back in his pocket. "All right, all right. Take him," he says, then spits a brown stream into the shavings. "Ain't even worth the four."

Carol and I stand side by side and watch the two men get into their trucks. My body turns to rubber. I wrap my arms around Carol.

"Thank you, thank you, thank you." I squeeze her as hard as I can.

"Easy does it, kid." She fakes that she's choking. "You're cutting off my airways and you're wrinkling my shirt."

But I just squeeze her harder.

"And I'm so sorry, Carol. I'm so sorry I hurt you. I miss you so much."

"It's OK," Carol says, smoothing out her flannel shirt.

"So what was that story about the old horse?"

"I wish I had one to tell. But I don't. Not this time. I was just trying to scare them off. Anyway, you were right. My stories are dumb. I think I just tell them to make myself feel better."

"Well, I could really use one of your stories right now." My voice cracks. She pats my back and lets me squeeze her one more time.

"I'm giving you something a whole lot better," she says as she walks to her car. "Take good care of Stinky. He's yours."

The barn is so quiet after Carol leaves. Almost everything is gone. All that's left is a pile of useless tack—Marge's halter with the broken buckle, Bob's bridle with the mismatched reins, Jasper's duct-taped halter, Sir Drake's busted breast-plate. Olive and Treasure and Stinky look at me over their stall doors like they're asking me the same question I'm asking myself. "What do we do now?" I feel for the stone in my pocket. It's warm in my hand, and the smooth side feels like glass.

From the end of the aisle, I can see that something's been written on the board. It's Wes's handwriting, but I'm not close enough to make out the words. I'm guessing it says *Goodbye, good luck* or *Thanks for nothing* or *Keep your chin up*. But when I get closer, I can't believe my eyes. Like my dreams are speaking to me. In neat cursive letters. In black magic marker.

You will see.

CHAPTER FORTY-SEVEN

God bless Flip Dixon. He offered me stalls for Treasure, Olive, and Stinky at his barn just down the road, at least until I come up with a plan. After I lead my horses into their new stalls, Flip shows me around the barn and introduces me to Jenn, his no-nonsense barn manager, and two teenage grooms, Pete and Mel.

"They can answer your questions if I'm not around. Just let Jenn know if your horses have any particular instructions. You can write their schedules on the board here." Flip points to a whiteboard next to the wash stall.

"You really saved my ass, Mr. Dixon. When I figure out what to do with a retired racehorse, an old-as-dirt toothless gelding, and a mare that needs more food than I can afford, you'll be the first to know."

"We're always looking for some extra help around here. Work-for-board is highly encouraged," says Flip. "Mel and Pete put in anywhere from forty to fifty hours a week so they can keep their horses here."

"Count me in for eighty hours until school starts," I say, heading out of Flip's big barn doors. "I'll be back here as soon as I wrap things up at Big Green."

At least Mr. Gibson is paying me to wind down the operations at Big Green. "Get every last bit of horse shit out of here" were his exact words. I spend the day removing feed buckets, hoses, old brushes, and torn blankets. I use a screwdriver to remove water bucket holders and stall guard latches. I even take away the hooks for the cross ties.

Everything here reminds me of how excited I was when I learned that the Big Green Barn would have horses in it again. And of the first day I saw Wes. How I spied on him before I had enough guts to walk into the barn and say hello. How I couldn't understand his no-speaking thing. How I got used to it so quickly. But also how his being here felt unfair at first. How I didn't trust him. How it didn't seem right that he was here and not my parents. But as time went on, it was like Wes being at Big Green Barn was how things were supposed to be.

I think of all the times I let him down. Like the time I let the horses escape. And the time I bungled the sale to the ranchers because I couldn't get over a small jump. And the time I wasn't there for Olive. The list is almost too long to remember. But he let me come back. He let me stay. He forgave me every time.

And that first day of lessons. How all of my posts and social media paid off. All those kids showing up and running around the barn. All those parents writing big fat checks to Wes.

I go to Treasure's stall and take down the picture of him racing in the Black Elk. I remember how I threw it in the trash because I felt like an idiot holding on to old dreams. And how, the next day, Wes had cleaned up the broken glass and hung it from a new nail, like he was telling me to never let that dream go.

I walk through the barn one last time. For a second, I almost forget it's empty. Quiet was normal in the evening after everyone was fed, when most of the horses were turned out, the chores all done, and the stalls cleaned. I used to love the quiet time. It made me feel peaceful. But this is a different kind of quiet. This kind of quiet just makes me feel lost.

Sadness rises in me, thick as swamp water. All I can do is sit here and let the scum seep into my mouth, then my nose, then my ears. I could shake this feeling by doing a quick chore like cleaning tack, but there's no tack to clean. There are no stalls to muck. No horses to groom. My head feels heavy. But I also don't want to leave. I want to lie down and sleep and wake up without thoughts.

The barn is so different in a Wes-less, horseless world. The beams that stretch from end to end strain and bow under the weight of the roof. The trim that Wes had repainted is already splintered and chipped. The glass panes are clouded, cracks snaking through them, and the holes in the floor tunnel into nothingness. It's like Wes's presence made these imperfections invisible to me. He is what made this place complete. I get up and stand in the center aisle, still holding the photo of Treasure. Outside, the field is empty. Even the breeze is silent.

Oh, Wes.

What really happened? How can I prove what I know— that Blake is the one who drugged Gator? I look for the answer in the spiders' webs, in the emptiness, in the faint slices of light. Even if no one else cares, I'm going to find out what really happened.

Then, thunder claps and rain starts pouring down. Ropes of water stream from the roof. The moment I step out from the cover of the barn, I'm drenched. I run across the field and into the woods toward Blake's cabin. I know exactly what I need to do. I'll make him tell me everything. Make him pay for what happened. He's the reason the barn is empty again. He's the reason Wes went away.

I march up Blake's muddy driveway. His truck is parked outside. Angry voices spill out of the cabin, louder than the pounding rain. Then the front door opens. I duck behind Blake's truck. It's Lexi.

"I don't give a good goddam about what you think. It's my horse," Blake yells.

"He could have bled out." Lexi's voice is shaking. Ragged. Like she's been crying hard. "You could have killed him."

I knew it! Why didn't I say something before? Why didn't I tell everyone what I already knew in my heart? That Wes would never do something like that. And why didn't I ever say anything to Blake all those times he was an asshole to Carol? Or when he was so distracted on his phone that he didn't control Rattler. When he shot the poor dog because of his own stupidity. Why didn't I open my mouth when he started bossing Wes around?

"No one needed to know," Blake says.

"But, Blake . . ." Lexi's voice utters something more, but it's too soft to hear.

"Any dumb bitch would have known to keep her mouth closed."

Again, Lexi's voice is just a murmur.

"The hell you are," says Blake.

Lexi runs.

Blake stomps out after her. "You get back here!"

She's barefoot. He chases her and she scrambles. She slips in the mud and falls. Blake stands over her.

"Fine. Wouldn't listen. You're useless." Then he raises his boot and kicks her. Kicks her with his foot in her ribs. Kicks her hard. Lexi makes a sound like she might throw up. Blake raises his other foot.

A courage rises up inside me. An animal power takes over. My legs and arms hum. I could pick up Blake's truck and throw it if I wanted to. Before I can even think, I'm in front of Blake with my fists flying and my legs kicking. I go apeshit bananas on him. He can't even see where my punches and kicks are coming from.

"This is for Conway!" I punch him in the stomach. He swings back at me and misses.

"This is for Loretta!" I kick him in the nuts. He bends over.

"This is for Rattler!" I punch him in the ear. He stands and tries to block me, but I get around his slow, drunk body and hammer on him some more.

"This is for Gator!" I punch him in the stomach again. The sour smell of alcohol seems to be in his sweat. He covers his crotch, but as soon as he moves his hands up to cover his face, I kick him so hard there he doubles over again.

"This is for Lexi!" I karate chop the back of his head.

"And this is for Wes!" I kick him in the ribs. He curls up on the ground. He groans.

I can finally back away. My heart is pounding so hard it feels like it could sprout legs and run right out of my chest. Lexi is leaning up against Blake's truck like she needs its help to stand. She's holding onto her side where Blake kicked her. She looks from Blake to me.

"Oh my God, Reese. Where did that come from?"

Blake is rolling around in the mud, groaning and cussing.

"I don't know. It's like I've been saving up to kick the shit out of someone."

Lexi takes a step forward and winces. She's standing in the middle of a giant mud puddle. I reach my hand out to her.

"We'll both feel better when his ass is in jail," I tell her.

My bleeding fingers hover for a moment over the dark puddle. The rain washes the blood from my hand, mixing me with the mud at my feet. When Lexi finally takes my hand, it's like I'm pulling her back into this world. Like she might have let the mud puddle swallow her whole. But instead, she steps out of the dark water and we run all the way to my house.

CHAPTER FORTY-EIGHT

I help Lexi up the stairs to my room. She holds her arms around herself like her insides are in pieces. I flick the light on and throw the layer of crap off my bed, clearing a place for her to sleep. She sits on the edge of the bed, looking down at the floor. Blonde cords of rain-drenched hair cover her face. She's so quiet. Like she's empty inside. I think of the snakeskin on the rock. I run a bath for her, wondering who Dad has with him tonight. I hope it's the one who takes the sleeping pills.

While Lexi's in the tub, I tiptoe downstairs to get her a snack. There's not much to choose from, so I grab a jar of peanut butter and a spoon.

I'm still straightening up my room, pushing things under the bed or into the bursting closet, when Lexi opens the bathroom door. She walks to the edge of my bed, not making a sound, and sits. I'm a little relieved that she's so quiet. Her voice has always been so annoying. Hearing it in my own house could just be too much.

"It felt good to do the right thing," she finally says. Her voice comes out cracked and low. Not the usual high and loud. Her forehead tightens into knots. Then she clears her throat. "When Blake blamed Wes, I couldn't eat. I couldn't sleep. I knew I just had to tell Sue the truth. I shouldn't have waited. When I finally texted Sue that it wasn't Wes, Blake saw it. And then he lost it."

Lexi looks around at all the horses covering my walls and galloping across my dresser. Embarrassing. They're the same decorations I've had since I was six. She picks up a picture of Mom from the Seabiscuit soap dish.

"Cool picture," she says. "Sitting bareback on a race-horse. Your mom was brave."

"Yeah. She almost gave my dad a heart attack."

"You know, Reese, I was actually jealous of you that your mom died. I know it sounds crazy. But it was like, at least you have a good reason to be sad." Her eyes search the room, trying to find the right words. "I wake up every morning wishing I was someone else."

"You? You're like the luckiest girl I know. You're popu-lar. You have the best clothes and you win at all the shows. I mean, look at you. Besides having an asshole boyfriend, you have the best life ever."

"That's exactly what I tried to make people believe. But it's so not true."

"You definitely had me fooled."

"I had everyone fooled. Even my own mother. I didn't want her to stop doing the thing she did best—giving me stuff. She buys me anything I want." Lexi sits up straight and raises her eyebrows. "I didn't want to burden her with my real problems. She'd just tell me I was being too needy."

"She actually said that?" I ask.

"She didn't have to. My mom's not a talker. Not about things like that. It was more of an understanding between us. The few times I tried to tell her how I was feeling, she

said feelings are fickle, don't be such a drama queen." Lexi
slumps her shoulders and tucks her hair behind her ears.
"I think I just wanted her attention. So when Blake paid
attention to me, it was like sitting in the sun after a swim in
a cold river. He was so sweet and nice and loving most of
the time. But when he drank, he changed. And even when
it was bad, it was better than being ignored."

I think about Lexi's mom. How she's never once come
to the barn. How she's always racing off somewhere.

"Mom hated Blake from the day she met him. That's
one of the reasons I kept dating him. Great way to treat
someone who gives you whatever you want, right?" She
looks back down at the picture of Mom. "It's so hard to
lose someone who's died, but maybe it's just as hard to lose
someone who's standing right in front of you." Lexi's eyes
are so full of tears she doesn't even have to blink for them
to stream down her cheeks. "When will she choose me?
You know what I mean?"

I think of my dad since Mom died. The way he changed,
grew a beard, dressed differently, dated more women than
I can count. As angry as that made me, that's not what our
fights were about.

"Yes. I know exactly what you're talking about."

<hr />

I leave my room, go downstairs, and throw a sheet and
blanket on the couch. I lie there, staring up at the ceiling,
listening to the groan of the refrigerator and the tick of
the clock on the mantel, thinking about what Lexi just
said. For a long time, I thought I was the only person with
that kind of pain. I thought everybody else had their life
worked out. Especially Lexi, with her perfect body, her

perfect riding gear, her seemingly perfect life. Her money. I thought she and everybody else operated their lives with some sort of a plan—a map or something that I never had. Like I was the only one finding my way alone in the dark.

The clock on the mantel ticks along, keeping me awake, moving time forward. What does time push into? Blackness? The unknown? Does it circle back around? When our time runs out, is there something else? Something not so terrible as time that just suddenly stops?

CHAPTER FORTY-NINE

Lexi is back in her own clothes, and we're having breakfast at the kitchen table. She pours milk over her Cocoa Puffs, puts the carton down, and shakes her head. "Where do you think your strength came from anyway? It's like you turned into a superhero or something. The Reese-inator!"

"Not gonna lie," I answer with a mouthful of Frosted Flakes. "I have no freakin' idea. I mean, all of a sudden, it felt like I could do anything."

Lexi chuckles. "You legit pummeled him. Like he didn't stand a chance. I mean, did you take martial arts or something?"

I almost choke on my Frosted Flakes. A milk bubble bursts out of my nose.

"Nice!" says Lexi. "Add that to your list of talents I never knew about. You're like a superhuman, ball-busting, nostril-bubble-blowing ninja. Come clean. What else are you hiding?"

I swallow my mouthful of flakes. "I was sort of in shock when I—"

"Reese Marie Tucker!"

Dad is standing in the kitchen doorway.

"What the hell were you thinking?" He walks in and starts pacing, then he stops and holds up his phone. "I got a call this morning from the police. The police! They said they arrested Blake while he was at the hospital. At the hospital!" Dad holds out his arms and shrugs. "You beat up a grown man?"

"He was pretty hammered, so it wasn't as tough as it sounds."

Dad starts pacing again.

"Well, what in the world would have made you think that was a good idea?"

"He drugged Gator and blamed it on Wes. I heard him admit it."

Dad stops pacing, puts both hands on the kitchen counter, and drops his head between his arms. He stares down at his feet for a long time and then looks up at me.

"No, Reese. That's not the whole truth. The whole truth is, you're out of control. And it's partly my fault." He shakes his head. "From now on, I'm just going to have to . . . keep a close eye on you."

"Mr. Tucker?" Lexi holds up her spoon like she's raising her hand in class. "Reese saved me last night. She didn't have time to do anything else but what she did. If it weren't for her, I'm not sure what would have happened."

Dad straightens up and looks from Lexi to me.

"Yeah, Dad. It's not like I'm going around looking for grown men to beat up. Besides, how about 'Gee, well done, Reese, are you OK? Did you get hurt?'"

"I think you would have been pretty proud of her if you'd have been there," says Lexi. "You should have seen her left hook."

"Yeah, and I didn't even know I had a left fucking hook!" Dad holds up his hand.

"Stop. Reese, please. Stop all this . . . craziness. Lexi, will you please excuse us?"

"Sure, no problem." Lexi scooches her chair back, puts her bowl in the sink, and walks out to the living room.

"Reese, all I want to say is, I get it. I've been a bad dad."

Normally I'd roll my eyes, but Dad looks teary and his lip is quivering.

"I've been a terrible example. But that's all ending. From now on, I'm going to be here for you. I'm going to do better." He takes my cereal bowl and rinses it in the sink. "And you need to quit swearing so much. Deal?"

I think about saying no fucking way, but Dad seems to be trying to change or start new or something. He already looks kind of different.

So I say, "Deal."

❧

The next morning, I'm sitting at the kitchen table, stirring my Captain Crunch. Dad walks past me to make himself some coffee. It's the first full day of Dad's being here for me.

"If Blake hadn't drugged Gator, if he'd have just listened to Wes, we'd still have a chance to save the barn."

Dad pours his coffee and sits down next to me.

"Wes and I would have made it happen. It was all coming together. Even though Wes felt like Gator wasn't fast enough, they still could have run a good race. Even without a win, there would have been nonstop business from people wanting their horses to train with Wes. Big Green Barn would have made another comeback, and we could have started up lessons again, and . . ."

"Reese, you're trying to keep snakes in a bucket," he says, like he can actually see all the thoughts sliding around in my head. "I wish I could help. But losing the barn was bound to happen. The thing about the horse business and the dreams that go with it is, one way or the other, you're going to be disappointed. This business is just too tough." Then he does something he hasn't done in forever. He asks me to lunch.

"Let's go to the taco place," he says. "We can talk, have a laugh, have some . . . fun . . . for a change."

"Because you have to keep your eye on me?"

"No, Reese. How about just because?"

"Fine. What time?"

"How about one?"

"Fine." I don't want to show it, but I'm actually excited to go to lunch with Dad. We haven't gone any-where together in forever. And El Taco is one of my favorite places. The waiters wear sombreros and bray like a burro if you order the special.

Dad and I choose a booth. Our waiter's name is Tom. He gives us our chips, salsa, and guacamole. I order the spe-cial—mainly to hear Tom bray. And when he does, Dad and I look at each other and laugh.

"He's good," says Dad.

"Yeah! He shows all his teeth and everything." I'm truly impressed.

We look at each other and laugh again. It feels good to be having some fun with Dad. Just the two of us. He raises his water glass.

Oh no. I know he's going to make a stupid toast.

"To—"

Then Dad looks past me. Big Bird is walking up to the table in her teased hair and leopard boots and red lipstick.

"Sorry I'm late."

"Dad. What the fuck."

"Scooch," she says and slides into the seat next to Dad. "Cookie gave me a lift and we were stuck at that broken stoplight in town, and I was like, crapola, I'm gonna be late. Hi, Reese. What are we toasting to? I need a drink. Waiter!"

While Big Bird's waving the waiter down, I look at Dad. He quickly looks away. I feel like I've been body-slammed. Like someone punched me as hard as they could in the gut.

"I'll have the special," says Big Bird to the waiter. When he brays, Dad and Big Bird laugh. The waiter goes to the booth behind us. I stare at Dad.

"He looked like a real jackass," Big Bird says through a laugh, as if she's the first to ever say that here. "What are the chances they have good margaritas here?" she asks Dad.

"That'd be a miracle," Dad says, flipping over the menu.

"Well, I don't believe in miracles," says Big Bird.

"Why the hell not?" I ask. "I mean, look at your hair. Isn't it a miracle it's actually that color and stays up that high?"

"Reese, leave her alone. What did she ever do to you?"

"Nothing. We were just talking about miracles, that's all."

"Really, Joe, it's OK. I was a teenage girl once."

"Newsflash, everyone!" I hold my fork like it's a microphone. "This lady was once a teenage girl. Talk about a fucking miracle."

"Can we pick another topic?" Big Bird asks.

"Why? You don't like miracles?"

Big Bird does a nervous laugh. "I said I don't believe in them."

"Well, you should." I say it louder than I mean to. "They happen. Trust me. I saw one with my own eyes. How do you think Olive got better? That horse was an ass hair away from death, and all of a sudden, she recovered."

Dad and Big Bird give each other a look like I'm a five-year-old who still believes in the Easter Bunny. And that really pisses me off.

"Hey, I know what that look means. And it's bullshit. You two weren't there. You didn't see what I saw. The horses I've been trying to tell you about. They came to the barn. They healed Olive."

Dad lowers his menu and leans toward me.

"Lower your voice please, Reese. Not here."

"Not here?" Now I'm practically yelling. I can't help it. "I can't tell you about the horses because we're in a taco restaurant that you hate because it gives you gas and makes your tinnitus flare up? Where then? Where can I tell you?"

Big Bird does a loud chicken laugh and then covers her mouth. The people around us go quiet. Dad's eyes dart around.

"Reese, please." He barely moves his lips as he talks.

A girl at the booth behind us loud-whispers, "That's that horse-crazy girl, right?"

"You mean Crazy Horse Girl?" says the waiter.

Heat crawls up my back and into my head. I know my face is getting red. I feel Dad's and Big Bird's eyes on me. That just makes it worse. I want to leave.

"Don't pay any attention to them, Reese," Dad says.

The waiter comes back. He's got a funny look on his face, like he's enjoying all this. "Can I get anyone another beverage? Some fresh guacamole?"

"Crazy Horse Girl has plenty of guacamole. See?" I scoop out the glop with my fingers and fling it into his face. Now people are gawking. Waiting. Hoping something else will happen. The waiter stands for a second—one eye covered with the green, lumpy dip. "And here's some salsa to go with it." The salsa hits his other eye. "And don't forget a drink." I pick up my glass of water and pour it over his head.

Dad and Big Bird sit there with their mouths open. Big Bird has never looked more like Big Bird—her pointy nose, her long neck, her big blonde hair all poofed up like feathers on her head. I take Dad's glass from his hand and pour his drink on the waiter too. When I slam the glass down on the table, it breaks.

Dad is up and he's pushing me toward the door.

"Someone should get the manager," I hear a man say.

"Should I call the police?" says the nose-ringed girl who seated us.

There is no braying as we leave, just the happy sounds of the mariachi band. Big Bird hustles out behind us, saying stupid things like, "Don't worry, we'll pay for the glass."

The waiter, his face still smattered with green and red, follows us out to the parking lot with the manager, who looks like he's fifteen.

The manager shields his eyes from the glare of the sun. "You know, we could have her arrested for that."

Dad partly guides, partly pushes me into the passenger seat and slams my door so hard the Jeep rocks. Then he turns to talk to the manager. "So sorry. Not sure what got into her," he says. "I'll take care of it. It won't happen again." Then he digs into his pocket for his wallet. "Here . . . for any damage . . ."

Big Bird is standing in the middle of the parking lot in her high-heeled boots, arms crossed, huge hair barely moving. "You go on," she says. "I'll get a ride from Cookie." As if anyone actually cared how she'd get home.

Dad says a few words to her before the Jeep leans with his weight as he steps up to get inside. He looks at me, at my hand. "Let's get you in to see someone."

There's a slit about half an inch long in the fleshy side of my palm. My whole hand stings. It's covered in blood. I press my other thumb on the cut to stop the bleed. "I'm fine, Dad. It was just a—"

"You're anything but fine, Reese." He jams the Jeep into reverse. "I should have done this a long time ago." He turns his head quickly one way and then the other before he jolts the Jeep out of the parking lot. He drives out onto Main Street, crosses Sleeping Deer and Waking Bear, and continues through Birdwood. His face is set. Fixed. Like he's decided his expression will never change, ever. He's a horse with blinkers. Just straight ahead. Focused.

"Really, Dad. I said I'm fine."

"We'll see about that."

He drives into the hospital entrance. A huge sign points to the right. GENERAL EMERGENCY. Dad goes to the left.

"Umm, Dad, it's back there. That was the—"

He nods. "I know where I'm going, Reese. I finally know where I'm going." He pulls into a parking space and comes around to open my door. He takes me by the arm and walks me through the parking lot, not to help me, not to support me, but to control me. I look at the entrance to the building, then up at the sign. Its letters are small and white. Like they're trying not to be noticed. Like they should only be whispered. Which is exactly what I do when I stand there and read the sign out loud.

"*Psychiatric Emergency.*"

CHAPTER FIFTY

"But, Dad!"

I want to run outside. I want Dad to drive me back to the barn. If I could just snatch the keys from him, I could drive myself there. But he holds on to my arm even tighter. Nurses swarm the hall. They're in and out, doing paperwork, checking my blood pressure. Who the hell knows why? They watch me from the corners of their eyes. They're alert to my slightest move, ready to spring into action.

"The doctor will be in shortly to do an evaluation," says a fish-faced nurse. "Meanwhile, this will help with the anxiety." She hands me a pill in a tiny plastic cup. I look at the pill, at Dad, at Fish Face. She nods. I put the cup to my lips and let the pill fall onto my tongue. She offers me water. I don't take it. The dry pill scrapes down the back of my throat.

"You two can wait in here," she says, leading us into a room with no white-papered table to climb up on, no one waiting to clean my cut and tell me I need stitches.

Then a man appears. He nods to me. "Reese? Hi. I'm Dr. Johnson."

"Dr. Johnson, I'm in the wrong part of the hospital. I just need some stitches."

He looks at my hand, pulls my thumb away from the cut, and it opens up again. "Looks superficial," he says.

"Great. We can go."

Dad sticks his leg out in front of me, blocking the door. "Sit down, Reese."

Dr. Johnson starts asking me questions. "Do you . . . aren't there? What . . . the accident . . . how often . . . see things . . . only you?"

I want to run, but my feet have grown thick roots that are burrowed into the floor.

"If you tell the truth," he says, and I can finally hear his words clearly, "this will go much more quickly."

I do want this to go more quickly. And if they know me and understand me, they'll know that I don't belong here. I'm tired of lying. For the first time in a long time, I tell the truth.

———— ❦ ————

Back in the waiting room, the white lights make everyone look green. The door opens and closes, opens and closes. Nurses walk in and out. Dad's chair is empty. When I talk, my mouth feels full of sand. I have to shape my mouth to say a word. Fish Face is filling out forms on the counter next to me.

"I have to get back . . . back to Wes."

"Who is Wes?" she says without looking up.

Then I remember. "He's gone."

"You can go too," says the nurse. "Once a bed opens up at Highlands."

"Highlands?"

"It's a great place, Reese." Dad is back. "It's on a lake," he says. "Lots of outdoor activities. It's only a couple of hours away."

When did he come back in?

"Dad, can we please go home?"

Fish Face leaves.

Dad sits next to me. "Soon," he says.

Another nurse comes in to give us the news. Highlands has a bed. Dad walks me back through the parking lot. He has my suitcase in the truck, already packed.

"When did you do that?" I don't know what's in it. I don't ask.

"You can come home . . . on weekends." His voice is different. He keeps stopping between words. "After the third week . . . once they get you . . . settled in and . . ."

We get into the Jeep and head west. The highway ahead of us is straight and points directly at the sun—a giant, burning match. We're on the stick driving straight into the flame.

"I should have done this a long time ago," Dad says.

A fence line follows us along the highway. Barbed wire stretches between posts, each post ticking off a word I don't say because any word would fail to convince him that this is all a big mistake.

"I've known something's been wrong for a long time, but I just didn't want to admit it. It scared me." Dad is squinting into the sun. "Baby? It's important that you know I'm doing this because I love you."

I miss the way Dad used to talk. His dumb jokes. His singing.

"You're not my dad. My dad doesn't talk like this. Someone told you to say this."

"All those therapists," he says. "That was just putting a Band-Aid on it."

Dad passes a stock trailer. Cattle peer through the vents. Giant red-and-white Herefords. I see a wet nose, a pair of glassy eyes, a switch of a manure-encrusted tail.

We drive alongside the Ghost Hawk River, which is churning with whorls and white rapids. The sun skates across the surface of Horse Thief Lake. We drive on. The dark orange dirt turns pink. A ghost of a moon slips between the clouds. In the distance, Smuggler's Rock looks like a ship at sea. A ship I'd like to be on. Our silence is so loud it makes my head hurt. We drive on.

When the road finally hooks around Smuggler's Rock, the glare from the setting sun is blinding. Dad puts his hand up to block it and lowers the tiny useless flap of a visor. I look to the side, away from the sun. The wind kicks up a pink haze.

Then, through the haze, I see them.

The horses.

They're charging toward us, their galloping hooves stirring up a cloud of pink dust. They're going to cross the road just ahead of us.

"Dad! Stop!"

"What?"

"Stop! They're heading right for us. Dad! Pull over! Pull over!"

When he finally manages to pull over, he lets the Jeep rest on the side of the road. He looks at me.

"Not this again. There are no horses, Reese."

But now the horses are so close they make the Jeep rock and sway and shake.

"It's just the wind." Dad leans forward and points to a massive dark cloud. "There's a storm just over there. Looks like a supercell. That would explain it."

A jagged streak of lightning cuts through the sky. Then thunder starts and doesn't stop. Dad's voice is swallowed by the roar.

But it's not just the wind. And it's not just the storm. The horses are everywhere. We are surrounded. Their bodies shift and drift inside the herd as they gallop by. They move up, move back, one horse sliding into the space of another. There's not an inch between them. Then I see the black one. He separates from the herd and comes toward my window. His huge body blocks out everything else. He lowers his head to look at me before he moves on. Dust rises and engulfs the entire herd. I can barely make out the horses now—just the splotchy pattern on a paint, the blaze on a forehead, the black of a tail. I'm wondering if they'll crush the Jeep. I'm wondering if they'll ever stop.

We sit there, waiting. Then suddenly, it's quiet. Dust floats back to earth.

"Reese," says Dad. "It was the wind. It was just the wind."

Then his phone rings, making him jump. It rings three times before he answers. It feels like an eternity.

"Flip?" Dad says.

"You better get down here, Joe. Treasure took off. I can't find him anywhere. And we've got a helluva storm coming."

CHAPTER FIFTY-ONE

Dad puts the Jeep in drive, does a U-turn, and guns it. When we pull up to Flip's farm, he's out in front, waiting for us. His face looks white.

"Jeezus, Flip," Dad says, climbing out of the Jeep. "You seen a ghost?"

Flip walks closer. His lips quiver as he talks.

"Tell you the truth, not so sure what I saw," he says. "Jenn and Mel and Pete are out looking for Treasure."

Hail peppers the ground all around us. Lightning flickers and thunder booms. We hear a loud crack. A huge oak near the main road is falling in slow motion. When it finally hits the ground, it rocks on its branches.

"Shit," says Flip. "That tree is on the fence line. Come on, Joe!"

We follow Flip's truck to the downed fence. The tree has taken out about fifty feet of fence on either side, making a wide opening to the road.

I look in every direction for Treasure. A herd of about ten brood mares and their babies are running around erratically. Pea-sized hail bounces all around them. Jenn and Mel and Pete pull up beside us.

"Sorry," says Jenn. "No sign of your horse. We have to get these mares in."

Flip rolls down his window and yells, "If they get out onto the main road, we got a real problem!"

"Park in the gaps!" Dad tells everyone.

Flip and Dad and the grooms park their trucks to fill in as much of the open space as they can. Then we all spread out on foot to fill the rest of the space with a human fence. But there aren't enough of us. And the horses are spooked. When the mares run up to us, we shoo them off. They dart around, looking for another opening. Then the whole herd turns around and disappears over the hill.

"We need to catch them near the gate," says Flip, "before this hail gets any bigger!" He opens the back of his pickup and hands halters to Dad and Jenn and the grooms.

We trudge through the field, trying to corral the horses into the corner. Hail bounces around us. Most of it's pea-sized but some of it's big as golf balls. The babies are scared. The mares are beyond spooked. As we close in on the horses, the mares start to panic, and the babies get underfoot.

"Stop!" yells Flip. "They're too spooked. This isn't gonna work."

We all head back to the trucks.

"What now?" Dad asks. "This isn't letting up any time soon."

More golf-ball-sized hail shoots from the sky. The wind keeps picking up.

"I don't know," says Flip.

"One of 'em's gonna get through," yells Jenn, "and then we won't be able to stop 'em."

The hail stings my cheeks and hands. I cover my head with my arms.

Then I hear that familiar rumble. The one that's like thunder. The one that's like a train coming. I feel it in my feet, my chest. My eyes search the field. Then I see them. The horses. Flip's horses! And leading the herd, galloping this way, is Treasure. He jumps the creek, and the mares follow. I walk out into the field, hoping he'll see me.

"Treasure!" I yell. Hail flies all around me, making it hard to hear. I yell louder. "Come 'ere, boy!"

He separates from the herd. He runs to me and reaches out his nose, snorting and stomping the ground. Then he rears up on his hind legs. He looks at me, front hooves high in the air, and then lands down softly. He swings to the side, his tall back right in front of me. Without thinking, I reach to his neck, leap up, and swing my leg over his back. My hands grip a tangle of his mane, and Treasure lunges forward into a gallop.

"Meet me at the gate with the leads!" I yell to the others behind me. Treasure thunders down the field, ripping through the tall grass, piercing through the air like an arrow. The hail stings my body like a million bees. The grass is a blur beneath Treasure's enormous stride. In a split second, Treasure and I catch up to the herd, and he's leading them back up the hill. A surge ripples through the herd. We all charge toward the gate. We're moving even faster. Then we run along the fence line, taking a straight path down to the river. Going downhill, I try to tuck back and grip tighter.

Flip's truck is about a third of the way up the driveway. I know he must be driving as fast as he can, trying to keep up. But when we pass him, we make his truck look like it's standing still. We fly by like we could be airborne at any second. Then we swoop back up the other side of the hill, leading the mares to the gate.

Treasure lowers his head and flattens out in the stretch. Flip guns his truck, but he doesn't have time to pick up enough speed to catch us. We're gone. Treasure is moving off from the rest of the herd so fast I can't hear them behind us.

"Whoa, whoa, boy!" My words slip behind us and disappear into the rumbling of hooves and breath. I couldn't stop Treasure if I wanted to. All I can do is grip his mane and become part of him. He knows exactly where he's going.

Dad, Jenn, and the grooms are at the gate just in time to catch the spooked horses. Flip's truck finally pulls up. I leap to the ground, bring Treasure to his stall, and then help lead all the horses safely into the barn. While Jenn, Mel, and Pete finish toweling off the mares and their shivering babies, Flip and Dad and I stand in the sheltered doorway of the barn, listening to the hail pounding on the roof. We watch it build, like a carpet of white marbles.

My head is still ringing with what just happened. All I can think about is how Treasure's legs moved, how it felt like he was flying, how far he stretched out between his enormous strides. I've never in my life gone so fast. I swear he must have set some kind of a record. My heart finally stops busting out of my chest, but my face is still burning from the sharp sting of the hail.

Then the hail stops. Dad looks at Flip and me and then out at the fields and driveway.

"Look at that," says Flip. "Damn turned the place into a sea of white."

"Speaking of turning white," Dad says, "what was it that you saw out there, anyway, Flip?"

Flip's eyes go wide.

"They all called me crazy." He points his thumb over his shoulder to Mel and Pete and Jenn. "I told Jenn I saw a herd of horses come out of nowhere. They went tearing through here, and your horse went with them. Jumped every fence on the way out."

Mel and Pete shake their heads.

"We didn't see a herd," says Jenn from one of the stalls behind us. She leans her head over the door just so she can do a big eye roll at Flip. "We just saw Treasure take off when the wind picked up."

Dad looks at me and puts his hand on my shoulder. "I guess some people just see things that other people don't," he says.

"You two sure you don't want to come in for some stale bread and canned tuna?" says Flip, trying to change the subject.

"Sounds delicious." Dad laughs. "But we'll pass on that. Listen, Flip. Good seeing you." Then he gives Flip the man-hug pat-on-the-back handshake. "Give me a holler if you need anything. We're gonna make like the Red Sea and part."

Dad's joke stops me in my tracks. I let out a laugh.

"Good one, Dad."

"You like that? There's more where that came from. How about, make like Houdini and disappear?"

I laugh harder.

"Or make like stockings and run?"

I laugh even harder. Then I can't stop. I laugh so hard, it's like I'm crying, and Dad and Flip start to laugh too.

"How about, make like an atom and split?" Dad says while he's laughing.

"You still got it, Joe," says Flip, laughing at me laughing. "You haven't changed."

Dad and I turn to go. Then Dad stops.

"Flip," he says, "you sure you saw those horses?"

Flip looks out across his back field, which stretches as far as the eye can see.

"You know me, Joe. I've seen a lot of strange things. But this one takes the cake."

Flip tends to his brood mares, and Dad and I walk to the Jeep.

"Where ya headed?" Flip calls after us. Dad looks at me, puts his arm around my shoulders, and calls back to him.

"Home," he says. "We're going home."

CHAPTER FIFTY-TWO

It's not like someone waved a magic wand and all of a sudden things were back to the way they used to be. That could never happen anyway. Not without Mom. But that night, it's like we started to see each other again. And it seemed like we had both changed some and we had both stayed the same some.

When we got home from Flip's, Dad made dinner. Hot cold cereal. He took my cereal out of the microwave and held out the bowl, sticking up his pinky finger like he used to. "Ta da!" he said. "A four-cereal combo for the bravest girl I know."

"I wish Mom were here to see him." Dad and I are leaning on the gate, watching Treasure peacefully graze in the field.

"Me too," he says. "She'd be sitting on him right now. Shorts. No shoes. Not a care in the world."

I laugh thinking about the photograph I have of her.

"When I first met your mom, I'd just spent forty-nine days in the wilderness . . . of my couch." He laughs. "I'd been playing for the minors. The big leagues had their eye on me. My father was so proud. He'd always wanted me to leave farming and make a life in baseball. I was about to start negotiating a contract." Dad's voice cracks a little. "But then when I was playing in Spokane, I got slammed stealing third and busted my shoulder. It never healed well enough to play again. Those forty-nine days on the couch were hell. But on day fifty, I decided to go to the laundromat."

"Mom was there." Hearing Dad talk about Mom feels like he's giving me permission to peer into a chest of lost things.

"That's right. I asked to borrow a quarter, and she asked me on a date. It didn't take long for me to fall in love with her. She was free and beautiful and saw things in people and horses that, hard as I tried, I just never saw." Dad watches a small plane make a white ribbon in the sky. "After my injury, I was afraid of taking chances. But everything your mom did had some risk. When she wanted us to start a horse business, I had every reason in the book why we shouldn't. 'Joe Tucker,' she said, 'you have so many excuses for not doing things, you may as well just stay in bed all day.'"

"I guess she had a point." I laugh.

"Right," Dad says. "So we leased the farm together. Every single day had its challenges. She said, 'What makes you think life is supposed to be easy?' The thing is, baseball had made life easy for me. Too easy. I wasn't used to tough. But your mom went along with tough times like they were no different than easy times. Once she said, 'Maybe we shouldn't judge our times as easy or hard. Or good or bad.' I was like, what does that even mean?"

"Well," says Flip, who comes walking up behind us, "maybe she was leaving you with something to chew on." Then he nods his head at Treasure. "That's some horse."

Dad shakes his head and looks at Treasure. "She was always right about horses."

Flip smiles. "Jessie sure had an eye."

"I didn't see it myself," says Dad.

"Dad thought he was stubborn as a mule and dumb as a goat."

"But Jessie brought him along with all the patience of a saint. She sure did show me I was wrong about him."

"And it looks to me like someone's ready to race," says Flip.

"You know, Flip, I was just thinking the same thing. Just when you think you're done with something forever." Dad laughs. "To be honest, I think he's even faster than he was two years ago."

"I wasn't talking about the horse," Flip says, putting his hand on my shoulder. "I've never seen anyone, and I mean anyone, ride a horse like that in my life. Don't know about you, but I believe in signs, and if you don't enter that race, I'll just have to do it for you. I think that horse is trying to tell you something. And something tells me you'll never be more ready than you are right now."

"You know something, Reese?" Dad looks at me and nods. "You are ready."

"Only thing is, I can't jump anymore."

Dad and Flip act like they don't even hear me.

"Looks like we're going to the Black Elk," says Dad.

"I'll be there," says Flip. "Wouldn't miss it. Not after what I saw."

Dad and Flip are talking like they know something I don't know. Dad nods at Flip, and Flip shakes his head and *tsks*.

"Just incredible," he says.

"But there's the jumping part." I shake my head. "I haven't been able to clear a jump in . . . forever."

"Details, details," says Flip.

"You can jump again," Dad says. "You just don't know it yet. But you will. Because you're a natural. And because you're just like your mother. Bravest girl I know."

CHAPTER FIFTY-THREE

When I open my eyes, it takes a minute for me to remember. Today is the day. I pull on my boots and take the path through the woods. And when I get to the end of the trail at the top of the hill, I watch.

I watch as the barn comes down. As the roof caves in and the walls fall to the ground with a dust-billowing thud. I watch from the top of the hill as boards crumble under thick tire treads, and giant metal jaws lift the strong beams into the waiting dump trucks.

I watch until I sense someone behind me. I don't need to look to know it's Dad. He's shaved his beard. I see his face, his dimple, his smile. No headphones. He isn't forcing his way to me. He doesn't even reach out for a hug. He just looks at me and I look at him and it feels like a beginning of something. Something I can allow.

He's older than I remember, and I wonder when the last time I really looked at him was. A web of lines and creases around his mouth have been hidden all this time by the beard.

We stand next to each other until every piece of Big Green Barn is hauled away, until it completely disappears, until all that's left in its place is the giant square of its brown dirt floor.

I fall into Dad's arms.

"I know things can't be fixed between us overnight," he says. He takes a deep breath, unwraps his arms, and holds my hands. I look up at him. "After your mom died, I couldn't handle even my own sadness. Your sadness on top of my sadness was just too painful." Dad's eyes fill with tears. "It's like I wanted to do anything but feel. I was pushing you off to a therapist instead of talking to you myself because I was afraid. Afraid of the pain I would feel."

Dad's words stop me. A frozen spot I'd been holding on to for a really long time deep inside my chest starts to melt away.

"Me, too, Dad." My own tears slip from my eyes. "I was so angry. Angry that Mom died and angry at you for dating and angry at you for asking LeeAnne to move in. Angry even that you changed how you dress. It's like all I wanted to do was make you as mad as I was."

"We're both afraid," Dad says. "Afraid of feeling."

Those words sound familiar.

"You're right, Dad. It's easier for me to be angry than show I'm hurt."

"It's easier to do almost anything than show we're hurt." Dad hugs me. "I've learned a lot recently, since I've been seeing your therapist."

I push him away. "Seriously, Dad? You have to sleep with her too?"

"No," he says, pulling me back to him. "I'm seeing her as a patient. You didn't use all the sessions, and I didn't want the money to go to waste. And she's actually been really helpful."

"Oh my God, Dad. That really scared me."

"Don't worry. I think I'm beginning to remember who I am. I'm finding my way back. What I'm really trying to say is"—he holds me away to look into my eyes—"I'm sorry, Reese."

"I'm sorry, too, Dad."

"I want to be here for you," he says.

"You are here."

"I mean, really be here. And to listen. Not just hear you. Really listen to you. You want to know the truth?"

"I'd like that."

"I think that terrible sound in my ears, the sound that suddenly went away, was an alarm I'd been ignoring for a long time."

"An alarm?"

"Like something trying to tell me that I wasn't tuning in. Not paying attention."

"Wow, you really have been seeing the therapist." I laugh.

"I owe it to you," he says. "And to myself."

"And I'll stop swearing so much. I know how much you hate it."

"That," he said with a laugh, "would be awesome. You promise?"

"Promise."

Dad squeezes me closer and kisses the top of my head. Then we don't let go of each other for a really long time. We watch the last drop of sun slip into the horizon. And for a moment, before the day goes away and the spinning thoughts inside our heads whirl us into the next one, just for a moment, we're sharing the same feeling. It's like I can feel us opening. Opening to each other again.

I'm so glad we're talking. Really talking. Words are important. Needed. But there are also words we don't have to say. Because as we watched Big Green Barn disappear forever, I knew we could both feel Mom right there with us.

CHAPTER FIFTY-FOUR

Lexi leads Treasure to the schooling field, and Dad and I follow behind her. When the field flattens out, she waits while Dad and I catch up. Dad lets Treasure smell his hand before he gently pats his jaw. When Treasure puts his nose to Dad's nose and breathes him in, Dad blows into Treasure's nose and laughs.

"Hello there, Treasure," he says. "I guess you found your way back too."

Dad puts one hand on Treasure's wither and leans forward, offering his other hand to me as a leg up. I let some of my weight fall into Dad's hand while I swing my leg over my horse.

"We have a lot to get over," Dad says, still holding my leg. "Let's start with that jump."

I ease Treasure into a trot and do a small circle around Dad and Lexi. Treasure's stride feels easy and smooth. He moves like his legs don't touch the ground at all, like he floats just above it. At the slightest signal, he breaks into a canter. I ease my hands up his neck to let him stretch out. Dad and Lexi watch as we make a larger circle. I can see Dad nod.

"OK, you're ready. Try the coop," he yells.

The coop—a wooden, triangular jump—sits at the edge of the field along the fence line. I grip the reins tighter and canter toward it. Treasure is moving fast.

"Keep up the pace," Lexi hollers. "You'll need to get used to it."

I look down at the uneven ground and then back up at the jump as I get closer and closer. I know what I need to do. I try to keep my arms out and my body relaxed, but just as we approach the jump, I pull back and catch Treasure in the mouth with a sharp jab. We're already in the air, but I'm off balance. When Treasure lands, I slide forward and fall to the side over Treasure's right shoulder.

"Shit!"

The ground moves toward my face. I wait for the pain, but the landing is soft. When I get up, Lexi has already caught Treasure and is walking toward me.

Dad jogs up. "You OK?" He's giving me *the look*. "I think you know what you're doing wrong. Just remember. You already know what to do. You just have to stop thinking about it."

We walk over to Treasure, and Dad puts out his hand again to give me a leg up.

"How exactly do I turn my brain off?"

"Try looking past the jump," he says as I ride off.

Again, I canter a wide circle. I give my body the speech about not tensing up. I try to imagine I'm Wes. I try breathing. Again, the fast-approaching obstacle causes the chain reaction of panic that makes me do exactly all the things I'm not supposed to do. I land in a heap so hard it feels like dust squeezes from my bones.

"Reese?" Lexi calls. "Reese? Are you OK?"

I can't breathe. I can't answer. Lexi kneels next to me.

"Don't move." She brushes my hair out of my face. She checks my eyes. I lie flat on my back.

"Reese. Reese, are you OK? What can I do?" Dad's voice is shaky.

Finally, the air returns to my lungs. "Yeah. Just got the breath knocked out of me."

He reaches out to help me stand. I let him pull me to my feet. My face is hot. Tears burn my eyes.

"Reese, hon, you don't have to do this. To be honest, there's part of me that's terrified and just wants to take you home so we can watch the game, eat snacks, and forget about this race."

Dad puts his arm around me. I nod, and we walk slowly toward the barn.

Lexi leads Treasure. I think about Mom. Her Treasure. Her patience with him. Her love for him. The story she knew he could tell. I wanted to be the one to help him tell that story, but I've failed them both.

When we're almost at the gate, I hear the sound of an engine puttering down the driveway. The unmistakable sound I've been missing with all my heart. I don't need to look to know that Wes is back.

He's barely out of his truck when I throw my arms around him. He's so still I can't even tell if he's breathing. When I press my head against his chest, it feels like a cement block. But I don't care if he thinks it's weird or that he's not a hugger. I don't let go. Then slowly, he lowers his arms around me, his chest softens, and I hug him harder. When Lexi leads Treasure toward us, I finally let go of Wes.

"I texted Wes," she says. "I hope that's OK. I told him if he's not busy . . . I've got an important job for him."

"Good to see you, Wes," Dad says. "Reese, I think this is my cue to make like a tree and leaf. Time for me to let the expert take over." Before he goes, he hugs me and says, "The bravest girl I know."

Wes notices the lime-green headband-bracelet thing that I'm wearing around my wrist. I hold it out for him to see. "I know. It's stupid. I'm not much of a knitter."

He takes my wrist, finds where I've knotted the thing, and unties it. I look at him, confused. He does a circle with his finger. When I turn around, he places it over my eyes and ties it behind my head. I know what he's doing. But part of me doesn't believe it.

"This is a joke, right?" I want so much to reach up and pull the blindfold off. He guides my foot to his knee, and I put my weight on it. I feel for the saddle and pull my leg slowly over Treasure's haunches. My feet find the stirrups, and I grip with my legs. Wes's hand on my calf is telling me to relax. Just like he did with Zadie.

"Reese?" asks Lexi. "What's going on?"

"Wes wants me to trot."

"Yeah, right." She laughs. Then she realizes this is serious. "OK, Reese. Just keep Treasure bending to the right, and he'll stay in a circle. You'll be fine."

"That's easy for you to say, Lexi. I'm the one blindfolded on a horse!"

"Wes just gave me a look, and I think it means he wants you to do the listening. He'll do the talking—through me. Get it?"

"Yeah, I get it. And it sounds insane for way more reasons than I can even begin to explain."

"Not sure, but I think he wants you to shut up. Yeah. Shut up."

"OK," I say. "Here goes nothin'."

"Tighten up a little on the right. You're a little off track."

"Well, that's because I can't see the damn track, Lexi. You wanna get on and show me?"

"No, uh, Wes wants you to figure it out yourself."

"This is the most ridiculous thing I've ever . . . not seen."

"It doesn't help to be mad about it," Lexi says. Her voice sounds a little louder. I must be cantering right past them. "That was me who said that. Not Wes."

"Yeah, thanks." My eyes hurt from trying to see through the blindfold. So much can go wrong when you're in the dark. Treasure could just stop. We could be heading toward a low branch. Anything.

"OK, let's try this," I tell Treasure as I let my fingers pull a little more on the right rein, bending his body slightly toward the inside of the circle. He's paying attention. "Good boy, Treasure."

"That's good, Reese. Now pick up a canter."

I shake my head. "This must be punishment for something. All the times I've made Wes mad. Is that it?"

"No talking, please," she says, like she's Mrs. Roth. "And remember. Riding is a feeling." Lexi uses the same words that came to me when I watched Zadie ride. They were just the right words then. And they're just the right words now.

I lightly press my right heel into Treasure's side. I can feel his muscles collect, his big, floating stride moving up, down, up, down, up, down. I can picture where we are in the field, but I can't tell if we are nearing the fence line or drifting toward the river.

"Am I staying in the circle?" I ask.

"Yep, you're doing just great. Keep going. Wes wants you to change leads through the center."

Suddenly, I can feel where the center is. I can feel the amount of pressure I need to press my leg, and I can tell how the slightest pull with my rein will signal Treasure to move across the ring we've created. As I sit here blindfolded, I remember what Zadie's mom said. When your sight is taken away, you have to rely on something else. And now I think I know what she meant. When there is no light, no one to show you the way, that's when you grow. Because you have to rely on something more than what you know. Something beyond what you understand. Even more than what you believe.

I shorten my right rein and keep a slow, steady canter. I can picture Treasure's movement, his shoulders going forward and back. My body relaxes. I can feel each stride but also everything between the strides. Each movement slows down for me. When Treasure reaches his legs forward, I know to bend my arms to give more rein. I can feel him stretch out and gather his legs beneath him. I can feel the slightest change. I reach my arms forward and let Treasure use his neck. Then when he leaves the ground, I am right there with him. I can feel exactly what I need to do.

"Woo-hoo!" Lexi yells. "Woo-hoo!"

Wes sets up more jumps. We sail over every fence in the field, and I feel like we could jump over anything. Anything.

CHAPTER FIFTY-FIVE

Trailers jam the field. Crowds fill the tents. Wrappers and cans and half-chewed apples already litter the grounds. Laughter rolls from one group to the next. A man in a tweed jacket knocks his pipe on the bottom of his heel, then packs it with sweet-smelling tobacco. Families eat candied corn and chicken wings and steaming bowls of chili.

Treasure holds his head high, taking in all the sights and sounds. Lexi backs him off the trailer and unwraps his legs. Wes gently places the tiny saddle on his back. Treasure turns to watch a girl in a yellow dress as her red-balloon bouquet bounces past him. The girl's dad points to the miniature ponies in the corral. Lexi reaches up to pat Treasure's head.

"Everything's OK," she tells him.

She leads Treasure, following Wes through the crowd. Dad and I walk behind them until we reach the roped-off paddock where the jockeys are gathering. I feel for the stone in my pocket.

"Jockeys!" The announcer's voice booms from the loud-speaker at a volume that would make even a bombproof trail horse spook. But Treasure doesn't flinch. "Please make your way to the start!"

Lexi adjusts Treasure's bridle, removes his tail wrap, and tightens the girth. Wes holds Treasure's head while Dad gives me a leg up to Treasure's back. People are yelling and laughing. Kids are screaming. A band is playing bluegrass. The sounds are all blending together, and my head is starting to hurt. I try to focus, but a rearing horse distracts me. My jaw is tight, my hands are clenched, my mouth is dry, and my teeth are clamped together.

A big paint gets into position. His seasoned jockey looks relaxed enough to ride through a storm and a fire and stay calm. A jockey on a sleek black horse looks younger than I am, but he seems ready, like he's done this before—like he and his horse are one. A huge, spirited Appy is giving her rider a tough time until he whacks her with his crop, but that just makes her rear and spin.

Then a jockey gallops up, all attitude, followed by a wealthy-looking man who must be the horse's owner and an entourage of overly helpful grooms. When they get closer, I recognize the owner. Sid Barker. And the jockey is the famous Australian who won the Black Elk last year by thirteen lengths. The one who harassed Wes at the Twin River Ranch when he was training Sir Drake. That total asshole, Patrick Miller. This time he's on a bay.

"I hope you like the view of my horse's ass, because that's all you'll be seeing of him from here on in," he says, swinging around so close to us that his horse's butt grazes Treasure's shoulder, forcing him to step to the side.

Lexi marches right up to the front of his horse and grabs the reins under his chin. "Excuse me, Crocodile Dundee, but I have a feeling that we might be grilling your tiny little

Aussie balls on the barbie by the end of the race, so good luck to you, mate."

The horse looks like it wants to rear, but she's got a firm hold. His handlers look on, their mouths hanging open. Patrick does a nervous laugh and walks his horse away.

"Oh, and you've got a massive bat in the cave," she calls after him. "A huge booger, dude. Hanging out of your left nostril. You should really do something about that."

When Lexi's on your side, you don't ever want her to shut up.

"Ladies and mental men!" Again, the loudspeaker booms and spooks the other horses. They bolt and rear. The Appy almost slams into us. I slip to the side but pull myself back into the saddle.

"Easy, boy." I pat Treasure's neck. He's listening to me. His ears twitch back and forth. "It's OK." I say it more to myself than to him.

The horses on either side of us are lathered and pulling on their bits. White knuckles and clenched fists hold tight with all their might. I look down at my knitted bracelet.

"Jockeys, please line up at the starting point!" The voice echoes back and forth. "And always remember, safety third!"

Then a crack of gunfire splits the air. Like a herd of frenzied warriors, we race toward the first jump—a rock wall. I do my best to hold Treasure back so I can jump clear of everyone else, but we're part of a herd. We all pour over it like a waterfall.

The next jump is a line fence. I hear hooves banging the top rails. *Crack!* One of the top rails has broken in two. Treasure sails over it nicely. The horses ahead of us are scrambling up a high muddy bank, leaving it slippery and slick. There's no way around the bank, and now there's no sure way up it. I hang on. Treasure makes it up the bank like he's sprouted wings.

Now we're gaining on the tail end of the pack. The paint looks lathered and tired. Treasure and I ease past him. But just ahead, Patrick's big bay still looks fresh. Treasure stretches out, and in a second, Patrick and I are side by side. He smiles at me. I give him the finger.

We reach the next jump at exactly the same time. It's an enormous hedge. My guts press against my throat when Treasure clears it. When we land, I'm thrust forward onto Treasure's neck. I slip to the side, my face inches from the bay's cutting, digging hooves. I heave myself back into the saddle. Treasure is now a runaway train. His instincts have taken over. But ahead of us is a hill, and on the top of that hill is a big, wide fence.

I know how these things go.

"Easy, Treasure. Easy." He's got hold of the bit and doesn't feel me pulling. If I could jump off now without killing myself, I would. Treasure kicks into yet another gear. Then I feel a shove. Patrick is swerving his bay into Treasure. He stumbles, pitching me forward. I almost slide over his neck, but he slows just enough for me to push myself back into the saddle. Patrick cracks his whip. *Thwack, thwack, thwack.* They steam up the hill toward the jump. I gather the reins. Treasure stretches out. In a blink, we're next to Patrick again. We reach the jump together. We arc through the air, Patrick and his bay right beside us.

And then they're not.

They're on the ground. The bay is scrambling to his feet. I look away fast.

That should have been me.

We're right behind the pack, their tails whipping in Treasure's face. Then he doesn't just take the lead. He runs like there's another herd to pass just ahead of us. He charges on until I can't even hear the other horses behind us.

When we reach the wooded part of the course, the dappled sunlight messes with my eyes. My goggles are covered with mud and horse sweat. I wipe them on my shoulder, but that makes it worse. I see only jostling movement, fragments of things—the trunk of a tree, a jagged boulder. As Treasure charges forward, branches dig into my sides. I tuck in close to Treasure's neck, my legs gripping him, my chest flat against his neck.

As we gallop deeper into the woods, the low hum of the Ghost Hawk River's current turns into a rushing roar. We round a bend, and just ahead is the crossing. The mossy bank silences the pound of Treasure's hoofbeats. He leans into the turn before the crossing, and I feel him lose his footing. The bank gives way and crumbles beneath us.

That's when I feel us fall.

Treasure and I land in the deepest part of the river, and the rapids are pushing us farther and farther downstream. I scream out, but the other riders are still too far behind. Treasure tries to keep his nose above water. I clutch his reins in my hand, but I realize I'm holding him down. I let go.

I hold on to his mane, but it's slipping through my fingers. Around me, water rushes past, carrying fragments of the forest. Leaves and sticks and moss. The sun ripples on the surface, but we're being pulled deeper. Fighting this current is like trying to stop a train. There's nothing I can do. Except stop. So I do.

As we're sucked deeper into the belly of the river, I think of the wounded foxes, Olive's baby stretched out still and silent in the straw, the spinning of the truck, the breaking crates, the flapping chickens, and the mouth of the rancher when he said the word "unnecessary." But then, like flashes of light, three words fill my ears. They're asking me to claim them. To recognize them. To own them.

You. Will. See.

The sound of hoofbeats vibrates through my chest. A figure blocks the light. I see the shadow of a mane and the flash of hooves. The wild black horse. He's in the water, standing firm, the waves parting around him. He moves toward us. I see the whites of his eyes, the pink of his flaring nostrils. He leans in with his big, powerful head and pushes Treasure toward the bank. I can feel Treasure's feet gain purchase. With another shove, we're up the steep, rocky bank. The black horse charges ahead, cutting a path for us and leading us up the hill. We're through the field. Then the rest of the herd is just a few strides ahead.

I look around.

The black horse is gone.

———◆———

Treasure sails over every jump, smooth and easy, like they're just part of the terrain. Before each obstacle, I sit perched above his withers, bending my elbows with each stride. The fears that once owned me have faded away. Before I'm over a jump, in my mind I'm already past it and on to the next one. I reach and stretch and let Treasure carry me over the jumps again and again and again. I give him all the rein he needs.

I let go.

Now there are only five of us left in the field. We're going into the last turn before the final jump. Treasure and I are right behind the pack, but we have no room to make a move. The horses are inches apart—there's no place to wedge ourselves in. The inside of the track is too tight, but pulling Treasure to the outside would take every bit of energy he has left.

Then the horse ahead of us moves to the right. Treasure and I move into the gap. Every time Treasure and I make a move, another path appears. The horses seem to part for us. We're between two horses who are running their hearts out. The only horse in front of us now is the big Appy. We're all barreling toward the final jump at the top of the hill. I tuck my body in behind Treasure's neck.

Leave something in the tank, I hear Dad's voice remind me, so I hold Treasure back. Two horses move past us. Their jockeys stretch their arms as far as they can, pushing with everything they have, but their horses are drained. They don't have anything left to give.

A few strides out from the jump, I reach my arms toward Treasure's ears, giving him all the room he needs to stretch his neck. His stride lengthens. He moves up alongside the Appy. Their hooves leave the ground. Time slows down. Sound stops. Mud flies. Sweat rains down. Legs reach and stretch. Treasure's feet hit the ground—a split second before the Appy's.

A nose ahead, we bolt over the finish line.

CHAPTER FIFTY-SIX

So somehow, miraculously, Trusted Treasure carried me over the finish line first. But once I'd done it—achieved the dream that had always been just out of reach—winning the Black Elk wasn't as important as I thought it would be. Don't get me wrong. I'm totally stoked that I won. But like Mom used to say, once dreams are reached, they're meant to turn to dust, giving you a chance to dream again.

What fills me now is the barn and all the life and events that happen in it every day. Days that string together to make a week, a month, a year. Days that are sometimes boring and sometimes busy and sometimes frustrating and sometimes magical. Days that all make up a life. My life.

Dad and Flip and Wes are partners now. At Flip's barn, I begin every day with the same routine I knew all my life at Big Green. But it's also my favorite time of year.

Foal season.

Mares need my round-the-clock care. And I help with the babies, getting them halter-trained and used to being handled. We all try to spot the foal that has the X factor. Like Mom always said, "You'll know it when you see it."

It's near the end of foal season. I've been in the barn every night for almost a month. Tonight everyone from the Big Green days is here—Dad, Wes, Lexi, Sue, Carol, and me. Flip is here too. Because tonight is extra special. Sue is almost positive it's Olive's turn to foal.

Because of Olive's history, Sue wants to be sure nothing goes wrong. We all have our cots and sleeping bags set up in the barn's aisle, and I'm first on duty. To pass the time, I'm knitting another hat for myself. Since the start of foal season, I've knitted scarves for Dad and Wes, a hat for Lexi, and socks for Sue and Carol. And they actually wear them.

There's no way I'm going to sleep anyway. I want to be there for Olive.

I think about what a miracle it is that Olive is here, how she got another chance at life, how the wild horses gave her that chance. And how they gave me another chance at life too. Every time I see them, it's like they are a reminder to me. They remind me to trust a feeling. Even if I can't understand it. Even if it doesn't make sense. They remind me to let go just a little. To allow some space for not understanding.

To loosen my hold.

I look up from my knitting and see a spider. She's sitting in the middle of her perfect design. The work she's done must have taken days. But right now she's resting. Or waiting. Waiting for a fat fly, waiting for tomorrow, or maybe just waiting for something to come and wreck her web so she can fix it.

Dream it up all over again.

I think of Sue's words. *We are fragile creatures.* I used to believe that horse people were tough. I thought we didn't let anything get to us, that we were a breed apart from the rest of the world. I was wrong. Horse people are fragile creatures too. We are. And being fragile is the thing that makes us strong. When we're fragile, we become more than that thing that gets trapped in our web or that stops us in our tracks and turns our world upside down. We become more than just the blood that rushes through our veins. More than a frame of bones that holds our muscles in place. More than physical. More than solid. We're more like light. Light that becomes even more beautiful when its path is interrupted. When it bends.

That's the only way you get a rainbow.

I hear Olive groan as she lies down. I run to her stall, slowly open her door, and kneel down next to her head.

"That's it, girl." I pat her neck, and then I call over my shoulder, "It's time!"

———————◆———————

I know what I want to name the foal the moment I see her little brown-and-white paint body begin to slip into this world, the same moment a rainbow dances on the wall of Olive's stall as the sunrise hits the rose quartz necklace I made for Sue. It swings close to her chest as she pulls on the foal's spindly little legs. Mom said rainbows are miracles. And now I know what she means. No matter how much they can be explained. As I watch this baby come into the world, I realize nothing explains the way I'm arcing into who I am meant to be.

"Welcome to the world, little girl," says Sue.

The filly lies in the straw, nodding her head, already trying to stand, while Olive licks her all over.

"Look at that. Mama's cleaning her up to show her off to everyone," says Flip. "She have a stage name yet?"

"Rose. I'm calling her Rose."

❧

After a few hours, mama and baby are ready for some turnout time in the nursery field. Wes leads Olive, and I follow behind with Rose. She's a late baby, and Olive seems to know she has to fatten her up fast before winter. But all Rose needs right now is Olive's milk, and this time, Olive's milk is perfect. We watch as Rose pulls her head out from underneath her mother's belly. Her little tail tick-tocks back and forth. She's staring at the edge of the woods. Then I see it too.

A fox.

He looks at us, crouched and still, a fat rabbit in his mouth. Then he jumps back into the thicket. But just before he does, I notice the tip of his tail.

It's missing.

"Conway!"

Wes looks at me and smiles.

"Just when I thought the day couldn't get any better."

While Olive grazes, Rose decides to play. She ventures away from her mother to follow a butterfly. Then she senses she's wandered a little too far. She does a mini buck, twisting and squealing before careening back to Olive, who gives her a sniff. For horses, that's as good as a hug. Then Olive gets back to grazing. I could stand here all day watching Rose's every little movement. I don't want to leave. But a couple of late mares need my minding.

I head back to the barn, but Wes puts his hand on my shoulder to stop me. I figure he wants to show me something in the field. But his expression is weird. Like something's caught in his throat.

"You OK?"

He nods his head, but he doesn't look OK. He clears his throat twice. He coughs and clears his throat again. He's making me nervous, so I make a joke.

"You hoarse?"

He doesn't laugh. He furrows his eyebrows.

"Still don't like that one? I know. Me neither. It's pretty stupid."

Then just when I'm about to try the why-the-long-face joke, Wes opens his mouth to speak.

"I need to talk," he says. "Will you listen?" His face looks as flushed as if he just ran ten miles.

"Oh my God, Wes! It's only something I've been waiting for ever since we met."

My voice is so loud he takes a step back. Then he looks out toward Olive.

"Words . . . ," he says, as if it hurts to speak, ". . . can kill."

I'm watching Wes, waiting for him to go on. I feel hypnotized. But looking away might make it easier for him. So I watch Rose dig in for a feed, stomping her feet and twitching her tail.

"I had a twin brother, Sam. And what I said to him . . . killed him."

"Bullshit, Wes. You can't kill someone with your words. That's not—"

"Trust me," he says.

His voice is soft. He speaks just above a whisper. I step closer to hear him.

"You can. You can beat someone down with words more easily than with fists." His chin quivers, but he continues. "I wanted him to want more for his life. He was the smart one. The one everyone knew was going to do great things. But when we watched our dad slowly die of cancer, it was just too much for Sam. It's like he gave up. After Dad died, I worked at ranches wherever I could. I found out I was good with horses. Sam stayed in our tiny town. Then he turned to drugs. When I found out he was addicted, I told him he was pathetic. That I couldn't stand to look at him. The next day, I found him on the floor. He had overdosed."

"And you've been punishing yourself ever since."

Wes nods. Tears fill his eyes.

"I'm so sorry, Wes."

"No one should be able to get away with saying shit like that," he says between his teeth.

"I know, but—"

Wes stops me.

"You don't need to tell me it's OK," he says. "That's not why I'm telling you. I'm telling you because when I drove away from the barn that day, I thought I had nothing left and no way to start over. I'm telling you because that day, something made me come back. Because I saw something."

"You saw something?"

"I was on the highway. I knew exactly where I was going, but I wasn't sure why I'd written those words for you on the board."

"*You will see.*"

"I meant to write goodbye, but I wrote that instead. Then I got in my truck and just headed west. All I could think about was all the time I'd been wasting trying to prove that my hard work had been worthwhile. Trying to prove that life is worth living. That my brother was wrong to take his life. When I see Smuggler's Rock up ahead, I pull off the road and I aim my old truck straight for it, as fast as it will take me."

My heart starts racing.

"Then I see them."

I know what he's going to say next.

"Coming out of the dust. And I hear those words over and over. *You will see, you will see, you will see.*"

"Wes. It's what I've heard all along."

"I had a feeling . . ."

"And that's why you came back?"

"I think it was a sign," he says. "A sign telling me there was still something left for me here. That I should be here. With all of you. That, and the text from Lexi."

"At least one of us has things figured out. And thank God, Wes. I missed you so much."

———————⌄———————

That night, Wes and I wait for the last mare to foal. I start knitting something new, but I haven't decided what it's going to be. I'm tired of scarves and socks.

"What are you making?" Wes asks.

And I can't help myself. "You. Will. See."

Wes smiles and walks off to check on the mares. He's on duty now, so I have a few hours to rest. I fall asleep, my yarn resting like a kitten on my chest. I dream I'm knitting my own web. I use all the colors I've known: the pinks of sunsets, the browns of snakeskins, the greens of water, the blues of sky. I use the colors of sadness and loneliness and fox fur and butterfly wings. When the web is done, I sit back and observe my beautiful work. But the wind picks up a tree branch that rips through the heart of it. So I knit again—another one, even more beautiful. This time, its edges are licked away by flames, and ashes float up to the sky. So I pick up my knitting needles and start another. I knit the colors of songs I've heard. The smell of air I've breathed. The taste of tears. This one is the most beautiful of all. I watch as it, too, is destroyed, this time by a swarm of munching insects.

But again, I pick up my tiny wands.

Then it's like I'm being tossed on the sea. My hand stops, mid-purl. I'm between the worlds of waking and dreaming.

I realize someone is kneeling next to me. Someone is lightly shaking my shoulder. I open my eyes.

Wes.

The mare must be ready. I get up and head to her stall. But Wes is pointing toward the outside. I follow him through the barn's open door. Morning fog is clinging to the field as if it's just begun to think about lifting. I rub the sleep out of my eyes. I hear hoofbeats. I hear breath. And then I see what Wes sees.

He leans close to my ear and whispers.

"They are here."

THE
END

ACKNOWLEDGMENTS

Even though they weren't really "horse people," my parents let me have a horse. I believe this story started percolating with the birth of Rambler, the foal of a mare we'd brought to North Carolina when my family moved from Ohio. I was nine years old. Mom and Dad and my older brothers and sisters spent lots of time waiting for me in the car while I fed and groomed and rode Rambler. They were all patient with my overzealousness, and one time, the entire family got involved when Rambler became ill and we had to take turns being with him through many nights to nurse him back to health. The vet said it was a miracle.

There are many people and experiences I'd like to acknowledge. Mom, for reading to us and always recommending books. Dad, for loving poetry and reading out loud, encouraging us to memorize his favorites. The horse stories that I read for a long time that became the bridge to appreciating great literature. Growing up in a house of readers—what a gift.

My brothers and sisters, who all played a part in my creative process. Ellen's talent as an artist and a writer has given me inspiration and insight. The stories Hans would tell when he came home to visit sparked an excitement about creativity that changed my life. Barbara's love and support in anything I tried and her own beautiful story-telling ability helped shape my love for writing. Martha's love for horses and her ability to catch all of them and take us for a ride, and her patience with me as a young horse lover. Steve's amazing natural horsemanship and skill to gallop beside a horse that didn't want to be caught, climb on its back and bring it in, taught me to appreciate a horse's spirit. Bob's sense of humor that surpasses anyone's I've ever known, and his ability to see irony in any situation. Sue's late-night reading to us from *A Wrinkle in Time*, and her stories of her adventures with her friends that I listened to on pins and needles. And Andy's and Pat's incomparable imaginations that made childhood memories feel magical.

I want to thank Bill Munton for opening the door to so many adventures with horses, and for encouraging me to write a long time ago. Tim Collins and Adam Goodwin for recent adventures. My riding posse, Tracy Egan, Julie Lake, Liz McKnight, and Andrea Caruso.

My husband, for his patience and love and for not asking too many questions while I was in the confusing creative process, and for teaching me the importance of putting time in every day and "bringing the ball down the field" a little at a time. Jay Michael, who has a story of his own to tell, for reading excerpts of my book early on, and whose passion for fishing and the sea are going to be great fodder one day. Quinn, for always having the best turns of phrase and for always asking me, "Mom, when is that book coming out?" Little did you know how much you impacted my work ethic.

Grub Street and The Work, for the classes and inspirational speakers.

Eson Kim, I still have my two-dollar bill. You were the perfect first instructor for my workshop in so many ways.

Louise Piantedosi, I can't tell you how extremely fortunate I feel to have met you. Thank you for helping make the editing process not only tolerable but a little bit fun.

Thank you also to all the early readers, for the encouragement you gave me. You kept my spirit alive. And you were what got this book through the rough stages. Betsy Horst, Arthur Vanderbilt, Julia Shivers, Lisa Borders, Sophie Westra, Annie Hartnett, Stona Fitch, Julie Lake, Tracy Egan, and Liz McKnight. I am so grateful.

And to Uncle Ernie, for reading a letter I wrote when I was very young and telling me I needed to write.

ABOUT THE AUTHOR

Christy Cashman is a mother, author, filmmaker, and active member of the Boston literary community. She is on the board of directors for the Associates of the Boston Public Library and is the founder of YouthINK, a not-for-profit mentorship program for young artists in the United States and in Ireland. In addition to *The Truth About Horses*, she has published two children's books, *The Not-So-Average Monkey of Kilkea Castle* and *Petri's Next Things*. Christy, her husband, their two sons, and three dogs live in Boston and spend time in Ireland and on Cape Cod. She is currently working on her second novel, *Beulah*, and on her third children's book, *The Cat Named Peanut Shrimp Cookie Fry Muffin Who Lives on Staniel Key*.

Author photo © Lindsay Ahern

SELECTED TITLES FROM SPARKPRESS

SparkPress is an independent boutique publisher delivering high-quality, entertaining, and engaging content that enhances readers' lives, with a special focus on female-driven work. www.gosparkpress.com

A Song for the Road: A Novel, Rayne Lacko. $16.95, 978-1-684630-02-8. When his house is destroyed by a tornado, fifteen-year-old Carter Danforth steals his mom's secret cash stash, buys his father's guitar back from a pawnshop, and hitchhikes old Route 66 in search of the man who left him as a child.

But Not Forever:A Novel, Jan Von Schleh. $16.95, 978-1-943006-58-8.When identical fifteen-year-old girls are mysteriously switched in time, they discover the love that's been missing in their lives. Torn, both want to go home, but neither wants to give up what they now have.

Bear Witness: A Novel, Melissa Clark. $15.00, 978-1-94071-675-6. What if you witnessed the kidnapping of your best friend? This is when life changed for 12-year-old Paige Bellen. This book explores the aftermath of a crime in a small community, and what it means when tragedy colors the experience of being a young adult.

The House Children: A Novel, Heidi Daniele. $16.95, 978-1-943006-94-6. A young girl raised in an Irish industrial school accidentally learns that the woman she spends an annual summer holiday with is her birth mother.

Beautiful Girl:A Novel, Fleur Philips. $15.00, 978-1-94071-647-3. When a freak car accident leaves the 17-year-old model, Melanie, with facial lacerations, her mother whisks her away to live in Montana for the summer until she makes a full recovery.

The Leaving Year: A Novel, Pam McGaffin. $16.95, 978-1-943006-81-6. As the Summer of Love comes to an end, 15-year-old Ida Petrovich waits for a father who never comes home. While commercial fishing in Alaska, he is lost at sea, but with no body and no wreckage, Ida and her mother are forced to accept a "presumed" death that tests their already strained relationship. While still in shock over the loss of her father, Ida overhears an adult conversation that shatters everything she thought she knew about him. This prompts her to set out on a search for the truth that takes her from her Washington State hometown to Southeast Alaska.